The Star Sailors

The Star Sailors

Gary L. Bennett

Authors Choice Press

New York Lincoln Shanghai

The Star Sailors

Authors Choice Press
an imprint of iUniverse, Inc.

iUniverse books may be ordered through booksellers or by contacting:

iUniverse
2021 Pine Lake Road, Suite 100
Lincoln, NE 68512
www.iuniverse.com
1-800-Authors (1-800-288-4677)

Original Publisher: St. Martin's Press, Inc.

ISBN-13: 978-0-595-35540-2
ISBN-10: 0-595-35540-4

Printed in the United States of America

To Susan
for sailing the stars with me

ACKNOWLEDGMENTS

Grateful acknowledgment is made to the following for permission to quote copyrighted material:

To Hart Publishing Company, Inc. for a passage from FLIGHT TO THE STARS by James Strong. Copyright © 1965, by James Godwin Strong.

To Les Presses de la Cité and E. P. Dutton for a passage from THE PRAETORIANS by Jean Lartéguy. English translation by Xan Fielding copyright © 1963 by Hutchinson & Co. (publishers) Ltd., London and E. P. Dutton & Co., Inc., New York. First published in France under the title LES PRAETORIANS and © 1961 by Les Presses de la Cité.

To Dover Publications, Inc. for a passage from THE LOST TRAVELLER by Ruthven Todd. Copyright © 1968 by Dover Publications, Inc.

To Edgar Rice Burroughs, Inc. for a passage from A PRINCESS OF MARS by Edgar Rice Burroughs. A PRINCESS OF MARS was originally published under the title UNDER THE MOONS OF MARS by Norman Bean (pseudonym) in *All-Story Magazine* as a six-part serial, February through July, 1912. Copyright © 1912 Frank A. Munsey Company. Copyright renewed 1939 by Edgar Rice Burroughs, Inc. Book form copyright Edgar Rice Burroughs, Inc.

To New Directions Publishing Corp. and Faber and Faber Ltd. for lines from "The Needle" from PERSONAE by Ezra Pound. Copyright 1926 by Ezra Pound. Reprinted by permission of New Directions. Also published by Faber and Faber Ltd.

To LIFE Magazine for a passage from "A Private Eye in Liverpool" by Richard Schickel. © 1972 Time Inc.

To Random House, Inc. for a passage from ULYSSES by James Joyce. Copyright 1914, 1918, by Margaret Caroline Anderson. Copyright 1934, by The Modern Library, Inc. Copyright 1942, 1946 by Nora Joseph Joyce.

To John Fowles, Anthony Sheil Associates Ltd., and Little, Brown and Company for the line from THE MAGUS by John Fowles. Revised edition copyright © 1977 by John Fowles. First edition copyright © 1965 by John Fowles.

To Atheneum Publishers for a passage from AFRICAN GENESIS by Robert Ardrey. Copyright © 1961 by Literate S. A.

To The New American Library for two passages from THE ODYSSEY by Homer, translated by W.H.D. Rouse. Copyright © 1937 by W.H.D. Rouse. Reprinted by arrangement with The New American Library, Inc., New York, N.Y.

To Curtis Brown, Ltd. and Farrar, Straus and Giroux, Inc. for the lines from WATCH THE NORTHWIND RISE by Robert Graves. Copyright © 1949, 1972 by Robert Graves. Published by Farrar, Straus and Giroux, Inc.

CONTENTS

Ah! if man would but see that hope is from within, and not from without—that he himself must work out his own salvation!

—H. Rider Haggard, *She*

To me, star flight appears as one of the great challenges of Nature, for I see the universe of stars as an arena that has been set for countless eons, patiently awaiting all comers. At any moment in time, any race—human or alien—that feels moved to pick up the gauntlet may do so. To whoever wins, the reward is survival.

—James Strong, *Flight to the Stars*

1

ASSIGNMENT

For the last week I've had the same nightmare. I am in a fortified city…It's a huge place, equipped with all the latest…technical refinements: 3-D cinemas, erotic clubs…drug-addicts…

…the city has many enemies. Emaciated and envious nomads prowl round it…

For this is my temptation:…to rise in arms against this outworn West and its rotting Byzantiums…

But on certain nights I remember that in the other guardposts there are friends of mine…and it's stronger than I am, I can't betray them. So I press the button and the nomads, bearded and tattered, but very much alive, with warm blood in their veins and healthy appetites, are sacrificed to the perambulating corpses in the city.

—Jean Lartéguy, *The Praetorians*

The quake hit suddenly. It tore through the overextended complex of shields in the underground base, stifling the control center and its necklace of sensors and alarm systems. The human-made tunnels, originally sculpted from stone by searing nullors, were now a writhing mass of rocks filled with dust and the roar of the violent upheaval.

Ben Wilson was not sure if he jumped or was thrown from his couch. He lay momentarily stunned on the rocking floor with his protective shield suit belt still clutched in his hand, just as it had been when he automatically grabbed it at the first mind-piercing alarm. His lungs were filling with abrasive dust and the first cauterizing vapors from the poisonous Calderan atmosphere. He coughed violently, spitting out black phlegm which he could barely see through glistening, tear-filled eyes in the dirty twilight.

Ben saw a suit light go on and a shadowy figure stagger in from one of the adjacent rooms, a figure encased in the invisible security of the guardian fields of force emanating from a jeweled belt. Ben scrambled to his feet.

"Sliger!" he yelled at the figure.

The figure moved toward him. A second tremor hit, hurling Ben against the wall, his bones snapping at the sudden change in momentum. He cursed out his pain. His belt was *gone!*

"What's happening?" Sliger asked, dazed. "Where's Marton?"

"No time," Ben shouted above the noise. "Get the hell out of here!" He pushed against Sliger's shield, indicating to Sliger that he should head for the main tunnel. Ben knew they had only moments to get out of their base, Ossa I, and that searching for the control center with its teleporter unit, a real promise of safety, was a futile exercise considering their present environment. In his initial burst of reflexive action, he briefly had one sardonic thought—they had failed to provide an adequate alternate escape system, but this thought was quickly submerged by others more directly related to his and his crewmates' immediate survival. Ugly, brown dust painted everything into obscurity. He could not see his belt in the quivering light emanating from Sliger's suit. He realized that the suit was probably damaged.

Within seconds, he saw Motsinger bleeding from several cuts. He had been thrown against the wall. Ben grabbed him and carefully guided him toward the main tunnel which led to their airship, the *Pelion*. With Sliger and Motsinger moving toward safety and no one else in view, Ben ran down the main tunnel toward the ship. Up ahead he could make out the dim reflection of the port lights, diffuse, disembodied eyes afloat in a sea of dust. He felt the cold, sticky sweat of fear contesting his reasoning and will to act.

The ground lurched beneath his feet, tossing him around like a mannequin. He bounced helplessly against one wall of the tunnel and then the other, his body on fire with bruises. He tried to brace himself but could not. He stumbled, rocks crashed about him. *The tunnel shield is gone!* His heart pounded. *How much longer before the seal goes?* He ran in a sort of crawling stumble down the rolling tunnel toward the dusty light ahead. His lungs ached, and his eyes burned from the gritty dust and toxic fumes. He could hear only a constant pounding roar, punctuated occasionally by the nearby crash of dislodged rocks. He felt ensnared in an ever-tightening trap of noise and dust.

End of third recording session.

Ben leaned back in his chair, letting his mental link with the recorder lapse into the passive mode. Tuning into the recording was every bit as vivid as the real experience—he was covered with sweat, that same cold, sticky sweat he had known so many years before. His muscles tensed then trembled. The antiseptic study with its quiet, metallic colors came slowly into focus and replaced the mental images of the collapsing tunnel.

He appreciated the cleanliness of his Fleet officers' quarters. No dust here, yet he was suddenly thirsty and felt an accompanying need to relax. He briefly considered the range of desensitizing agents available from the automat and decided on his favorite: straight, old-fashioned ethyl alcohol, chilled but not with ice. It was detoxified, of course, as was everything in his society.

Why record my life at all? he wondered. He hoped to add something meaningful to the static body of literature on galactic exploration. He hoped that his limited experiences before the imposition of the Perimeter would provide an impetus to explore again, allowing people to feel the excitement and danger of opening up a new world for humanity.

He had followed his father to Caldera and had tried to make something of value out of that primitive and lifeless world. Now, in his mind's eye, the winds roared across Caldera's hot, waterless surface, everywhere scouring and shaping the rugged mountains which contorted the surface. That same wind shaped his dreams. How could anyone appreciate the volcanoes and quakes which lashed across that blasted surface? Survival—tough, brutal survival— that was the lesson humanity had learned in the Tellurian Pleistocene epoch and had had to relearn on Caldera. And in both places weaponry had made the difference. He saw no stigma attached to using a nullor for survival. Like it or not, civilization existed because of weapons.

He snorted suddenly. The liquid had caught in his throat. *Slow down.* He was breathing hard again. He craved air untainted by dust and deadly gases.

He thought about what to record next, trying to decide how far to go before quitting for the day. Tomorrow he would be leaving for Earth to take command of a training flight, so it would be many weeks before he could finish his recording. He also had to consider how to handle the delicate matter of Fleet Commander Sedmak's presence in the investigation of the failure of Ossa I and what Sedmak had said to him when he was indicted for illegally using a nullor to save two of his crewmates. Sedmak had helped him realize the need to use weapons to preserve human civilization.

Sedmak! He smiled wryly. The Fleet Commander was probably his only real friend. Yes, he owed a lot to Sedmak. Matthew Sedmak had been a Sector Commander when Ossa I vanished on Caldera, but he had taken an interest in Ben by supporting his entry into the Fleet Academy even after the potentially disastrous investigation of the Ossa I incident and the ban on his use of nullor weapons, a ban which made him a useless commodity on Caldera. Yet, even here in the Space Fleet, fate continued to torment him. What was there to do in a society which had, in a few short years after his graduation, erected a Perimeter that halted all further space exploration? Where were the positions of power now? All he had on this infernal Perimeter base was a ship command and a shrew of a mate, the nagging bitch daughter of his Base Commander. He ought to have told them all where to shove off. But what else did he have? It was *his* miserable society. Still, it needed him more than he needed it. And that was why he stayed.

He strained back in his chair and stared at the still recorder. His body felt loose, almost afloat from the effects of the alcohol. He closed his eyes, and images tottered wildly like the dizzy gait of a drunk. The *Pelion* rolled and pitched with neck-wrenching violence as Ben fought to keep it level. They were flying away from the remains of Ossa I in a ship that had lost its inertial control system! He gulped air, forcing his stomach under control. He felt his fingernails cutting the palms of his hands. He had single-handedly piloted the ship to safety.

He was still feeling the druglike effects of an induced but unneeded sleep the next day as he slumped down in his passenger couch aboard the Fleet supply ship that was taking him to Earth.

"Going far, Ben?" someone asked.

He squinted at the man seated across the aisle and recognized the pinched-looking face of Zworykin, a Fleet engineer assigned to the Fylgan base.

"Earth," Ben replied tersely. "Got a ship to command out of there." He did not feel like talking to anyone.

"Where to?" Zworykin continued, his gimlet eyes on Ben. "From Earth, I mean."

"Shamash. Routine assignment. No big deal." Ben was bored. He activated the telepathic link on his couch so he could passively monitor the upcoming flight by noetronic means. Shielded by the protecting fields of the ship, this was his only way to "watch" the liftoff.

Zworykin settled on his couch. "Never seems like there are any big assignments anymore. Not like it used to be, before we had the Perimeter." His voice had an aimless quality, as if its owner did not care whether anyone was listening. "Still, the Perimeter serves some purpose. Keeps us engineers busy keeping it together." He chuckled to no one in particular.

Ben cleared his throat loudly in the middle of Zworykin's laugh. *You wouldn't make staff engineer on a tug. The Perimeter suits your closed mind.* Then Ben locked Zworykin out of his thoughts and tried unsuccessfully to consider the launch.

The supply ship lifted off the Perimeter base along an ejector beam that guided its supporting stem of blazing energy flux. Through the noetronic link with the scanner, Ben "watched" the rapid recession of the airless satellite that had been his home these past few years. Behind it loomed the mother planet and the cool, red sun.

Without scanner magnification the satellite Fylgan became just what it was—one small stone in the kiloparsec-wide Perimeter, simply another piece of that loosely knit, empyreal collection of unwanted planets, planetoids, space stations, and patrol craft which surrounded the Federation. These pieces in turn were supported by a more elaborate, widely dispersed set of unmanned sensor units and concealing screens.

When he considered what made up this vast ellipsoid, he felt fortunate in having drawn an assignment to Fylgan. At least he had not been cramped in some space station. He had a ship command, and someday he would have a larger command. Then he could do something about this ovoid cage humanity lived in.

He hated the Perimeter. He hated every vacuous cubic centimeter of it. He experienced brief moments of vivid awareness in which he almost gagged on the thought that his whole purpose in life was to keep humanity inside the Perimeter.

Enough! He forced his mind onto a Fleet training aid in the link. His rage against his prison was useful only in controlled doses; it kept him going, but he must not allow it to consume him.

The ship flashed out of metaspace and decelerated toward a lonely, oval-shaped space station adrift by itself light years from any star system, an isolated vanguard of Sector K-10. Probably put here because it filled up a blank space on some Sector Commander's quad-dem map, Ben thought as the ship made the necessary field tie-ins with the station.

"Well, so long." Zworykin was standing over him.

Good riddance, Ben thought to himself as he stretched. "Have fun," he said.

"Not much chance of that. Seems the main sensor unit on the station is out. Have to stay and fix it." Zworykin moved away.

"Sensor units don't go out," Ben called after Zworykin. Ben knew that they could fix themselves.

"This one did," Zworykin said, then disappeared in the direction of the teleporter room.

A blue-suited crewmember came down the aisle. "We may be here longer than we planned, so if you'd care to get off for a while…"

Taking her advice, Ben beamed from the ship's teleporter room over to the Perimeter station, checked in with the Fleet duty officer and then headed for the local Fleet club.

The club was a small, cozy room with homey Tellurian furnishings and conventional quad-dem artwork which made a person forget his or her loneliness while encased in a station woven by humans from powerful fields and made to look tangible. The clubroom held too many people.

He shouldered his way through the bodies and voices to the automat, where he ordered a Tellurian vodka and had the computer provide him with a list of personnel on board. Then he scanned the list while sipping his drink.

"Welcome aboard, Commander."

Ben looked up at a tall woman wearing the insignia of a Base Commander, then suddenly he recognized her—an old classmate from the Academy. "Raya Kireyev!" He shook her hand warmly. "I didn't know you were in charge here. I just came in on the supply ship. On my way to Earth. Looked like an extended stopover so I thought I'd come aboard."

"Where're you stationed now, Ben?"

"Fylgan."

Her wide, tense-looking face relaxed somewhat. "Perimeter, too?"

He nodded. "Yeah. Gets a little lonely." He gestured with his drink toward the other people in the room. "Popular place."

"We've had an equipment breakdown. Part of the crew is off duty." Her gaze shifted to a point just past his right ear.

Ben stared at her. *Jumpy.* He could sense it every time. "Yeah. I heard. One of our engineers is supposed to have a look at the situation. Zworykin, his name is."

"If you've got a few minutes, Ben, I'd like you to stop by my office."

"Fine. Be glad to." Ben followed her down an adjoining corridor and into a small, typically functional Fleet office.

"I've got a favor to ask," she began when the door had sealed behind him. "You probably know we're under a comm silence order here."

Puzzled, he said, "No, I didn't know."

"Fylgan isn't under comm silence?" It was her turn to be puzzled.

"It wasn't when I left. Why? How long has this been in effect?"

"Several months. That's all I'm at liberty to tell you. Nothing leaves here except through cleared channels. No routine messages in or out anymore."

She spread her arms in a tired gesture that ended almost in a shrug. "This whole sector is sealed off. That's why I asked you down here. I'd like you to take a message to my husband." She placed a sealed letter on top of her desk. Ben looked at the name and address written on the envelope. "He's on Earth," she said. "I just want him to know everything is all right." Anticipating his reaction, she added, "Ben, it's an honest letter. I'm not divulging any secrets. You have my word as an officer, but you can read the letter if you still have doubts."

"Be glad to take it," Ben said as he slid the letter into a concealed pouch in his uniform. As a result of the years of intensive training he had undergone with her, he knew that her word was good. Like all Fleet personnel, he was trained to detect falsehood and he knew there was none here. "What do you people do to warrant such attention from the front office?" he asked.

"The usual thing. Mostly passive monitoring of the stars beyond our part of the Perimeter."

Ben laughed. "We must have lucked out on Fylgan. All we get is the internal stuff. Very little outside work." He used these remarks as an opening to find out about the disabled sensor unit. It was peculiar that a Perimeter base should lose the use of the very item that had caused it to be placed under a communications silence order. But she evaded every attempt of his to learn more about the problems and secrecy of this base. Deciding that Raya was not in a mood to reminisce about their common past and that he could learn little more about the problems besetting this desolate station, Ben stood up to go.

"Thank you," she said quietly but with obvious feeling.

"Any time." Ben gave a friendly salute and left the office.

Restless, he walked the silent, shadowless corridors which had the emotional appearance of gray despite the presence of relaxing colors and other pleasing sensory images that originated in some hidden psych machine. No sound arose when his black boots touched the soft floor.

Ben passed many rooms, some containing one or two operators lost in idle conversation, most filled with the dim glow of untended equipment. Damn lax operation, he thought.

A sonic warning penetrated his skin. "Please do not pass this point," said a placatory mechanical voice that came from nowhere. "You will need a Fleet Secret certificate and a special clearance from the Base Commander to proceed beyond…"

Ben ignored the rest of the words. He stared for a moment at the forbidden length of corridor, knowing that to proceed further meant instant paralysis from a hidden stunnor beam, then he turned to retrace his steps.

"Ben! Hold up a minute!"

He whirled to see Zworykin coming from the room at the end of the restricted corridor. Now what the hell is he up to? Ben wondered.

Zworykin rapidly walked toward Ben, his hair now as rumpled as his cheap clothing. "Got to get an instrument scanner," Zworykin mumbled in his speaking-to-no-one manner.

"Fine," Ben muttered practically to himself as he walked alongside Zworykin.

His eyes suddenly bright, his manner direct, Zworykin turned. "Would you help me get my stuff together?" Without waiting for Ben's answer, he darted into a nearby unoccupied room that was filled with a girandole of sensor controls.

Ben followed Zworykin into the room, where he found the engineer frantically dashing about, peering into compartments and collecting tools.

"You ought to get a basket or a tractor beam," Ben said, annoyed with all the wasted motion he saw.

"You're right," the engineer said. Near to where Ben stood, Zworykin found a control panel for an internal tractor beam, and he used it to collect the parts into an orderly ensemble. Zworykin's eyes darted about the room. "Ben, that sensor was sabotaged." Zworykin's voice was hushed, uneasy.

"Huh?" Ben was not sure he had heard Zworykin correctly.

"Nothing wrong with it. Oh, they've got sloppy maintenance here. I'm not giving them any promotional merits on their upkeep. But that unit was sabotaged. Someone neatly fixed it so it couldn't receive any data."

"Do you know what it was monitoring?"

At that moment a uniformed crewmember appeared in the doorway. "Find everything, Zworykin?" The newcomer glared at Ben. "I didn't know you had company."

"Ben was on the ship with me," Zworykin nervously replied as he introduced them. "He's passing through to Earth."

"Nice to meet you," the crewmember said in a flat voice as he turned to accompany Zworykin and his tools.

Part way down the corridor, Zworykin turned back to Ben. "I'll be staying on for a while. Fleet orders. See you back on Fylgan." He resumed walking toward the sealed-off area.

Ben stared after the two retreating men with their cargo of invisibly supported material moving between them. Well, something is sure as hell out of whack here, he thought. He knew from long years of Fleet life that it was useless to probe beneath the unease to the unanswered questions. There were reasons for this kind of unusual activity, that much he felt certain about. He would play according to the rules and see what happened.

He stopped at the clubroom for another drink, hoping to catch some conversational clue about the mysterious behavior aboard the station, but all he heard were the usual off-duty complaints, magnified perhaps, and a certain conversational standoffishness that had not been evidenced earlier. He was glad when he was summoned to return to the ship. At least he could bow out gracefully.

The ship had severed its field lines with the station and was now easing away from the station on the repulsive power of its invisible pellor rays, the complement of a tractor beam. As soon as sufficient clearance was obtained, the ergon impeller would be activated, accelerating the ship to luxon speed. Then metaspace and another base, leapfrogging around the Perimeter before returning to Earth. Ben was still bored. He yawned and scratched. His hand touched the blue synthetic fabric of his Fleet uniform. *Nothing!* He sat up, feeling carefully. *The goddamned letter is missing!* He found no fault in his concealed pouch. Quickly, he summoned a crewmember and requested a search of the teleporter unit, then he sat back, stiffly annoyed.

The crewmember returned in a few minutes shaking his head. "Nothing, sir. Do you want us to check with the station?"

"No, forget it," Ben said in a distant tone, then he slouched in his seat, glaring. Slightly mortified, he guessed what had happened: *those bastards scanned me before I left, and they refused to transmit the letter!* He had been beamed off while the letter remained aboard the space station, shrouded in a communications silence blacker than the void through which it moved. Evidently, even Raya was unaware of the extent of station security. He supposed that his acceptance of the letter constituted a breach of station security, yet there had to be some trust between officers. She would not violate security. The blackness moved inside him. He was chagrined at having been outsmarted by some teleporter operator.

The slow trip to Earth resumed with sporadic stops at other Perimeter bases. People got on. People got off. Equipment transfers were made. There was a noticeable laxity at some of these bases. *The Federation is feeding on itself and dying,* he thought bitterly. *These people feel a lack of purpose in what many of them have devoted their lives to.* He likened them to abandoned legionnaires sent out to guard a dying empire. Silently, he cursed the politicians who had willed this stagnation of the visions and adventurousness of man.

He felt even more contempt for the people in charge of these bases. They were afraid to shit without first getting approval from Fleet Headquarters. Ball-less wonders. Afraid to make a decision. He knew *he* still had the talent and the will to make decisions without studying a problem to death or crawling to Earth for guidance. He shook his head in disgust as the ship departed from its last stop before Earth.

The supply ship exited from metaspace well "above" the plane of Sol's ecliptic and soared "down" on a stream of fire from its ergon impeller until it was safely captured in a Tellurian guide tube and steered to the Fleet base on the Atlantic coast of the North American continent.

Within minutes of the landing, Ben contacted Raya's husband, passing along a fabricated message from her while ducking his inquiries about the communications silence. Only for a friend would he have made such a diversion from his carefully planned schedule.

He spent the next few days going through the usual ship commander check-in procedures and briefings, then he received orders to report to Ron Carson, the Base Commander, for a courtesy discussion of the assignment.

The human receptionist in Carson's outer office motioned for him to enter. The door to Carson's office dematerialized in welcome, and Ben walked into the sunlit room now open in front of him with its official-looking desk, chairs and table. Carson, appearing as militarily correct as his furniture, stood waiting for him behind the desk. Ben was only dimly aware that the door had sealed behind him because his attention was instantly drawn to the tall, brown-haired man who moved in from the side of the room.

"Commander Sedmak!" he nearly blurted out but caught himself, then saluted both Sedmak and Carson. People generally were in awe of this large, powerfully built man, every centimeter the Fleet Commander that he in fact was, and Ben was no exception.

"At ease," Carson said crisply.

Carson looked quickly at Sedmak, excused himself and went into an adjoining room.

"It's good to see you again, Ben," Sedmak said, shaking his hand soundly. His grip and his voice were rather like the rest of him, almost larger than life. "Have a seat," he added as he sat down at the table. "It's been a long time since Caldera. How long has it been?" His voice resonated throughout the room in a not unmusical baritone.

"Over twenty years," Ben replied as he sat down, facing Sedmak. "I understand that it's been a successful alteration." Clearing his throat a little nervously, he continued, "I might add, I owe you some thanks for altering me."

Sedmak smiled. "You owe that to yourself."

Ben waited as Sedmak paused to pick up a folder and to adjust a small, portable visual scanner unit.

"I understand you stopped briefly at a station in Sector K-10 on your way here." Ben looked into his commander's probing, steady, gray eyes and then at the slight upturn of one corner of his mouth. Ah, yes, Ben thought. He knew about that, too—about the letter. "You always challenge the rules, Ben. I really believe you like to make things happen."

"It was a personal letter." A defiant tone.

"It might not have been."

"I like to think I can trust a fellow officer."

"So do I. You're lucky it was not a real security infraction *and* that I have other plans for you."

Ben leaned forward, eager now that answers to some of his questions might be forthcoming. "What's going on out there? There's been a comm silence imposed throughout that whole sector. And rumors of a main sensor unit being sabotaged on one of the stations."

Sedmak's eyes narrowed slightly. "You've got good ears. You're probably lucky to have gotten off that station."

"Is it true?"

"Yes." Sedmak moved his body a little closer to Ben. "But that information is Fleet Secret. So forget it."

Ben shook his head in amazement as he leaned back in his chair. "Incredible. Those stations only have Fleet-cleared personnel. That's pretty frightening if we can't trust our own people."

"It's a very ugly situation. A lot of unpleasant things have been happening throughout the Federation. People are openly moving against us. Sabotaging a Perimeter base is perhaps the most brazen act so far, but for certain people it was necessary that that sensor unit and others like it be eliminated." He paused. "I'll say some more about that later."

Curiosity hammered at Ben. "But who? Why?"

"I think you can guess the who and the why." Sedmak sat back in his chair and took a deep breath. The afternoon sunlight played lazily about him. "But then it's understandable, since we now have a reason to go beyond the Perimeter."

Shock, like a slight noetronic jolt, ripped through Ben's mind, loosening a barrage of questions into jumbled bits and pieces which refused to realign into any systematic order. Floundering at this heresy, he finally managed, "It's really serious…uh…whatever it is that's happening?"

"We think so, yes. I want you to take a look at this." Sedmak activated the scanner, retrieving information from the data-storage center. Ben saw a series of numbers and years come to colorful, three-dimensional life on the screen. He recognized those numbers as the annual toll of ships lost before the Perimeter was established.

"Have you wondered why so many ships were lost without a trace?" Sedmak asked, his eyes fastened on Ben.

"A lot of us have, yes."

"And why we have done so little about it?"

Ben started to respond with the standard Council explanation, but Sedmak continued speaking:

"I know the reasoning which justified abandoning those ships. I can appreciate how thinly stretched our exploration support was in those days. Even now, within the Perimeter, we're still badly spread out. But suppose I told you that we may have a clue as to what happened to one of those lost ships. Wouldn't you want to investigate?"

"Yes, sir."

"Then you've got more curiosity than our Council. They want the whole matter silenced. Take a look at this."

The visual image on the scanner changed, and Ben watched a capsule summary of an early exploration trip pass across the shining screen, followed by the news that the ship had been lost shortly after arrival at its destination. The life-support monitors in the Federation were very succinct: *no evidence of life remained on the ship.* The missing starcraft was written off, and the years passed in the capsule summary until a few months ago…

Ben immediately sat upright, his gaze fixed on the screen in front of him— the greenish-blue ball floating in the blackness of that screen had just become an unfathomable globe which spat out warped planetary radiation. The Perimeter bases in Sector K-10 were still unable to explain the change.

"We don't know exactly what's going on out there," Sedmak answered the intensely surprised look on Ben's face, "but we mean to find out. The standard safety rules, not to mention our present legal restrictions, keep us from actively probing it in any manner. So, until further notice, you are to refer to this planet only by the code name 'Gordius.' And outside of the select group of people whom I will identify as being cleared to work with you on this mission, you will not discuss this information with anyone." Sedmak placed his powerful hands in front of him on the table.

Ben nodded his acceptance of Sedmak's orders.

The hands now slid gracefully around the folder. "Council has seen all the data," Sedmak continued, his voice and eyes pressing the importance of the matter, "but they do not believe the time is right nor the resources sufficient to open the Perimeter. For the present, they have imposed a strict comm silence order on Sector K-10, and they have classified all the new information we have on Gordius. *Classified!*"—his tone was scornful—"that shows how desperate they are. However, *I* plan to send a ship to Gordius. And if that ship brings back the evidence I think it will, then the Federation will be in for some radical changes in thought."

Sedmak paused until the boldness of his scheme made its full impact on Ben. It was unsettling to Ben to hear the Fleet Commander's proposal to disobey his superiors in Council.

His desired effect achieved, Sedmak continued talking: "The ship has got to be crewed; first, because I trust humans more than I trust machines; and second, because I can justify a crewed training flight as a cover, while I can't justify any robotic probes inside our supposedly well-explored Federation." Sedmak's expression grew increasingly conspiratorial and intense as his big voice diminished. "Ben, I need someone I can trust to take charge of such a ship. There are many of us who would give anything to go, but your rank leaves you free enough to do it without question. And I know you have the capability to do the job. Will you go?"

"Yes," Ben answered firmly without the slightest hesitation, as he had anticipated the request. He paused, then added, "You said many of us. How many are involved?"

"More than you might suspect but not as many as I would like," Sedmak admitted, his gray, foglike eyes stabbing at him with a diffuse inner light, a sharp contrast to warm Sol outside. His voice swelled now, and he rose to his feet and began pacing. "Ben, you've seen the stagnation of the Fleet. Even a blind man can see it. And what is happening to the Fleet will eventually happen to the whole Federation as more and more people realize that they are sealed in a trap of humanity's own devising. Even before the Perimeter was established, there were many of us concerned about the missing ships and other inexplicable phenomena. Now I am in a position and have a justifiable reason to do something about it." His powerful figure stopped, he faced Ben and said with almost theatrical deliberateness, "Suppose we're not alone with our Federation, Ben. Suppose another group is waiting out there for us and does not want us to explore."

"Well, that has always been a remote possibility, but now—"

"Now, exactly. In this job, I have to consider all the possibilities. We have had a long period of peace—the longest real peace in the recorded history of humanity—and almost daily, because of our lack of exploration, our inward oriented society, we eliminate another potential weapons system. If we were to run into a problem with other beings from beyond the Perimeter, then the Federation could very well cease to exist. In a word, we're defenseless.

"I have arranged for you to command a modified training ship called the *Odyssey*," Sedmak continued briskly. "Before this mission is over, the name may be very apropos.

"You will be briefed later on the modifications which have been made to the ship, the shield suits and the general flight plan. You've got a little more than a week before the crew assembles for the official preflight checkout, which gives you plenty of time to learn the real plan. As far as the crew and the outside world are concerned, you're on a routine training flight to Shamash. We can't take any chances on anyone knowing the real mission. That will be disclosed by you to your crew when you get there. Too many people in our midst are suspicious of all flights right now, especially one that might involve a crew sympathetic to crossing the Perimeter. Which is another reason why I and others with known sympathies like mine can't risk going."

Sedmak again made some adjustments on the scanner. Three names appeared on the screen. Ben caught his breath at the sight of the first one. In his effort to absorb all that his assignment entailed, he had momentarily forgotten his original orders, which had the names of the men assigned to him for the training flight. The first name brought everything back into a chilling focus. Sedmak smiled and gave him a sly, knowing wink. "Other than you, I want an honest, unbiased crew. These men are not part of any conspiracy. Still, they were not arbitrarily picked. In a sense, they each represent a different viewpoint, a different personality, which when added up leads to a whole approach that could convince humankind of their findings. For that reason alone, it's important that you all return." In a firmer voice, he added, "Understand that carefully—*I don't want a crew loss situation!*"

The screen changed to a tridem picture of the first man on the list. Ben looked carefully at the image of Lt. Richard J. Highstreet, Jr., as he liked to absorb every detail about his crews, know how they functioned and how to make them function. Highstreet was a Tellurian by birth and like most of his kind, a mixture of many races. He was tall and angular, dark haired like Ben, with brown eyes in a dark-skinned face a trifle too small for his head. Highstreet was over ten years his junior.

Sedmak looked from Ben to the picture. "Other than the obvious reason for sending Highstreet, he's a damned good pilot." He cleared his throat, the first sign of unease Ben had ever witnessed in Sedmak. "Normally, I wouldn't prejudge a crew to its commander, but these are difficult times. Highstreet is probably the best of the three for running a ship. I would look to him as a second-in-command. He's smart and thinks for himself. He originally came to our attention in other ways—some problem at the Academy and a bad experience on the Perimeter. These incidents were not his fault, and I think he has matured as a result of them."

The screen changed again, revealing the second man on the list: Lt. Gregory I. Sheldon, a science officer from Ziolkovsky. Like Highstreet, this man was tall with a heavy tan. His fashionably cut brown hair and serious gray eyes, looking like somber slits of mist, stood out in light contrast to his skin. Ben observed that Sheldon was a descendent of some Tellurian northern hemisphere emigrants who had grown up on Ziol with its hot deserts. Sheldon was almost twenty-five standard years old and a specialist in astrophysics and systems analysis.

"Sheldon is a quiet one, a loner and an outworlder," Sedmak said. "I understand that he and Highstreet are good friends, even shared an assignment together. And he also knows your third crewmember, which makes him a common link.

"Normally, I wouldn't send someone like Sheldon on a mission like this—he's too cerebral, an introvert—but I think he will have a personal interest in this because of the massacre on Ahriman." Ben briefly recalled the Ahriman incident, in which a team of explorers were mercilessly tortured and killed by the planet's inhabitants. The event provided added support to those who opposed space exploration. "Don't underestimate him," Sedmak went on. "He's a damned good scientist, and while he isn't geared for Fleet service, he does have a tremendous will to succeed."

Ben refrained from making any comments, preferring instead to review the three dossiers in private. He wondered whether his selection had been discussed in the same cryptic manner.

The screen changed tridem pictures again to show another Tellurian, Lt. Arthur W. Cooke, who with his reddish hair and blue eyes looked much younger than his recorded age, only five years younger than Ben and ten years older than Sheldon. Like Ben, he was of medium height. Ben knew that Cooke had a strong background in planetology and in operating the payload and logistics systems on starships.

Ben was puzzled by Cooke's unfathomable stare from eyes as enigmatic as they were clear. They were like small, pale-blue ponds, penetrable yet somehow closed to him.

"Cooke is a Syncretist and a bit of a rebel," Sedmak said.

"Why send a Syncretist?" Ben was angry. "You hinted that they—"

"I know, I know," Sedmak responded to Ben's sudden outburst. "They hold no love for us. I blame them for the Perimeter and for the current mess we're in. But these are only my feelings, extrapolated from their desire to remake the Federation."

"But why send *him?*" Ben repeated. "You might as well give me a programmed self-destructing ship. He's a weak link in what so far seems like a pretty solid crew."

Sedmak blew out a lungful of air, fatigue evident in this expulsion of wind. It was obvious he had covered this ground before. "He's a recent convert. He wasn't raised among them." Pause. "We have a pretty good idea of the mental trickery they're capable of using, but he hasn't shown any unusual behavior, so we're guessing his Syncretistic sympathies result from a conscious desire and not subconscious training. Sheldon's known Cooke for some time, so he can probably be used as a guide in judging whether Cooke has changed. Cooke has *shown* no deviant behavior." Sedmak's face was in shadows. "I agree that we're taking a calculated risk with him; however, if you find what I believe is out there, we'll need Syncretistic support to turn Council around. Also, his presence takes a lot of suspicion off this flight. He is good at his job, but all I can offer you is a warning: keep him under surveillance and remember that *he may just be the most important one on your ship.* So bear with him."

"What if things get rough out there?" Ben asked. He needed to define the limits of his authority once he left the Federation.

"Carson will go over the procedures and contingency plans." With a knowing smile, Sedmak added, "As Carson will show you, we've even given your suits a little extra protection. We've tried to anticipate every possibility without giving away the real mission."

"I'm also thinking about the Fleet conditioning," Ben said, remembering the agonizing emotional aftermath of Ossa I, when he successfully fought the punishing guilt which had been imbedded in his mind by the Calderan administrators as a part of their overall precautionary measures to prevent the use by individuals of lethal devices such as nullor weapons around living organisms. His conditioning on Caldera had been limited in scope compared to what the Fleet imposed on its more widely traveled personnel. He had faith in his own abilities to cope with the problem of conditioning, but what about his crew? Would any one of them in a true crisis situation refuse to save himself or other members of the crew if it meant killing?

"You'll have to do the best you can, Ben. I don't have the power to alter that conditioning. I know you'll avoid situations that would force you to test it. We want answers, not trouble."

The screen went blank, leaving the room in semidarkness. It was getting late.

"I've got to leave now," Sedmak said as he handed Ben the folder of personnel data. "Carson will take care of the details, although he doesn't know all that you know about the mission; I've tried to compartmentalize the information for security. We'll give you all the help we can. I've even gone so far as to permit you to use my official seal for emergencies, but otherwise I'm going to stay behind the scenes. As far as you know, I had nothing to do with any of this. If need be, we can program mental blocks to any probing in the event the mission fails. Short of having a shipborne nullor, which is illegal, and concealing screens, which would arouse suspicion, I think you'll find the equipment to be the best the Fleet has, which is a damned sight better than what you had at Ossa I." Sedmak shook Ben's hand firmly. "Be careful, Ben, and good luck. Come home safely."

2

EARTHSIDE

He could not say what he meant by freedom, for he realized that, in truth, he had not been freer at home than he was in this queer city, but there the hedging rules had been less obvious, or had affected him, personally, less than they did here.

—Ruthven Todd, *The Lost Traveller*

The reddening disk of Phaëthon loomed above the low, yellow-and-greenish-brown foothills to the west, mixing rays of orange-red light with dark, oblong shadows below to create a paintpot of color outside. Midsummer was at its fullest on Armstrong and despite being inside the environmentally controlled flyer, Richard Highstreet felt hot just from seeing Phaëthon.

On an impulse, he banked the tubular flyer and aimed it directly at the eye-singeing red flare. Phaëthon seemed to beckon him onward with the promise of a gateway to an earlier, more pleasant time. He wanted to forget that he had just left his three-year-old son behind in the care of his in-laws. He had left his son alone just as his father had left him.

Phaëthon reminded him of another heat—the heat of the African continent in that long-ago summer when the Highstreets had still been together. He thought back to the last family outing before his father took command of the spaceship *Leos* to explore the Sangraal star system. He remembered camping near a lake in the midst of a green Elysian jungle. His father's gift for storytelling transformed the dark forest, nurtured by ample rain and idyllic weather, into a kind of Miocene Eden, where humanity's simian forerunners had quenched their thirst in order to live so that the human race could be born. In the midst of this paradise, Richard's father had spoken of living solely for life itself. Then he went off to die.

Highstreet thought of the parallels between his life and his son's. Would the pattern go on? he wondered as he "watched" the human-made geometric figures of yellows and greens and browns on the plain below. His mind moved with the scanner, and he "felt" the wind around him as he guided the silent flyer along on its invisible pellor rays.

Within thirty minutes, he was over the coastline of the Aegir Ocean, skimming along above the dark, prostatic fluid which pounded the sandy beaches in a ceaseless, orgasmic rhythm like some Precambrian ocean stirring with the first motions of life. The early Tellurian planetologists had established on Armstrong what existed naturally on Earth: a delicate interglacial balance between Armstrong's polar and equatorial oceans, which made the beautiful Aegir coast possible. Sinking Phaëthon caught the darkening water and turned it green-orange. Here, he and Jan had made love for the first time, alone in a cove with the shining green water wetting the yellow-brown sand around them. Afterward, she had climbed a small wet boulder near the waterline, letting the salty, seminal sea breezes caress her naked brown body. Here she had paused to gaze at the vibrating ocean. He had looked up at her as she asked in a thoughtful tone, "Can even your space be more beautiful?" At first, he had merely nodded, knowing that each environment had its own peculiar beauty. Finally, he had quietly said, "I suppose that had I lived centuries ago I would have been a sailor." His mind saw her then as she turned to him, her long, brown hair blowing lightly across her smiling face, and said, "You are a sailor, my dear Odysseus—a star sailor."

Damn! He did not want to think about her. She had left him. And now he was leaving their son because he had been ordered back to Earth. He jerked the flyer up from the beating waves and soared silently over the rocky coastal cliffs.

In another half-hour he caught the snow-covered Aesir Mountains, which looked like majestic white fangs whose sky-piercing tops sparkled red in the final light from Phaëthon. Beyond them, fingers of darkness clutched eastward, forcing Richard to rely on his scanner for the remainder of the flight to the Tamil spaceport. He relaxed in his couch, totally at ease in the air and happy to be in control of a flying device. While a casual pilot would probably rely solely upon the automatic controls, secretly hoping that nothing would go wrong, Richard commanded the flyer himself, as he had within him the confidence borne of long hours of intensive and extensive flight training at the Space Fleet Academy. Through the mental teaching machines, he had learned to navigate, to control different ships, to make repairs and to control his physical and mental processes even to the extent of functioning as a computer. Like all officers in the Fleet, his mind had been noetronically filled with a vast supply of information, giving him a complete working knowledge of space travel and exploration so that in an emergency he could automatically recall and use this information. This method of learning complemented his own style of thinking. He had an almost algebraically terse reasoning ability that radically condensed the intervening algorithmic propositions to the point where his decisions and responses seemed instantaneous. Life was a one-time affair, with no room for elaborate analyses of every decision or for recriminations about past mistakes. Still, there were moments when he thought about Jan, about his old friend Jerry Whittaker, and about the unease he felt as a result of staying with the rule-laden Fleet.

Initially, this noetic education had been a mentally expanding experience but now as he gazed at the scanner-lit landscape below, he knew that his education had served him only to pilot trivial craft like this flyer. Any civilian could do that much. There was nothing useful to be done with his education. Exploration was finished. He had sought professional rejuvenation through assignments such as his postgraduate work in the Science Officer Corps of the Fleet, yet now his only compensation in the Fleet was visiting the explored Federation planets, where he could still muster an interest in the beauty of the life forms there. That was all that was left—life, so hold on to it. All around him the dark Armstrong night moved its black cover over the places the scanner and sensors left.

Two hours later, he was inside the spaceport. Gone now was the freedom of flight. In the spaceport he experienced again all the organized frenetic activity which he had come to associate with and dislike about Earth. Jan had lovingly shown him a more open and relaxed way of living, a way more in concert with the outworlds such as Armstrong than with his home world, beset as it was with skillfully hidden but ever-present behavioral controls. Now that Jan was gone, only Greg Sheldon and Coni Sanderson, of all of his friends on Earth, could be counted on to understand his feelings. That helped make the trip home bearable.

The spaceport bar was nicer than the bars he usually frequented on Earth. A colorful quad-dem painting swirled behind the bar counter, casting a cheerful, multicolored glow on the three or four other people silently drinking inside. He was surprised that the bar had a human bartender at that off-hour. He ordered one of the local beers and took it to a twilight-shrouded booth.

"Well, don't speak, stranger," a woman's voice chided him.

Richard looked up at the dark form of a woman silhouetted against the quad-dem painting. There was something familiar about the voice and stance, head thrown back at an angle. "Mary! Mary Whittaker! Sit down, please."

She slid into the booth facing him, a drink held in both hands. "Long time, Rich."

"Well, I guess it has been. Two years? Three?" He smiled, happy to see this direct, energetic woman. "You look as beautiful as ever."

She wrinkled her long, narrow nose in mock disgust. "And you're revolting…as ever," she drawled. "So how is it we meet in this cosmic way station? You first." She crossed her long legs, tugging at the knees of her blue uniform.

"Just finishing up my leave. On my way Earthside to perform the exciting and original assignment I've been volunteered for. How about you?"

"Just about the reverse. I've been on patrol in K-10 for the past few months, and now I'm rotating Earthside for some leave. You leaving on this next flight?"

"Right you are, you lucky person." Mary shook her head, grinning, then asked, "How's the family?"

Richard took a mouthful of his beer before replying, "Not too good. Jan's off on Goddard, and Richie is staying here with her parents."

"You break your contract?"

"No. We're just separated. She doesn't want to break it."

Mary smiled and placed a hand on Richard's. "That's good. If I know Jan, she'll be back."

"How about you?" he asked, seeking to change the subject.

"Still free and single. The Fleet keeps me busy."

"No other problems?" he asked cautiously.

She gave a short, mirthless laugh. "No. They've left me alone for several years now. I think they're finally convinced that I had nothing to do with what Jerry did."

Sadness hit Richard as he remembered the frantic chase beyond the Perimeter that he and Greg Sheldon had been part of, the Fleet ship *Guardian* slicing its way to Ormazd in search of—*forget it!*

"You really loved him?" she asked, her voice telling him that she understood his thoughts about her brother.

Richard took another drink, then he stared at the hint of white foam clinging cloudlike to the side of his glass. "Yes. He was my best friend at the Academy. He was too good for all of this. I still feel rotten about what happened." She touched him again, her voice soft now. "You weren't to blame. You didn't know."

He drank again, hoping to think other thoughts. How many times had he and Jerry drunk beer and chased women while at the Academy until they were almost busted? He could not guess at the answer. They had had fun, too much perhaps, as if in pleasure they found release from the frustration of knowing that even before graduation they could never go beyond the newly established Perimeter. Jerry had spoken only once about his anger at the Perimeter, on that night several days after Sedmak had announced to the Academy during their second term that Council had decreed the establishment of a Perimeter. Jerry and he had gone later to an image shop, only to end up in trouble with a robot patrol because Jerry, in his stoned state, got out of line with them. Richard blamed the Perimeter for Jerry's failure to finish the Academy; Jerry was justified in leaving, since the Perimeter meant that there was nothing for him to look forward to in the Fleet. He, Richard Highstreet, had been the dumb one. He had stayed on, putting up with every degrading assignment, sacrificing his freedom like a fully controlled automaton, in the hope that one day…

"You say you've been out there in K-10," he said to Mary, remembering something his father-in-law had told him just before he left the westcountry of Armstrong. "Do you know what's going on on Vesta? I heard a rumor about some equipment problems and political demonstrations."

"I don't know anything about Vesta. We stayed in space all the time I was in K-10. Occasionally, we docked at a space station. Otherwise, just lots of flying." She twisted her glass and watched the motion of the dark fluid. Without raising her eyes, she added, "But something funny *is* going on in K-10. Sensor units have been sabotaged. Crews aren't working."

He looked closely at her dark, handsome face.

She lowered her voice and leaned toward him. "There's a rumor…you're bound to hear it sooner or later, Rich; we heard it at one of the stations…something about some signals being received from the Sangraal system."

Sangraal! The word reverberated inside Richard's head like a sonal blast. The second planet of that yellow main sequence star which whirled well beyond the Perimeter had swallowed up his father, sealing his fate in a cavernous void of silence. "Is it true? Which station? When? Who?"

"Whoa, Rich, slow down. Look, it's a rumor, a hot one, but it's still a rumor. Sector K-10 is closed off under comm silence, so there's no way to verify the rumor. We may have been the last patrol ship to come out. Except for me, the others have returned to patrol duty. What I've told you is probably classified by now. I'd tell you to stay out of it if I thought it would do any good."

Richard finished his beer in one long drink. "Let's see how our ship is doing." He stood up and held out his hand.

Richard felt more in touch with himself by the time he reached Earth and was once again walking along the familiar grassy path that led to the garden apartment which had been his home with Jan and Richie. Mary had been a lovely traveling companion. She was a fine person, easy to be with, and she was a realist. She, like a number of people in their highly mobile profession, accepted the terms of their nomadic life and declined exclusive conjugal arrangements or contracts of any sort. He knew, however, that several of the men she paired off with when circumstances brought them together were friends of many years standing. He would call her as soon as he got settled in the apartment.

Richard and Jan's apartment was located at the edge of the sprawling ancient city, near the Fleet base. The apartment fronted a splendid harbor; Richard admired the aquamarine vista. The bay was used almost exclusively for recreation now, as commercial transportation had long ago been transferred to the teleporters. Although the teleporters provided almost instantaneous matter transportation, people tended to walk out of doors more frequently here than in most cities. Richard noted a number of people, couples mostly, walking along the pathway bordering the water. A delicate yellow-green fuzz softened the tips of the tree branches in the little park by the apartment. He inhaled the refreshingly cool salt air and let himself into the apartment.

He tossed his flight bag onto a sofa and ordered a whisky from the automat as he placed a call on the communicator. The three-dimensional visage of a mature, dark-haired woman reflected back from the communicator a feminine version of himself.

"Hello, mom. I just got in."

"I see that. Welcome home." Her hazel eyes searched his eyes for a moment. "How do you feel?"

"Fine, mom, just fine. How about yourself?"

"Perfectly all right. Your brother is here, that is, not here this moment, but here. You two haven't seen each other in ages, have you? Are you free tonight for dinner?"

"Uh, sure, mom."

His mother ignored his hesitation and the fleeting look of dismay in his expression. "See you in an hour or so," he added. Richard could take his cocky, arrogant little brother on a good day, but he'd hoped for a quiet evening with his mother, whom he both loved and admired. He had not seen Ken in nearly a year. Richard hoped that during that time Ken might have mellowed. His last visit with Ken had ended up like so many others before it. Ken had derisively put down Richard's profession, strongly implying that Richard was desecrating their father's memory by staying in the Fleet. In Ken's view, space was nothing but a human graveyard.

Richard turned from the communicator and looked around the bright, open rooms with their traditional furnishings. They were cheerful, but he was now indifferent to them, as if they were a smile on a stranger's face. The silence echoed the many words that had been left unsaid between him and Jan during the preceding several months. The combined resentment and guilt that accumulated during his absences crippled communication between them, even though they went through the ritual of confrontation, contrition, reconciliation. He did not blame her for the way she felt. She had her own life to lead. She had not married a goalless traveling man, but he became one for a number of reasons, none of which satisfied her. And the reasons did not satisfy *him* any longer. Lately, the restrictions on flights had confined him to Earth and so now he had little interest in his career in the Fleet.

Yes, he had been bitter when she left, bitter about her leaving him, bitter about the purposelessness of his life. "You might as well break the contract!" he had yelled just before she walked out the door on her way to join the mission to Goddard. Then as now, images of another couple, locked in death, flitted through his mind. *They* had stayed together. But he had only partially understood while denying a much greater truth. He could still see the tears in Jan's sad, brown eyes as she turned to face him from the doorway. "I love you, Richard, but you can't see that. I won't break the contract!"

He realized now that her decision to leave was a valiant effort to give them time to start over and that she had understood their relationship better than he. He knew, too, that it was wrong for him, a man disenchanted with his unfulfilled dream of exploration, to deny her the right to her dreams. They were still legally bound to each other, but Richard knew that her outworlder morality had been shattered in the pleasure palaces of Earth, and he dreaded her long absence on Goddard. He had picked up too much on Armstrong and from her to recapture his earlier Tellurian nonchalance about sex and love: they were too precious to be wasted casually.

His only consolation was her parting words: "I love you. I won't break the contract!" He had pulled his life together, fueling his efforts with his father's admonition to live life and with a lesson taught to him from a graveyard in the forbidden regions beyond the Perimeter.

Through the windows, ribbons of soft light flew linearly from a sun-saturated cloudbank as Richard fixed a second drink. One more call and then I'd better get going, he thought.

The communicator responded to his command, and in less than a minute its artistically colored screen changed into the comely face of a young, blonde-haired woman. He had turned the communicator up to full magnification, and his throat caught at seeing her so clearly before him, as if she were in the room with her sybaritic smile and slender lips colored pink against the paleness of her skin. Upon seeing him, sudden excitement flushed her. "Hi, Rich! When did you get back?" Her voice spoke of music, some ancient harmonious way of speaking that had died when technology became ruler. She had girlishly small bones smoothed over by the firm roundness of a young woman. He had never seen all of her, and he knew he never would. Even now, her overconcealing outworld-type swimsuit locked the pleasure from his eyes. The vertical lines of her caressingly long, yellow-white hair, together with her bone structure, gave her face just enough ovalness to keep it from being round. Her slender nose was small in keeping with her overall size, and it had a certain youthful cuteness about it. But the eyes! Large and round, full of intelligence and awareness, green with spring, radiating with lambent life. Yet, those eyes, like her face, hinted at some quiet sadness. He wanted her in this room, this moment. In a society where ugliness and deformities had been scientifically eliminated, he still felt that Coni Sanderson was the most beautiful woman he had ever seen. He wished he could tell her this. Certainly, Jan would have been proud to hear it, but Coni was different—such a compliment would bring winter to those glistening eyes. Coni, the ice princess: he often wondered what she was like in bed.

"About an hour ago," he answered her question. "Hey! You look wet. If you were any more real, you'd dampen my floor."

She laughed, the sounds playing like musical notes on some responsive scale within him. "We had just come in from swimming when you called."

He wished more than ever that she was with him. *Jan's been gone too long.* "Is your old man around? I'd like to talk to him."

"Sure." She called off-image. One thing you had to say about Coni, she never flirted, he thought. Either one of them could have made several suggestive remarks, but flirting for her was unthinkable. He used to wonder if her attitude of nobility had roots in the terror of her past. She was damned fortunate to be alive, not to mention being in love with the one man who could do the most good for her.

A lanky man moved into the image, his skin set darkly against hers. Coni smiled up at this newcomer, her arm in his. "Hello, stranger!" the heavily tanned man said. "Welcome back!"

"Jeez, Greg, you look pale! You need to get out of that apartment."

Greg Sheldon quietly laughed, the dryness of his voice creating another contrast between himself and the fantasy-making woman beside him. "How about coming over tonight?" Greg said, and Coni quickly added, "Please do, Rich. Despite what Greg says, I know how to fix old-fashioned meals."

Richard returned Greg's laugh and shook his head. "Much as I'd like to, I can't. Another lovely woman beat you to it, my mother. However, I would like to talk to you later tonight, Greg. Try to get up to speed before tomorrow."

Puzzled, Greg looked at Coni. She nodded briefly, silently. "Sure, Rich. What time?"

"Make it about 2200. I'll meet you at the High Tide. Then maybe you can show me the latest night spots."

"Not a chance," Coni said in a playfully firm tone.

"We'll behave," Richard said. "I'll see you later, Greg." The images vanished, leaving him feeling more lonely than ever. This feeling was aggravated by the knowledge that his schedule would keep him from seeing Mary until he returned from Shamash. He gathered his things together and walked into the bedroom he had shared with Jan, where he slowly undid the hidden fasteners that held together his sky-blue, custom-fit uniform and ankle-length black boots. What to wear tonight? he wondered.

He left his mother's apartment by 2130, satisfied that his family obligations had been met. With a relaxed gait he strolled toward the harbor and his rendezvous with Greg Sheldon. He felt a twinge of guilt about the emotional suspense that always preceded these family get-togethers. What was the problem? His mother had exhibited her usual concern about his safety. Wisely, he had not told her about the rumor he had heard from Mary Whittaker, even though he told her that he had seen Mary. Ken behaved a little better than usual, but it was not the same without his father.

The High Tide was a run-down bar and cafe located near the harbor. Its appearance had been purposely contrived through the artful use of period marine motifs to give it the atmosphere of a seafarers' retreat. The interior decor consisted of rope trim, scoured plank floors, limp swatches of netting draped across walls, and well-worn, heavy wooden furnishings. The place was popular with the younger Fleet officers, which was why Richard always felt at ease inside. Richard looked around the semidarkened room where the only sources of light were actual lanterns and hidden imagers, the latter making the walls appear illuminated by bluish-green light reflected from rolling ocean waves. Several noisy spacers pressed close to the High Tide's one claim to fame—an authentic, well-stocked, greenly lit glass aquarium located along the wall opposite the entrance.

Seeing no sign of Greg, Richard sat down at an empty wooden table that faced the entrance. He ordered a whisky from the automatic bartender, one of the few contemporary variants allowed in the High Tide. The owner, a portly man named Bernie Dworski, had deliberately taken on weight, wore tight-fitting striped sailor shirts and an unneeded black eye patch just to give the place a more authentic look and perhaps to counter the anachronistically automatic bartenders.

Richard had barely started to sip his drink when the old, wooden door opened under the guidance of Greg Sheldon's shadowy hand, and Coni Sanderson entered the room like a leucothean spirit wafting in on a sea breeze. The other noises in the room subsided briefly as Coni stood there looking for Richard. Several people could be heard sucking their breath at the sight of her. Richard waved and she glided to his table, with Greg close behind. Richard stood and shook her hand and then Greg's. "What a pleasant surprise to see you both. Sit down—the drinks are on me."

As usual, Coni ordered a nonalcoholic tropical beverage, and Greg ordered a whisky. Smiling at Coni, Richard said, "My crack about seeing the nightspots with Greg must have gotten to you." Coni returned his smile somewhat blankly but said nothing. Richard leaned back in his chair and admired Greg's clothes. "Jeez, you look fashionable. Who would guess that inside those colorful clothes beats the heart of a dyed-in-the-wool reactionary? Earth seems to have treated you okay while I was gone." He paused for effect. "All kidding aside, I'm glad to see you."

Greg raised his mug in salute. "Always glad to drink your booze," he replied, his laugh covering them like a soft, dry fabric that had been sonically cleaned. "How was Armstrong?"

There was a burst of argumentative phrases from the spacers standing near the aquarium, which caused Richard to emphasize his answer. "Peaceful as always. Sure was glad to get away from here." Greg's eyes narrowed slightly at the sudden noise, obviously concerned that Coni was staring at the spacers. Richard continued, "I don't think I've ever needed a vacation as much as that one."

Greg focused on him. "Richie make out okay?" His eyes were back on Coni.

"Yeah. He really likes the place. Didn't want to leave," Richard answered without pause. With anyone else he might have been annoyed with the apparent interchange in the center of attention but he knew that Greg's Fleet training permitted him to follow numerous activities at the same time, so he overlooked the shifting of Greg's eyes.

More raised voices. There was a sound of glass grating against glass, followed by the frenzied splashing of water. Instantly, Richard turned to see what was happening. The aquarium was literally frothing with greenish-white foam.

Coni yelled something that was lost in the racket, then she ran to the aquarium before Richard or Greg could stop her. She viciously struck one of the spacers with enough force to knock him aside. Greg darted after her.

Coni smashed her tiny hand through the glass cover, shattering it into large jagged pieces. Richard leaped after Greg. Everyone else in the room seemed frozen in place.

Misty, dark clouds of blood swirled through the churning aquarium as Coni frantically groped in the water searching for something. A dark shape materialized out of the foam and clutched her hand.

She screamed in pain and fear. Greg grabbed her arm, but she twisted away and then pulled her hand out of the water. A small tube of black flesh clutched her hand with tiny tentacles.

"A Cetian bloodsucker!" Richard blurted out his fury as he, too, tried to help Coni. She resisted both men as she swung her hand repeatedly against the remaining broken segment of the glass cover in an effort to slice up the creature. The injured tentacles tore at her flesh with a renewed vigor born in desperation, while Coni's and the creature's blood mingled and gushed over the glass and into the water.

The creature dropped lifelessly into the water as suddenly as it appeared, adding to the dark stain inside the glass cage. Only then did Coni allow Greg to hold her. "Damnit! Somebody get a medicator!" Greg shouted as he pressed Coni's torn hand to his body in an attempt to stop the flow of blood. "Don't worry, honey," she murmured. "I can heal it."

Dworski dashed into a back room and quickly returned with a small home medicator.

"It's all right now," Coni said, holding up her hand, which was covered with ugly scabs but no longer bleeding. She refused aid. "I can fix it at home. There was no poison."

Flustered, Dworski asked, "What happened?"

"Someone tossed that bloodsucker into your tank," Greg answered in an icy tone.

Dworski turned to the three or four spacers who were helping their fallen comrade get up. Dworski's bulk now worked to his advantage, and the spacers backed away from their image of a hulking giant. "You dirty bastards!" he growled. With a fluidity that belied his weight, Dworski threw a chair at the huddled spacers, causing them to scatter. "Get the hell out of my place before I call the robot patrol!" he yelled with rage, chasing them from the room.

"Greg, I had to do it," Coni said quietly. "That creature was causing such pain. Those poor fish." She looked up at him for support. "It's all right now, isn't it?" Her voice drifted off into a tremulous whisper, mingled with the tense murmured sounds now filling the room. "It's all right," Greg answered. "I'll take you home now."

Richard felt awkward standing there. "Is there anything I…"

Greg shook his head. His face was drawn and anxious. "We'd better leave before a patrol starts to nose around." He guided Coni toward the door.

Richard moved past the remaining customers and held the door open for Greg and Coni. "I'm coming with you," Richard said very quietly. "Just in case there's more trouble."

Greg held his eyes on Richard for a moment but said nothing as he walked Coni out the door.

Somehow the three of them managed to get through the darkness to Greg and Coni's apartment without contacting any patrols or other people. Inside, Greg sat about ministering to Coni, who finally asked to be left in bed with their medicator. "You go talk shop with Richard, I'll be okay," she persisted. "Modern medicine has taken care of me." Richard sensed a slight bitterness in her words. He knew what she meant—artificial blood in an artificial hand.

After leaving Coni in the bedroom, Greg returned to the living room, where Richard stood waiting. With a sigh, Greg slumped into a chair, weakly motioning for Richard to sit on the sofa. Then Greg stared morosely at the wall. Finally, he spoke, almost to himself, "What kind of person would do a thing like that?"

Richard started to answer then stopped himself. He suddenly wondered whether Greg was referring to the incident at the High Tide or the earlier, more terrible event on Ahriman. "Let me get you a drink," he offered, feeling that he should be doing something.

Greg nodded without feeling. "I shouldn't have let her come with me, but it's our last night together and she was so insistent. And she felt very lonely."

Richard got up and ordered two whiskies from the automat, then he turned on one of Greg and Coni's sonic quad-dem paintings, pleased to have the music and four-dimensional images glide through the room like a living poem reaching out to all his senses. From previous experience, he recognized Fontana's *Dancers of Cytherea,* one of Greg's favorites.

Richard took a drink from his glass. Greg appeared to be relaxing amid the playful images and sounds of the painting. By way of changing the subject, as well as getting to the point of the evening's meeting, he asked, "What's up on this flight to Shamash? Seems a little funny to be screwing around with training flights these days."

Greg shrugged, his face momentarily lost in the shadowy images of wild dancers cavorting to the increasing tempo of the music. "I don't know. I was as surprised as you when it came up. I figured that the timekeepers had finally caught up to the fact that recently I've been on Earth more than off it. But why they put you on it? I don't know. You've had your share of training."

"I guess all we can do is look at the bright side. We'll be out there flying for the fun of it, no purpose other than that."

Greg spat out some air. "Wilson may not be fun."

"How's that?"

"Some of the troops tell me he can be a real prick. He lacks our scientific attitudes. He tends to follow all the old militaristic 'I-run-this-ship' kind of crap." Greg took a sip from his drink. "Carson had one of his dull receptions again last week. I met Wilson there. He'd just got in from the Perimeter a few days before. He's kind of aloof. Cold s.o.b. Coni didn't take to him either."

"What about Cooke?"

"I met him six or seven years ago. Surely I must have mentioned him to you. Anyhow, when I met him, he had just graduated from the Academy and was returning from an assignment. Kind of funny, really. Coni introduced us. I thought he was a rival for her, which is probably why I never liked him. It turned out that he was a friend of a woman Coni had met several years before that. Coni still keeps in touch with her—I don't know why, they had some differences of opinion—but I haven't seen Art Cooke in years. The last I knew he was stationed somewhere in Eurasia. Keeps him close to his Syncretistic roots."

"Is he one of those?"

Greg nodded.

"Shit, you were right—there may not be much fun on this mission." Richard stood up. "Care for another?"

Greg emptied his glass. "Sure." He handed Richard his glass and then excused himself to check on Coni.

When Greg returned, Richard handed him a fresh drink. "She's resting," Greg said simply. "Medicator indicates everything is okay."

Taking his own whisky, Richard returned to his spot on the sofa. "I ran into Mary Whittaker at the Tamil spaceport."

"Oh?" Wariness sounded in Greg's voice. "How is she?"

"Looks okay. She said they've finally left her alone." Richard shifted his weight by leaning against the arm of the sofa. He came directly to the news that was troubling him. "Greg, what do you know about signals from Sangraal?"

The music had subsided, and the ghost dancers had moved away from Greg's darkly impassive face. "Nothing. This is the first I've heard of it." Without recourse to his Fleet-learned sensitization, Richard believed him. He had known Greg Sheldon for about five years and never once had known him to lie. The man just was not capable of it. "What's the story?" Greg asked.

"Just a rumor Mary picked up in K-10." His fingers gripped the icy glass. "Still, I want to check it out." He thought for a moment. "You know, it really pisses me off. When we go to Shamash, we could just as well go to Sangraal. A slight change of injection coordinates and at metaspace speeds we'd be there in no time."

"Forget it, Rich. We'd never make it. You saw what happened the last time someone tried that."

The image of the patrol craft *Guardian* streaking in furious pursuit of a stolen trade ship flashed through his mind. "Yeah, you're right." Damn, he did not want to think about that incident. Mary had been enough of a reminder. "I just can't help thinking about what happened to him."

"I know. But the law *is* the law. And there's some strong muscle in it. I'll try to check around tomorrow morning before we leave, see if I can learn anything. But don't count on it. People aren't talking much around the comm center."

Richard nodded. He should not have expected more. He remembered something else. "Hey, you're into Neo-monadism and all that political crap— what's going on on Vesta. I also heard a rumor about that place."

Greg furtively looked around the room then leaned over in his chair to get closer to Richard. "It's pretty bad. All I've heard is rumor, too, but there's a small-scale rebellion out there. The Fleet has been keeping it under tight security. I've never seen anything like it. One rumor has it that the Syncretists took over one of the continents, destroyed some Fleet sensors and are now tampering with the educational system."

"What the hell brought that on? Sounds like something out of the twentieth century."

"Or worse. I've experienced what can be done with an altered teaching machine. It doesn't take too many subtle hints planted in the subconscious until you've got a whole new person. I still turn cold every time I enter a link."

"Yeah, I remember your saying something about that. Those weren't Syncretists, were they?"

"No," Greg replied, his voice losing some of its secretiveness. "Just well-meaning psych machines. But spare me from another. Fortunately, I found that just knowing about it was sufficient protection. That's how I got into Neo-monadism."

Richard shook his head, simulating disbelief. "I never thought we'd ever see a revolution. The old Judeo-Christian-Muslims claimed their Satan had his ass tossed out of heaven, so I guess there'll always be a few diehards who can't stand paradise." He lifted his drink in toast. "To paradise," he said with obvious sarcasm. "Maybe we'll see a little of that action—Vesta is practically next door to Shamash."

"I wouldn't count on it. The *Odyssey* is just a training ship."

"Doesn't matter. I've seen enough action *outside* the Perimeter. I don't need any inside it." Forget the *Guardian* he told himself.

"What's puzzling about this is why the sensor units were hit and why they resorted to physical action. That's just not their style. Something must have really gotten to them."

"Desperation maybe," Richard suggested.

"Maybe. At first, I refused to believe the rumor because it was so out of character for the Syncretists. But sitting here on Earth you hear a lot of talk from spacers, and the rumor was persistent. No details and nothing in the news, just a persistent rumor."

"I'm beginning to think that whole sector is fucked up. If the Fleet is classifying a story, it must be serious. I can't ever recall anything being classified."

The communicator interrupted, signaling a call. At a nod from Greg, Richard manually actuated the unit and stood back as his mother's body appeared lifelike in the room. She greeted Greg and turned to Richard. "I'm glad I tried to reach you here. Have either of you had the news key on?"

Greg shook his head.

"No," Richard replied. "Haven't had mine on since I got back. Why? What's up?"

The icy cold from his drink seemed to cover his body as she replied, "They've just reported Mary Whittaker missing."

3

INCIDENT ON FREY

…whatever I may do…will be prompted solely from selfish motives, since it gives me more pleasure…than not.
—Edgar Rice Burroughs, A *Princess of Mars*

Greg stepped off the levitator on the forty-seventh floor and walked the length of the corridor to the apartment he shared with Coni. His eyes instinctively retained their normal squint in this brightly lit corridor, slicing a horizontal section across its vertical appearance, with the upper and lower borders made fuzzy by the diffraction patterns of his eyelashes. He rubbed his forehead briefly and concentrated his mental powers on erasing the dull ache which grated at the backs of his eyes. He felt rotten. Fortunately, it was quiet, and no one else was afoot in the hallway. Not that it mattered—he and Coni knew very few of their neighbors.

The apartment door opened at his presence and he stepped inside, mindful that Coni might yet be resting. The living room was still gaily lighted in a manner reminiscent of a midafternoon sun, causing the geometrically contemporary furniture to appear like happy, angular creatures briefly frozen in play. She always liked lots of light. It did not bother him. He was used to more light than Sol put out.

The quietness of the apartment knifed his ears, causing him to briefly tense up. He had expected to find her resting on the sofa and absorbed in soothing music as she had been when he and Richard had left. But she was not there waiting for him, and no music or quad-dem paintings greeted his senses.

He looked in their bedroom and found her asleep, blonde hair splashed across a pillow, with covers, so out of place in an environmentally controlled bed, pulled tightly about her. He felt a childish rush of affection. She was so damned beautiful! He blotted out the origins of that beauty—it had almost made him impotent one night just thinking about it. She had been that way before, so she was justified in looking that way after. He leaned over the bed and softly kissed her cheek. She stirred slightly, a hint of a flickering smile on her lips. Her hand had renewed itself. He stood up and left her to her sleep.

Too restless to sit down, Greg walked through the apartment. It had been a difficult night—first the trouble at the High Tide and now Mary Whittaker's disappearance. He had accompanied Richard to the police station and back to his apartment without having nerve enough to tell Coni what had happened. That event would have to come later.

In the bathroom he paused to examine his face in the mirror, surprised as always at its dark contrast with the pastel colors around him. He had grown so used to being on Earth that he assumed he looked like its inhabitants. He looked closer at the mirror image then dabbed some cream about the corners of his eyes. Despite the scientific skin conditioning he had received on Ziol, he was certain he was seeing lines forming around the corners of his eyes. *Been squinting too long. Even here. Only way to see.* It was his own fault. His skin had originally been meant for the dimly lit, mist-filled wintry seas of Europe, not the hot Tehuti desert of Ziol. Fortunately, his eyes no longer got bloodshot.

He caught sight of a bottle of pills and swore. *She had induced sleep again! Damn!* He should never have left her alone after what had happened, especially with his departure so close, he thought. She could get so morose at the thought of his leaving.

Greg returned to the living room and ordered a mildly sweetened cafnex, a hot, nontoxic alkaloid stimulant, from the automat. He felt tired, tired from talking to the authorities about Mary Whittaker, tired from the realization that he had deserted Coni. Too tired to use his Fleet-learned mental powers to fight his emotional fatigue. He sat down on a soft, adjustable sofa, at ease in the contours of his body shape. His beverage floated silently in a cup beside him, held aloft by an unseen tractor beam.

He rubbed his forehead again and covered his eyes. He knew Mary Whittaker. He had met her through Richard after he and Richard returned from their Perimeter assignment. She was a friendly, warm person, very happy to be in the Fleet, very enchanted with spaceflight. Now she was gone. Missing with no clues or motives. People did not disappear in this peaceful, crimeless society without a very compelling reason. Certainly not Mary Whittaker, who had no problems, except one and that had been settled years ago. Even though she had sincerely forgiven him, not just in words but in her actions, he still shared some of Richard's guilt for being on the *Guardian* when it flashed beyond the Perimeter to chase that stolen starship to Ormazd. When they were assigned to the Perimeter, the two of them had often half-jokingly talked of going beyond it, yet neither had imagined that their chance to do so would cost them so dearly.

Greg drank slowly from his cup. Where was Mary now? To dramatize their concern, he and Richard had personally visited the police as soon as Richard finished talking to his mother. Richard told them that Mary had returned to Earth with him (this they already knew) and that she had left him at the port. She did not reach her destination, an apartment shared with two other Fleet officers. No one seemed to know where she was and why she had not checked in. Richard had been the last-known person to see her. After losing Jerry, this was a bitter blow to Richard.

Thinking back on her disappearance, Greg realized that the prevailing mood in the Fleet was consistent with such an act. For weeks, he had been aware of a growing malaise, the sudden silence around the comm center, the rumors about Vesta. Secrecy. People moving stealthily about on mysterious tasks. Mary's disappearance blended with this wholly new emotional feel of the base. He knew he had a suspicious mind, a condition he justified as necessary in order to fight off the mental tampering which had been practiced upon him by his childhood teaching machine. Now it might be necessary to have a suspicious mind in order to survive. People just did not disappear. He suspected the worst.

Had she been removed because of her knowledge about Vesta? But who would do it? The Fleet? It wasn't their method of operating, yet the Fleet was not operating normally anymore. The Syncretists? They had never done such a thing, yet weren't they rumored to be in rebellion on Vesta? Why would anyone do it? And how was it accomplished? The Tellurian authorities had access to special locators. If she were alive or on Earth, they would find her. But so far she had not been found. Was she off-Earth? Only the Fleet could successfully perform that feat. Had she been physically and mentally changed to fool the locators? That was insane. The Syncretists were rumored to have those illegal capabilities (and if they did, might not the Fleet have them also?), but he refused to believe it. There were special protective screens which could block out a locator, but the average citizen did not have access to them. Again, was it the Fleet or the Syncretists? Most likely the Fleet had her on a special assignment in keeping with all its other recent unusual activities. No sense considering the other possibility—that she was a victim of an illegal nullor attack.

Surely some police sensor would have detected such an event. Besides, people didn't murder one another.

Before he had left Richard's apartment, and while his thoughts were still forming, he had warned Richard to be careful. If Mary's disappearance was in any way related to her duty in Sector K-10, then whoever wanted her out of the way might reason that she had passed undesirable information on to Richard. Richard had chided him, laughing at the very idea of a conspiracy and arguing that Mary would return shortly. Richard was too open and too trusting to do anything about his own safety. Even now Greg resisted an urge to warn his friend again. The authorities would probably have Richard under routine surveillance and that should be sufficient protection. He would call him later in the morning.

Greg stood up and stretched. Even though he felt tired, he was restless. Maybe he should take one of Coni's pills, he thought. It would be so much nicer pressing against her warm body than standing there alone.

Taking his cup with him, he walked toward a wall, letting the window unfold before him. The city sparkled around him, alive with radiant lights. In a few hours Sol would beam its golden rays from across the distant harbor, and he would feel better in the warm, natural light of a star almost as bright as Ra.

Ra! He longed to stand on the desert hills near Konstantin, the capital of Ziol. There in the Tehuti desert he could watch the westerly descending sun of Ziol paint the rugged desert mountains all shades of orange, blue and purple, a varied mixture of colors that defied in a primordial manner the human-made greenness so prevalent surrounding Konstantin. How often he had seen the rays of stellar photons streak across the gulf, separating him from that afternoon reddish sphere to strike the peaks, causing them to flame and sparkle as multihued gems of some ancient fire god. *The early explorers named you well.* His only change would have been the ultimate one, Amen-Ra. For there was the source of life energy, the home of ka.

But he was here on Earth, enveloped in buildings and people. Coni preferred it that way. She liked living on Earth, where she was protected at the center of the Federation. He could not blame her, not after what she had been through, yet he still felt that the mind was a delicate object and that too much communion with others could warp and break it like the sudden exposure of plastic to heat. Each encounter left its impression. He was aware of everyone around him, but he built a barrier so he could be himself inside. He believed that the price of total empathy was total loss of self. In this sense, he saw the desert not as a symbol of death but of life, life freed of the overpowering distractions of civilization.

Seeing the city before him with its fluidic lights speaking of activity, he craved the opposite: the peaceful freedom of the Tehuti desert. He had played in that desert as a child and explored it as a young adult, always pleased with the rugged beauty of that quiet muse-filled temple. If a person was to survive in Tehuti, he had to think just as humans had been driven to do by all of Earth's deserts, beginning with the terrible Tellurian Pliocene epoch which had started the human race down the magical path to thought.

Greg was brought back to the present by a flash of light outside his window. Across the harbor, a starship was landing, its light energy muted to protect the environment. He always thrilled at seeing the globular radiance of a starship silently gliding down a guide beam to land. That's what it was all about—being able to go where you wanted, return when you wanted, dart into the solitude of space and see the blazing stars firsthand. As a youngster he had stood one night in Tehuti, staring at the brilliant points of light above him, and he had cursed the Perimeter which closed them to him. But he had made out better than most—he had found Coni and that made it all worthwhile.

Remembering the work he had been doing earlier that day, he turned from the window and walked to the desk in the adjoining study room. He left his cup in the clutches of the tractor beam and stared with unseeing eyes at the computer-assisted analysis he had been engaged in for the past several days. He could not work on it now. She had asked him to try once more before leaving for Shamash, and he had again done his best. Still, he could not explain the tortured planet Ahriman, where she had been dragged screaming with pain into a mind-wrenching maturity unknown to their race. And his failure to explain that place only added to her belief that it was not natural, that it had been created by diabolical creatures just to satisfy a sadistic whim.

Damn-it-all-to-hell! He pounded the desk with impotent fury, unable to contain his anger yet frustrated by his inability to act. *Why her?* She had been so young, so innocent, so beautiful! How old had she been? Thirteen? Fourteen? What a helluva initiation into the concerns of star-bred adults.

He collapsed into the chair before the desk, weak from frustration. He had been eighteen standard years old when he met her. Although she was two years younger than he, she was wiser in the ways of the Federation. She had seen many planets and traveled considerably, while he was on his first trip off Ziol. He had not known then that her parents had been culturologists, once busily engaged in exploring planets with alien life forms. His parents were middle-level managers at the isolated Fleet base near Konstantin, concerned only with staying on peaceful Ziol. He was a lonely, out-of-place outworlder, she a daughter of Earth, the mother of the Federation. They had met during the prelaunch preparations of the starship *Avalon*. He had been captivated by her from their first meeting; she was to him the perfect woman and, despite their different assignments, he looked for every opportunity to be with her. Yes, he thought, those were exciting times, and he had felt doubly blessed by having met her and by being on the exploratory flight of the *Avalon*.

The mission of the *Avalon* was to study a solar system located on the Perimeter of the Federation. This solar system, and its main sequence star, were named Jotunnheim, a whimsical reference to the presence of several Jovian-sized planets. Initial surveys had shown that Jotunnheim II, an inner Tellurian planet, had life and had once even supported a civilization.

Coni and one of her guardians, Dr. Tom Lippert, shared an assignment as the two sole members of the cultural group aboard the ship. They were a hedge against the remote possibility that intelligent life might still exist in the Jotunnheim system. Greg had been fortunate to be there at all. Possessing more interest than experience, he had been assigned as a technician to the astrophysics team under Dr. Nat Imamura. It was Nat who had introduced him to Coni, obliquely mentioning that he should be careful with her because her past had not been very happy. Still, something in her manner and in her expressions told him that she welcomed his presence.

She in turn had introduced him to Art Cooke at a prelaunch party. Art was a young Tellurian Fleet officer whose principal Fleet interest was restructuring planetary systems to fit humankind. Greg had not liked him; first, because he was jealous, which emerged later on as unjustified because Art and Coni were friends by virtue of Coni's acquaintance with Art's lover; and second, because Art had lost no time in ridiculing Greg for his outworld political ideas, including his libertarian Neo-monadistic philosophy. Art had spoken in fervent tones about a new unity of the human race in which all the people would eventually merge their essences to achieve the common good. Such a society, he had argued, would have no need to explore anything but its collective mind. Greg had been thankful that Art was not a member of the *Avalon* expedition, for he could not have peacefully borne Art's constant proselytizing.

When the *Avalon* arrived in the Jotunnheim system, Greg's time was quickly taken up with astrophysical studies. Under Nat's direction, and with increasing excitement, Greg scanned this system of massive, hydrogen-covered giants—a planetary system composed mostly of the dominant Jovian planets, with their multicolored atmospheric bands set against a background of amber; hulking spheres which dwarfed the two smaller Tellurian planets closer to Jotunnheim. Greg now saw in a very personal way the artistry of science and mathematics. Mathematics per se was like grammar to him, an exercise in the proper connection of symbols. Science, like literature, took these symbols and following pertinent grammatical rules made complex sentences that described the physical

Universe. An equation could be as beautiful as a Ziol desert sunset when one understood the meaning behind it and the intricacy of the logic which had given it birth.

While Greg worked his long hours, Coni would often join him, since there were no tasks on these gas giants that required the talents of a culturologist. She would usually sit quietly in the room with him, reading or studying with a mental link. Her interest in his work centered mostly on the influence of planetary development on life.

As the time for their flight to Jotunnheim II neared, Coni became the active one, planning with Tom Lippert the exploration of the initially chosen two sites that contained debris from the vanished civilization. He still remembered the breathless way she had run from a meeting with Lippert into the laboratory where he was working. How exquisite she looked with her long, blonde hair flying and her sea-green eyes sparkling! Oh, how he had wanted to kiss her then, but she held back in her happy excitement. "Greg, Tom wants to send down two separate teams to examine the cultural bases for this civilization. He would lead one team, and since I'm the only other specialist on board, I get to lead the second team. And," she added triumphantly, "I've picked you for a teammate."

"Hold on, woman." He slid an arm across her delicate shoulders and squeezed gently. "I'd sign up with you in a picosecond but what about Nat and Tom? What do they say about all this?"

"Tom has talked to Dr. Imamura, and they agree that you're not needed here. You've learned enough theory to help me. Besides," she smiled in a shy, adorable manner, "you can make an honest woman out of me."

"I'll make something…" he said, laughing, "but for now I guess I should ask, 'What are my orders, boss?'"

"Kiss me."

And he did.

Their studies on Jotunnheim II were exercises of the most laborious detail, for they were forbidden to interfere with the planetary environment. It had been clear from the *Avalon's* initial investigations that the debris of the vanished civilization was so intimately mixed with the soil that only with slow, painstaking efforts by researchers spending considerable time on the planet could the expedition safely uncover the past of Jotunnheim II. So Greg and Coni worked on the surface out of a small, prefabricated base which resembled a giant, spread-eagled, green cephalopod with truncated tentacles more than it did a human habitat. Greg was quietly concerned about their privacy when they were joined by Yüan Ai-ling, a thirty-year-old Tellurian paleopedologist, but Ai-ling was too open and too happily gregarious for this feeling to last. She had that innate ability to put people at ease, engage them in conversation, and make them laugh. Her graceful, slender build matched Coni's, and her almond eyes and dark-brown complexion complemented Coni's green eyes and light features.

Jotunnheim II was a planet at peace with itself. Strange birds, flying reptiles and insects darted and flew through its still air, unconcerned about the sudden presence of human explorers. The planet had its share of varied animal life, but nothing more advanced than a few lowly root-eating mammals and tree apes inhabited Jotunnheim II. The planet was like a dehumanized caricature of Earth. Because it was so peaceful, Coni suggested the planet be named Frey, and this was accepted by the others in the *Avalon* expedition.

Two days before Ai-ling was scheduled to complete her assignment, Greg stepped out of the shower, sonically dried and clean. He felt refreshed as he smeared his protective cream over his body. *It has been one damned long day with no results. I need a break.* In point of fact, it had been almost three days of continuous work with the three of them struggling to complete the necessary studies before Ai-ling's departure. Donning a clean pair of shorts, he walked out of the shower room and along the corridor to the central living room. He passed Ai-ling's room, where he saw her small, naked body resting on her bed as she studied with the aid of a mental link.

Greg walked into the living room and surveyed its sparse furnishings. Through an open doorway he saw Coni standing before the computer console. "Hey! How about something cold and wet?" he called. She did not turn around. Her small shoulders were slumped forward either in study or defeat.

"Damnit, Greg, I can't make any sense out of this planet," she said almost to herself, her frustration made evident to him by her uncharacteristic swearing. "If these remains we've uncovered mean anything, it's that Frey had a relatively highly developed culture, at least equal to first century Rome, yet I can find little else besides the building stones to support that claim. The recaller says this civilization existed perhaps as recently as two standard centuries ago—or even less, the data are a little peculiar—and then some cataclysmic event which our astronomers never saw destroyed it in a manner that almost left it hidden from us. How? Where is this culture? What happened here?"

He went to her and put his arm around her. She was obviously tired. Like him, she rarely used stimulants or forced mental control, preferring instead to operate on her own natural life force. He wished Ai-ling were there to supply some amusing diversion. His problem was that he was just as serious in his pursuits as she was in hers, and he lacked the ready reply that would put her at ease.

Her heavy breathing showed the sharpness of her frustration. "Greg, have you ever wondered why our part of the Galaxy, particularly what we see beyond the Perimeter, is so sparsely populated by intelligent creatures of any kind? It's almost as if by design."

Greg desperately wanted to lighten the mood. With an obvious attempt at jest, he said, "Careful now, you'll have me believing in gods next."

She stared up at the ceiling and silently whispered, "Or devils."

Greg looked sharply at her, instinctively tightening his grip on her. He had never heard such a hushed, fearful whisper in his life. She slid out from the clasp of his arm and walked to the other end of the console, where she added in a manner that told him she no longer was aware of the two words she had just spoken, "We have enough gods, a whole government full of people who are trying to restructure our lives."

Greg wanted to grab her and shake her out of this mood but he held back, afraid of the possible consequences of such action. Remembering Ai-ling, he decided to make light of her remark. "That's heresy coming from a culturologist. Or maybe it's self-serving, since we're now so standardized that you people have no cultural diversity to study."

"I'm serious, Greg." She seemed almost ready to cry, and he felt like an ass for jesting with her. "At times, this whole social system of ours gets me down. Our individuality is a sham—you and I don't differ from each other enough to warrant the name individual. Maybe you're right—maybe I am bitter about the lack of cultural diversity. I do believe that diversity represents human experimentation, a search for other ways of functioning. And it clearly has survival value." Almost bitterly she added, "Your scientific mind ought to appreciate that fact."

Greg was cautious now. He knew that in their private moments, they were supposed to be isolated from the *Avalon*. Still, he could not suppress the fear that if they were ever overheard, they could expect more of the same psychological reorientation which had been worked on him as a youngster—and this time it might not be so gently persuasive. He studied Coni for a few minutes but she seemed unaware, as her eyes focused away from him on the screen image of the darkening green jungle outside. Night was fast approaching. He agreed with her statements: the Federation placed a premium on conformance, which was a natural outgrowth of the successful elimination of crime and other socially deviant behavior, but he wanted very much to have this conversation later, when they were away from the confines and pressures of the base.

He groped for something to say that would pull her back to their Federation civilization. Gently, almost consolingly, he said, "At least our lack of diversity has stopped human fighting."

"Yes, and in its place we have lifelessness. And it leaves us so…so…defenseless." She had begun by being angry, and she was ending almost with a sob.

It was evident to him that she wanted to speak about something in particular, but she lacked the ability to bring herself to do so. She wanted to talk; in fact, she seemed to need to talk, yet he sensed that her conversation was skirting her real concern. Was it Ahriman? he wondered. Tom Lippert had told him before they left the *Avalon* that she was the sole survivor of a massacre by aliens on that profaned world. Lippert had also subtly suggested that Greg offered the kind of stability Coni needed. Greg also remembered Lippert's warning about her fragility, so he refrained from forcing her to the point of release. Perhaps, if he maintained the proper atmosphere, she would unburden herself. Recalling his impromptu political discussion with Art Cooke at the prelaunch party and her unspoken reaction to it, he softly asked, "Are you one of Art's Neomonadists?"

Coni's green eyes suddenly focused their ocean light on him with an intensity that Greg found discomforting. "And what if I am?" Greg felt taken aback by this new intensity. Then he saw the tears in her eyes and went to her. "Greg, I don't want to be mean to you," she said. She cried a little longer and then dried her tears. She pressed her face against his chest and spoke very softly, her voice still quivering. "Greg, I wanted very much for you to be a part of this and a part of me." She placed her left hand on his chest. "And I guess I want to be a part of you."

He leaned down and kissed her. As he did, he could see that her green eyes were moist again. He sensed, not so much by her words or actions but by a meeting of their minds, as if he were telepathically linked to her, that she was reaching out for him. "I love you," he said softly. He felt her begin to cry again. He held her tightly and caressed her soft, blonde hair as he whispered her name several times.

They stood like that for several minutes, then Coni whispered so softly that Greg could hardly hear her, "Did you mean that?"

"Yes," he answered, "I love you."

She was quiet for a moment, seemingly lost in thought, then she spoke again, "Can you love someone you hardly know?"

"I love you," he said again. "And I always will." He felt her smile as she pulled closer to him.

He could have held her forever, feeling the sensuousness of her supple body blending into his. Finally, he became aware of a more rhythmic beat to her breathing, and he saw that she had fallen asleep, standing there relaxed in his arms. *You were more tired than 1 thought.* But he could see that it was a peaceful sleep. She looked relaxed, almost happy. Carefully, he carried her to her bed and made her comfortable for the night, then he returned to the living room.

Ai-ling, now wearing a simple smock, was seated on the sofa studying some reports on a portable scanner. She smiled as he entered. "Is she tucked in?"

He nodded as he walked to the automat to order a drink. "It's been a long couple of days."

Ai-ling sat back from the scanner. "You two ought to take it easy. I don't know why Coni is in such a rush. If she's trying to finish before I leave, I can always stay a few extra days. Hell, I don't have anything that pressing. This could be the last major exploration inside the Perimeter, so we might as well take our time and enjoy it." She glanced at his drink. "Will you fix me one?"

He ordered her drink, then said, "I think I'll see if we can't take tomorrow off. Maybe relax a little, take a walk outside. That is, if you're serious about staying over."

She accepted her drink. "I think *you* should get *her* outside—she hasn't been more than one hundred meters from the base since we beamed down. I'll hold the fort down while you're gone."

"Ai-ling, I'd like you to…"

"No, you wouldn't. You're just throwing out a line of outworld chivalry. You two are the most lovesick pair I've ever seen. Besides, I don't feel like playing chaperon."

Greg smiled. "You aren't."

"That's for sure. Otherwise, I'd have to weld both your bedroom doors shut."

He felt the warmth of embarrassment on his face. "Well, I guess I'd better finish her computer study or I'll never get her to take tomorrow off." He had more on his mind than just the computer work. He also wanted to think privately about his talk with Coni. Ai-ling smiled at him as he turned and walked into the adjoining computer room. He sat down at the base console, absently staring at the glowing data screens as he tried to sort out his emotions and thoughts. He knew Coni wanted him and that she was trying to reach out to him. *Am I the stability that Lippert mentioned?* There was something hidden inside her, most likely a remnant of her fearful experiences on Ahriman. He did not know how to handle the situation, since the psychologists had left few personal complications for humans to face. He felt he had been honest with her: he loved her very much and he always would.

Another level of his mind digested what was flickering across the data screens, causing him to suddenly focus on the contents of one of the screens.

The computer had evidently finished analyzing the materials collected that day and even with his untrained eye, he could see that the computer was having trouble sorting the data.

"Ai-ling, would you come here a minute." In an instant she was standing by his side, her hand resting on his bare shoulder. "You're the soils expert—what do you make of that?"

She chuckled. "You've got a preponderance of extrusive material coupled with a weird distribution of plagioclase feldspars and ferromagnesian silicates." She clasped his shoulder. "And a pretty good eye for soils. Too bad that doesn't include paleopedologists."

"Well, if you don't care…"

Her hand tightened. "I care, Greg. Don't ever think that I don't. You've found something unusual. Every expedition does. Those soil and rock samples you took today are different but before you call in all the wizards, especially Coni, how about letting me take a crack at it…*tomorrow*. We *all* need some rest."

"Aye, aye, skipper." By rank and experience she was the chief scientist at the base, although Coni was in charge of the overall investigation at the site. Greg stared at the screen, watching the shifting data. "You know, that's the first extensive set of soil and rock samples we've gotten around the material left by the Freyans. I wonder if the two items are related?"

"The *Avalon* has the same data," Ai-ling replied. "Let them worry about it tonight."

"You're probably right," Greg said as he stood up. "All that shower and drink did was make me sleepy. I'll see you in the morning." He turned, kissed her softly on her cheek and walked out of the computer room, across the living room and into the corridor leading to his room. As he entered the corridor, he paused to look back. Ai-ling was seated before the console, lost in study of the unusual material. Greg smiled to himself as he walked down the corridor. Ai-ling was more dedicated than she cared to let on. He looked in on Coni, saw that she was in a deep slumber then went to sleep in his own room.

Greg awoke to the warm golden rays of Jotunnheim filtering through the skylight. The auditory sensors transmitted the sounds of the jungle outside. He lay on his back, enjoying the feel of the sunlight on his naked body, while the room came alive with the busy chatter and buzzing of jungle creatures. He had slept longer than he had planned, but he could not bring himself to get up; it was just too peaceful. His door opened, and he looked up to see Coni step inside wearing a brightly colored outfit, her yellow hair radiating in the Freyan sunshine as if it contained its own sun. She looked like Nefertem and Neith joined in one beauteous living prayer to light and life. She was smiling, and Greg could tell that she felt more refreshed than she did the previous night.

"I swear you're turned on by that sun-blackened body of yours, the way you keep exposing it." She walked over and leaned down to kiss him. Her soft hair caressed his face, and her hand braced against one of his nipples, causing delicious shivers of excitement to stream out like a sunburst from that spot. "Why don't you get organized, sleepy, while I fix us something to eat?" She darted away from his clasping hands and laughingly skipped down the corridor.

Coni had breakfast ready when Greg arrived in the living room. Ai-ling was not there. He looked in the computer room and saw from the data log that she had spent most of the night working. He walked over to the breakfast table and sat down beside Coni. "Ai-ling still sleeping?" he asked.

"Yes," she replied as she passed him a steaming cup of cafnex.

"Looks like she spent most of the night working," he observed.

Coni looked puzzled. "What on?"

Greg evaded her question and felt guilty for doing so even as he remembered Ai-ling's request and Tom Lippert's warning. He decided to wait for Ai-ling to make the announcement.

They ate slowly while Coni talked happily about Frey and its beauty. She did not speak about the previous night, so Greg said nothing about it either. It was the first relaxed meal they had had together since the hectic exploration of Frey had started. As they finished eating, Greg asked her if she would like to take some time off from work and just enjoy Frey. At first, Coni was reluctant, pleading that she must finish the environmental aspects of her work before Ai-ling left. Greg persisted in his request, noting that Ai-ling could stay longer if necessary. "You said this place was beautiful," he added, "so why not add to it by joining me for a walk outside. You ought to enjoy the planet you named."

She sat silently for a few moments then slowly replied, "All right, I'll go with you. But we mustn't be gone too long."

While Greg cleaned up the breakfast remains, Coni notified Tom Lippert and the *Avalon* of their plans to spend the day walking through the nearby forest.

"You're not going to wear that here, are you?" he asked as she put on a shield belt. "There's nothing out there that can hurt us."

As if to answer him, the skylight rays of Jotunnheim ignited the human-made jewels on the belt, firing them to incandescent brilliance. In design, the belt crossed functionalism and art. Greg knew that within that belt and its silent gems rested the manifold power to provide complete life support and protection, vastly augmented sensor and communications capabilities, and levitation.

Her face was grim. "Just taking the proper precautions. You'd be smart to do likewise."

"No, thanks." He dropped into a playful swordsmanlike crouch, parrying at her with an imaginary sword. "I'll take my chances."

She was not amused. "I'll see if Ai-ling wants to join us." She returned shortly, followed by Ai-ling.

"I think I'll stay inside and keep the place under control," Ai-ling said. When Coni left the room to get something, Ai-ling quickly asked, "Does she know about the material?"

Greg shook his head.

Ai-ling was relieved. "Please don't tell her until I've had a chance to thoroughly check it out. I don't want her to get excited about this, not yet anyway."

"You put in a long night. I thought you were the one who took things easy." She smiled and winked at him.

As soon as Coni returned, Greg escorted her to the main portal, and they stepped outside into the noisy, humid jungle of Frey. Hand-in-hand they strolled through the green plants that surrounded their base. Green-leafed trees were everywhere, some with tops that came in clumps like green cauliflower, others hanging seductively limp like filmy emerald gowns. Here and there white flowery trees seemed to float amid the jade background like beautiful pale clouds. Greg immediately noticed how good it was to feel again the natural warm air against his skin and to hear the birds and small animals talk to one another as they ate and played and mated. The air was alive with the stimulating smells of growth. Even though Coni did not have her belt activated, he thought the mere presence of such a belt was a psychological barrier to full enjoyment of the environment. At first, Coni was hesitant in her walk but gradually overcame this and grew relaxed. She seemed very cheerful, and she would often stop to look at a flower or try to coax some small animal out of hiding. Greg did not know if it was just Jotunnheim above or seeing her so happy that caused him to feel a warm glow as he walked with her. He found it hard to understand why she had been reluctant to accompany him. She was more a part of this life-filled forest than he.

In the afternoon they paused near a small clearing that contained a little stream which must have come from the mountain near their base. Here they stopped to rest. Coni sat against a large, leafy tree, and Greg placed his head in her lap from where he could see her lovely face bordered by her gently moving breasts. Above her rode Jotunnheim, sending its yellow rays through the misty blue sky into the overhanging dark-green foliage. Such beauty, he thought. Am I glad we didn't get stuck with that boulder-strewn mountain valley on the other side of Frey where Tom is. Here is Frey at its best. He felt very content and at peace as they talked easily of their thoughts and plans. When their conversation seemed the most relaxed, he saw her face suddenly grow serious.

"I'm sorry I was such a bitch last night," she said softly, not looking at him.

He held her right hand in both of his hands and kissed it. "You weren't a bitch. I'm afraid that I was the nasty one. I should have been more considerate when you were so tired."

"You weren't nasty and you *were* very considerate."

"Coni, I don't want to probe, but why do you push yourself so? What are you looking for on Frey?"

"Remember what we talked about last night?"

"Yes," he answered, not wishing to see her get upset again.

"I think you can understand some of what I want to find on Frey." She paused to look at him, her face very solemn. "Art was right about you."

"How's that?"

"You look so open, so a part of things on the surface, but your Neo-monadistic philosophy still shows through. I guess that's partially why I was so angry at you last night for playing with my ideas."

"I apologize. In a way I was a little defensive. Too many people would shrug off my thoughts as outworld nonsense and of little use to the human race or to the Federation. I'm a pretty selfish individual, so I guess I've built up too many barriers to keep others from hurting me."

"Yet, you say you love me."

"It's a very peculiar feeling. I'm physically attracted to you, as you're very beautiful." He sensed a fleeting current of tenseness pass through her. "But I find myself thinking of you as being as important as myself. I guess I'm still showing my selfishness."

She leaned over and kissed him softly on the lips, then smiled as she straightened up. "I like your kind of love. You haven't demeaned yourself, you've elevated me. I wish I could tell you or show you how much that means to me."

They were silent for a while. Greg watched some birds fly over the clearing and then he said apologetically, "I suppose I should say something in defense of my selfishness. It's not at all what people usually mean by the term. To me it's a desire to live and be one's self. To preserve it, it means allowing others to live freely. I guess it represents a means or ability to survive. I don't know if that still makes me a Neo-monadist or not."

"It doesn't matter," she answered softly. "I knew where you stood when Art first tried to provoke you at the party."

Greg broke off a blade of green grass and put it in his mouth, briefly tasting its bitterness. He suddenly felt very pensive. "You know, I sometimes think there are only two types of people who can really appreciate freedom: those who enjoy life as an end in itself and those who enjoy just being themselves."

She stroked his brown hair. "Those same people could also exist with certain kinds of tyrannies." He felt that she was testing him.

He smiled. "Not really. No one can enjoy life or be himself when tyranny rules. Anyhow, I am oversimplifying. The key word for me is 'appreciate.' I didn't mean to imply that these types are best equipped to create or defend freedom. Obviously, there are as many shades of human behavior as there are people. I was just generalizing to illustrate my views.

"As for undoing tyrannies or creating an atmosphere for freedom, we need two other types: those who are unhappy with the status quo and those who have the capability to organize and lead us to something better. But these same people can also be a danger to freedom once it exists. That is why I say there are only two kinds who can genuinely appreciate it: one because he enjoys experiencing without restrictions the intrinsic beauty of life, a total unquestioning acceptance of it, without upsetting it, with an unwillingness to prevent others from enjoying life since he realizes how good it is; the other because he realizes that he is unique in the Universe and is willing to live and enjoy that uniqueness. Some would consider him selfish. I say his role in life has been too little understood and too long maligned. He wants to be free because only then can he follow his own pursuits."

Coni looked back at him with a quiet seriousness, her eyes magnifying the verdure about them, focusing it into his own eyes. "And you are the latter?"

He stretched out on the grass, his head cradled in his hands. "I sometimes feel that all four types are fighting within me and that it may take an outside catalyst to force one type to dominate. But yes, I believe that I am predominately selfish. However, as I said before, not in the sense that people commonly think. I just want to live, Coni. I want to be free, and I am willing to accept responsibility for my life and for my actions." He suddenly laughed. "You know, maybe that's why you think I'm so open—I've got a selfish interest in avoiding chaos by being honest."

She laughed along with him with her musical laugh that he loved so much to hear.

"I was just thinking," he continued, "that space and time and energy are so intertwined that one can almost draw an analogy between humanity moving through time and a starship moving through space. Like the ship, we're shielded in our own way, but even the crew of the ship has to make some hard and correct decisions, as I'm sure some dead explorers will undoubtedly verify." He saw her hands nervously clasp each other, and he realized he had stupidly and inadvertently come too close to her past.

Coni looked at him solemnly, apparently unaware of his brief look of concern, then asked in a quiet voice, "Which am I?"

Looking more evenly at her now, Greg replied, "That is for you to decide. You must make your own choice."

For several minutes Coni listened to him discuss his philosophy of life, then she said, "But Greg, you can't just spend your life in some cerebral home debating philosophy. Your body lives and is an integral part of you. The two are not separable. That is why we are here rather than a machine. We can integrate the abstract and the tangible. We're constantly made aware of the conflict, the dichotomy, but there is none if we simply are ourselves, as you said. Man can unite the two since he is both and they are really one."

"Have I said anything to conflict with that?" he asked with a laugh. "With your Circean enchantment and mystery, I'm sure I'd have no trouble uniting the two."

She smiled at him.

Greg looked up at the small amount of sky framed by the jungle and noticed that Jotunnheim was farther to the west. He quickly jumped up. "Hey, we'd better get back before it gets dark. I don't want to spend a night out here without my suit." Teasingly, he added, "We don't know what kind of demons really prowl this place at night."

Greg looked down at Coni and saw that she was staring at him, her face a mask of fear. He swiftly knelt beside her and kissed her. "I'm sorry. I was only joking."

She stood up quickly and said, "Let's go." She started back down the trail before he could move.

Greg was puzzled and somewhat hurt. What had he said that caused her to change so? He rapidly caught up with her. She was walking very fast and her face looked frozen, as if it had been drained of life. Even her luminous green eyes appeared devoid of their usual luster. He could tell that she did not want to talk, so he accompanied her in silence.

The green jungle haze darkened quickly now that Jotunnheim was setting, and the foliage blocked its rays. Greg found himself longing for Tehuti with its wide-open vistas that permitted a person to see seemingly forever. The Freyan jungle no longer represented life, it represented a collection of obstacles that had to be surmounted if they were to return before dark. He was not personally concerned, because like all the explorers he had been implanted with the necessary accouterments, such as mental direction finders and chronometers, that helped him find his way through the jungle. But Coni was another problem—she moved like a person in fear, which seemed so unreasonable to Greg. The Freyan jungles were virtually harmless to humans. The few poisonous insects and reptiles were of no concern because they had received immunizations against their venom and stings. He almost wanted to call to her, "Why the hurry?" but he kept silent.

He tried to slow the pace, but she was insistent in her desire to hurry. As they moved through the ever-darkening forest, Greg silently cursed himself for not having updated his night vision. The jungle seemed to grow more silent as the darkness increased, then suddenly he heard a noise in the trees overhead. He looked up to see first one and then several dark, manlike shapes moving through the trees.

Coni shrieked. At first, too startled to move, Greg froze, then he reacted as he saw Coni flee blindly down the vanishing path. Her suit was on!

"Coni, come back!" he yelled as he ran after her.

With her suit's pellor ray, she was faster than he, and he found himself throwing caution aside as he chased her. The dark shrubbery tore at him, scratching his unprotected skin. Several times he tripped, and each time he cursed the absence of the belt which would have overcome these obstacles. Finally, he caught up with her near their base clearing and attempted to block her path.

"No! No!" she cried over the suit communicator. Her breathing was hard. "I won't go back. Let me go. I won't go back to *them!*" She was screaming now and then she fired the stunnor, knocking him senseless to the ground. She had mercifully used a low-power setting, and he came to in time to see her run into their quarters. She sealed the main portal after her. Greg wasted no time on it. He ran to a small emergency door and mentally activated the controls which enabled him to get in.

Cautiously, he crept along the silent corridor, alert for any motion or sound. All he sensed was the hum of the base equipment. Where was Ai-ling? He found the supply room and quietly entered it, closing the door behind him. He quickly tore through the supply cartons until he found what he wanted—a spare suit belt. He had no time to argue with Coni, not as long as she was wearing a suit belt and was prepared to use its stunnor. He put on the belt and activated it, then, feeling more secure, he stepped back into the corridor.

He found Ai-ling lying unconscious on the sofa in the living room. It was apparent that she had been stunned. The life monitors in his suit told him that she was unconscious but otherwise all right. Coni was working at the base console to seal off the base.

"*Coni!*"

She whirled toward him and shrank back against the wall, obviously torn between her love for him and her fear. "Please, Greg, help me!" Her green eyes showed only terror, yet he knew it was not directed at him. She seemed to be looking past him to the closed door, as if she expected some demon to burst through at any moment. She would not let him come closer to her. She was jumpy, always ready to move.

Greg tried talking to her, but she was not listening to him. Her whole being seemed to be concentrating on something outside the building. It was a stand-off: he could not stun her and she could not stun him. In desperation, he opened an audio comm link to Lippert's base, all the while frantically thinking of something to say to Lippert that would not alert his companion or the *Avalon*. He hoped that the *Avalon* was not actively monitoring their suits. He was not ready to have his love reoriented by a psychological link as he had almost been while a student on Ziol.

"Lippert here." The disembodied words sounded sepulchrally in Greg's ears.

"Tom, this is Greg." He watched Coni closely, but her trancelike state seemed to make her unaware of what he was doing. "Tom, remember that stability criterion we talked about?"

There was a pause and then Greg heard Tom say hesitantly, "Yes…" He could sense Lippert's concern.

"Well, I've found some…some,"—he was grasping—"some feldspars and silicates that don't meet it." *That should take care of the* Avalon. "Can you take time off to beam over for a look? I promise a good dinner." He thought that last part was pure gold and had he not been so concerned over Coni, he would have congratulated himself on the ruse.

Tom Lippert agreed to beam over and then signed off. Greg walked down a corridor to the teleporter room and quickly activated the teleporter unit. He stood ready with a spare shield belt. There was no sense in letting Tom Lippert enter their base unprotected. Greg's wait was short. Tom Lippert swiftly materialized and stepped into the room. The concern etched in his face showed Greg that he had understood the purpose behind Greg's invitation. He immediately saw Greg's suit and the spare belt.

"My god, Greg! What has happened here?"

Greg briefly told Lippert about Coni's flight through the jungle, trying to minimize the stunnor attack on Ai-ling and himself. "I don't know what got to her. She was apprehensive about my remark about demons and then a band of tree apes—at least they looked like tree apes, I didn't have my night vision—startled her into complete panic."

"Damn, I was afraid of this," Lippert said with apparent agony. He walked down the corridor in the direction Greg indicated, refusing to wear the prof-fered belt.

They found Coni at the base console. She whirled at their arrival, a look of surprise flitting across her otherwise terror-stricken face. Tom Lippert walked slowly toward Coni while speaking to her softly, reminding her that he had saved her once before on Ahriman and urging her to deactivate her suit. She focused on him, struggling inwardly, then the suit shield was down and she was running to him. He held her in a fatherly embrace as she cried bitterly and uncontrollably.

"Tom, *they* were out there," she gasped in a quivering voice interspersed with convulsive sobs. "Please take me home, Tom. Greg took me out there." Her voice was like that of a lost little girl crying out for comfort and security.

Lippert spoke to her in a very soothing tone, telling her that she had only been frightened by some harmless tree apes. Greg looked on as Tom gave her a serenogen. Very quickly Coni grew calm and her breathing more rhythmic.

"She's okay now," Lippert said without emotion. "Please take her to her room."

Greg carried Coni to her room and carefully placed her upon her bed. He knelt beside her to brush some of her yellow hair away from her face. She looked so peaceful now. He kissed her lips lightly and returned to the living room.

Ai-ling was lying on the sofa, propped up on a pillow. Her dark eyes were dreamy and she seemed to be having trouble focusing on Lippert, who sat beside her with a medicator in his hand. The application of the medicator brought her back to full consciousness. After Tom explained what had happened, Ai-ling shook her head sadly. She sat up, pulling her knees up under her chin and brooded for a minute. "That poor girl. I know you said it was there, but I never realized there was so much fear…so much terror." She then looked at Greg sadly.

Greg looked quickly from Ai-ling to Lippert, who was now standing. "Tom, tell me what happened out there. What's wrong with Coni?"

Lippert ignored his question and looked at Ai-ling. "Were the recorders and comm systems off?" he asked in a matter-of-fact tone.

She nodded.

Lippert breathed a sigh of relief and sat down. "How about a bourbon and water, Greg?" Mechanically, Greg started to comply with Lippert's request when Ai-ling suddenly stood up and waved him to sit down. "I'll get it," she said dryly. "We could each use one."

Greg was too unsettled to sit down. He paced the room while firmly clutching the drink Ai-ling had made for him. "This is all tied in with Ahriman, isn't it?"

Lippert nodded, his face drawn. He accepted his drink from Ai-ling and sipped it. Ai-ling sat down again, curled her feet under her and beamed her eyes into Lippert's face.

"There's a lot about Ahriman and the Sanderson Expedition which was not widely released," Lippert began. "Some was held back to protect Coni, some to protect a few bureaucrats. And I suspect some was also held back to keep the public from taking Sanderson too seriously. He had some offbeat ideas." Lippert paused to take another sip of his drink. He sadly shook his head. "Such a hellhole makes Caldera look like paradise." He paused and then resumed speaking in more analytical tones. "Anyway, we went to Ahriman because our probes showed the planet had once held an advanced civilization. You know the story—somehow the planet had been knocked into a highly elliptical orbit that threatened to eventually plunge it into its sun. We went there to study this civilization and see if we should break the Federation code and interfere in the natural destiny of the planet.

"You cannot imagine the fierce storms and climatic changes which racked that planet. It was hard to believe that anything remotely like us could have built a civilization on that world, but we found that the civilization antedated the catastrophe that ruined Ahriman. All we found of its inhabitants were cave-dwelling brutes, vaguely apelike but of a low order of intelligence."

Greg instantly realized the connection and regretted his teasing remark about demons.

Lippert continued: "These creatures were more beastly than man himself. We set up several exploration sites, with Coni and her parents at one of them. It's not clear what happened except that during one of those freakish storms, their camp shield was penetrated and the Ahrimanians got inside."

Lippert paused and looked sadly at the floor. He held his drink in both hands and rocked it back and forth nervously. "They killed all the men and took the women back to the caves. Coni was the only one who survived the ordeal—the damage to the dead was so extensive, so complete, that we couldn't even use renascent techniques." Lippert paused again. "We tracked them and finally got her out. It was pretty awful what they had done to her." Lippert's breathing came in sob-like gasps. "It was as if they wanted to tear the source of human life right out of the bearers of it. I've never seen such carnage!" The glass dropped from his hand. He covered his face, his voice now muffled and agonized. "They had tortured them to death, one by one, holding Coni for last. And so she saw her own mother…somehow she kept her sanity…we found her a torn, bloody mess, more dead than alive."

Greg was rigid, his fists tight. He grew oblivious to everything in the room except for the words issuing from Tom Lippert's mouth. Ai-ling's breath came through clenched teeth, her dark eyes damp with tears.

Lippert leaned back and looked fully at Greg. "The physical scars were the easiest to mend." (So that's why she disliked being called beautiful, Greg thought.) "I assure you she looks just as she used to. She always was remarkably beautiful.

"But she suffered severe brain damage. We could easily repair the obvious damage—don't forget: she passed her tests for this flight—but all we could do for her emotionally was bury the whole incident. I would not permit the authorities to do anymore, because I could not bear to see that wonderful girl turned into another Federation zombie." The bitterness in that last remark almost froze Greg where he stood. "I think her father and mother would have made the same choice. I couldn't tell you more, because I did not want others to be able to unlock the hell she has inside. I've told you both this much because you deserve some explanation for what happened here tonight, but I ask you to keep it to yourselves. In retrospect, I should have trusted you, Greg. In fact, I should never have permitted her to come out here, but she wanted to do what her parents did. They were also culturologists, as you know. Maybe it's her way of proving herself after Ahriman."

Greg shook his head in sorrow. "I wish I had known. I have been such a bastard around her."

"No, Greg. She loves you, and I think she needs you very much. I think you can see now why I felt you would be a good companion for her. You grew up in a stable environment. Ziol is a lovely planet, I've been there. But more importantly, you have an attitude toward life that I like. Coni followed her parents too much, and I think you can finally give her the strength to be herself."

"What happens next?" Greg asked, nodding toward Coni's room.

"Treat her with patience and care. If you like, I'll stay the night, but I think she'll be all right tomorrow. If I stayed, the *Avalon* might want to know what you found. Please keep this from them."

Greg nodded his agreement.

"I think she should learn to rely on you," Lippert added with a dry smile, "since I have an idea that you'll be around her more than I will. By the way, was there anything to your remark about the feldspars and silicates? I'll have to make some report when I return."

Greg glanced at Ai-ling. Her eyes acknowledged his request, and she answered Lippert: "Yes, Tom, there is something very unusual about some of the material we found. There appears to be an excess of extrusive material with an atypical distribution of plagioclase feldspars and ferromagnesian silicates."

At Ai-ling's request, Greg had the computer put the analytical data on the screen. Lippert looked at it for a while and mumbled several times about how interesting and unusual it looked. Finally, he clapped Greg on the shoulder and said, "I've got to get back. Why don't you transmit this information to us. I'll call you tomorrow to see how everything is going."

After Lippert left, Ai-ling approached him and clasped both of his hands in her smaller, more slender ones. "Don't be so glum," she said quietly, her dark eyes searching his face. "It wasn't as bad as all that."

"How you can say that after what she went through and what happened here tonight?"

"That's the whole point, Greg. Despite what she went through and the panicked state of her mind, she cares...about both of us. How long were you unconscious?"

"A few seconds. Why?"

"And I'd guess a few minutes for myself. She could have paralyzed us all night instead of temporarily knocking us out, She was very frightened, Greg, but not so frightened that her fear overpowered her desire to protect us." Ai-ling smiled prettily and stepped back to slap him playfully on the shoulder. "I think you've got a swollen head—Lippert made too much of you. Don't get so noble and proud. She survived Ahriman without you. She is one helluva woman, and personally I think you need her as much as Lippert thinks she needs you." Laughing now, she added, "Well, what are you hanging around here for? I can run this place. Your place is down there." She indicated Coni's room.

He smiled weakly at her. "Thanks, Ai-ling. Do you think it's all right if..."

"Don't thank me. Tonight I lost a potential lover or two. There's too much seriousness around here. Yes, it's all right if you sleep with her—she's not going to go psycho if you crawl into her bed."

He walked across the living room then paused at the entrance to the corridor leading to Coni's room. He turned back to Ai-ling and smiled. "Thanks, anyway."

"Will you get going, dummy?" She was trying to look stern. "I'll cover for you. Sleep well."

Coni was lying just as he had left her. He unfastened his sparse, two-piece suit and crawled into bed beside her. Confident now that he would not disturb her, he snuggled against her, one hand instinctively holding one of her breasts. "I love you," he whispered to the sound of her deep breathing. He kissed her cheek and neck then stretched out to sleep.

He awoke to sunlight and soft crying.

"I'm sorry, Greg. I'm so sorry."

He put a finger to her lips and then took her in his arms. She continued to cry for a long time. Finally, she pulled back and inquired about Ai-ling and Tom Lippert.

"Ai-ling is fine. There's no need to worry. Tom left last night. They're both covering for us."

"Did he…did he tell you about me?"

He could see that she wanted him to say no, but she knew the answer could only be yes. She started to cry again, that same quiet crying which tore so mightily at his emotions. He tried to hold her again but she shook her head.

"Do you love me?" she asked. It was like a cry for help.

"Yes."

"Always?"

"Always."

"How…how much did Tom tell you?"

"Enough."

"I want you to hear it all and then tell me if you love me."

"Coni, I love you. I don't care about Ahriman. Put it behind you."

"Ahriman." She spat out the word bitterly. "Greg, I thought I could take it, I really did. The doctors did wonders for me and Tom and his wife took very good care of me, but I'm not strong enough to carry it off. I need you so desperately, I guess I'm just as selfish as you claim to be. I want you to help me cope."

"Do you want to cope?" He was testing her,

"Yes," she whispered, tears running down her face.

"Then tell me."

Greg listened to her story, all the while filling with rage again because of what this young woman and her family had suffered. He had always considered himself unemotional, but her quivering, whispered story of the atrocities committed on her and the others left him sick and angry. He could not imagine any creatures performing the kind of beastly tortures she described. At times as she talked, he sensed that she felt guilty about her survival in the midst of such hideous carnage. Several times she alluded to an inner, powerful will to live, coupled with what seemed to her now to have been a surprisingly flexuous response to all that had happened to her. She had wanted to live regardless of the cost.

When she finished her story, her eyes were dry and pleading. This time she did not resist his holding her, and he told her again of his love. She cried again, from relief now rather than injury. Finally, she fell asleep, and he laid her back on the bed.

Greg and Ai-ling sent routine reports to the *Avalon* and did their best to cover for their lack of activity while Coni slept. Lippert called several times under one pretense or another, and Greg assured him in coded fashion that Coni was all right. Late in the afternoon she came out of her room and joined them. She smiled weakly, enough to tell Greg that everything was again normal. Ai-ling left them alone.

He fixed a cafnex for her, which she drank quietly. He caressed her hands and she smiled at him, wrinkling her pretty nose slightly.

"Feel better?"

"Yes."

"One more question and you have my silence forever. Why did you really come on this expedition?"

She stared silently at the dark beverage before her, then looked up at Greg. He felt relieved that she could face him again and talk with confidence about her life.

"Dad had a theory about…Ahriman. He believed that the planet was not placed in that orbit by some cosmic accident."

Greg looked at her questioningly.

"There were a lot of reasons for his belief," she continued. "There was nothing in the space near Ahriman that could cause such a catastrophe. Of course, dad knew the cause might have been swallowed by Ahriman's sun, even though the computer never gave what dad considered a good account of the natural phenomena which might have produced that erratic orbit.

"Anyway, whatever caused Ahriman to take such an erratic orbit also wiped out its civilization. We were fairly certain that both events occurred simultaneously."

"And the cave creatures?" Greg asked cautiously.

"Dad said they were the mutated remnants of the vanished civilization, almost like lemures. But no one believed that mutations could occur so fast and so completely. Dad believed that the Galaxy harbored some terrible race which had fiendishly destroyed Ahriman. He issued a few speculative reports on them. He even had a name for them—Apollyoni."

"It sounds a little farfetched."

"The only proof we really had was the hatred of the cave creatures. Even though they had not progressed to space travel and therefore could not have lost a space war, they knew we were from the stars. They understood this fact and both feared and hated us for it."

"Did you capture one and put a link on it?"

"Yes, but we learned nothing. That's why I'm here now—I want to prove that my father was right."

Greg chided her in a gentle voice: "That's not good science."

Coni gave him a slightly angry look. "Science has nothing to do with this." Then she relaxed, smiled a little and stretched out a hand to him. "I'm sorry. You're right, of course."

Greg kissed her hand, then she continued, "Dad used to talk about the old concept of an ecological niche. He said that humanity, now living in harmony, has removed all enemies, so perhaps nature provided one."

"The Apollyoni?"

"Yes," she answered quietly. "He was concerned that we might very well be entering our version of the Mousterian period of culture." She paused for a moment, her penetrating green eyes showing now the faraway look of one lost in thought. "In a way, I think everyone should share some of dad's concerns." Her leaf-flecked eyes focused on him again. "We live in a uniform collection of planets protected by our Perimeter." She shrugged slightly and spread her arms. "There is nothing that says we should continue to struggle. We have enough to amuse almost everybody. Man can stop right now if he desires, *but the Universe moves on.* Eventually, humanity will face a challenge, if not from the Apollyoni then from something else, either a natural challenge or one contrived by some other form of life."

Greg avoided disputing anything Coni said. He doubted very strongly that the Apollyoni existed, as the very concept seemed mad to him. It resembled too closely the ancient practice of ascribing bad happenings to evil gods, except that now, in her enlightenment, Coni was speaking of evil beings instead of evil gods. Greg felt certain that the Federation would have discovered such a race if it indeed existed. He could, however, envision the mind of a young girl raised in the innocence of the Federation grasping wildly at the musings of her father in a desperate attempt to explain the evil she had suffered. Despite their secular environment, Greg believed that Coni, in her own way, had simply reinvented Satan.

Coni and Greg spent the rest of the day talking. Greg felt very close to her, and in spite of his disbelief in the Apollyoni theory, he could not bring himself to talk her into undergoing psychological treatment. He loved her too much to turn her over to the machines. In the recesses of his mind was the idea, the romantic hope, that their love for each other could do more for her than all the scientifically devised mental therapy in the Federation. Such an attitude was alien to his scientific bent, but he was emotionally involved now both in his love for Coni and in his distrust of the links.

As they talked, Greg noticed that Coni grew more relaxed and confident. Greg believed that the worst of her ordeal was over and that she trusted him and felt better having him with her. That night, for the first time since her panic in the jungle, they made love. She cried afterward in a kind of happy way and then fell asleep in his arms.

In the morning, he awoke to find her cheerfully fixing a meal and straightening up their little base. Ai-ling smiled at both of them from her seat at the base console.

"It's about time you got up," Coni said with her musical laugh. "We've got to earn our keep."

He kissed her. "You're a slave driver." He winked at Ai-ling who flashed him the okay sign. "How do you feel?" he asked her in a serious tone.

"Great! I'm ready to get back to work."

While Greg ate, Coni reviewed her notes and the computer studies from her last piece of work. As Greg was checking their equipment in preparation for their next task, Coni suddenly asked in a very concerned voice, "Greg, did you know that the computer was having trouble sorting out the building material we uncovered? It bears no relation to the surrounding 'natural' material."

"I was aware of it," Greg answered a little warily. He had caught her emphasis on the word "natural." Ai-ling had entered the living room and was watching them both very closely. "I talked to Tom about it," he said.

"What does he think?"

"He plans to investigate it. I suppose we should turn the problem over to the planetologists. There's undoubtedly some explanation for the unusual distribution of materials."

Ai-ling added, "I've studied it, too, but I can't explain it yet."

Coni activated a closed visual comm link with Tom Lippert and asked him about the extrusive material.

"I haven't made much sense out of it," Lippert replied. "We've found similar stuff at the lower levels, but the recent material near the surface is no different from that found naturally on Frey. I've turned *my* data over to the *Avalon* for further study." Greg understood that Lippert's emphasis on the word "my" was meant to let them know that he had covered for their recent inactivity.

"Tom, this may be what we're looking for!" Coni exclaimed.

Greg looked at her sharply, but she was concentrating on her conversation with Lippert. Ai-ling's face showed concern as she, too, turned to Coni.

"I don't understand," Lippert said, puzzled.

"The Apollyoni!" she cried excitedly. "This unnatural extrusive material could have been produced by them if in the process of destroying the Freyan civilization, they disassembled and then reassembled the building material."

Lippert was silent for a moment, Greg was afraid to breathe, and then Lippert spoke in a soothing voice. "We have no proof of that, Coni. Before we make any statements on this matter, I'd like to find out what the *Avalon* discovers."

Greg could not see Lippert's face, but he could tell from his voice that he did not believe in the Apollyoni hypothesis. It was obvious to Greg that Lippert was trying to gently dissuade Coni from invoking her father's opinions about one planet to explain unusual behavior on another.

Coni was visibly upset over Lippert's unwillingness to support her conclusion, but she agreed to wait, as Lippert suggested. When she finished talking to Lippert, she went back to work in a very quiet, determined manner. Greg made himself as unobtrusive as possible, keeping the tractor beams busy recovering more material from the Freyan past. Even Ai-ling was subdued, as if she feared that any talk would set Coni off again. Once he heard Coni muse aloud about the Apollyoni having such trouble with their weapons of destruction that they inadvertently created some unnatural extrusive material.

By the end of the day, Greg was relieved that Coni seemed to have forgotten her brief conversation with Lippert. Several days later the *Avalon* signaled that a deposit of this unknown material had been found in the northern regions of Frey. It was hypothesized that the Freyans must have been impressed with the deposit's different qualities and carried it all over the planet. The planetologists showed how under the right conditions the material could have been created naturally.

After the report was concluded, Coni sat down with a dejected look on her face and bitterly commented, "The Apollyoni have fooled us again."

Greg walked over to her, sat down and put his arm around her. She closed her eyes and rested her head on his shoulder. He massaged her neck and back.

"I'm so tired, Greg. I'll be glad to leave here."

Greg was not certain whether she was finally breaking the hold Ahriman had on her. He felt that if she could accept the report from the *Avalon* and get away from her work, she would soon forget the Apollyoni and perhaps someday could bury Ahriman.

"After this is over, let's take a long vacation, just the two of us," he said in a warm, firm tone.

She smiled and kissed him. "I'd like that. Maybe we can go to Ziol and see Tehuti. I feel the need for some wisdom and"—she paused—"some magic."

The *Avalon* completed its basic exploratory work a few months after unraveling the mystery of the extrusive material. Greg was not completely satisfied with the results of the Jotunnheim II exploration. Many questions remained about Frey and its civilization. Still, Greg realized that in a way this would make many theorists happy—there were enough data to make the problem interesting but not enough to curb all speculation.

In a way, Greg felt that his only regret on leaving Frey was contained in the feelings he had when Coni remarked as they left the attractive, enigmatic planet: "I made a mistake in naming this place Frey. I should have called it

Belial." That remark seemed to take the final gram of bitterness out of her. Thereafter, she never spoke about the Apollyoni influence on Frey.

Greg sat brooding in his chair, his mind still filled with images of Frey. He became aware that he had been gnawing on a callous that he had, over time, chewed on his finger. So much had happened since Frey. He had followed Nat's advice and entered the Fleet's Science Officer Corps. He had met Richard while on the Perimeter assignment and had then gotten involved in the flight of the *Guardian* beyond the Perimeter. Poor Mary Whittaker, he thought. Life starts out so simple and despite our best efforts to keep it simple, it gets so involved, so messed up. He hoped that his life with Coni balanced out the incident he and Richard had shared aboard the *Guardian*.

Greg stood up and stretched, feeling his muscles and bones snap into place. He looked once more at his computer study of Ahriman. There were no Apollyoni, even if he could not satisfactorily explain through natural phenomena what had happened to that planet. And Mary Whittaker would turn up, safe and normal. It just had to be. Sure he believed in the worst. Who wouldn't in a society where every effort, every device worked for conformity? But the Universe was basically sane—it had to be. Young girls were not sexually and physically tortured because some aliens ruined a planet. And Fleet officers did not simply vanish.

But then why had Jerry Whittaker tried to escape? Why was there a Perimeter which conveniently cut off planets like Ahriman from further study? Perhaps someday even Frey would be defined as outside the Perimeter.

4

INJECTION

Come, or the stellar tide will slip away.
Eastward avoid the hour of its decline,
Now! for the needle trembles in my soul!

—Ezra Pound, *The Needle*

Greg's vision grew lighter. The sleepy darkness receded on an ebb tide of dreams. He squinted at the Sol-like artificial light which floated mistlike across the bedroom as he stretched his arms and legs on the bed. *Jeez, I hardly slept—it wasn't worth even trying to sleep.* He knew he would probably feel worse today for trying rather than just foregoing sleep. It was damned hard to sleep. His mind had been so alive with thoughts. Images had battered him all night, refusing to be stopped by the fortresslike walls of his mental control. He could not deny them passage across the moat that separated his subconscious from his conscious.

Mary Whittaker was missing. The remembrance of Frey. The unsatisfactory explanations of Ahriman. Coni's injury at the High Tide. The upcoming voyage of the *Odyssey.* He owed Mary more than he was doing. He and Richard both owed her something, for Jerry's sake. He lamely justified his inaction with the excuse that he had to attend the preflight briefing today and then lift off this afternoon for Shamash.

Coni stirred. He rolled over on his right side and placed his left arm across her chest. Her breathing was still deep, but she was slowly waking. She blinked her eyes open then looked at him and smiled. He kissed her. "I love you," he said softly.

She turned to him, her arms around his neck as she pulled his head to her. "I love you, darling," she replied in a soft, serious voice. "I love you very much." Her eyes shone in the Sol light, sending the iridescent light of moist green grass and leaves out to him.

"How do you feel?" he asked, his lips brushing lightly against hers as he spoke. "Fine," she answered. "I'm almost healed."

He kissed her again while his left hand caressed her soft right breast, excitement building within him as she pressed closer to him, arching her back to feel all of him. Their tongues met like moist sensual fingers searching out some exotic handclasp. He felt her nipple harden, so he moved to touch her other breast. He kissed her neck, her collarbone, her breasts. He felt the warmth of her breath on his head, and the way her yellow hair fell about her naked shoulders was like a radiant glow from some golden star. He carefully pulled the covers from her and undid the filmy garment she wore.

He wanted to weep for joy! He wanted to tell her how beautiful she was! He wanted to worship her! But he was silent, silent with feeling. She flowed like water, there were no angles to her. Her breasts rose gracefully, and her hips were smooth-rolling curves that blended into shapely legs. His mouth moved across her breasts to her flat stomach and then to the maiden hairs that beckoned him with their dark-blonde promise of sunshine and life. She was alive with him, moving with him, holding him to her. He moved up again and entered her, feeling safe within her. He laughed to himself when he thought about the comments on their different sizes—she *was* built just right for him! She was part of him, moving against him like a gentle current spreading warmth through his body.

They came together, he pressing down on her in frozen yet relaxing release, she driving up against him in a spasm of ecstasy.

He lay on top of her, breathing easily now and trying to keep his weight from pressing too hard against her small body. She smiled up at him. "I like it so much better this way," she said. "You're wonderful."

"I'll never replace a pleasure palace," he laughed, showing he knew the implication of her remark.

She pouted. "What do you know about them?"

"I'll never tell."

She raised her head and kissed him.

The world was not organized right. He knew this. What had nature intended for humanity? Probably nothing more than had been intended for all life—replication. The rest was up for grabs. Well, the act was pleasurable, the most pleasurable natural experience he knew. Certainly more pleasurable than spending a day at the Fleet base. So why did he have to get up and leave?

He rolled off her and lay on his right side watching her. His left hand moved softly along the lines of her young body. "I love you." She smiled at him.

They lay like that for several minutes, touching, murmuring words of affection, then she asked, "What time did you get in?"

"After midnight. Quite a bit after to be exact." He brushed his tousled hair out of his eyes. "Had a bit of a problem. Mary Whittaker is missing."

"Oh, no!" It had taken Greg some time to break the story of Jerry Whittaker to Coni, but she knew and understood Richard's and his concern for Jerry's sister. "What happened?"

He shrugged. "We don't know. She arrived with Rich on the flight from Armstrong and then simply vanished. The authorities are investigating." He kissed her lightly. "Don't worry—I'm sure everything will turn out okay." He wished that he believed that. He got out of bed.

"Where are you going?"

"Got to get dressed m'love. Duty beckons. Today is the day and all that nonsense."

Darkness clouded her eyes. "I wish you didn't have to go."

"We've been lucky. I haven't had much off-planet work in a long time. I'll be back in a few days. How about spending the time with Tom and his wife?"

"No," she said as she sat on the edge of the bed. "I think I'll putter around here. Maybe swim a little."

"By the way, I looked at those calculations again. Not much luck. If you have time, take my user's card over to the base and ask Stan Arkin or Jim Colton to go through them for you. A sort of check on me."

She smiled slightly. "I'll wait until you get back. Anyhow, I trust you—you are the Fed's best astrophysicist."

"Ha!" He started into the shower. "But I'll keep you around just for saying so."

She smiled broadly and stretched, her breasts going firm now. "Well, at least you're the best astrophysical lover I know."

He was out of the shower in a minute and quickly donned his dark-blue uniform and black boots. The old outer skin. He hardly knew the uniform existed. He looked up and saw her leaning against the edge of the doorway. She was still naked and pressed her breasts and legs against the doorway in sensuous invitation. "Don't go," she pleaded. "Please don't go."

He looked at her in utter helplessness. He was too weak where she was concerned. This flight was part of a reward and punishment cycle. The Fleet was too moody now. Too many unusual things were happening to make this a pleasant flight. And Coni was the reward for staying.

He walked to her and put his arms around her. "I need you, Coni. Please bear with me on this trip."

He thought about that remark later as he walked along the gleaming white walkway toward the low, sandy-brown flight operations building, where he and his three crewmates would assemble for the preflight briefing. He did need her. She was life to him just as the springtime around him was life to him. He saw her eyes in the carefully trimmed lawn and in the billowy clouds of green that topped the nearby trees. He was lucky to have her. Where was Jan now? And Art's woman, Vanessa, where was she? Yes, he was the lucky one.

He started to climb the handful of white steps leading to the main entrance of the flight operations building.

"Greg! Hey, Greg!"

He turned and saw Richard running up the walkway after him. "No rush, fellow. We're early. How's Coni?"

Smiling, Greg answered, "She's okay."

Richard's face was impassive; no emotion was written there. "They found Mary."

Greg stopped. He did not like the sound of his friend's voice or the look in his eyes. "Is she all right?"

Richard's face came alive with lines of concern. "Hell, I don't know." He looked around them. "Can we go some place to talk?"

"Sure. As you said, we're early. Let's take a walk." Greg moved down off the steps, and Richard followed him as he started on a new path around the building toward a small, dark pond that separated this building from its twin, the planet operations building a few hundred meters away.

"She showed up in Africa, some fukken Syncretist settlement near Bamako." He turned to face Greg as they walked. "I don't know what to make of it. She told the investigators that she was through with the Fleet, through with every last bit of it. She said she finally found peace. She doesn't want to come back. She doesn't even want to see her friends or relatives. I asked to talk to her but with no luck."

"What do the investigators think?"

"Her story checks out. She says she went under a screen to get away from us long enough to put it all together. All the studies of her check out."

Greg walked in silence, his head bent and his arms crossed over his chest. "Rich, I don't like it," he said. He stopped near the black water pond and faced Richard. "I don't like it one damned bit." He looked down at the pond, exhaling a tired lungful of air. "I meant to call you this morning to see what happened and also to tell you that I had no luck in learning more about the Sangraal signals. This whole incident with Mary has got me bothered. She comes back to Earth from Armstrong, presumably okay. She's been in K-10, where she says people are getting signals from the Sangraal system. That's the sector against which the Syncretists have rebelled and over which the Fleet has imposed a complete comm silence." He sucked in some air as if seeking buoyant support. "Care to hear some paranoia?"

"I'm listening."

"Suppose you were a Syncretist and learned something that could mess up one of your sacred ideas, for example, the Perimeter. Suppose something was going on beyond the Perimeter that threatened to force the Fleet to go out and investigate. Wouldn't you do everything in your power to stop such action? Wouldn't you force the Fleet to silence all bases receiving information that might necessitate such an investigation? Wouldn't you silence anyone who might return and who knew about this 'something'?"

Richard's mouth opened in disbelief. "You mean to tell me that the Sangraal signals, the K-10 silence, the uprising on Vesta and now Mary's change are all related?"

"Yes," Greg replied simply. He felt defensive in the face of Richard's incredulity and finally added, "And probably a number of other events, too."

"That's pretty farfetched. I can't buy it, Greg." Richard shrugged, hands open. "I admit that some weird things have happened recently, but I don't buy all this conspiracy stuff." He shook his head. "It's got to be simpler than that. Someone got to Mary and played on her concerns about the Federation. She got sucked into Syncretism before she knew what hit her."

"Well, at least you agree that they can be mighty persuasive."

"If you mean by that that they can pull a few illegal mental tricks, I'll agree with you there."

Greg turned back toward the path they had just taken. "All I ask is that you think about all of this. It's been bothering me all night, and this morning on the way here I made the connection. I don't expect you to believe me, but just think it over. Mary just wasn't their kind." He started walking down the path. "We'd better get back before our new ship commander gives us a demerit for tardiness." Greg felt relieved that Richard would be off-planet for several days. Greg had not been able to warn Richard again that he might be the next missing person. An image seared through Greg's mind—*Art, the Syncretist.* No, it couldn't be, he thought. *His* presence was pure coincidence. Or was it?

The briefing room was an unaffected rectangular room, containing a simple, functional table in the center and formfitting chairs around it. A small scanner occupied the center of the table, where it could suck up everyone's attention by being the only item of note in the entire room. Of course, the walls could convert into large scanner screens, but for now they were simple washed-out structures caught in the artificially simulated light of Sol. No one was in the room when Greg and Richard were cleared to enter.

Greg immediately walked to the automat. He felt unsettled since he had put his facts together. The true scientist would be out verifying the hypothesis. "Coffee, tea or milk," he said in mimicry, knowing that the first two existed in the automat in highly changed forms from their original namesakes and the last was a synthetic, nonfat, creamy-tasting white froth.

"Fix me a cafnex," Richard murmured as he slumped into a chair opposite Greg.

Greg made two cups of cafnex and handed one to Richard. He was raising the warm liquid to his lips when the door opened. Ben Wilson entered, followed by Art Cooke and Ron Carson. There were brief greetings and introductions. We're all here, Greg mused. The final pat on the back from the Base Commander. Just like the old days. He did not feel at ease in the presence of Wilson and Carson, and he noticed that Richard and Art did not either. "Anyone for some cafnex?" he asked the silent trio of newcomers. Wilson shook his head, his face impassive. Art made his way past Greg to the automat. Carson smiled and said no.

They all sat down with Richard, Carson and Wilson on one side, Greg and Art on the other. Wilson shuffled a few papers then spoke quickly and forcefully: "You've all seen your orders and had a chance to study the proposed flight plan, so I won't spend much time reviewing that. We'll make this a direct flight to Shamash. When we get there, we'll do a quick recon and return. I want all systems checked out before we launch, and we'll follow standard procedures all the way to Shamash and back. Highstreet—you're on as assistant ship commander and lead science officer. Cooke—you take the payload systems and planetology. Sheldon—you've got the systems monitoring and astrophysics. Just because this is a training flight is no reason to slack off. I've got my own ideas on training, so stay alert all the way through. You've got four hours before liftoff to get your systems in order. I'll inspect it at 1400 and then we go. Any questions?"

No one had any questions. Wilson resumed speaking about the technical aspects of the flight plan, and he used the scanner to illustrate his procedures. He briefly questioned each man on his duties and then turned the meeting over to Commander Carson.

Carson spoke for a few minutes about the importance of the mission and the benefits derived from diligent training. His voice was quiet and inducible in contrast to the forcefulness of Wilson's. Greg tended to dismiss Carson's speech as the usual preflight bullshit except for Carson's unusual emphasis on team action and success. Dramatic bullshit, Greg decided. If they can't get our interest one way, they liven it up another way. As far as he was concerned, the flight was so routine, so tedious, that he would have to force himself to stay awake. He figured his only problem would be staying out of Wilson's way.

When Carson finished, Wilson said, "Okay, let's get to it."

Greg looked at Richard while trying hard to conceal his smile with his cup. The rumors circulating around the base had not been false—Wilson *was* an autocratic commander. Every crew is entitled to at least one sonofabitch, he thought. It comes with the uniform.

Now that he had his assignment, Greg was eager to get going. However, Richard had other plans. "You go on ahead and keep the ship commander company, Greg," he said after the others had left. "I'll be along shortly."

"There could be some tests built into the prelaunch checkout," Greg protested. "You ought to get started now."

"Wilson may be tough, but he's not chickenshit," Richard observed. "If there's any testing to be done, it'll be for real."

"So what's keeping you from going to the ship now?"

"I think I'll try to reach Mary once more. If necessary, I'll beam to Bamako. Okay?"

Greg nodded. He should be trying also. He turned and walked out of the room to catch a levitator to the launch operations building.

From the levitator he stepped onto the wide main concourse of the sprawling launch operations building near the guide tube holding the *Odyssey*. The roof was down today, replaced by a shield screen which allowed the dwarfed humans a chance to see the glimmering starships silently floating in their invisible tubes of force. The *Odyssey* was a small starship, about sixty meters in length at its longest dimension and adequate for training, Greg judged. He stood, hands on buttocks, and looked up at his new home and marveled at this almost blinding white, elongated globe whose energy was mercifully muted by the surrounding force screens. The *Odyssey* glowed like some miniature star except that it held more energy than any star, and with its vaporous appearance, it was, in a sense, less real. No features marked its shining surface. It was uniformly constructed of potent fields.

Greg walked to the nearest teleporter unit. A remote clearance scan was made of him, and he was permitted to enter the teleporter. The sending instructions were preprogrammed, based on his known orders. In an instant, the large sunlit concourse was replaced with the uniformly lighted mechanical features of the teleporter room on board the *Odyssey*. He stepped from the teleporter beam tube and walked out of the room to examine the ship. Even though he understood the physics of starships, he could never quite get used to the fact that what appeared to be a gaseous ball of energy from the outside looked so solid and homey inside. Every comfort had been built in. The color schemes were chosen to agree with the personalities of the crewmembers. The interior decor and arrangement of equipment was what Greg used to call "inspirationally neutral"—it did not excite him, but its functional neutrality did not depress him either.

There were times when Greg wondered whether the physicists were right in their theories about starships and metaspace. Perhaps when he entered a starship, he was reduced to the same plasmatic energy he had seen from the outside. Perhaps this whole image of solidity was artificially created in or by his mind to lend a sense of "reality" to the vaporous state of a starship. Had it not been for the synchronal exclusion principle which precluded him (at least to the best of known theory and practice) from being simultaneously anywhere else or anything but what he was, he might have also wondered about the ability of the teleporter to contribute to this effect.

A central hallway connected the control room at the forward end with the ergon impeller, penetrator and metadrive at the aft end. Since the ship was slightly ellipsoidal, with its longest axis aligned with this hallway, he could justifiably think of a forward and aft end even though the terms had no practical meaning. The ship was isotropic as far as guidance and propulsion were concerned. It had its own inertial control system which maintained a Tellurian gravity equivalent regardless of motion so the ship could move in any direction at any time and at any speed or derivative thereof. Despite this isotropy, Fleet custom had kept the forward and aft terms whenever it was apparent what was meant. At that moment, Greg was actually horizontal relative to Earth's surface.

Radiating about the central hallway were the individual rooms for the crew, the payload compartment, flight operations equipment and the teleporter room. All this was a luxury because a basic starship did not need the volume.

Greg stepped into the room assigned to him. It was no different from others to which he had been assigned. On most flights, especially the now rare training flights, the Fleet still maintained its old custom of providing all the necessities and luxuries for the individual crewmembers. Greg had only to show up. His personality profile was known, and his tastes and idiosyncrasies would be accommodated. He resisted a temptation to plop on the bed. He was sure Wilson would not approve.

Greg walked to his personal locker and took out a shield belt. He fastened it carefully around his waist and tested it. Satisfied with its performance under test, he was going out the door when his eyes caught the small quad-dem picture near the door. Coni! She was there, smiling at him and as alive as if she were in the room with him. He swore briefly. He had never taken her picture on a flight. He preferred to carry her in his mind, where she was all his. She knew that. And the Fleet knew it. So why was the picture here? He walked out the door, a little unnerved yet afraid to cancel such beauty by turning off the picture.

He entered the control room and found Art stretched out in the rear crew-mate's recliner, which would serve as his duty station. For some reason, long buried in outmoded Fleet engineering and tradition, those craft with a four-person control room always had the ship commander's recliner at the front, with the assistant commander's and system monitor's recliners located side by side, separated by an aisle, and to the rear of the ship commander's recliner. The payload monitor's recliner was located aft of these two recliners and on a line with the ship commander's recliner. Two portals on either side of Art's recliner facilitated travel into and out of this rhombus-shaped arrangement.

"Hello," Greg said. "Hard at it, I see."

Art looked up, his lighter complexioned face blank. "You're getting perceptive in your old age." His tone was cold.

Greg walked over to his recliner, which was to the right and in front of Art's. He felt nothing as he sat down, but he knew that invisible fields were ready for his mental signal to activate the reclining chair. These fields would course through him, feed him, care for him, eliminate his wastes and provide secondary environmental support during the flight. One thought—that's all it took to activate the recliner.

Greg mentally signaled the recliner to swivel so he would face Art. "Sorry I didn't get much chance to talk back at ops. Wilson was all business, and Rich had a few things on his mind."

"No matter. We'll be seeing each other quite a bit the next few days." Greg saw that Art had his recliner in full operation and was hooked to the telepathic link with the *Odyssey*. Greg judged from the tone of Art's voice that he was paying only partial attention.

"How's Vanessa?" Greg asked.

"Okay."

"Coni's been asking about you both, especially since this assignment came up. She hasn't heard from Vanessa in several months."

"She's been busy off-planet."

Greg laughed. "I swear she gets off-planet more than the Fleet. Where to this time?"

"Vesta." Art's eyes were now searching his face. Greg was not sure if he flinched upon hearing Art speak that word. *Does Art know?*

Clearing his throat, Greg went on, "More educational work or just a vacation?"

"A little of both. How's Coni? I haven't seen her in years."

"Same as always." *I can be noncommittal, too.* "Ever figure the odds on a flight like this?"

"What do you mean?"

"Three people with common acquaintances. I don't know if you recall but I worked with Rich on the Perimeter once. Also, one could wonder why only one gender."

Art shrugged. "The only thing that puzzles me is why the flight in the first place."

"I think I'll get to it," Greg said as he returned his recliner to the forward-facing position. "1400 is creeping up on us. How're you doing?"

"Almost finished except for some late cargo they haven't put on yet."

Greg activated his recliner with the appropriate mental signal. Then he established communion with the telepathic link. Through his mind and the telepathic link he was now part of a vast noetronic circuit of thoughts and sensory data. There were no visual controls or instruments in this room, but they could be called into play from their concealed storage locations. No screens or other vestiges of old-fashioned spaceflight adorned this silent control center. Everything he needed to do his job was in his mind. He could dart throughout the ship and by virtue of the ship's scanners and sensors, he could be anywhere outside it. All the functions he needed to control he could mentally handle through the link. He was now an integral part of the ship in the ultimate manner, assuring uniform operations between crew and ship.

He always entered a telepathic link with a feeling of deep reluctance. He knew there were ample laws and regulations which protected the privacy of his inner thoughts. Only the conscious, ship-related communications of his mind could be sent into the link. Yet, there was always the danger that something more might surface or might be made to surface. He did not want to share his thoughts and feelings with others.

The shipboard telepathic link was very much like the teaching machines he had used as a child, those advanced scientific organa which directly fed the student's mind with the desired knowledge while providing illustrated examples as needed to ensure that the information was properly understood before subtle tests were administered. His learning had been painless and fast, although it had taken an effort on his part to learn in this manner. Later, when he diagnosed the intent of some of his lessons, he likened the teaching machines to an enemy army tearing at the stone walls of his mental castle. Once inside, they were capable of doing anything, he thought. Even now he preferred reading to the links because reading permitted him to select what he wished to absorb. Now he could consciously evaluate the material before it became a permanent cerebral fixture.

Still, the links of the teaching machines *were* a superior means of learning; they could provide vivid noegenetic images of history and literature, making the past live through showing the historical interrelationships between science, art, literature, commerce and philosophy. But Greg had often wondered if the truly imaginative person required such assistance. Would not the imagination suffer like an untended flower if the links were overused?

At fifteen standard years, Greg had noticed a trend in his literary and sociology lessons. Thinking back on it, he realized that the trend had been developing for some time. It was a subtle development but it was there. He had seen a definite sequence in novels that emphasized a more outgoing life, as well as a sequence in sociological studies that described people who were more concerned about those around them. It was difficult to be sure of his suspicions, but discussions with his friends revealed to him the unobviously different approaches in their educational experiences, and this helped confirm his belief that he was being psychologically reoriented.

His first investigation of the teaching machines had consisted of a study of the history and philosophy of the educational system. What was it like? How had it got that way? What were the goals and standards? And most important, was it permitted to tamper with a person's mind? He kept his opinions to himself, as he had felt sufficiently wary of the dangers of the course he was taking. He had studied by himself, but the links had provided most of the information.

From the beginning of his education, Greg knew that the present social and technical level of the Federation resulted from a compromise between two factions that had fought to shape humanity's future. One faction, which included the Syncretists, represented an interventionist view of humanity, wanting to use the new technology to remake man, to engineer him physically and mentally in order to build a utopia. The other faction, which included the Neomonadists, was more libertarian in its approach, preferring the primacy of man and desiring to shape his technology and society to fit that primacy. There were, of course, variations: interventionists who sought the total submergence of the individual; libertarians who sought to prevent any changes; and, as in all human history, there were those who sought dominion over their fellowmen. But these variations and extremes were no more than minor perturbations in the tug of war between the two main factions.

Human history at times of change seemed cyclic, a pull this way then a pull that way, but if rational minds were operating, the outcome was often a compromise, as if each view was somehow relevant to a part of human nature and only a compromise could approximate the answer. Extremes served to galvanize action, while rationality thrived best in moderate environments.

And so man tampered with himself, with his environment and with his society, but each new adjustment was made with the view of preserving what man had been, preserving that innate individuality which had permitted man to go out to the stars. It had been like a drumming in Greg's mind: *we will make you physically well and long-lived but you will stay you; we will educate and pro-vide for you but you will stay you; we will ensure your mental health but you will be you.* Simply stated, the biologists had recognized that the abstract concept of nature had had more experience than man in selecting survival traits.

But what constituted good mental health? Greg still occasionally pondered this problem. Is the inmate fit to judge the doctor? By whose standards do we judge? If man is to remain an individual, then deviations must be permitted, Greg had reasoned. Despite the rigid laws governing the use of the link, Greg could conceive the fundamental problem by drawing an analogy to a tenet of old-fashioned criminology: one cannot stand idly by while a killer walks the streets. And in his mental ways maybe he was a "killer" to someone or to soci-ety. Did he not represent an anachronism in an age of mental union? His indi-viduality had legally survived the embryologist's skills, but could it survive the link?

Even then he had had perpetual mental debates: "If the State had con-structed my personality, would I be any less happy since I would have known no other existence?" He would wonder what his life might have been like cen-turies earlier. My health, my education, my opportunities have all shaped my personality, he thought. But he had concluded that deep within there existed a basic *him*, an intrinsic self modified only in its interrelationships with the out-side since these interrelationships could be changed; therefore, freed of the biologist, he existed basically unchanged. How I am may change, he thought, but what I am does not.

Just as he was now on guard in the *Odyssey's* link, he had openly opposed the reorientation that had been practiced upon him some ten standard years before, probably even earlier than that. The very knowledge of what had hap-pened, what was in fact still happening, served to protect him. It was sufficient to simply ignore or filter what the teaching machines imparted. It was this experience, coupled with similar experiences of his friends, that had caused him to become enmeshed at that early age in Neo-monadism, a sort of extreme libertarian philosophy. This occurred even though he could not com-mit himself to the ultimate tenet of Neo-monadism—the rejection of organ-ized society—since the Federation had in its own way given birth to him, but he could, in more cogent terms, argue, "I exist. I am happy. Let me lead my own life." Eventually, he discovered the paradox inherent in his attempts to convert others to his way of thinking: if he wanted to be left alone, then he would have to leave others alone.

Greg pulled his thoughts away from the silent presence of the link and con-centrated on the tasks before him. He was responsible for monitoring all systems aboard the *Odyssey.* He ensured that the engines, the shields, the scanners, the sensors, the life-support system and all the other computational and flight devices worked as a team with the crew so the men could carry out their assigned mission. Ben Wilson and Richard would be busy with the major flight decisions and with astrogation. Greg had to keep everything else functionally active while Art handled the direct flight hardware and payload aspects of the flight.

He enjoyed being the systems monitor while in space because the task fit in with his general interest in all scientific and technical fields. He had no real specialization except astrophysics; therefore, systems monitoring suited his desire to think of technical problems in terms of the complete system. The mental link with the ship did have its rewards: it was a vitalizing experience to feel the awesome intricacy and power bundled within a starship. He could sympathize with the joy experienced by the biologists when they conducted their scanner and sensor studies. The experience of mentally linking with the ship was like being a part of the life process: the convolutions of the mind, supported in fluids and dispensing signals along a multitude of paths in response to sensors, and the rhythms of the heart beating to push the precious red liquid through the network of life.

With the aid of the computer, Greg sequentially went through the learned and ordered checklist. He would activate a device after receiving the go-ahead from Art, run it through the functional acceptance checkout procedures and then integrate it into the whole shipboard system for final testing. With human participation, it was a long process, one he would not normally do since the computer was perfectly capable of doing it without him, yet this was what Wilson wanted and so he would give it to him. (The term "computer," a carry-over from earlier centuries, always seemed so limiting to him because a computer was now much more than a high-speed calculating machine. The *Odyssey's* computer was actually a superposition of mensatronic fields with intelligence, reasoning powers, decision-making capabilities, self-healing faculties and almost unlimited storage and input capacities. It was more than equal to the biologically enhanced minds of its human partners. It acted as the central brain for the complex ship-borne nervous system of controls, sensors, propulsive units and life-support.)

He looked up and saw Richard climbing into his recliner. Richard shook his head slightly, answering his question about Mary before he could ask it. Silently, Richard entered the link.

Greg was aware of both Art's and Richard's presence. He knew Art was checking the hardware and he felt? sensed? knew? (how could he really describe what was in his mind?) Richard's review of the flight plan. When Greg and Art finished, Richard reviewed their work.

"A-Okay," Richard said aloud. "You guys keep this up and I'll sleep to Shamash."

Ben entered the room on schedule and conducted the final review. Greg noted that Wilson was very thorough in reviewing every detail of their preparations.

Stand by to receive cargo, Ben thought on the link. Art activated the teleporter unit. When the last-minute equipment was on board, Art used an internal tractor beam to position it carefully by remote control into the assigned locations in the payload compartment.

Final review of your checklists, Ben continued when Art had finished. *Flight operations?*

Go, Richard replied.

Systems?

Go for launch, Greg answered.

Flight hardware and payload?

All go, Art responded.

Ben relayed this information to Launch Control and requested clearance for launch.

Odyssey, *you are cleared for launch!*

This communication, which told them that Launch Control had activated the final protective shields around the *Odyssey* and had prepared a clear ejector beam, echoed in Ben's mind as he went through the final, well-learned procedures for launch. His three crewmates were similarly engaged in making their own contribution to a successful launch, mentally working according to well-established launch procedures. This was a moment of oneness, a moment seldom experienced in automated launches, a moment that carried with it a peculiar pleasure of union of purpose that Ben enjoyed. Through his telepathic nexus with the crew and ship, Ben was aware of the complex operations being performed to make the launch.

A quick telepathic question brought affirmative responses from the other three crewmembers and from the *Odyssey's* computer-controlled instrumentation and controls systems. In a quiet voice that hid his anticipation, Ben said aloud, "Well, here we go."

Under the guidance and control of the crew, the launch operations were initiated. The confining and stabilizing fields of the ergon impeller were built up until the desired field topology was established. The engine injector forced a burst of energy into the space defined by the fields. The fields began to vary temporally and spatially, enclosing the energy and compressing, confining, and reducing instabilities. As Ben mentally probed the engines, only training kept him from a feeling of actually being pulled into a Charybdis of energy. When the critical energy flux was reached, the injector provided a continuous flow of energy at this flux level.

With the aid of the link, Ben sensed the measurements being made by the ship's instruments. He could feel the field strength building up to contain the additional energy. Instabilities and anisotropic effects were eliminated as the fields established a self-consistent flux-field equilibrium. The proper phase mixing had been accomplished.

Ben mentally activated the launch controls. The fields focused the energy flux and ejected the hellish flood into the launch shields. The *Odyssey* streaked away from its berth, following the ejector beam on a path away from Earth. Protected by the ship's inertial system, the crew was physically unaware of the liftoff, although mentally, through the scanners, they were vividly aware of the launch.

Ben felt good about the launch. It was seldom that such semiautomatic, human-controlled flights were made, yet the crew had lost none of its early indoctrination. The mental reflexes had been excellent, and there had been no failure in alertness.

The *Odyssey,* existing and moving more like some ethereal focalization of field lines than a tangible object, rose out of Earth's atmosphere and moved along a gradually "rising" trajectory which would take it "above" the plane of the ecliptic. Ben went through the post-launch checkout, then, satisfied that everything was functioning correctly, he placed the ship on automatic control and broke with the telepathic link. There was a moment of familiar disorientation as the mental hub of activity was replaced by the quiet of the control room.

Ben turned his recliner to face the crew. He could see that his crewmates were also experiencing that same brief disorientation which resulted from the transfer from a totally mental communication to a partial or totally verbal one. On his right sat Richard Highstreet, his long, tanned body bent in absorption with the mission. From the aft end of the room Art Cooke returned his gaze with that same unfathomable stare he had seen on the scanner image in Carson's office. Glancing now to his left, Ben saw that Greg Sheldon was still keeping track of the flight even as he listened to the world around him.

The crew sat or lay back in their life-supporting recliners, nodes forming the points of a four-cornered diamond. In a brief, uncharacteristic spirit of whimsy, Ben saw not the diamond but a mythological conjurer's circle, an apt symbol for a crew telepathically linked to achieve certain goals.

"It was a good launch," Ben said with a friendly smile. "It shows that the old training is holding us all in good stead. We can all look forward to a routine training flight."

There were brief nodes of acknowledgment. Ben had not expected more, since the training flight had been hastily put together, and it was not the sort of routine operation which a good crew could look forward to with any sort of enthusiasm. Since to the others the flight was an end in itself, it probably seemed to them somewhat unorthodox. Soon they will learn just how unorthodox it is, Ben thought to himself.

Art was the first to speak. "We received some excellent liftoff images. It was quite a beautiful scene. If you have no objection, I would like to replay them and record them."

"That's fine with me," Ben replied. He wished to keep Cooke under surveillance just to assuage his misgivings about him, but he knew he could not stop Cooke from taking some time off; he did not want to arouse the crew's suspicions. Once they entered metaspace, it would be a different story. Turning to Greg, he said, "Sheldon, I'd like you to review the mission path to Shamash." Looking at Highstreet, Ben went on, "Rich, run a probe of the surrounding space." Highstreet nodded. "Otherwise, I think we're in good shape for injection, so I see no reason why we can't relax and enjoy the trip. However, since this is a training flight, I would like to have someone linked up with the ship for the duration of the flight. Being the noble type"—again he smiled—"I'll take the first link."

As the crewmembers began their newly assigned tasks, Ben reminded them, almost as an afterthought yet in a tone that carried authority and implied a meaning deeper than a literal one, "We will, of course, be conducting some training exercises prior to injection. Everyone should stay alert throughout this flight."

Richard watched as Wilson returned to his mental link with the ship. Cooke was already lost in his recapture of the launch images and in his own emotional response to them. Richard glanced over at Greg, who was busy with his review of the mission path to Shamash. Greg, apparently aware of his glance, looked over, smiled and signaled with his right hand that all was okay. Richard returned the smile and then linked up to the *Odyssey's* scanners.

No matter how many times he had done this, the effect was always overwhelming. There he was, mentally shot into the black void—he, Richard Highstreet, a tiny speck rising from that blue-white precious stone called Earth as if the field-like *Odyssey* were some sort of scientific dream conveyer. By linking through the multifaceted scanner system he could see Earth, the Moon and other nearby objects from any vantage point and with an almost unlimited sensory range. He closed his eyes in awe of the mental vision of the life-giving orb that was his home. His mind reached out, first to the Moon, then through the scanners to all the surrounding space.

He could follow the energy flux from the ship, feel the wonder of life in this Solar System and sense the immensity of space around him. There were no boundaries out here. The whole effect was intoxicating in a strangely Promethean manner. This was why he was here, on this ship, even if it meant performing a routine training flight to the Shamash star system.

It seemed to Richard that he had always had this yearning to be in space. To feel the ship under his control. To view worlds as no native could ever directly see them. Spaceflight had given man a new perspective, and he aimed to absorb it all. He had looked forward to this phase of the training flight, with its prospect of practice mission exercises, because it was more demanding than a routine cargo flight and was vastly more interesting than the more direct interstellar teleportation.

A sudden remark from Wilson brought Richard out of his musings. "We're in a good position to try a rendezvous with Mars. Should be useful as a recon practice. Everyone ready?"

Richard immediately broke his total link with the scanners and added a connection with the ship's instrumentation and controls network. He saw Greg and Art Cooke performing similar linkups. He could not help noticing the differences in the two men's expressions: Greg approached the task before him stoically (was there a hint of anticipation hidden here?), and Cooke seemed bored by the whole operation. The mental link was completed. Once again each crewmember became part of a whole, a separate entity, cells linked to make the organism.

"I would like to simulate a pullout of metaspace followed by a rendezvous," Wilson verbally continued. "To aid in the simulation, I am channeling us off the usual communications. We'll go this one on our own. Now to swing back in and around to catch Mars."

The team functioned automatically in response to Wilson's orders. That living-nonliving symbiosis with the ship carried them on. Wilson, enmeshed in the overall control of the flight activities, was handling the flight, with Richard as his backup. Each was pulling the various systems together with his mind and the *Odyssey's* computer so that the engine functioned as planned. Richard always thought the linkup verged on schizophrenia—each mind controlling the ship through the computer, yet each could still function on a level that shielded him from the others' inner thoughts. Greg had locked in on the operational systems, specifically concentrating on the engine, his mind sifting the facts, making decisions and guiding the flight operational systems through the desired functions. Cooke was reviewing the hardware aspects of the control system, his mind actively darting throughout the control system, checking and probing. Peripherally, Richard was aware of the trend data that had been suitably blended and sent flowing through his mind. The ship was, for all practical purposes, the fifth and most important crewmember: through the computer it pulled the other four together into one integrated personality.

The fields within the *Odyssey's* engine refocused and redirected the energy flux at Wilson's command. The *Odyssey* shifted course and began an out-planet approach to Mars. Richard kept track of the scanner operations as well as the overall system functions. He felt the old thrill of moving through space. He was elated.

They were coming in on a sweeping trajectory, each crewmember performing as if Mars were in fact an unknown world instead of the red warlord of the ancients. Time passed swiftly, as each one was busily engaged in making up his part of the telepathic link to the ship. Cooke confirmed that everything was ready for the deceleration and inspection orbit about Mars. Perfunctorily, as required, Cooke mentally stated that there were no obstacles to the reconnaissance mission. Greg approved the operational checks and had the *Odyssey's* shields ready for increased power.

Take it in, Wilson mentally flashed to Richard.

Richard quickly overcame his surprise, took command of the *Odyssey* and moved the craft into a standard recon orbit. Cooke began a full scan of the planet, while Greg ascertained that the ship's systems were ready for instant departure or landing as required. The rendezvous was being performed efficiently, Ben noted to himself. Again, Fleet training was paying off.

The crew experienced the proximity of Mars through the scanners. They felt the presence of life, sensed the human traffic and viewed the desolation peculiar to Mars. The god of war's namesake indeed looked in places like a wasteland left by some ancient and terrible war. The planet was not a stranger to the crew but under the simulated reconnaissance procedures, it seemed a little alien, leaving Richard slightly uncomfortable as he went through this phase of the exercise.

"I want you to abort the recon mission and pull back to metaspace injection mode—now!" Wilson commanded.

Richard quickly issued the appropriate mental commands. The computer cleared the previous operations, coordinated the scanner inputs and initiated the departure. Cooke and Greg integrated their efforts with the overall system requirements. The engine pulsed to new life, and the *Odyssey* "climbed" rapidly away from Mars within fractional seconds of Wilson's command. The drive for metaspace speeds, coupled with safety considerations, meant a rapid ascent "above" the ecliptic.

Take it through some evasive maneuvers while maintaining metaspace injection goal! Wilson's mind was now commanding on the link.

Again, the crew quickly responded. Richard adjusted the *Odyssey*'s trajectory to avoid imaginary forbidden zones which Wilson randomly selected. At the same time, Richard held to his goal of reaching metaspace injection velocity. Greg monitored the mass detector and the shield.

Hold this acceleration and regain initial trajectory under evasive action.

Richard was too busy to consider Wilson's reasoning, and he silently cursed him for the mental exertion required in this semiautomatic flight even as he experienced the pleasures of command. The *Odyssey* again altered its trajectory and moved in erratic fashion toward their previous injection point. Richard felt Wilson's mind probing for defects in the system. So far everything was holding up. Then Wilson signaled his desire to take command again. Carefully, the two men exchanged control functions. Wilson held the ship in its evasive pattern then flashed: *Stand by to acquire injection gate.*

Greg double-checked the energy flux, confirmed the velocity and put the metadrive on standby status. Cooke prepared for the shift of control functions from world space to metaspace, while Richard stood by to back up the commander. Richard sensed the breathless anticipation of their impending departure from all that seemed real.

Wilson had smoothly made the transition in systems operations. Mechanical messages blurted into the link from many sources: *Shield good. Mass detectors okay. Isolation factor nine. Controls ready for locking.*

Beta point seven! came the mental signal from the computer, telling the crew that they were traveling at seventy percent luminal speed.

The scanners confirmed that they now had the desired amount of isolation for injection.

Beta point eight!

The controls were locked on the injection point for automatic acquisition. The ergon impeller was nearing its limit.

Beta point nine!

Suddenly, Richard had the mental impression that they were not alone—another object looking for all practical purposes like a twin of the *Odyssey* now seemed to be with them. He started to signal this fact, preparing to abort the injection, when "nine" after "nine" whirled through his mind. Then Wilson and the computer, in unison, flashed: *Inject!*

5

METASPACE

...it's better to die attacking the future...than to be shot down
while in retreat to an increasingly irrelevant past.
—Richard Schickel in *Life* Magazine (17 March 1972)

The *Odyssey*, traveling at near luxon speed, cut its ergon impeller as the penetrator in the metadrive pulsed to life. Energy flux, drawn from beyond the luxon barrier by the penetrator, converged at the *Odyssey* and was focused, thrusting the *Odyssey* across the barrier. For one swift instant of time, the *Odyssey* became a singularity in the energy-momentum map of world space, and then it vanished from world space to be reborn in metaspace as a superluminal entity. But to the inhabitants of world space only the void remained where once the *Odyssey* had "existed." The trip along this cosmic Bifrost had begun!

Greg, conditioned as he was by the *Odyssey's* life-support and control systems, as well as by many previous injections, still felt a brief sense of disorientation, a sense of having been disassembled and then reassembled in such a way that everything was at once strange and not strange. It was as if he had entered *Erebos* and now understood Circe's remark about "double-diers." He quickly shook his mind free of the feeling by invoking his Fleet training. It's just in my mind, he thought. It's just in my mind.

The ship was now operating under seemingly new laws that were really generalizations of the old ones that governed world space, but new systems, consonant with the metadrive, were functioning now to preserve the effect of a world space existence: an oasis of world space rationality in a desert of strangeness. Man was taking his world with him.

The ship flashed to the crew's minds the successful barrier penetration signal. The four crewmembers relaxed in their recliners. Wilson disconnected himself from the link as the computer took charge of the *Odyssey*.

"So far, so good," Wilson commented dryly. "I'd like to continue the watch procedure. Sheldon, you maintain a link with the ship. Rich and I will review the shield and tractor beam status. Cooke, you're on your own time, but stand by to relieve Sheldon."

There it was, Greg thought: a series of simple, direct statements. Like programming a computer.

Art stood up, stretched, gathered his recording equipment and left the control room. Richard, who started to speak, stopped himself, his face showing unease as he took his cue. He broke his link and began discussing the shield and tractor beam checkout procedures with Wilson. Greg briefly listened to Wilson's comments as he took over his watch.

"Rich, I want to make damned sure the shield and beam will work when we need them, regardless of other system malfunctions."

A puzzled expression was added to the ill-at-ease look on Richard's face. *"When we need them?" "Other system malfunctions?" Wilson is carrying his role too far. I would have been less dramatic.* Greg made a mental note to talk privately to Richard later on.

Greg mentally shrugged off any further thoughts of the shield and tractor beam checkout. Ship and crew operations would be routine until they reached the Shamash system. He leaned back in his couch, closed his eyes and began reviewing the post-injection checkout that the ship was making. The activities of his crewmates ceased to concern him; his world was now locked into his mind, what data the ship telepathically fed him and what he consisted of. Everything else was nonexistent. Almost automatically, he sequentially tapped into the various scanners, mentally viewing the *Odyssey* and its activities, all the while receiving a steady flow of trend data on the flight.

At times like this, Greg found it hard to keep his thoughts totally on the job. The mental training he had received in the Fleet had been too good to permit him to miss anything unusual while in the link, so he never felt guilty about what his conscious mind was concentrating on. He could dwell on a single subject or let his conscious thoughts flow unchecked like a meandering cerebral stream bringing life-giving fluids to the stationary cellular landscape of his mind. It fascinated him that in the midst of ship-induced activity, he could rise above it, almost as the waters moved around Scylla, flowing unchecked by the localized effect. The routine chores needed no thought, he had learned. It is only when faced with the unusual that man thinks. But Greg enjoyed the routine because now his conscious thoughts could go unshackled, and he no longer had to worry about personal contact with the others and the accompanying need for directed thought. Enmeshed in a regimented computerized ship checkout, he was free.

Being in metaspace never ceased to amaze him. He enjoyed the privilege of participating in one of the greatest scientific feats in the history of the human race. Metaspace was such a wildly unconventional place, with its weird physical behavior, and yet the *Odyssey* had entered this mad ocean with such ease, merely by using the penetrator. In the simplest of mental images relating to the entrance to metaspace, Greg thought of the ancient quantum mechanical analogy of tunneling. The penetrator maximized the capability of a ship—which by virtue of the ergon impeller was moving at almost luxon speed—to penetrate or tunnel through the luxon barrier. Metaspace was that space inhabited by objects with superluminal velocities; a space where proper masses, lengths and times were mathematically imaginary and hence unobservable to subluminal beings; a space where infinitesimal amounts of energy led to almost infinite speeds. The paradox of metaspace travel lay in the fact that an infinitely fast particle was present everywhere on the supercircle of its trajectory, a sort of metarelativistic uncertainty principle that meant velocities of an order less than any of the infinities, and hence finite world times, were required to complete the metaspace jump from injection to exit.

Caution had to be exercised in selecting an injection or exit gate, since singularities in the energy-momentum map of world space could be dangerous, particularly near stellar systems. As a consequence, the Space Fleet operated through predetermined injection and exit gates or "jump points" safely removed from galactic objects. Special mass detectors and standard starship shields were used to protect a starship in the event of an astrogational error. The detectors, which were modified scanners, could penetrate the luxon barrier, ensuring that injections or exits were not made in the presence of other objects. The shields acted as a backup to the detectors in that they screened the ship off from its environment in the event the detectors failed to function properly, causing the ship to cross the luxon barrier at the wrong place. The shields, of course, had a primary function—to protect the ship from the debris of space during the mercurial flights.

It had taken an extensive effort to develop life support for humans in metaspace. It was not sufficient just to discover the metadrive principle. Before it could be tried with humans, scientists had to overcome the maze of relativistic effects that would plague the operator of a subluminal starship approaching luxon speed: the Doppler shift and accompanying hard radiation, aberrations, the apparent complete rearrangement of the Universe. But once in metaspace, man was on his own, sharing a strange existence with other superluminal entities. If the metadrive failed, he would be cut off from his own world space. Sometimes, Greg thought, it was like humankind traveling to the stars on the river Styx.

Greg's conscious thoughts suddenly ceased their ramblings. Something in the link input did not check out correctly! Consciously, he focused strongly on his heretofore subconscious review of the operations on the *Odyssey*. *What the hell have I been doing?* He opened his eyes and saw only Wilson in the control room. Greg supposed that Richard was on some errand for Wilson or else was off duty. He was aware that Wilson was still checking the shield because he could sense Wilson's probes through the link. Rather than spending time tracking down everyone's activities, Greg decided to continue rechecking his previous work. A quick mental review showed that he had finished the standard checklists and had been reviewing the pre-injection attitude when his subconscious signaled him.

Again the flash of warning!

Greg's mind plunged to the source of the problem. He could see it now as he skimmed through the scanner recordings. The injection coordinates and attitude did not coincide with those implanted in his mind from the mission plan.

The Odyssey *was not headed for Shamash!*

"Ben, I think we've got a problem," Greg said. His words seemed absurd to him when he considered the immensity of the problem, which at the same time caused him to doubt the data he was receiving. At metaspace velocities, he knew that erroneous injection coordinates could at best delay their trip while they worked to correct the error and at worst could send them well beyond the Perimeter, if not outside the Galaxy.

Wilson simply looked at Greg with blank eyes.

"Our pre-injection coordinates and attitude do not check with the ones we should have used for Shamash," Greg added.

Wilson now stared hard at Greg. Finally, he said, "I know."

"What do you mean, you know? Right now, as far as Shamash is concerned, we're lost."

"No, we're not lost," Wilson replied decidedly. "I know where we are and where we're going, but I'm going to ask you to keep to yourself this change in our mission."

"I don't understand." *What change of mission?*

"Give me a few hours to finish what we've started, then I'll explain everything to you and the others. For now I want you to consider this whole activity to be Fleet Secret."

Greg did not want to question Wilson. Nevertheless, Greg could not accept that the Fleet would sponsor such a mission change without informing the crew. He considered the possibility that the change was some sort of test. *No one uses security classifications anymore, except when it pertains to recent comm center activities!* "On whose authority is this being done?" Greg asked.

Wilson gave a telepathic command, and Greg's mind suddenly filled with the unmistakable official seal of Fleet Commander Sedmak. "Any other questions?"

Greg shook his head. He knew that this was no longer an ordinary training flight and that all the rules he had expected to play by were now inoperative.

"You will have to excuse me then," Wilson said. "I'd like to take over the watch." Wilson was already on the link, in charge again.

Greg nodded dumbly, broke his link and got out of his recliner. Conflicting emotions fought within him: he was curious to know what this mission was, and he was anxious about this now unorthodox flight, so much so that he wanted to object loudly and violently. But he remained silent. He almost hated the mental control which produced his silence, even though he was willing to give Wilson the benefit of his doubt. He walked out of the control room as Wilson settled back in his recliner, now in charge of a ship whose destination was considered too secret to tell even the crew!

Ben relaxed as the door sealed behind Sheldon. He had not really expected anyone to be alert enough to see through the cleverly disguised injection before the *Odyssey* exited from metaspace; however, he had considered the possibility and was prepared for it. Long ago, he had learned that developing a set of options for every conceivable eventuality and the accompanying controlled responses enabled him to act purposefully while others were trying to understand the problem. Sheldon was overwhelmed. Still, Ben did not like using Commander Sedmak's seal even though it was necessary to convince Sheldon of the authenticity of the new mission. He knew that Sheldon was disturbed about the change in destination, but he also knew from Sheldon's background that he was reliable. Sheldon would not talk, not even to his old friend Richard Highstreet, at least not for a while, and by that time the *Odyssey* would have reached its real destination.

Ben probed the ship quickly and expertly. He wanted no more problems. Satisfied that all systems were functioning properly, Ben relaxed in order to let the trend data from the flight pass through his mind. He experienced a pleasant sensation as a result of being in charge of the ship, and he appreciated his position all the more when he considered his struggle inside the static Fleet to get into a ship commander's recliner.

Greg walked listlessly down the corridor leading to his room, heavy from the emotional conflict caused by his curiosity and concern about the modified mission. For once in his life he would have liked to talk to someone about all this, to be able to verbally sort out his thoughts and feelings. This was not the kind of situation that lent itself to a systems tradeoff study of alternatives. The indicator on Art's door showed that he was in, but Greg had no interest in talking to him. Richard's indicator showed an unoccupied room. *Probably aft checking out the shields. What the hell can I say to him anyway? It's all Secret.*

He entered his room, letting the door close silently behind him, and gave in to his earlier urge to plop on his bed. He lay there for several minutes, hands behind his head, and stared at the ceiling. He did not even look at the moving painting of Coni. Were they being diverted because of some emergency akin to the problems in K-10? Was the *Odyssey* part of some strike force being sent to Vesta? What was so special about this crew that they were being sent on a secret mission? Where the hell were they going anyway? And why? Calm down, he told himself. Whether he liked it or not, time was carrying all of them toward the exit gate, and the more he knew about his immediate future, the better off he would be. He had to sort out the data he had. He knew the pre-injection coordinates, attitude and the current flight plan. All he had to do was check them against the Fleet atlas to see where they were really going; that is, if Wilson let him use the computer and if Wilson did not change course in meta-space.

His door signaled Richard's presence and then opened at Greg's command. Greg did not get up; instead, he indicated that Richard should sit down in one of the available chairs. "What's going on?" he asked by way of a greeting. "I thought you were aft working on the shields."

"I was," Richard replied as he sat down. "Wilson is taking this trip very seriously. Can you imagine actually going aft to directly probe the engines and shields? It's a big fukken waste of time. Got any cafnex?"

"Yeah." Greg pushed a button near his bed, and a tractor beam brought a steaming cup out of a wall portal to Richard. "Something bothering you? You looked kind of funny right after we jumped. Anything to do with Mary?"

Richard shook his head slightly as he drank from his cup, eyeing Greg from over its rim. After swallowing, he replied, "It's funny all right. Maybe weird would be a better word. Did you notice anything unusual just before we jumped?"

"Like what?"

"Like a duplicate of the *Odyssey* traveling right behind us."

Greg laughed. "Now that's impossible and you know it. We were the only ones around the jump point. You 'heard' the isolation factor count."

"So, what were *you* doing when we jumped?"

"Monitoring all the bloody systems as a good monitor should."

Richard smiled triumphantly. "Which goes to show you couldn't have known what was going on outside the ship. Wilson and I were the only ones 'watching' the whole flight. And I tell you I did 'see' a double of this ship."

"Well, it had to be some kind of hallucination or spatiotemporal echo because there is no way another ship is going to get close to us without our knowing it, particularly when we're about to jump."

"It was there!"

"All right! All right! I'm not arguing with you. Some weird things have happened at these velocities."

Richard leaned back in his chair and let his cup float in the web of the tractor beam. "Thanks for the support. But you're probably right—it wasn't really there."

Greg groaned. "Oh, come on, Rich. First you say it was, now you say it wasn't."

Richard smiled. "It was there all right, but not from the outside. Think about it: no one has ever recorded such a phenomenon before. I believe the other ship was an image concocted right here in the *Odyssey*."

"Pardon me while I climb to a higher level. It's getting deep around here."

"Knock it off, Greg. Wilson was probably testing us. Do you realize that I blew it by not aborting the jump when I saw something was definitely wrong."

"Not wrong. Just funny."

"Screw you," Richard said, getting up. "I've got to get back up front and report to Wilson. I think I'll confess my sin and accept his reprimand."

Greg was thinking fast now. *Should I tell him? Should I let him go back to Wilson and get sucked into this new mission without any warning?* "I've got a better idea. When you get up front, if Wilson still hasn't said anything about your 'sin,' why don't you review the pre-injection data and see whether the 'other ship' really existed. If it doesn't, or didn't, then there's no sense getting chewed out for something that either didn't happen or can't be proved."

"Good idea. If it weren't for your brains, I don't think I could stand you." Richard thought a moment. "Except if it isn't there, then the implication is that I'm crazy."

"We'll tape it up to motion sickness."

"Ver-ry funny. But I'll play your little game since it at least gives me—Hey! Who gave you the painting of Coni? It's very real-looking." Richard walked over to examine the small moving image. "I thought you didn't go for this sort of stuff."

"I don't. I probably should talk to Wilson about it. Somebody evidently thinks I ought to be reminded of Coni, as if I needed to be."

Richard walked to the door and smiled lewdly. "Well, if you decide to throw it out, I'll take it."

"Lecher!" Greg yelled in mock anger as he threw a pillow at Richard's hastily departing figure.

Richard took several running steps down the passageway and then slowed to a walk as he entered the control room. Wilson turned as he entered, his eyes framing a question.

"Everything checks out," Richard said as he sat down.

"Good. I've put together some contingency plans of the sort one might use in a real exploration emergency. They're on the link now. I'd like you to study them. I also plan to have Sheldon and Cooke study them in their rooms."

Richard did as he was told. He would follow up on Greg's suggestion when he finished with Wilson's contingency plans. But he never got the chance, because Wilson's plans were more involved and more numerous than he had expected. The man had thought of some of the wildest emergencies!

The computer signaled the approach of the exit gate from metaspace. Wilson relayed the message to the crew and requested their participation in the exit operations. As Greg and Art returned to their recliners and rejoined the link, Ben Wilson was already busily increasing the *Odyssey's* energy in order to slow it down to the point where the luxon barrier tunneling probability was maximized.

Stand by to acquire exit, Ben flashed the mental signal to the crew.

Greg monitored the metadrive as it boosted the energy of the *Odyssey,* thereby slowing down the ship. He put the ergon impeller on standby status. Art took over the direct control systems, ready to make the switch from metaspace to world space. Richard mentally moved throughout the entire ship, alert and ready to replace anyone or anything.

The shields were operating normally, and the mass detectors showed the exit to be free of obstacles. The inertial system was functioning correctly.

Beta two came the mental signal from the computer.

The scanners confirmed the report from the mass detectors that the world space exit was isolated from any obstacles.

Beta one-point-five!

The controls were locked on the exit gate for automatic acquisition. The penetrator was nearing its limit.

Beta one-point-one!

Then the decimal numbers got smaller and smaller in a blinding whirl as the beta values converged to unity. Ben and the computer flashed as one: *Exit!*

6

RETURN TO WORLD SPACE

…had the youthful Moses listened to and accepted that view of life, had he bowed his head and bowed his will and bowed his spirit before that arrogant admonition he would never have brought the chosen people out of their house of bondage nor followed the pillar of the cloud by day.

—James Joyce, *Ulysses*

Suddenly, the scanners were alive with scenes from world space and with the vitality of the ergon impeller. The magnified scanner space ahead was filled with a yellow main sequence star surrounded by several planets. Art was momentarily distracted by his required post-exit tasks, by his desire to be certain that he had properly recorded the scanner images for later use and by his relief at successfully completing the jump. He did not immediately see the implications of the images registered on the scanners. But the distractions were momentary, and he quickly "saw" that the *Odyssey* was approaching a yellow main sequence star whose color verged on white and not orange and whose mass, radius and luminosity were greater than Sol's and not less as would have been true for Shamash. Art checked the independent sensors. But the scanners did not lie. There were too many planets and the spatiotemporal topology was wrong.

He immediately flashed a specified mental warning signal on the link. He added aloud in a voice barely concealing his concern, "We're off course." He looked at his crewmates, straining to read their faces from his aft location. Highstreet's mouth was set, and the furrows between his eyebrows were exaggerated. Greg seemed less concerned; his face was immobile. But like Highstreet, he was telepathically probing on the link. Greg started to massage his forehead with his left hand, shielding his face as he moved his fingers above his eyes. Art could not see Wilson, who was the only crewmember going through a routine post-exit sequence of operations.

Wilson was turning his recliner around when Highstreet caught his breath suddenly and shouted, "Sangraal!" His face was pale, almost yellow against his tan, and his expression was a mixture of surprise and something akin to dread. Art looked quickly at Wilson. *That bastard knows what has happened!*

"That's correct, Rich," Wilson said slowly. There was no other sound in the room. Greg still had his eyes covered and Art sensed his presence in the link, but Greg was no longer actively probing.

"What went wrong, or should I make that why?" Highstreet's eyes narrowed as he turned his full attention on the face of his commanding officer.

"Nothing went wrong," Wilson replied quietly. "This is our real destination." There was a short pause; they waited uneasily for him to continue. "The mission to Shamash was a cover for the real destination which, as Rich said, is Sangraal. We are acting under special Fleet orders, and until now this whole operation was classified Fleet Secret." He nodded to Greg. "Sheldon can testify to the classification."

Three heads turned toward Greg.

"Sheldon knows little more than you do at this point," Wilson quickly added. "He discovered that Shamash was not our destination shortly before we exited. He knows now that this is an authorized Fleet secret mission. I want to emphasize that this mission is considered extremely important to the Federation and is regarded as highly dangerous. While you were probing our destination, I activated all shields and alert systems. If there are any problems, we must be prepared for an emergency jump to a set of safe coordinates programmed into the ship. That's why I've had you studying those contingency plans. Now—"

"Who authorized this mission?" Art interrupted harshly.

Wilson glared for a long moment at his interrogator.

"Sedmak," Greg answered for Wilson, breaking the dismayed silence. He turned his recliner so that it faced his three companions, then he added, "The security classification seems to be for real, Art. I find it just as hard to believe as you do." He faced Highstreet from across the central aisle. "I'm sorry, Rich. I wish I could have told you sooner…I did what I thought was right, but if I had known…" His voice trailed off, and he glanced down at the floor.

"He was acting under my orders," Wilson explained. "We had to operate in this manner because the stakes are high and the risk is great. I cannot emphasize enough the importance of this mission to the Federation and "—he paused briefly—"perhaps to all of humankind."

Art felt anger building up within him like a plasma being driven to higher and higher kinetic temperatures.

Wilson continued slowly but firmly now. He was reasserting his command and serving notice that the time for dissent was past. "You were all picked for special reasons. Each of you has some talent or quality necessary for the success of the mission." He looked at Highstreet. "Our final destination is Sangraal II, which was explored many years ago. I'm going to replay a bit of history for you on the link."

Art's mind filled with the image of a large starship lifting off from Earth. He felt all the thrill of that beautiful experience while the link coursed its way through his mental connections. As the ship climbed rapidly away from Earth, the link began to explore its contents. Art knew that this was a medium-sized exploration ship that appeared to have a larger than normal contingent of bio- and socio-scientists. Then he saw the ship commander, a tall man with black hair and brown eyes, a man of familiar handsomeness—*Highstreet!* Suddenly, he realized that it was Richard Highstreet's father, and the unclear events of the past few minutes began to coalesce in his mind. He was aware of the ship's name, *Leos,* and the memories of a story filed in the recesses of his mind surfaced as he mentally opened the gate which the Fleet had taught him to control.

His mind impressed some order on the memories and link images, and he knew the sequence now. He knew about the *Leos* expedition to Sangraal, how the ship had safely arrived at Sangraal and then went almost immediately to the second planet, a green and blue world bathed in white clouds circling the distant yellow-white main sequence star which some ancient lunar astronomer had named Sangraal. It was a star system located much closer to the galactic center than Sol and around the galactic rim so it was not visible to the naked eye of anyone in the Federation. It was a remote system by Federation standards of exploration but an exciting one because it was known to harbor life.

The link went blank. All contact had been lost as the *Leos* approached Sangraal II. There were no signals from the life-support system. Then came the images of the brief Fleet investigation, with the inevitable decision of the investigating board, a decision so characteristic of that period: "The Board concludes that there are no available ships or probes to investigate the loss of the *Leos* and still leave full support to the other activities demanded by the members of the Federation. We therefore recommend that Council place the Sangraal system off-limits to further exploration until such time as a suitably prepared and protected search mission can be undertaken in a manner designed to protect the Federation. We also recommend continuance of the automatic concealing screens to protect the Federation from any potential hostile probing from the Sangraal system." As usual, the detailed systemized study of the alternatives supported these conclusions, and Council acted to implement them.

Art saw the lines of strain in Highstreet's face. Well, he thought, there's a man with a stake in this impossible mission, whatever it is. He felt a wave of resentment against Wilson sweep over him. Wilson was part of the problem that had led to tragedies like the loss of the *Leos*. Art disagreed strongly with the philosophy prevalent until recently that permitted badly needed starships to go on unnecessary exploration trips beyond the protection of the Federation. Humanity needed to consolidate its newly formed Federation and build a good economic, technical and, most importantly, social basis before allowing flights like that of the *Leos* to proceed. He recognized Wilson as a man who would push onward beyond the safe confines of his own civilization, and he knew such men were responsible for the destruction of the *Leos*.

But to Art, the awful, final folly of the expedition to Sangraal lay in the flight of the *Odyssey*. With substantially the same weak basis that had permitted the *Leos* to leave Earth on its final mission, the *Odyssey* and its crew were being asked to go out alone beyond the protective Perimeter in search of the missing ship, compounding the earlier madness. It was unheard of in the Federation.

The link noted that over the years the Sangraal system had been constantly monitored by the usual omnifarious, screened sensors so that everything about the system could be studied without the study being detected. Still, Sangraal II remained as it had been before the *Leos* arrived, a bright world of life traveling its uncaring path through space and time. Then, only months before the flight of the *Odyssey*, the planet changed, becoming an unfathomable mystery spitting out erratic signals. There appeared to be no set pattern and no spatial or temporal alignment in these signals; they were merely short, random bursts, followed by long periods of silence. As the monitors gathered these signals and analyzed them, it was discovered that a Fleet Alert signal could be extracted from the irregular bursts. The odds against the Alert being a random event were overwhelming. The inescapable conclusion was that *someone from the Fleet or else someone (or something) with knowledge of Fleet procedures was trying to signal the Federation!*

"Now you know why we're here," Wilson said simply. "This is the only case in which a ship has disappeared and years later we received a signal. It is particularly significant that it is not a cry for help but is rather the coded Alert signal. There is one final scene worth noting, now that we can finally actively probe Sangraal II again."

The image of a ghost planet filled Art's mind, a disquieting image in which nothing was distinguishable but a blackish-gray mass that defied all attempts to scan it. Art felt that he was seeing something dead and shrouded in mists, yet he could not analytically justify his feeling. He was relieved when the image was quickly replaced by extensive calculations and observations which showed no credible natural cause for the catastrophe, since the abstract in this case was less disturbing than the actual object.

Wilson spoke again: "I might add that that image of Sangraal II was taken from Federation-based monitors and supplemented by our own scanners. It represents the best we can do from here, but we hope to do better when we get to Sangraal II. We have brought some improved scanners made just for this task. But as of now, all we know about Sangraal II is what you just saw. However, you may probe Sangraal II at any time, and you're also free to redo any of the calculations and review the history of Sangraal. But a quick check of our sensors will tell you that from here, with those clouds, Sangraal II appears to be lifeless."

Highstreet leaned back in his recliner as if to relax, but his cordlike facial muscles reflected inner tension. Through the noetronic circuit of the link, Art sensed Greg redoing the calculations and checking the data, but he also sensed that it was a perfunctory operation performed by a man already convinced of the outcome.

"And how do you intend we carry off this…recon mission?" Art asked.

"We are to try to determine what happened to Sangraal II and, if possible, to the *Leos*." Ben ignored Cooke's predictably hostile attitude. "There is concern that whatever happened here could happen elsewhere."

"Then why the secrecy?" Cooke asked. "Why can't we just openly come here? In fact, why couldn't the Fleet send a probe instead of a crewed mission?"

Ben was not used to discussing command decisions with his subordinates, and he was losing his patience with Cooke. Only his respect for the wishes of Commander Sedmak held him in check. Distastefully, he realized a more personal touch was needed. "Art, you know as well as I do that the Federation has been badly torn by the curtailment of exploration. We don't want to cause more problems by looking into a potentially disturbing occurrence that may have a natural explanation.

"I would like to have information gleaned from an unmanned advance probe, but we have had too much trouble scanning Sangraal II to expect to learn much over that distance. We wanted people here, people who could deal with any problems that come up and suggest, *in situ*, ways to solve the problems and be able to report their findings when they returned."

Art could hardly hide his contempt for Wilson's answers. The reasons for not sending a probe just did not make sense. There was a false note in Wilson's explanation. He knew for certain now that Wilson had not told the crew everything. He had to get away to think and to search out the truth. He felt confined by a man who was commanding this venture from a vantage point of more knowledge than he cared to release, by another who was momentarily haunted by the ghosts of his childhood and by a third who was as indecisive on the matter as he.

"Ben," Art persisted, "suppose there is some sort of problem here that is not due to natural causes but to an alien accident or design. That would be like some of the contingency plans we just studied. What precautions are we to take?"

Wilson placed a hand palm down on the armrest of his recliner and stared at his spread fingers. "First, the *Odyssey* is completely screened off from the Federation. It has been so since we entered metaspace. This is to prevent any of our signals from providing a clue about our origins to the potential aliens Art mentioned. The screening includes the flight recorder." Like Highstreet and Greg, Art looked at Wilson in disbelief. "Fleet Control is monitoring a decoy which will tell them we're on a slow flight to Shamash." Art saw Highstreet nod knowingly to Greg. "We could not take the chance that someone or something with hostile intentions would follow our signals back to the Federation. We do have an internal flight recorder which will keep a complete record of the mission. For a backup device, I plan to leave a hidden passive monitor which will receive a short-range coded version of the data in the flight recorder. If for any reason the flight recorder ceases to transmit to the monitor, the monitor will assume the *Odyssey* has"—he paused for a very brief moment—"ceased to exist and it will retransmit the data when it is free to do so. Both the flight recorder and the monitor will broadcast in such a way that the recorder does not identify the location of the monitor and the monitor does not lead anyone to the Federation.

"The only negative aspect in our screening operation is that we were not able to obtain the necessary large-scale concealing screens to hide the ship or us from locally based scanners. Unfortunately, the Fleet may not know what we're doing but anyone or anything here does—or will!"

"Surely, the sensors monitoring Sangraal have picked us up by now," Art protested.

"Yes, I'm sure they have," Wilson replied. "Except their data will be classified until we return. Sector K-10 has the primary responsibility of monitoring this part of the Galaxy. That sector is under comm silence."

Greg had a twisted half-smile on his face. "I suppose it is self-evident that the maneuvers around Mars were designed both to confuse the three of us about our entry into metaspace and to get rid of the Fleet monitors so they would follow the decoy."

Wilson nodded. "Don't think those maneuvers were just for secrecy. We may need and use them."

Highstreet continued digging for the increasingly disconcerting details of their situation. "Except for the decoy and classifying the sensor data, these are all standard procedures even if they haven't been used in years. If I follow the logic of these procedures, we must be carrying a destruct system."

Wilson nodded silently, his face reflecting the grimness of Highstreet's voice.

"What about weapons?" Art asked,

"High-power stunnors in the suits and a very strong shipboard tractor beam," Wilson replied.

Art stood up. "Ben, I'd like to check our payload and other hardware just to be sure everything is in order." Art had him now. As the payload specialist for the mission, it was his responsibility to perform all the necessary hardware checks. If Wilson refused, he would open himself up to more questioning about what they were carrying. Art thought he saw a fleeting look of suspicion cross Wilson's face.

"Okay." Wilson stood up and inhaled deeply. "Let's get moving. Art, go ahead with your inspection. Be sure to check out the ship remotes. Sheldon, I want you to run a full-up systems analysis for all test conditions, including the contingency plans. Rich, review the emergency exit procedures and establish a recon trajectory to Sangraal II that provides maximum security and escape possibilities."

The pace quickened aboard the *Odyssey*. Wilson was back in form, issuing quick, direct orders, galvanizing the crew to action and pulling them out of any debilitating debates. Art broke his link and walked out of the control room, relieved to be free of the others long enough to consider the situation and the real purpose behind the mission. Of one thing he was sure: Wilson had not told them everything, and Art did not want to think about the implications of any missing information.

He moved silently along the corridor, checking remote links and installations as he went while his thoughts examined the many implausibilities: the sending of a crewed ship, the ease with which the Perimeter was penetrated, the absolute secrecy of the mission. There was a flaw in Wilson's story, a flaw that Art knew tangibly existed on the *Odyssey* perhaps buried in the last-minute cargo, the same cargo which was probably the source of the decoy. His present predicament was without precedent—the Fleet just did not operate in this manner. It was almost like a mental examination, and he felt that it would all end shortly. It just did not seem real.

He went through the remote checkout of the payload and the other shipboard hardware almost mechanically. His mind was filled with thoughts about the *Odyssey,* its real mission and the events which had started him on this mysterious trip.

Art thought of himself as one of the new breed of humans—people who had grown up in a technological world. His life began as an artificially fertilized egg in a life-sustaining bath of nutrients. Parental participation or presence was of no importance because the Tellurian state provided his necessities. The trauma of childbirth and childhood, the dangers of parent-child incompatibility and the other evils associated with the old-style nuclear family were supplanted by an enlightened movement toward a completely state-controlled population. This style of living provided the kind of stability and biological perfection for which humanity had striven so long.

His early interest in science had developed as a natural outgrowth of his desire to apply humanity's technological achievements to moving humanity toward a cohesiveness more substantial than that which the Federation had achieved with its union of diverse worlds. (He knew that that union was almost nonexistent, since the Federation was in fact a rather loosely knit confederation of planets, and its Council was not much more than a policy-making body.)

Art saw his way of life as the vanguard of what the Federation must become, so it seemed natural that he leave his syndetical childhood home and attend the Space Fleet Academy. It was a chance to carry the message of "the way" as he saw it to the farthest reaches of the Federation.

Art was ill at ease with the world that awaited him. The ambitions and relatively heightened egoism in the outside world cut into his deeply held views on the imminent perfectibility of the human race. He did not, of course, find the egoistical grossness of earlier centuries but he certainly found the descendants of that grossness. The fundamental reason for the cultivation of those qualities he objected to was obvious; in fact, he was now a part of it—space exploration. The tenuous but persistent exploration and colonization of new worlds required society to reward and encourage those who had the ambition to extend the Federation. But Art saw these same people as potential disrupters of his desired social order, one in which all humans were united for the common, peaceful good.

He found little support for his views among his comrades at the Academy, and he was not particularly surprised at this once he properly assessed his new world.

Only in one sense was he sympathetic to what space exploration had done for humanity and its outlook on the Universe: he appreciated the paramount Federation rule regarding the sanctity of life. Although the known Universe was filled with planets, the majority were either too hot or too cold, too massive or too poisonous to bring forth a successful and highly developed life form like man, leaving the human race to ponder its near absolute uniqueness in its part of the Galaxy. Art learned that when one has seen the desolation of the majority of those lifeless orbs, then one appreciated the almost religious reverence with which the Federation beheld any life it discovered. The corollary to this rule demanded total noninvolvement in the affairs of any discovered worlds developing their own civilizations. Intelligent life forms must not be contacted unless their level of advancement showed them capable of withstanding the cultural aftermath of the contact. Humanity knew that its Tellurian history was filled with the strife and disruption which unenlightened colonialism had produced. The human race needed nothing from these worlds, so it confined its colonization to those planets which were uninhabited or filled with undeveloping, nonintelligent lower life forms. The Federation had instilled in its citizens the command that only with a cosmic catastrophe could one circumvent this corollary.

Art was fascinated by the idea of creating new worlds from the lifeless ones which humanity so often found. This fascination was in keeping with his goal of creating a new social order, since he fully realized that he might have to start his new society in a place other than Earth. He specialized in planetology at the Academy, where he learned how to study and explore a planet and finally how to change it to support human life. Because his interests were planet-oriented, he served most often as a payload specialist on routine Fleet space missions, converting only to planetological pursuits when he was on-planet.

Since he shared so little with the differently motivated students at the Academy, he spent his free time with likeminded people from the outside world. He often traveled to the other continents of Earth, seeking the beauty and interesting people there. He loved to record the multifaceted scanner images of Tellurian beauty and experience them later on, an endeavor which he practiced during his inactive periods on long space flights. In this way, he felt more a part of his world.

It was this love for nature that brought him to Vanessa Shklovskii, the one who most closely shared his thoughts and visions. He had gone to the forests of the huge Eurasian continent to spend several standard weeks of his leave camping. Such a beautiful coincidence, he had thought later, that she should be out walking on the same hill where he was recording scanner images of some deer. She was the most open, direct person he had ever met, and she had that certain grace and intelligence which smoothed over her directness. His mind always carried that first image of her, her lively, penetrating brown eyes and her lovely face, so sensuously caressed by the eddies of her soft, space-black hair. Her voice still spoke to him with its husky tones, almost hypnotic with the sexual suggestiveness that she was to show him that first night she spent in his camp.

His new view of the future had begun about noon of the following day. He had accepted her invitation to visit her home, and now they stood atop a grassy hill from which he could see a cluster of environmentally designed modern buildings nestled in the small, green valley below. Vanessa stopped on the hilltop and held his hand. She stared at the aesthetically functional buildings for a long moment while the soft forest breeze caressed her flowing hair. Finally, she turned to him and smiled. "This is home," she said simply.

"Very lovely place," he replied, kissing her softly.

"Art, before we go down there, there are some things I should tell you." Her tone was more serious now.

He nodded but said nothing, preferring to let her speak.

"Like you, I grew up in a syndetical society." Still holding his hand, she looked from him down to the elegantly simple buildings below. "Only I didn't leave it."

"Syncretist?" He knew the answer even as he asked the question.

She nodded her positive response. "I didn't want to be so deceptive last night, but I had to know what you really thought. I love you for your thought of uniting humanity, and I want you to meet my family."

"I'd love to."

"Will you stay with us?"

He laughed. "Until my leave runs out or you kick me out, whichever comes first."

She laughed, too, and then hand-in-hand they started down the hill to the forest community.

He met many people in those first hours in the community, yet not once did he feel like a stranger or an outsider. It was like coming home. He felt very much at ease and very much a part of Vanessa's home.

When he had seen the main buildings and met many of their occupants, Vanessa took him to her room, a simple but nicely furnished open cubicle located just off what appeared to be a large "family" room. Oblivious to passersby, she quickly changed clothes and then excused herself for some community activities. As she was leaving, she called his attention to a link and told him that if he was interested, he could study some of the Syncretistic philosophy while she was gone.

After she left, he restlessly paced the room, touching and looking at its contents. Occasionally, he spoke or nodded to someone who walked by. He admired these people for designing harmonious and unified living quarters. (They had even revived the old custom of eating together!) But he felt a pang of jealousy when he considered what this implied about Vanessa. He quickly checked himself. Had he not been raised in such a fashion? Had he not made love to most of the young women at home? Vanessa's home was like returning to his own: he could experience the joy of being with true people again.

Now feeling a little more at ease, he lay back on a couch and connected himself to the link. Immediately, his mind was alive with the Syncretistic world.

Syncretism was a philosophy and way of life which had arisen from the social upheavals of humanity's early experiments in technology and society. The roots of the philosophy were old but the approach was new, taking as it did much from humanity's technology. It was an attempt to fuse together the best that the human race had developed and to discard the rest.

He experienced again through the mental link all the divisions which had rent human societies. He felt the strife which came from differing religions, differing political systems and differing economies. Historical man had been like some terrible creature possessed with the demon of destruction. But analysis showed that this demonic fury could be tamed. The Syncretists looked at human society and selected the best. They sought peace and security through a new unity of humanity based upon a scientifically derived code of ethics which supplanted the mysticism of the ancients.

Humanity must grow up as one and experience the same things. Here, Art saw again the advantages of the mental links. By living together openly, without reservation, by accepting each other and freely exchanging thoughts, humanity could replace distrust and fear with love.

Each new advance in the biological and social sciences was viewed with hope by the Syncretists, hope that the solution to achieving complete unity was at hand. The mental link could be used to completely open one mind to another (Art was surprised at the frankness with which this illegal act was discussed), the behavioral theories could be used to establish the conditions which favored unity and the scientific techniques of the biologists could be used for the final structuring of the united society of humanity.

Art experienced each new revelation of Syncretistic thought with a tremor of excitement. They had gone beyond much of his thinking because their approach was more revolutionary than evolutionary. But he knew they were right. They had simply taken the same observations he had made about humanity and carried them to their logical conclusion.

One had to harmonize the conflicts arising in human society. The continued development of the human race demanded this. To Art and to the Syncretists, the choice seemed clear enough: actively work toward this unity. It seemed like a logical extension of his own desire to proselytize to the Federation about the advantages of his own childhood.

Political, social and economic action would have to be taken to overcome the divisiveness of the Federation society. The Syncretists looked with favor upon all attempts to unify humanity, and they were displeased with activities such as space exploration, which tended to divide humanity by establishing separate, independent worlds. Here again, Art was in sympathy with the Syncretistic viewpoint. Humanity should stop its present tenuous exploration and consolidate what it already had. Art found himself in total agreement with the idea of using political means to achieve the goal of total unification. In fact, he felt ashamed that he had not considered it before. He blamed this on the looseness of the Federation and the absence of a strong political force. He knew from history that political means were extremely useful in achieving a desired goal. Besides, a united campaign was in keeping with the Syncretistic philosophy, while his desire to proselytize was a deviation, an expression of individual will without consideration of the good of the group. He now saw a new reason for his Fleet career: an inside persuader for unification before humanity became too divided. He would work to hold the line on space exploration. Waves of excitement moved over him as he exulted in this new goal of his life.

The Syncretists viewed humanity with almost religious devotion. It was part of their desire to coalesce the divergencies of humanity's societies: focus on humanity itself, think about the commonality. It was the ultimate in anthropomorphism. Art's mind filled with the image of a man and a woman. The colors were blurred and then the two sexes merged. He could only envision the oneness of a human's physical being: the one head, two arms, single body and two legs. Humanity was all, and the union of humanity was goodness. Art could almost feel the fervor build within himself. He had never thought about humanity in such religious terms.

It began to make sense to him. If the human race was ever to be brought together one had to stress the positive, common, binding aspects and downgrade or eliminate the differences. Art had always sought this union for all humanity, and he saw that by making a godlike being of this sexually, racially intermixed hominid, the anthropocentric Syncretists had gone far toward making unity an attractive and desirable goal. Humanity was all, and all would be for Humanity.

United, humanity would be like the pre-death world of the life-filled Precambrian seas. Merged by links and the common learning experience, the ultimate effect would be that no one would die. Humanity would now be one giant reservoir of thought—the true god and the true strength. Art knew the Syncretists had elevated philosophy above all the historical definitions because they no longer dealt strictly with politics, morals, economics or social organization. Instead, they went to the very core of humanity by using all the sociological and technological tools at their disposal.

Art felt the almost indescribable euphoria of discovery and of knowing that there were others of a like mind. As the link finished, Art felt content. He relaxed and then dozed on the couch.

He awakened to the feel of warm lips on his, of soft hair falling on his face and soothing hands fondling his body.

"Wake up, dreamer," Vanessa said with a light laugh. "You'll sleep your life away."

Art put his arms around her and pulled her to him. "As long as I've got you, I'll be glad to."

She pulled him up to a sitting position. "Then you would miss our nightly meditation. Come to the family room."

As he stood up, Vanessa deftly connected him to another mental link which he guessed was located somewhere else in the building. He felt images enter his mind. Joyous thoughts. Erotic thoughts. Expectant and pleasing thoughts, but mostly the former, as if some highly desired event were about to occur and people were waiting in suspense for it. He felt a little disoriented by the flood of many minds and a little surprised that it was possible to openly link so many minds. He momentarily closed his eyes to sort out his mental images, eliminating the distraction of other visual images. Then he felt Vanessa in his mind. She was soothing and warm, exuding love and tenderness. He was so overcome that he hardly noticed her undressing him. He opened his eyes and saw that she was disrobed and had almost done the same to him. Had he wanted, he could not have stopped her now.

When she finished, he held her close, feeling her lissome body against his as they kissed. Then she took his hand and led him out into the large, central family room. There he saw most of the community also disrobed and lying on couches, cushions and other devices, some of a highly amatory nature. He felt a warm glow of welcome fill his mind, and he immediately felt at ease.

Vanessa led him to an empty couch, where she lay back and pulled him to her. Their lovemaking began at a deliciously slow pace, which she controlled. He was aware, through his mental links with the others in the room, that they, too, had started to make love.

Art felt Vanessa's lithe body move against his as she selectively sought out and excited each of his erogenous areas. He kissed her mouth, her face, her hair, then moved his lips along her neck to her breasts and nipples. His lips and hands caressed her stomach, her maidenly loveliness and her slender legs. He experienced an uninterrupted stream of erotic images of extraordinary plasticity and vividness. He knew he was receiving more than just the impressions of the others in the room. The link was filling him with ecstasy, with music and color and taste and touch and smell. It all moved in kaleidoscopic fashion until the final blending of synesthesia overcame him completely. The music surged into beautiful colors ranging over the whole spectrum, and his other senses became sharper and transmuted. He felt as if he had transcended time and space, that this aesthetic experience was all.

Again, Art saw the image of the man and the woman, their distinctions blending into one. But the image was sharper now. He was in Vanessa and she was in him. He felt a joyous release into her and simultaneously felt her fill with happiness. Around him he sensed the plateau of passion of the family. *Humanity was all, and the union of Humanity was goodness.* The image was one, and he felt an indescribable peace and unity. Around him he experienced an almost religious sigh of approval uttered as a mantra to achieve unity with the Universal Mind.

Gradually, the link faded and Art sat up, still holding Vanessa. He saw the other family members separating but still holding to each other, and he also saw that all of them were happy. Soon, he was among them, guided by Vanessa in a pilgrimage of ultimate personal communication. The family members moved about, touching and holding each other without reservation. He felt at one with them, and he knew the correctness of the deification of humanity. Unity was his goal: the warmth and concern of being together.

He felt so content and relaxed that he experienced the unusual that night— he slept a peaceful sleep in Vanessa's arms.

The next day, Vanessa was up early and was soon busily engaged in several tasks. When she returned and after they ate with the others, she took him to the central operations building to meet that month's collective of administrative coordinators, a group known as the Syndic.

She ushered him into a large room with a semicircular table around which were seated over twenty people. They were apparently expecting him. Vanessa introduced him to each coordinator and then indicated that he should sit in a chair near the center of the table. Then she stepped back to the rear of the room.

The one who seemed to be the chief representative for the coordinators spoke: "On behalf of all of us, I would like to welcome you, Art. I hope everything has been to your liking."

"It has," Art answered enthusiastically.

"You have had a chance to explore our ways, and we have explored you," the prolocutor continued. "What do you think of us?"

"I believe in what you're doing and I want to help you," Art replied with a sincere feeling of commitment.

"Thank you," the prolocutor said. "I'd like to go over some of the things you learned yesterday before I ask you any further questions. We are familiar with your background, and we know about your home in North America. We have chosen to become a part of the Syncretistic movement because we believe a larger union is necessary to overcome humanity's divisiveness. We hope that someday your home will join us.

"Right now we are approaching a crucial test. Despite our small but growing size, we have been able to persuade many members of the Federation Council that their current direction will only lead to chaos and further divisiveness. In particular, I am speaking about the Federation's commitment to explore the Galaxy. Council has been quietly studying and debating this commitment, and I believe it will shortly vote either to sustain or abolish that commitment. We have been working hard to see that Council changes its commitment to one of internal unity. We believe, as you do, that humanity must be united before proceeding with more forays into space. We feel it is a strain upon our society to support this flimsy, far-flung Federation while continuing to explore ever farther from the home world.

"If we could hold the Federation to its present size, we could divert our talents and resources to uniting humanity so that we can face the Universe not as a collection of individuals but as a mighty, unified intellect. I hope you can appreciate why we have taken this active approach to the affairs of the human race. While we appreciate your home experiment, we believe that humanity must be actively united. Humanity has been torn apart by its self-induced environment, and we must be the glue that binds humanity together. But the glue does not miraculously appear at the broken edges—*it must be applied.*"

The prolocutor paused and looked into Art's eyes. His voice resumed almost in a whisper, "Will you join us?"

The room was quiet. Art felt all eyes on him. "Yes," he answered.

Vanessa was at his side, her hands around his neck. She kissed his cheek. The coordinators smiled and spoke warmly to him. One by one they came to him and congratulated him. Soon, he was surrounded by happy people. As the prolocutor embraced Art, he said, "Welcome. There is much we must talk about, particularly your role in the *new* Federation. But for now, go with Vanessa and enjoy the rest of your leave. We will talk later."

As Art and Vanessa left the central operations building, Art turned to her and said in mock seriousness, "That was some show. It was almost like facing Tomás de Torquemada himself."

She punched him playfully. "They just wanted to welcome you officially."

"What if I had refused?"

She smiled her mysterious smile. "We knew you wouldn't."

He hugged her as they walked through the center of the community. He felt good. Sol was shining warmly through a brilliant deep-blue sky, the air smelled of blossoming trees, and he heard the sounds of life from the community and from the nearby forest. This is Utopia, he thought. "I love you," he said solemnly. She pressed closer to him.

"Art, let's go for a walk in the woods." Her tone was solemn now, too, hinting at something unsaid.

"I'd love to." With his newly established, link-formed closeness to her, he sensed that something was troubling her. "What's the matter?"

She held tightly to him. "I've made a previous commitment for this afternoon, and I want to be with you now."

He felt a little slighted. "What sort of commitment?"

Relieved at the chance to explain herself, Vanessa sighed and then quickly spoke, "I have a distant cousin in North America who is a friend of a family of explorers. Evidently, these people have adopted a young girl who survived some catastrophe in space, but they have now been given a brief assignment off-Earth. They wanted my cousin to take care of the girl; however, she has some conflicts with her own schedule, so she suggested sending the girl here because she thought we could help her. To make a long story short, the girl is arriving late this afternoon and I'll be taking care of her."

"Will we find some time to be together?" Art asked anxiously.

"Yes."

"Is she a Syncretist?"

"No," Vanessa replied. "She knows little about our movement. As I said, she had some traumatic experience on an exploration trip. Her real family was killed, and I understand she was damaged physically and psychologically. It's all okay now, and I'd like to give her a peaceful stay. I won't talk about the Syncretistic movement unless she is interested." She smiled her mysterious smile again. "But if I can interest her, I will."

Art and Vanessa spent the remainder of the morning walking through the evergreen trees near the community center. They watched the squirrels and birds. They laughed together and made love together while coupled through a portable link.

He was almost resentful when Vanessa suggested that they start back so she could meet her new responsibility. They arrived at the teleporter room shortly before the start of transmission. Art felt slightly annoyed and nervously paced the floor while Vanessa stood silently watching the receiver.

Precisely on schedule, the unit activated and the girl materialized. Art had stopped his pacing and stood watching the girl from the far side of the room. She seemed momentarily uncertain of her surroundings as she came out of the beam, but she quickly regained her self-control. Vanessa went to the girl, introduced herself and embraced her warmly, then led her to Art.

"Coni, this is Art Cooke," Vanessa said. "Art, I'd like you to meet Coni Sanderson."

He took her hand. Something twinged in the recesses of his mind, but he ignored the feeling because he was so surprised at and almost in awe of her. He guessed she was at most fourteen or fifteen standard years old. She was a little smaller than Vanessa and more conservatively dressed, yet she was so incredibly beautiful that Art scarcely noticed her clothes and could hardly speak. If she were older and he were not so in love with Vanessa, he knew he would seek her out. She smiled a little shyly up at him but her handshake was firm. Her face, her figure and her flowing blonde hair spoke of natural youth and beauty. Her eyes held a hypnotic fascination for him. They were the clearest green he had ever seen, and intelligence was written in them. And they also told him of some sadness that far transcended her years. She was not at all what Vanessa's description had led him to believe. He felt she had an inner strength that belied any traumatic experience.

Vanessa took Coni to the quarters assigned to her. Art was pleasantly surprised and a little relieved that Coni would not be staying with Vanessa. If Coni was as unfamiliar with the Syncretists as Vanessa claimed, then it was best that she not be suddenly exposed to their customs. Art noted that Vanessa did a good job of explaining community life to Coni. She said just enough to tantalize Coni, but not enough to unfold the whole story. Coni was a little tense from the trip and the events leading up to the trip, so Vanessa and Art left her to relax in a tranquilizer shower and agreed to join her for an evening meal.

On their way to Vanessa's room, they were stopped by a member of the Syndic who excitedly reported that a major pronouncement would be forthcoming from the Federation Council during the next day.

"That can only mean one thing," Vanessa said in a determined manner after the coordinator left, "Council will rule on its commitment to further exploration. If we've done our work, I think we'll be entering the first phase of a new and better civilization."

Art walked silently hand-in-hand with Vanessa to her room. He only half-listened as she talked about the possibilities concerning a change in Council's commitment to space exploration. His mind was pondering the differences in the two women he had just been with: Coni, the beautiful, quiet girl who held within her some private hurt; and Vanessa, the lovely, determined woman who opened herself to the world in her desire to change society for the better. There was an inner hard core to Vanessa that was, in its own way, as mysterious to him as Coni's unknown suffering.

They made love along with the others in the family room. For Art, the joy and pleasure equaled that of the previous evening. After their group caressing, Vanessa and Art dressed and joined Coni for dinner. He felt relaxed and happy. He listened quietly while Vanessa and Coni talked. They exchanged information on common acquaintances. Despite their different temperaments, he could see a friendship forming between the two. Vanessa seemed to transcend her missionary zeal and took a genuine interest in Coni. He wondered, sitting there as an almost dispassionate observer, whether Vanessa might secretly consider Coni a potential convert and would work toward her conversion. He sympathized with Vanessa if she was indeed trying to interest Coni in Syncretism because he knew the wisdom of the Syncretistic society and through his enlightenment, he now appreciated the need for an active participation in changing the Federation. He was certain that if Coni suffered from some terrible experience, then the collective support of the Syncretistic minds could soothe, comfort and cure her. He thought that perhaps this might be Vanessa's true goal because she skillfully put Coni at ease.

Late in the evening, the trio broke up, with Vanessa and Art agreeing to meet Coni the next day for a walk through the woods and a tour of some of the facilities in the village. After parting with Coni, Art and Vanessa walked home with joined hands under a star-filled black sky.

"She certainly seems normal enough," he said, allowing his earlier mental observation to verbally materialize.

"Not really," Vanessa answered, as if she were speaking not to him but to herself. "She has been helped, but she is very tense and very much alone. I think we can help her."

He marveled at this woman who was willing to give so much of herself to help others.

When they reached Vanessa's room, neither felt like resting, so they talked for a while and then Vanessa suggested that Art study some of the other link information on the Syncretistic movement. Later, they made love, and Art sensed through the link that a part of Vanessa's mind was concerned with Coni.

As the sky lightened, Coni signaled that she was awake. Vanessa and Art joined her for a brief, nourishing breakfast and then the three of them left the village for the nearby woods.

Coni seemed rested after a sound sleep, a sleep which he and Vanessa had not needed. He also noticed that Coni appeared a little more relaxed than she had on her first day with them. He hoped that Vanessa was right and that they could link with this girl and help her. To all outward appearances, she seemed normal enough. She was bright and happy, with an easy, musical laugh.

Near midday, Vanessa suggested that they return to the village. On the return trip, he observed that Coni was more outgoing than she had been when they started their walk. She talked about her interests, her friends the Lipperts, who had taken her in and for whom she felt much affection, and she also talked about life. There was a frankness to her that Art liked, even though he did not always agree with her views. He also noted that her parents and her personal tragedy were never mentioned, nor did she hint at them.

When they arrived in the village, they discovered many people moving about in the village center, talking excitedly and smiling and laughing easily in a sense of joyous release.

Even though they suspected what had occurred, Art and Vanessa asked the first people they came to what had happened. From the smiles and happy voices came the news, "Council has voted to suspend further exploratory missions. They're going to limit the size of the Federation. We're on our way!"

Art hugged Vanessa and kissed her hard. She smiled happily at him, and he could see his own smile reflected in her brown eyes. "Yes, we're finally on our way," she said quietly and with relief amid the joyous throng in the village center. "Let's find a link and see how the Council debates went. I can tell we'll be celebrating tonight." She held him tightly.

They turned to go to Vanessa's room when they noticed that Coni was no longer with them. Vanessa and Art looked at each other, each silently asking the other, "Where did she go?" They quickly looked through the crowd, then Vanessa pointed to the woods and called out, "There she is, Art. Something's wrong. We'd better go to her." He looked where Vanessa pointed and glimpsed Coni disappearing into the trees.

Quickly, they broke free of the crowd and ran with an effortless gait into the woods. They found Coni seated on a fallen log on the side of a hill, her face pointed at the horizontal slice of sky and away from the village. When they got abreast of her, Art saw that her face was painted by two wet lines which extended from her sea-green eyes along the length of her face. She said nothing to them but continued to stare silently at the blue expanse of sky between the vertical trees on the hillside.

Art stood slightly back while Vanessa approached Coni. "Coni, what's the matter?" Vanessa asked, her soft voice full of concern. "Have we done something wrong?"

Coni silently shook her head.

Vanessa placed a hand on Coni's arm and knelt beside her. "May we help?"

Again Coni shook her head. She remained motionless for several minutes, her eyes fixed on some unseen spot in the sky. Finally, she wiped away her tears and smiled a weak yet bitter smile. "I'm sorry," she said.

"Is anything wrong?" he asked. He had never seen such behavior and was extremely concerned about her.

Coni looked at him with eyes that seemed intensely green, because of the combination of the sunlight streaming through the trees and the redness of her tear-filled eyes. There was also a new inner intensity in her verdurous eyes which he found vaguely disquieting.

"Yes, there is something wrong," she said quietly. Her voice was terse, clipped in style. Both Vanessa and Art looked carefully at her now. Coni made no move to arrange her disheveled hair or clothes. "There is something wrong with a society that will cut itself off from its future and laugh while it is doing so."

"The Council ruling?" Vanessa asked softly.

Coni nodded.

Art felt a need to explain the ruling to Coni. He knew that if she understood the real effect of the ruling, then she would be able to calmly face the new era they were all entering.

"It doesn't necessarily mean that we are cut off from our future," Art said slowly. He wanted to be cautious in order to avoid upsetting Coni. He must be wary until he understood the cause of her anguish. "There are many possible futures for humanity. Space exploration is just one. Just as Council vetoed further exploration, they can later recommend a continuation of exploration."

"What other immediate future is there?" she asked bitterly. "Space travel has allowed us to diversify, and it has brought about a second Renaissance."

Art felt the wisdom of the Syncretists well up within him, and he wanted to convey to Coni his Syncretist devotion. "Perhaps the frontier of the mind is our future. If we could unite our mental powers, think what a potent force we could be if we continued to explore and colonize."

Art saw Coni's pretty mouth take on a grim set. "Your collective strength means little to the individual who has to face a hostile world alone." Her voice was still filled with bitterness. Like the sadness he had seen in her eyes, he felt that her bitterness was an emotion not in keeping with her youth. "Instead of teaching people to rely on machinery or others, we should teach them to rely upon themselves because in the final accounting, we must each stand alone."

Vanessa tightened her hold on Coni's arm and spoke in a soft, soothing voice, "There is a strength in the collective mind that transcends even this final accounting."

Coni stood up suddenly. She looked from Vanessa to Art with eyes that looked like emeralds illuminated by lightning. "There is a different kind of strength," she said grimly. "The strength of an individual to overcome all odds in order to become the master of her own destiny."

Vanessa slowly stood. She spoke again with a quiet voice. "I grant you that, Coni, but neither individual nor collective strengths has to be exclusive, and certainly neither depends upon space exploration."

"That's where you're wrong," Coni replied in a sadly bitter tone. "The collective depends upon the proximity of its members. If we continue to explore, or if we spread out the Federation, then we must rely upon the individual."

"Grant us the time to consolidate our exploratory gains," Vanessa pleaded.

"If we stop now and turn inward, we are doomed," Coni replied angrily. "My parents were culturologists. They understood the need for diversity, and they knew that a unified, inwardly oriented society would stagnate. If we don't explore, if we don't seek new stimuli, we are dead as far as the Universe is concerned."

"There is time later for all of that," Vanessa said. "First, we must face the task of overcoming humanity's divisiveness. The urgency to explore is not as great as the urgency to unify."

"The urgency to explore may be greater than you realize," Coni replied, her anger beginning to give way to crying. "I left my parents and friends out there"—she pointed to the sky—"dead on a godforsaken planet that defied all analysis." She began to cry again. "They died because a planet had been restructured to resemble somebody's warped idea of hell."

Vanessa put her arm around Coni's shoulders only to have her move away.

The associations clicked in Art's mind as his earlier mental twinge became a spasm of suddenly connecting thoughts. He silently cursed himself for not unlocking sooner the history stored in his mind.

"The Apollyoni?" he asked softly, still wary of upsetting Coni further.

Her eyes fastened on his, revealing a fierce, raging hatred. "Yes," she said, the word sliding from her mouth like a sudden blizzard in the middle of her heated crying.

"Coni, I know about your father and his ideas, but it's just a hypothesis," Art said soothingly. "There is no evidence to support it."

"And there never will be if we stop exploring." Only the tears were left now, glistening like faint parallel streamlets from two green fountains. "You talk about uniting humanity and using human technology to do it. But where did that technology come from? From experimentation. From hypotheses and theories and analyses and more experiments. We cannot stop experimenting because then we stop growing. You're damning the scientific method. You're damning rational thinking if you believe we can leave the Apollyoni as a hypothesis not to be investigated. Just like you're damning humanity with this—" And she moved her hand in a sweeping gesture along the outline of the village. With that, she turned and walked back to the village.

Vanessa looked from Coni's departing figure to Art. Her eyes were hard and questioning. "What have you done to her? What are these Apollyoni?"

"The musings of a man frustrated by his inability to explain natural phenomena," Art answered solemnly. "Coni's father tried to advance the idea that there was a race of beings who traveled the Galaxy leaving a wake of destruction in their path. It's an irrational idea and unsupported by any evidence. Mere diablerie. He died trying to find that evidence, and now his daughter, in her grief, is caught up in his beliefs. Forget her, Vanessa. She has an emotional block to us. Only complete mental reconditioning can overcome such fear and hatred."

"Then we'll do what we can to help her," Vanessa said in a determined voice, her look telling him that she, too, now remembered the incident on Ahriman. "If she won't come to us, we'll go to her."

Vanessa turned from Art and quickly ran after Coni. Art followed them at a distance. He watched as Vanessa caught up with Coni. He could see them talking. He sensed the concern and pleading in Vanessa's face, and he noted Coni's stubborn movement toward the village. The two women walked out of the woods and through the village center, which was not as populated as it had been. Heads turned as the two women passed without greeting anyone, still absorbed in their conversation. Art followed as they entered Coni's residence.

He waited around outside listening to Vanessa's voice, which seemed so soft and full of concern. He sensed an almost hypnotic quality about her voice. Satisfied that all was well, he entered the room. Vanessa was seated beside Coni, her arm about her. Vanessa was speaking softly into Coni's ear. He noted that Coni was visibly relaxed and apparently oblivious to his presence. Vanessa carefully undressed Coni and then herself. She led Coni to the tranquilizer shower.

When they emerged, Coni seemed to see him for the first time. She smiled dreamily, and he could see that her eyes lacked their earlier fearful luster. He marveled at Coni's mature beauty, her smoothly flowing youthful lines, and he watched in awe as Vanessa led her to her bed, embraced and kissed her and then put her in the bed. In a matter of moments, Coni was asleep. Vanessa quickly but silently dressed and then walked past him out of the room. Art hurried after her.

"How is she?" he asked, now concerned about both women.

"She's okay now," Vanessa answered in a matter-of-fact tone. "I had to hypnotize her and use my portable link to calm her down. There is an awful amount of pain and suffering inside her. It's terrible what happened to her. I'm surprised she controls it as well as she does. I couldn't take all of it. It would take several minds or a psych machine to work on her, and I'm not sure we want her *that* reconditioned."

He walked the rest of the way with her in silence. Once they got to Vanessa's room, she excused herself and left him alone for several hours. He spent the time using a link to review the Council ruling. Despite Coni's concern, he knew that Council was right. He realized that Coni was too emotionally involved in the decision to consider it dispassionately and from a wider vantage point.

When Vanessa returned, she barely spoke to him. She went right to her couch, lay down and turned on a link. He was visibly hurt, but Vanessa closed her eyes to this. He knew he had handled himself badly and had possibly interfered with Vanessa's desire to get through to Coni. Neither got up to participate in the evening ritual, and he watched through the night as Vanessa lay there attached to her link. He did not know if she slept, if she received images or if she was just thinking. Toward morning she got up, uncoupled the link and came to him.

"I'm sorry," she said simply, holding him. "I had a duty today and it just didn't work out. Still love me?" There was no emotion in her voice.

"Yes," he said, kissing her firmly. Even as the happiness of being with her again swept over him, he realized that a new element had entered their relationship: implicit in her words was a warning that she had certain tasks which took precedence over his feelings.

As he continued his payload checkout, he thought back to that scene in Vanessa's room. Their relationship changed after that incident. He returned to the Academy. When events permitted, he spent as much time with Vanessa as possible but just as his new assignments in the Fleet required him to travel a lot, she also traveled extensively in her efforts to advance the Syncretistic way of life. Even now she was on Vesta in Sector K-10 doing only her coordinator knew what. Increasingly over the years, Art found himself, in her absence, putting his energy into the same cause. He had wanted to spend his life with Vanessa, but like her he had come to realize that they must be the generation to sacrifice so that humanity could have a new and better society. He had found his fulfillment and sense of belonging in the Syncretist movement.

Over these same years he had followed Coni's activities. He knew that she and Vanessa had remained friends despite their differences, and he was a little jealous when Coni went to live with that upstart outworlder Greg Sheldon. Art had even felt a little consternation when he was assigned to this training flight with Sheldon. He had not particularly liked Greg because of his apparent solitary, almost antisocial, personality and archaic outworld ideas on individuality. Moreover, he had not liked taking precious time away from Syncretism for what he considered a needless, routine training flight.

He laughed bitterly to himself as he thought about the so-called training flight. He was certain that Council knew nothing of the real purpose of the flight and even if it had known and had approved, *he* could have stopped it had he known in time to inform the Syncretists. He knew this flight was counter to everything which the New Society needed. He wished he could contact Vanessa.

His mind was filled with these thoughts when something in his probing of that last-minute payload consignment triggered an alarm in his mind. *Something had been cleverly disguised for protection against routine probing!* The concealment was so ingenious that it almost fooled him but he had been expecting the worst. The disguise had fooled several automatic port-checking devices, and it had fooled him during the prelaunch checkout. Quickly, he focused all his mental attention on the alarm. The results of his mental search almost caused him to start with surprise, shock and disgust. He knew he had found what he was looking for—the terrible secret piece of evidence that refuted Wilson's implication of official support. He quickly recorded the data and with an angry set to his face walked rapidly back to the control room. His three crewmates turned to face him as the door opened to admit him.

He stood in the doorway, staring hard at Wilson, his mind torn with anger and disgust at his commanding officer. "You said that this mission had official support."

Wilson stared back at him without answering.

"Well, if it has official backing, why are we carrying nullor weapons?"

7

DESTINATION

'My name is Ozymandias, king of kings:
Look on my works, ye Mighty, and despair!'
Nothing beside remains. Round the decay
Of that colossal wreck, boundless and bare
The lone and level sands stretch far away.
                    —Percy Bysshe Shelley, *Ozymandias*

No one spoke.

Richard and Greg looked from the angry face of Art Cooke to the starkly impassive face of Ben Wilson. Art and Ben had locked eyes. Finally, Ben spoke in a hard voice, "Would you explain your accusation?"

Art's face was slightly flushed, and his anger seemed to effuse from his whole body. "You know goddamned well what I'm talking about. There is a complete set of modified shield suit belts in the payload compartment. They've been modified to include nullors." His voice almost cracked as he verged on a scream, "That is illegal!"

Richard looked at Ben with a mixture of disbelief and concern. "Is he telling the truth? Are there nullor weapons on board?"

Ben nodded affirmatively. The hardness in his face seemed to give way to a look of fatigue. "Please sit down, Art. I'd like to explain why we have the nullors."

Art shook his head. He glanced anxiously at Richard and at Greg. "This is more serious than you realize." He pointed at Ben. "He is specifically forbidden to use nullor weapons under any circumstances. That is a known ban, Ben, and no amount of crappy explanations will get you out of that one. You know what this means, don't you?" Art looked again from Richard to Greg as if pleading for help. "This mission does not have any official sanction. It is an illegal mission set up for hell knows what kind of mischief."

Ben's eyes narrowed and his muscles visibly tightened, but he remained impassively seated in his recliner.

"Ben, I want you to contact the Fleet," Art pleaded. "Tell them where we are. And tell them we're going back. We've violated so many laws that we'll be lucky to keep our minds intact."

Ben stood up slowly, his fists clenched, his mouth set in a rigidly tight line. Somehow he seemed larger than his actual size, and his look seemed almost as black as his hair. "I'm not going to ask you again, Art. Sit down and let me explain." Ben's voice was hard and cold, and he spoke forcefully. Richard and Greg were as taken aback as Art at this almost totally unusual display of brute force.

Art looked silently at Ben for a long moment, his outward anger at his commander giving way to a look of pleading. "Ben, can't you see this is wrong? We're in serious trouble. We've violated almost every rule of exploration." Ben said nothing in reply. Finally, under Ben's unyielding stare, Art sat down.

Ben breathed a sigh of relief. He looked at each member of his crew. "Art is right. The suit belts have, in addition to the normal stunnor, a nullor which can be activated under the right conditions. The link can explain that later. Art is also correct when he says that I am forbidden to use nullors under any circumstances."

Richard and Greg each started to speak, but Ben waved them silent and continued talking: "The reason I am forbidden to use any nullor weapon is because I once used such a device to save two crewmates and in the process came close to killing them," Ben said in a tone more defiant than apologetic. "It was a chance I believed I had to take even though it violated the literal interpretation of the law on weapons."

"It also violated the intent of the law," Art said in a quiet but determined voice. "Weapons of destruction are not to be used around living things."

Again, Ben looked tired. "Art, I don't want to debate the law just now. I want you to understand why those nullors are necessary."

Richard spoke quietly. "Ben, despite the ban on your use of nullors, Art still has a point. These weapons are placed under strict control. Why are we doing this, if it does not have Council sanction?"

Ben sat down while continuing to look intently at each member of his crew. "What I told you before about Sangraal II is true. I did not elaborate on the events leading up to this mission because I felt they were not germane to the actual conduct of the mission."

Greg interrupted in a slightly urgent tone, "But surely you must have known that we would discover the nullors. If not, at some time you would have had to tell us."

Ben nodded his agreement. "I was hoping after we landed on Sangraal II. There was even some hope that we might not need to use those belts. You might never have known about them."

"What else have you hidden from us?" Art demanded. He no longer trusted Ben but felt a need to keep probing. Ben had learned enough mental and emotional control to protect himself from the normal evaluations a Fleet-trained person made of his speech and bodily actions.

"Nothing," Ben replied. His voice barely hid disdain. "We have on board one of the most powerful tractor beams in the Federation, as well as special scanner equipment designed, we hope, for Sangraal II. I will admit that the tractor beam could be used as a sort of shipborne weapon. You know how controlled all spacecraft are—it was only possible to install suit nullors; anything more elaborate would have been detected. In all other respects, the *Odyssey* carries only what any simulated exploratory flight might be expected to carry." He paused and stared past Art toward the closed door. "I will say this: those nullors are there for your benefit because I and several others like me care enough to want you to return safely. If I had my way, this ship would have a nullor, too."

There was an audible gasp from several of the crew at hearing what almost amounted to blasphemy.

Ben stood up again and gestured vigorously with his hands and arms. "I mean that in all seriousness. I even wish I had the time to rig up the suit nullors to work as ship nullors without destroying the ship in the process. Sangraal II is a planet which defies analysis. We cannot probe it. It has probably cost us the lives of the crew of the *Leos*. And now we are receiving a Fleet Alert signal. Something is wrong on Sangraal II and that something is very likely dangerous to us."

Art spoke again, this time in a slightly placating voice. "Ben, these are matters for Council to deal with. They are not our concerns. We have no right to jeopardize the whole Federation by our unauthorized presence here."

"Ben, let us know the complete story behind this mission so we can judge its merits," Richard asked, also in a slightly placating tone. "Does Council know that we're here?"

"Rich, the less all of you know, the better," Ben responded. "If the mission fails to turn up anything, and you do know what I know, then you are asking for a memory erase of the whole experience."

Art shook his head with obvious disgust. "You people are desperate. Memory erasures are as illegal as this whole damned mission."

In an icy voice Ben replied, "Are they as illegal as using links to probe other people's minds?"

Art flushed. "What do you mean?"

"I'm speaking about some of the techniques, or should I say tactics, used by the Syncretists."

Art leaped from his recliner, his body shaking with rage. "What we have done is for the benefit of humanity. We want to unite all of humanity. What you are doing with this mission is opening up all the old divisions. Who is behind this mission? He's the one who needs a memory erase."

"It's obvious who's behind this," Greg said quietly as he looked from Art to Ben. They each looked back at him. "Unless Ben has more tricks at his disposal than I give him credit for, it's obvious to me that only one person could have set up this mission: Sedmak himself. I would also guess that Carson was or is in on it. Nothing goes on at a Fleet base without the cognizance of the Base Commander."

Ben did not immediately respond to Greg's statements. Richard asked, "Is Greg correct?"

"Yes," Ben said simply.

"Sedmak!" Art exclaimed with abhorrence. "That anachronistic bastard!"

Ben moved toward Art, prompting Richard to stand up between them. "Art, I need you for this mission," Ben spoke quietly, almost in a hiss as his teeth were clenched. "I need you for reasons you don't even understand yet. But so help me, as long as I'm running this ship, if you ever say another word out of line, I'll see to it that you're stunned for the rest of the mission." The room was again quiet. *"Do you understand?"*

Art nodded.

"Now I want everyone to sit down," Ben said coldly. As soon as Art and Richard were seated, Ben sat down. "I made a mistake in how I played this one. I apologize." He looked at Art. "I misjudged your reactions. I wanted very much to come out here, do a quick check and return, hoping to avoid involving you in the rest of the operation. I was wrong in that assumption.

"You all want to know the details, so I'll tell you what I know. You won't like it but I'm asking you to hear me out.

"Art was correct when he said this mission does not have official sanction. Council was secretly apprised of the Fleet Alert signal and the apparent change in the appearance of Sangraal II. They debated the idea of sending some kind of probe or crewed craft but decided against it, probably for the same reason they set up the Perimeter." Ben and Art glared at each other. "We have never had a situation like this. No lost expedition has ever signaled back after this many years, assuming it is the expedition that is signaling."

Art quickly interjected, "Or it was a ruse of Sedmak's to get Council to back a mission like this."

"Be real, Art," Ben replied. "If the signal were a ruse, then when Council failed to support this mission, it would have been the end of the whole business." He shifted his body slightly and resumed his earlier speech:

"For a moment, let's forget about all the artificial rules we live by. Forget the Federation and Fleet regulations. Try to think about Sangraal objectively. Years ago, we had evidence that Sangraal II had life. We did not know the extent of development of that life because our probes were not as good then. Also, we tended to send out expeditions rather quickly, and by today's standards, based on limited data. We did know, however, that Sangraal II was a Tellurian-type planet.

"With this in mind, Council approved the flight of the *Leos*. Richard's father, who was a very capable ship commander, perhaps one of the best in the Fleet, was placed in charge of the flight. Since we knew that Sangraal II harbored life, the *Leos* carried a larger than normal contingent of bio-and socioscientists. There was guarded optimism that we might at last find a race as intelligent and as advanced as we.

"You've experienced the history of that flight on the links. The *Leos* vanished. Not a single clue was detected from our sensors within the Federation. That in itself is unusual. In almost every other instance of a crew loss situation, we've had some clue as to the nature of the problem. Sensors, scanners and flight recorders don't just quit. Life-support systems try to function. But from the *Leos*—nothing!

"And to add to the dilemma, we could no longer passively monitor Sangraal II for the *Leos*. We aren't even sure that the *Leos* landed or beamed down an exploratory party. It was as if a shield had been erected around the planet. Even from here we can't really probe Sangraal II, although we know it is there. And we know it appears to have changed recently.

"I grant you that it was stupid of the Fleet not to have immediately dispatched an armed rescue ship, but those of us interested in Sangraal II now were not in a position then to do much about it. Perhaps, given the facts and Fleet capabilities at that time, we would have made the same decision. Based on what we know now and what was made known then, I believe the Fleet played down the significance of the *Leos*. Again, this may have resulted from the inability of the Fleet to do anything about the tragedy.

"But think about those intervening years of silence. Think about that ghostly planet shrouded in secrecy all those years, then imagine Sedmak's concern when he learned that Sangraal II was now sending out signals, Fleet Alert signals. And all this occurring at about the same time the planet's image changed.

"Remember, Sedmak has a dual job. All we have ever really functioned under is his space exploration and commerce job, but he is also charged with the defense of the Federation. Even if the public and most of us in the Fleet do not think about the second job, I can assure you that *he* does. It is just as important to him as his exploration job. Whether we like it or not, we have a military function.

"Suppose the disappearance of the *Leos* is not the result of some accident. Suppose, for the sake of argument, that someone or something decided that humanity should go no farther in this region of space. If so, they know about us, but we have gone on for years oblivious of them."

Greg asked, "If this is so, why haven't they come after us?"

"I'm only throwing out ideas," Ben answered. "Who knows why this alleged alien race has not sought us out peacefully or militarily. Perhaps the *Leos* was able to destroy itself and prevent them from learning about the Federation. Perhaps our failure to send a rescue ship or our establishment of the Perimeter set up the conditions that kept us apart. Or perhaps," he added ominously, "they are preparing to attack and are even now secretly probing the Federation."

"This whole idea of an extra-Federation race is pure guesswork," Art said. He looked at Greg. "It smacks of Sanderson's theory of the Apollyoni."

Greg started to reply, but Ben waved him off. "Go back to the link for a minute," Ben said. They each did so as Ben telepathically activated a preselected data dump from the computer. "Think about the number of lost ships, several of which, like the *Leos,* remain unexplained. Now think about some of the planets we have found, planets such as the one where Sanderson died, planets which fit no logical explanation. Even Frey"—he glanced at Greg—"one of the last within the Perimeter to be explored has some potentially unusual features about it.

"Suppose, in a typical military fashion, we assume the worst and prepare for it. Perhaps there is a race, such as Sanderson's Apollyoni, which seeks to destroy or drastically alter all life it encounters. If nothing else, as scientists we should at least investigate to see if Sanderson is correct."

"Sanderson was wrong about the Apollyoni," Art retorted. "Every planet described by the link has a natural explanation. Maybe it is not always neat or simple, but there is always an explanation. Similarly, I'm sure each lost ship has an explanation. So where does this put us?"

"In the Sangraal system, Art, prepared as best we know how for any eventuality," Ben replied. "Let me make you a proposition—allow me to complete the mission, and if we find nothing unnatural, when we return I will resign from the Fleet and accept without contest whatever legal punishment Council or the

Fleet wants to exact." He paused to look hard at each one of the three men in front of him. "I will gladly record that pledge on the flight recorder for permanent record."

The other three did not speak for a few moments. Each knew that Ben Wilson had given them a proposition which was heavily weighted against him. And should the punishment be carried out, his useful professional life would be finished.

Art thought for a while and then spoke, "I'll go along with this mission on three conditions. First, I want you to record on the flight recorder for transmittal to this passive monitor the complete story of your part as well as Sedmak's and Carson's part in this flight. I want all the names called out. Second, when we return, I want to select the exit gate so that, without interference, we can return the flight recorder to the proper authorities. As a backup, I want the monitor activated before we leave, and I want the destruct mechanism deactivated before we leave. Finally, Ben, I don't want to land on Sangraal II. Let's make this a quick recon and then return."

"You ask a high price," Ben said with a hint of sadness. "You realize that you are asking me to betray many people and ruin their careers, if not worse."

Art nodded his acknowledgment.

"Art, you're asking Ben to destroy the lives of a lot of people," Richard interjected. "You know how something like this can grow out of all proportion. If you insist on implicating others, leave it at Sedmak and Carson. The authorities would arrive at that conclusion anyway. Remember, some of the people involved in this may be innocent, or they may be dupes, or they may even be operating from motives entirely different from those of Sedmak or Ben."

"I want this whole conspiracy exposed," Art replied bitterly. "These people are violating the very concepts of the Federation and of Council control of the Fleet. They are acting as some kind of self-appointed, autonomous government whose actions amount to treason. They must be ferreted out and stopped."

"Art, let the authorities handle this," Richard urged. "There is no need for us to condemn the whole group until we know all the facts."

"We know enough to condemn them," Art retorted angrily. "You're letting your personal involvement in this mission cloud your thinking. That's why you picked him, isn't it, Ben? You knew he would be so interested in finding his father that he could be counted on to overlook your illegal action." Both Ben and Richard started to reply, but Art continued: "And Greg. He's so in love with Sanderson's daughter that he'd go along with you in the hope that somehow this mission would help her." Greg looked sharply at Art. "Yes, I know about Coni's suffering, Greg. In that sense, she should be here, not you. When she learns of the negative results out here, then maybe she can finally rid herself of this Apollyoni nonsense." He laughed bitterly. "You claim to be a Neo-monadist, yet you are going along with this militaristic clique."

Richard interrupted. "Your reasoning for the selection of the crew doesn't make sense, Art. If Sedmak or Ben had wanted an obedient crew, why were you selected?"

Art shook his head. "That's the one point in the plan which has me puzzled."

"I think you know the answer," Ben said quietly.

Art laughed mirthlessly, then in a voice filled with scorn he said, "Do you seriously think that somehow I can be exploited or used against Syncretism?"

"No, Art, that's not how Sedmak saw it," Ben replied quickly in a calming tone. "In a sense, you may be right about why Rich and Greg were chosen, but Sedmak said they each came to his attention for other reasons. I'm sure he scanned thousands of names in selecting this crew. In fact, I was selected just like the rest of you and learned about the real purpose of the mission shortly before launch. I don't pretend to know all that he considered when he selected each of us, but I'm sure consideration was given to the effects of Richard's father and Greg's partner. But Sedmak was impressed with the capabilities of all of us—he believes this crew has what it takes to complete the mission.

"You were correct in associating your selection with Syncretism, Art. Sedmak appreciates the power and influence of Syncretism. He realizes that without Syncretistic support, nothing will come of this mission, even if we find what we fear is the case. There has been no attempt to reorient your thinking, Art. Sedmak is not dumb. Any analyzer would immediately detect the slightest attempt at reorientation. Furthermore, I have no intention of interfering with your activities as long as you don't jeopardize the mission. His hope and mine, too, is that you will faithfully report all that happens. Now, do you see why I need you?"

"You're going to pay an awful price for that need," Art said scornfully. "Regardless of Sedmak's rationale for selecting this crew or his misgivings about Sangraal II, he has no business operating without Council sanction. It is not up to Sedmak to make these decisions. Council, which is elected by *all* the people, decides on these matters.

"In the interests of all humanity, I insist on all three of my conditions."

Ben stared hard at Art. "I accept with one qualifier: if something unusual occurs during our recon of Sangraal II, such as the sighting of the *Leos* or its crew, I reserve the right to land should it be necessary. In return for my accepting these three conditions, I expect no further trouble from you."

After a brief pause to consider what Ben had said, Art replied, "I agree."

The tense atmosphere in the control room seemed to be expelled, and each crewmember visibly relaxed.

"Give me a few minutes to make the recording," Ben said. "Art, you may monitor it. When I'm finished, we'll resume our work." He turned to Richard. "While I'm making the recording, Rich, I want you and Greg to maintain a full-alert status and be ready to move out at the slightest unusual happening."

Richard and Greg set up a full, active monitoring of the *Odyssey* and the surrounding space. As Ben had said earlier, the shields and all systems were activated and the *Odyssey* was programmed for instant action. To each of them, the apparent lifeless space around them and the solar system toward which they were rapidly traveling seemed more sinister now than they had ever thought possible.

Both Richard and Greg sensed Ben activating the flight recorder for personal use, and they also sensed Art's presence on the link. Neither felt inclined to monitor this activity. Each was silent, preoccupied with his own thoughts.

When Ben finished his mental recording, he turned to Art. "Are you satisfied?" he asked, almost accusingly.

"Yes," Art replied without emotion.

Ben looked at each of the three crewmen. "Does anyone else want to add to this recording?" Richard and Greg gave the briefest of negative nods. Neither met Ben's eyes.

Again, in his emotionless tone, Art said, "I would like to add a few thoughts about the mission and my reasons for letting you continue with it."

Ben said nothing; he simply nodded his assent. Richard and Greg again turned their conscious thoughts back to the *Odyssey*. They could each sense Art working with the flight recorder. Art's personal use of the recorder ended after a few minutes, and Greg, as the systems monitor, duly noted that the flight recorder was now back in fully automatic operation.

Ben mentally through the link and verbally signaled for the attention of the crew. His recliner was turned so that it still faced the others. "Until we return to the Federation, I want everyone at his duty station. The *Odyssey* will remain on a full-alert status during this time. Art"—and here there was only the slightest, almost unnoticeable, hesitation denoting that anything had ever been amiss— "I want you to keep checking the hardware for all systems. See that our payload equipment is functional, including"—and he paused again—"the monitor and the tractor beam; and probe each of the Sangraal planets for any sign of life or for anything unusual. Greg, maintain your systems monitoring and probe every damned cubic centimeter of space for anything out of the ordinary. That includes Sangraal itself. Rich, I want you to stay in parallel with me on the inward flight so you can back me up or take over as necessary. Also"—he glanced sharply at Art as if in anticipation of trouble—"keep the tractor beam ready for whatever use we may have for it." Art did not speak. Ben continued. "I will take the *Odyssey* in on a standard star system recon just to double-check what we presumably already know. We check each planet and satellite closely, as if we were 'seeing' them for the first time, all the while paying close attention to Sangraal II. As you know, we have no evidence of life anywhere in this system and no evidence that the rest of the Sangraal system is anything but a natural stellar system, but in case any of you get complacent, just remember: the *Leos* disappeared without a trace, and Sangraal II is still shielded from our best scanning equipment."

Ben rotated his recliner to face the forward end of the *Odyssey*, and each of the four men began to carry out his assigned tasks.

When they were satisfied with their various tests of the ship and the star system, the crew moved the *Odyssey* into a spiry reconnaissance trajectory past each of Sangraal's planets. At the outermost planet, a whirling hydrogenous sphere, they left the monitor disguised as a part of the natural field and radiation belts. They swung past seared and battered Sangraal I and moved around Sangraal itself to head outward toward the cloud-covered second planet. The crew raced to catch this spherical wraith, spinning along its almost circular orbit some 160 million kilometers from Sangraal.

Looking as they did from space, where they were unable to penetrate the clouds which seemed to actively defy their scanners, the crew saw that Sangraal II still had the gross features they already knew. The planet had a diameter of thirteen thousand kilometers and based on a computer analysis, a mass slightly more than that of Earth. Again, based on their extra-atmospheric observations and computer analyses, they were aware of the negligible oblateness of the planet and that the planet had almost no inclination of the equator with respect to its orbital plane, which in turn placed the equator almost within the plane of Sangraal's equator. And the crew noted a day whose duration approached twenty six standard hours. They also observed that Sangraal II was an unprotected target for extra-planetary radiation, since its magnetic field no longer existed. This had been another of the puzzling changes noted earlier by the Federation sensors and now confirmed by the *Odyssey*.

Greg was greatly intrigued by this hidden planet, and he made several weak attempts on his own to penetrate the cloud cover of Sangraal II. He mused to himself, "Whoever lives there must be like the Cimmerian people, wrapped in mist and clouds. Dead." He wondered if this was not how Aornum looked.

As the *Odyssey* moved into orbit around Sangraal II, Art continued his active probing of the planet by devoting all of his energy to this task. He activated the special scanners which had been brought especially for

Sangraal II. As he brought the full complex of scanners up to power, he saw that he could begin to penetrate and analyze the upper atmosphere which, at first, seemed to consist of some kind of blackish-gray, swirling mass of gases filled with ashlike particles to the point where this upper atmosphere resembled a mobile emulsion. He noted that the ash itself was responsible for his earlier failures to penetrate the atmosphere. As Art penetrated deeper, he found very little free oxygen. The atmosphere consisted largely of water vapor and ash, which immediately told him something of the still hidden surface and helped explain the blackish-gray clouds which concealed the surface. Art also noted other compounds, including hydrogen, carbon dioxide, ammonia, methane, boric acid, hydrogen sulfide and some relatively unusual combinations of hydrogen, silicon, nitrogen, oxygen and certain other metallic elements.

Deeper and deeper he probed. He felt as if he were actually in the turbulent atmosphere of Sangraal II, fighting to clear away the floating ash that screened his scanners. All around he sensed the violence of the gases in motion and the thrust of vast electrical discharges which were quickly absorbed by the floating ash. He fought against the atmospheric interference, redoubling his efforts to penetrate to the surface. He called forth his own vast mental powers and pushed the scanners down into the mists, boring through, he felt, like some powerful searchlight.

He burst through the shroudlike atmosphere to "see" the horrible panorama of a planet destroyed. Throughout the whole spectrum of sensory experience, he "saw" the burned and twisted remains of a planet which, he thought on the link, must have experienced some stellar bath to have been so radically changed from the greenish-blue life sustainer that was previously scanned from the Federation only a few months ago.

The rest of the crew was mentally with him, moving now over this Phlegraean surface. Art led the way across the warped and gnarled landscape. He probed and analyzed, all the while furnishing data and evaluations to his crewmates.

The surface was a dark gray that verged on black, somewhat like basalt in the normal visual spectrum, a spectrum which Art ruefully noted they would never see on this planet because of its atmosphere and surface. He was thankful for the scanners and their ability to recreate the surface in a fashion that made sense to his mind.

He could only describe the surface features as harsh and tortured, like the ancient face of some battered and bleak derelict of space. He and his crewmates saw twisted ranges rising above hummocky plains. The undulating nature of the plains seemed to suggest fluidity. Aside from the plains, it was a savagely rough land of barren rock, large rifts and long chasms separated by flat-topped plateaus—all overlaid with jumbled fractures and uplifts. Art was awed by the massive faulting of the crust and the chaotic mixture of massifs, ridges and talus-filled troughs which seemed to him more the work of some insane practitioner of macramé than anything conceived by nature.

Initially, Art thought that the planet was covered with solidified lava. But as he analyzed what the scanners gathered, he realized that this was not the true surface. He saw the influence on the surface of volcanic activity, but the surface was seriously distorted by planetologic incongruities. This surface was like nothing he had ever studied in the Federation.

He saw evidence of what appeared to be massive, solidified lava fields covered with the blackened remnants of ejected, molten rocks. In places the debris seemed pyroclastic in nature, as if formed as a result of some awful explosion. There was also evidence of violently ejected, welded rhyolitic tuffs known as ignimbrites scattered over a surface which he could only describe as scoria, since it looked so much like the solidified lava froth that marked the slag of volcanic activity. Certainly, the vesicular nature was noticeable.

Elsewhere he found jagged, broken blocks which adjoined relatively smooth areas where the surface appeared unbroken, ropy or billowy. Interspersed with the various surface features like weird synclinal basins were deep hollows and giant, dust-filled basins. Occasionally, he saw openings of tunnels and caves but like so much on this mysterious planet, he was unable to penetrate them.

His mind ached as he sought to unravel the mystery of the surface. He had the full resources of the *Odyssey* at his disposal, but he was no better than a savage gazing at a pile of rocks.

It's all one twisted mass, he thought on the link. *It's hard to separate the surface into fragments or lava. There is evidence for both extrusive and intrusive material, but there is no evidence of volcanoes, fumaroles, calderas, anything. It doesn't make sense.*

He tried repeatedly to penetrate the surface, but the special scanners, operating at full power, could not go beneath it. He tried the full scanner spectrum repeatedly and still the results were negative. He was unable to probe the planet any deeper. He could only analyze its surface with the scanner, which acted as his eyes.

Ben, this planet is like some kind of energy sink, Art thought on the link. *It is almost totally impenetrable—any beam we use on it will be totally absorbed without any effect. Even a nullor would be useless against that stuff. All that passes through is gravity but somehow I'm prevented from using that 'frequency' for internal probing. Shields, tractor beams and pellor beams may function for a while but it's as if a field barrier has been built to stop anything we could ever throw against it. This planet defies all rules—it shouldn't exist.*

Ben: *Keep probing.*

Art's only other quantitative datum was the temperature of the surface. As he had expected from his mental trip through the atmosphere, the surface was too hot for water to remain liquid. Nowhere could he find any water, either magmatic or meteoric. But he noted for the benefit of the crew that even the temperature was inconsistent with the other observations he had made.

The temperature does not fit my idea of an energy sink, he observed through the link, *yet if this planet had undergone any kind of volcanic or other planetary activity sufficient to produce this monstrosity, it would still be hot—hotter than it apparently is. There hasn't been enough time to burn off the surface of a planet and cool it to just above the boiling point of water. The original temperatures must have easily exceeded 3000 K. It would take decades to cool this much lava—if it is lava.*

He continued his mental exploration. In places he found what appeared to be cinders and pumice coupled with fine dust. But even the dust could not be penetrated. It seemed to Art that the dust particles themselves had established an interlocking net of fields which effectively stopped his scanners.

He mentally reviewed the facts in an effort to put some order into what he had observed. As he did, he also initiated a series of calculations on the computer. He knew that Sangraal II had once been a tropical, Tellurian-type planet. Now it was a burned-out hulk. Sangraal had not undergone any unusual activity in those years, so the source of the burned-out sphere had to be based within or near the planet itself. He could only imagine volcanic activity, but the scale of damage was too immense to be natural. He knew that even if one could postulate extensive crustal penetrations which could release such massive amounts of molten material, the now relatively cold, solidified and seismically stable remains were also not natural. He could not imagine a planetary surface which defied the best analytical tools of modern science. Even the collapsed remnants of dead stars could be probed. Nor could he imagine how such incongruous remnants could coexist. He saw no evidence for crystals or phenocrysts. He felt that the cooling should have permitted some crystallization, but he found no visual data to support the idea of crystallization. The surface had cooled as one big, uniform, amorphous mass. He did not understand how the planet had suffered such damage.

The rest of the crew were still with him in his observations, so they were aware of his attempts to analyze the planet.

Ben called for a complete study by the computer of all possible causes of the destruction of Sangraal II. Almost instantly, he and the others were supplied with a wide-ranging set of phenomena, including hypothetical astronomical events, planetary instabilities (including consideration of the possible effects of the engines of the *Leos*) and wars. Permutations and combinations of these phenomena were freely considered, as was the possibility that the *Odyssey* was actually scanning an illusion. The computer factored in the conditioning events and ordered the causes by probabilities. Immediately, the mind of each crewman was filled with òne very apparent conclusion: *Sangraal II had been destroyed by unnatural phenomena—and that argued for the interference of some intelligent life form.*

This conclusion was followed by the hypothesis that the recent change in Sangraal II and the transmission of the signals might be bait to bring in another human ship.

No one spoke for several minutes after that. Each silently considered the information he had received.

"We'll make one last attempt at deciphering this planet and then we'll return home," Ben finally said. Turning to Art, he continued, "Send a standard recon communication signal to the whole surface. We'll keep it up for one planetary day and then leave." To Richard and Greg, he said, "Maintain the full-alert status and keep probing for any explanation of this planet."

Art shrugged. "I don't see how anything could be alive down there."

"There are still a few tunnels and caves," Richard said, hope reflected in his voice.

"Even if someone had survived all this and lives in those lava caves, he could never receive our signal," Art said in reply. "Unless he has a receiving unit on the surface and there is no evidence of such a unit."

Ben glanced sharply at Art. "Nevertheless, turn on a full spectrum comm signal. And keep analyzing the planet."

Art activated the standard reconnaissance communication signal. Sangraal II was immediately bathed in a burst of energy which carried signals of intelligence over the full range of conceivable communications devices. Concurrently, he activated a receiver which monitored all emissions from Sangraal II and analyzed them for signs of intelligent life.

Once these tasks were completed, Art resumed his study of the surface. Now that everyone was resigned to the enigma, the initial pressures of trying to understand the planet lessened thereby enabling Art to move mentally over the surface with a more relaxed attitude.

For Art now, the surface took on a nightmarish beauty. He saw the ash-filled gray mists moving silently across the almost black, angular landscape. He imagined freezing some planet at the moment of birth. It would look like this. But this planet had been frozen at the moment of death.

Art had visited many Federation planets and had studied the rest, but Sangraal II was unique. Never had he seen such total desolation. One word kept surfacing in his conscious thoughts: *malpais,* the badlands.

He knew it had taken considerable energy to produce the scorched, craggy surface, and he believed rather strongly that the *Leos,* no matter how belatedly it appeared to have acted, had been responsible. He felt certain that a full analysis of data by Federation scientists would support the Syncretistic argument that humanity need explore no further. Somehow, he thought, the *Leos* caused this horror. He imagined an abandoned *Leos,* its shields failing, spewing forth a searing torch of death. He thought about the terror which had been visited upon this planet, and he was thankful that the Syncretists had had the courage to set up the Perimeter. He reasoned that there was some unknown planetary quality which no one had foreseen, and despite its apparent rarity, he felt it would be sufficient to warrant continuing the cessation of galactic exploration. He laughed silently to himself—Ben would return with his data, but it would be used against him and his kind. Sedmak had unwittingly brought about his own downfall.

Art did not believe in the Apollyoni. He saw the concept as a natural one for Sedmak to embrace because it would justify his going beyond the Perimeter. It would open up all the old divisions, further fragmenting humanity. To Art, the Perimeter represented an ideal human-made cradle within which the human race could be nurtured to greater awareness of its unity. There are no demons outside the Perimeter, he thought, only those that exist inside the minds of the Sedmaks and the Wilsons.

He felt sorry for Richard and Greg. Very likely they would be severely disciplined for failing to act as decisively as he had. He also sympathized with their backgrounds and how they had been used. Perhaps with time, he mused, they would see the wisdom of Syncretism, and all the hurt would end. Yes, this is the grave of a world, he thought sadly, a monument to humanity's stupidity.

Art's thoughts were interrupted by the receiver suddenly commanding the crew's attention. *Someone or something on Sangraal II was sending out a signal!*

8

LANDING

Which are you drinking? The water or the wave?
—John Fowles, *The Magus*

All *stations maintain full alert,* Ben commanded on the link. *Stand by to leave.*

Safe behind the ship's screening devices, Greg's trained mind studied the signal, analyzing it for some evidence of deceit or some attempt to control or destroy his mind. It was a standard precaution but one which Greg employed with an almost personal vengeance.

"It can't be," Art said in amazement. "That planet is dead." He continued his analysis of the signal. "It must be some sort of strange reflection of our comm signal."

Turn off our recon signal, Ben commanded through the link in response to Art's comment.

Art quickly cut the multifarious recon communications signal, but he was dismayed to discover that the planetary signal continued unabated.

"Someone must be alive down there," Richard said in a voice that barely concealed his excitement. "Perhaps there are survivors in the tunnels."

"It's probably some natural emission from that energy sink," Art replied. "Maybe our signals or the ship have triggered something." He almost added, "...just as the *Leos* did."

"Let's stop the hypothesizing and try to get some data," Ben said coldly. "Art, have you found its location?"

"Yes," Art replied. "It's in the northern hemisphere on the side facing us. The signal seems to be totally random. There is no spatial or temporal order to it. It's not even aimed at us or at anything in particular."

"It's just like the signals the Fleet has been receiving," Greg added somberly.

"Scan the area," Ben ordered. "Find the source of the signal."

Art mentally closed in on the area of the signals. He raced over the blackened surface until, through the scanner, he hovered over a narrow, twisted channel amidst the contorted, rocky landscape. The channel, which began at one end in a relatively open space bordered by high vertical walls that housed a large shallow cavern, ran its crooked course over more than five kilometers, disappearing finally into the black desert as a narrow slice. He knew the signal was coming from this cut in the surface, but he could not find a source. The channel seemed as dead as the rest of Sangraal II. The sides ranged from four meters to over thirty meters high, and they were as jagged and treacherous as the surrounding milieu. He decided that this channel was nothing more than the result of whatever had happened to Sangraal II. Perhaps it was the hollows of a collapsed tunnel. He had seen other rifts like this.

The signal continued.

Art began a detailed examination of the channel. He looked as closely as the scanners permitted at the rocks, the sides of the channel, the rocky, ash-covered floor and the tops of the walls. He strained at each stony particle, and he tried to probe the vesicularly appearing debris of the slag that was Sangraal II.

The signal continued.

Art fought to maintain control of his temper as he gradually narrowed his search down to the one end of the channel which was particularly tapered and twisted. He "saw" that a human could barely get through such a place.

The signal continued.

The end of the channel in this direction was marked by a large, angular, black rock. He could not probe around this rock, yet the signal was very strong in this area. He suspected that the source lay somewhere near the rock. Damn this energy-sucking planet! he thought angrily. He started to examine the rock and its environs.

The signal ceased.

Ben and Art cursed simultaneously.

"Keep searching," Ben ordered. "There must be something down there. Rich, is everything still okay here?"

"Yes," Richard replied.

Art continued to probe the tortuous, magmatic-appearing trench. "Nothing," he said bitterly.

Greg shifted his weight in his recliner and pressed the fingers of his left hand against his head. He seemed to be concentrating on something. "Ben," Greg said quietly, his eyes still closed in concentration, "that was a Fleet Alert signal. Just like the others."

Art glanced sharply at Greg. "That's a lot of crap, Greg. I received those signals—they were just so much static. A bunch of comm noise."

"Damnit, it's the truth," Greg responded angrily, his eyes on Art. "Go through my analysis if you don't believe me."

Art and Ben traced Greg's steps through the computer. Art's eyes never left Greg's.

Richard, busy with the ship alert, glanced over at Greg, "True?"

"True," Greg said simply.

"It all checks out," Ben said.

"Coincidence," Art snorted. "Greg had to pull every trick in communications theory to come up with that Alert signal. Just as Sedmak must have done. There's a natural explanation for that signal." He looked at Ben. "You're treating this as some kind of Siren."

"In more ways than one, Art," Ben replied. "We're going to land."

Art's mouth opened as he struggled to say something in this moment of disbelief. "Ben, you're violating your promise. You can't land."

Ben glared at Art. Ben's face was hard, and his mouth had an angry, tight set to it. "I said I wouldn't land unless something unusual occurred. I'm taking this ship down. It's up to you to keep your part of our bargain."

"Damnit, Ben, this is insane!" Art exclaimed angrily. "For all we know there's nothing down there. Greg could have read too much into that emission. And even if there is something down there, we could endanger the whole Federation by landing."

Greg looked hard at Art. "I didn't read too much into that emission. You checked me out. Did I bias the conclusion?"

Art said nothing.

"Well, damnit, did I?"

Art gave a slight shake of his head. "It doesn't matter whether or not you did. The point is that we have no business being here. That signal could be a trap. It could be a cover for some kind of scan of this ship. I say let's get out of here."

Richard momentarily submerged his monitoring to his automatic subconscious level. "Suppose the *Leos* or its crew is down there. Do you propose to leave them?"

"There's nothing down there," Art answered in a loud, angry tone. "You've been over the planet as much as I have. Nothing lives there."

"What about the caves?" Richard asked in an equally angry tone.

"There's no cave where the signals originated," Art retorted.

"Behind the rock," Richard said sharply.

Art breathed a sigh of exasperation. "Hell, who knows what's under or behind that rock or any rock on this hellhole. There's no device on the surface for sending signals. And no signals are going to penetrate that surface."

"That's why I intend to land," Ben said with a determined voice. "We searched the planet from up here and found nothing. I intend to put our scanners on the surface, in that trench, and we'll search it from one end to the other."

"That channel is over five kilometers long," Art said. "With our poor scanning capability we could spend days down there and still not find anything."

"Art, listen to Ben," Greg said in a placating tone. "Suppose we forget the artificial rules, as he asked us. Can't you acknowledge that there is something unusual about that channel? If we could determine what it is, then perhaps we can finally forget Sangraal II."

"Greg, you continue to amaze me," Art said disdainfully. "I still remember the so-called individualistic outworlder, the champion of the ideal of going your own way. Now here you are supporting a treasonous, militaristic clique bent on destroying the very freedoms you profess to believe in. You're contradicting yourself."

Greg looked at him with eyes that seemed filled with some sad knowledge. "Art, either way I go, I am damned," he said quietly. "I've thought about what you and Ben said. Ben is asking me to betray my government. You are asking me to betray humanity. I have no choice. I say we land."

"I hope you realize what you're saying," Art said bitterly. "The flight recorder has copied your little speech. You're now as guilty as Ben."

"But not for the same reasons," Greg said. "And that is what is important to me."

The crew sat silently for a few moments. Finally, Art shook his head in apparent exasperation and looked up at Ben. "If you must investigate further," he said in a quietly earnest tone, "then send down some robots or beam someone down. Don't put the whole ship down there."

"I can't risk it," Ben replied. "You've seen how that surface sucks up our signals and distorts sensory images. The robots may not accomplish anything, and I don't want to lose one of us because of interference with our teleporter beam over this range. The ship is the only thing strong enough to make it down, so, like it or not, we'll have to go as a group."

Ben led them through the landing sequence. The link was now in full operation—four minds fused with the computer to monitor and control the

Odyssey. Scanners and sensors continued to probe the Sangraal star system and its second planet.

Ben manipulated the fields within the ergon impeller and redirected the *Odyssey* from its orbit. The ship moved effortlessly and silently into a path that enabled it to make an exploratory swing around the surface at close range. As the ship neared the atmosphere of Sangraal II, Ben placed the ergon impeller in a standby mode and activated the invisible pellor beams to guide the *Odyssey* across the planet. Ben closely watched all flight indicators, making sure that the danger of which no one spoke but all knew would not arise, the very real danger that the pellor beams would not be sufficient to enable them to land safely on this strange planet.

Quietly but swiftly, like some spirit from another dimension, the *Odyssey* dived into the depths of the misty atmosphere surrounding Sangraal II. The ship shimmered continuously as its shields opened up a path through the ash-filled, murky air. Closer and closer the *Odyssey* approached the surface, while its scanners and sensors probed at a rapid rate.

Ben leveled the ship off when it reached about eight kilometers above the surface. He was satisfied that the pellor rays could do their job. The *Odyssey* glided ghostlike through the swirling mist, while below and unseen except by the scanners, stretched the blackened hulk of a planet. But for the faint glow from the *Odyssey* and its shields, the planet was a grim world of darkness. Only the occasional motion of the atmosphere with its quickly concealed electrical storms and the infrequent sizzling of water hitting the mysterious crust below yielded any auditory sounds for the scanners.

Greg felt an almost womblike sense of security in the *Odyssey.* He was too busy monitoring the ship to be more than peripherally aware of the new enhanced view of Sangraal II, but that awareness was sufficient to let him know now more than ever that Sangraal II was an alien, inimical place to be exploring. Despite the surface temperature, the planet brought up long-forgotten terror tales about cold, misty homes of the dead and their hideous killers. The blue skies and occasional green vegetation of Ziol were not here to comfort him. A feeling of apprehension sprang from deep within him, and he could not immediately trace its causes. He knew that he would have to be ever vigilant for danger, and he also knew that he could trust nothing on this planet. Automatically, as he had been trained to do, he considered every conceivable sequence of events, and he reviewed the contingency actions needed to protect the ship and its crew. He knew the others were doing the same, and he felt certain that Ben would have a ready response for anything that happened.

His concern about the planet and what it could do to them were not sufficient to distract him from his tasks. Through training he had learned how to
control his emotions and bodily processes. Yet, he allowed a certain amount of
emotional concern to remain as a sort of backdrop to his main mental activities. In this manner, his feelings fueled his alertness and cast his activities into
a surrealistic light, giving the ship's systems the appearance of functioning in
an unreal fashion. And he sensed that they, too, were aware of a feeling of dread
and were responding to it as if activated by a living nervous system. He compared the whole link-derived scene with standing on Ziol, but a changed Ziol,
as if Ra had shifted its spectral emittance so that the light, instead of yellow,
was now dark and foreboding, and the trees and rocks and deserts looked eerie
and unnatural.

Are we go for landing? Ben flashed through the link.

Three affirmative acknowledgments greeted his mental question.

In stillness, the *Odyssey* rapidly descended toward the blackened ground
until it hovered just above the mysterious channel which had beckoned them
with its phantom signal.

Art, probe that area around the narrow end of the channel, Ben ordered
through the link.

In a few moments, Art flashed back, *Still nothing.*

Stay alert, Ben added. He adjusted the pellor beams to allow the *Odyssey* to
drop quickly into the open space at the wide end of the channel. He held the
ship afloat a few meters above the channel bottom and cautioned the crew to
probe carefully and be ready for an instant departure. But the scanners only
recorded the lifeless, uncaring regolith, which had become so horribly familiar
to the crew. Satisfied that there was no immediate danger, Ben sent out a disguised signal through the flight recorder to place the monitor in a temporary
holding cycle. Then he moved the *Odyssey* into the bulbous cavern and carefully positioned it above the cavern floor. The cavern floor was below the floor
of the channel, making it possible for Ben to obtain almost total concealment
for the *Odyssey* by moving it back from the cavern entrance while keeping it
out of direct line of sight. He tried to complete the concealment by using the
tractor beam to maneuver rocks into a camouflaging pattern about the
entrance, but the rocks remained unmoved.

We'll leave it here, Ben signaled. *We can tolerate the drain of this soil acting
upon the pellor beam, but I don't want to chance putting stresses on the shields at
this time. We may need them for other purposes.* Ben signaled for a status report
from each of his crew. Assured that everything was operating as designed, he
signaled back, *Rich, stay on the link. You're in charge. Keep all systems, including
the beams and engine, in standby status. Art, I'd like you and Greg to join me out-*

side. After receiving three acknowledgments (Richard's somewhat reluctantly for he also wanted to go outside), Ben broke his connection with the telepathic link and rotated his recliner to face the rest of the crew. Aloud, he said, "Art, I want you to go through all the procedures and make the necessary preparations for our trip outside. Make sure we can get in and out without contaminating ourselves or this planet. Get our gear ready for beaming outside. Be sure that everything is protected. Have our new shield suit belts ready and link them to the shipboard scanners so we can 'see' what is going on when we get outside. Greg and I will meet you at the teleporter unit."

Greg completed a post-landing systems check of the ergonic neuroglia of the *Odyssey,* then he joined Art in readying their equipment to beam off the ship. Ben arrived five minutes later to oversee the disembarkation procedures, including the donning of the new suit belts with the separately powered nullors. Ben pointed out that the nullor provided a suicide device. He grinned slyly. "A little extra bonus—in case the suit shield fails." They each knew that Council policy dictated that any explorer who was captured or in any danger of compromising the Federation was to annihilate himself or herself by collapsing the suit shield. This was just one of many ways of preventing any information about humanity from coming under alien ken. Knowing that he had a redundant means of self-destruction and no identifiable enemies on the planet, Ben decided against activating the timer for the automatic destruct system. Art refused the new belt Ben offered him. He looked disgusted. Turning to Greg, Ben said, "Take Art's belt—just in case."

Step by step they followed the disembarking procedures: first, the activation of the suits and a link with the ship, then the transmission of the exploratory equipment and finally…

We're going out now, Ben mentally stated to Richard. *Watch the shields.* Turning to Art and Greg, he said aloud, "Well do a quick but thorough search of this channel, starting at the other end where the source of the signal seemed to be located. Stay in sight of one another and be damned careful. Rich has orders to maintain comm silence unless it is absolutely necessary to do otherwise, and he is to leave at the slightest hint of trouble, so we'll be on our own once we beam out. Any questions?"

Neither Art nor Greg spoke.

"I'll go first," Ben continued. "Wait for my signal before joining me."

Ben stepped past Art into the teleporter unit and with an expressionless face vanished from the ship.

How is he? Greg flashed to Richard.

Okay. No problems. He's looking around now.

Several minutes passed. Art and Greg waited impatiently while Richard mentally fed them images of Ben exploring the cavern and then moving into the clearing which marked their end of the channel. His every act followed the established Federation guidelines and precautions for an initial planetary exploration.

When he finished his initial examination of his new environment, Ben asked Art to beam a rock inside the *Odyssey*. Art used a tractor beam to maneuver a shielded container into position in the teleporter unit. He and Greg looked on expectantly as the teleporter energized.

The container remained empty.

Shit! You can't move them and you can't transmit them! was Richard's only comment.

Greg smiled mischievously at Art. "Looks as if it was a good idea to land instead of taking a chance on beaming someone down here."

Art stared sullenly at Greg, his face a mask of defiant darkness. He did not speak.

The ensuing silence sucked at Greg's ears until he almost wished they had not agreed to help conceal the *Odyssey* by avoiding communications from the ship.

Greg was relieved when Ben finally guessed the problem and signaled Art to teleport from the ship. Now it was his turn.

He paused for a moment to glance at the room and equipment around him. Beaming off a ship was almost as uncanny to Greg as entering metaspace. He activated the teleporter. He felt a tingling sensation of decomposition and recomposition, even though he knew that his imagination was at work again. All he saw was the almost instantaneous exchange of surroundings. Like some sort of montage, the teleporter was simply replaced with the stark walls of the cavern outside.

The link from the belt through the relay unit to the special scanners on board the *Odyssey* was complete. With the aid of the scanners, Greg could "see" clearly around him; it was as if he were standing in the beautiful yellow glow of Ra. Because of the dusty atmosphere, it was a limited vision at best, but even this provided some comfort. Behind and above him was the *Odyssey,* a slightly ellipsoidal, pulsing interaction of powerful fields invisibly suspended above the cavern floor.

Greg "looked" at his new surroundings. He expected to feel some awe or apprehension at this unreal world; instead, his mind simply observed and cat-alogued facts. He was fascinated by his detachment which made this planet seem like others he had been on. Perhaps, he thought as he touched his belt, the suit is responsible for my detachment. If I could really feel this world, I might become more aware of it. He disliked the stimulants and controls built into the belt, because he felt they hampered the natural functioning of his mind. He quickly deactivated these devices, hoping that by doing so he would be brought into empathy with his new environment.

The walls of the cavern, like the rest of Sangraal II, were a dark gray that verged on black. The walls showed every evidence of having once been molten. He had the feeling that he was standing inside the remains of some gigantic bubble forged from the melted soil of Sangraal II.

He "looked" at the ground beneath his feet. It seemed to consist of firmly packed pumice, ashes and cinders. The dust did not appear to cling to anything except itself. Here and there were rocks of various sizes. He knelt and examined some of them. They were confusing, as Art had concluded. At first glance, they looked like pyroclasts. Their density did not preclude such a conclusion, but closer examination revealed many unusual features. Certainly, he surmised, they had been molten and probably explosively formed. But they refused to admit to any probing. Some of the rocks were quite large, as if they had been formed by freezing large clots of magmatic material. Many of the rocks showed a frothy porosity, which indicated they had once been charged with gases.

Greg walked up the inclined floor of the cavern and stepped into the opening outside. As the others had indicated, there was no sign of anything hostile. He watched as Art and Ben sorted out the equipment. They had already rolled several of the larger fragmented rocks into the mouth of the cavern. Peripherally, he was also aware of their initial discussion of the failure to transmit the rock selected by Ben.

Greg glanced back at the walls which bordered the clearing and the channel ahead. The walls were steep, rising almost vertically to the blackened milieu several meters above him, and they showed the lavalike markings of heavy scallops. Like the walls of the cavern, the ones outside in the channel appeared to have been molten at one time, as if something had furiously scorched its way through this spot, leaving only a bubble and a channel to mark its path. He marveled at the energy necessary to accomplish this change in a planet.

The air was filled with mist and ash, but he had no trouble "seeing" through this material at short range. If he tried to "look" at distant objects down the channel or at the turbulent sky above, he discovered the ash-filled mist gradually overwhelmed the scanners. He had to put forth a special effort to overcome the clouding of his "vision." He did not care to think what it would be like in such a place without a shield suit and the special scanners. Aside from the poisonous vapors, there would be no light—literally a black death.

He walked over to where Ben and Art were working. In this uncanny place, his two crewmates with their shield suits seemed like apparitions superimposed on their strange environment. In a sense, he supposed they were no different from the *Odyssey* in this preternatural world—they were mere fieldlike alien manifestations of mythical disembodied spirits whose true physical presences were somewhere else.

Got your bearings? Ben asked through his suit link. By now all contact was direct between the three of them or was made through the disguised relay unit.

Yes, Greg thought in reply. *Need any help?*

Not right now, Ben answered. *Let's test our nullors and then move out.*

Art stayed with the equipment as Ben and Greg walked to the far side of the clearing outside the cavern. Greg noted that Art was still "watching" them with the same look of disgust he had shown when they first donned the special belts.

Greg felt a little uneasy about using a nullor. He had used them in training but never in a real situation. In the case of these death-dealing devices, Greg was in total sympathy with the Federation edict prohibiting their use around living organisms. To Greg, the nullor represented the closest thing to the long-sought-after ultimate weapon. There was no undoing the damage once a nullor had been used. In theory, they could be made large enough to destroy anything or everything.

Try it on the wall, Ben thought.

Greg instinctively pointed his right hand at the wall, although it was not necessary to aim the nullor in that fashion. Was he afraid he could not control it, or did he want it removed as far as possible from him? He flinched mentally as he brought out of his mind the specific command he had learned for this special belt.

He started as a brilliant ray seared its way from the shield around his hand to the wall at which he pointed. The air crackled. Greg was momentarily surprised by this unforeseen reaction. He knew the nullors were *controlled* destructive devices, and he had only intended to nullify the wall and nothing else; therefore, only the wall, not the air, should have been affected. Then he quickly realized that the energy absorbent ash in the air was responsible for the occurrence of the ray. In some manner, the ash was interfering with the nullor to the extent that the belt power he had used to map a part of the wall onto null-space was forced to visibly bridge the gap between him and the wall. Damn planet, he thought. Nothing is normal here! In spite of the intervening atmosphere, where the beam touched it the wall instantly flashed into a brilliant white spot. He quickly cut the nullor, feeling both a little disturbed at its use and worried about possible damages. He did not know if these feelings resulted from his own beliefs or from those superimposed on him by the Federation.

The white spot vanished with the cessation of the nullor. Greg could only stare in wonder at the undamaged wall. Although his suit sensors had already given him the results of the nullor test, he instinctively walked over to the wall and touched it with a shielded, sensor-fed hand. *This stuff is impervious to anything,* he flashed on the link. *The suit says it's no warmer than before.*

Was that full strength? Ben asked.

Yes.

That should demonstrate that the safest place for the Odyssey *is inside the cavern,* Ben's thoughts flashed over the link. *I would like to take some of this stuff back with us. I'll make another attempt to get a sample when we return.*

Greg moved out of the way while Ben checked out his nullor. When he finished, Ben asked Greg to check the belt meant for Art. Greg did so, but he felt no better at having to repeat the unpleasant operation.

Feeling a little sick? Ben asked on a short-range mental link meant only for Greg.

I'm okay.

I just thought the Fleet conditioning might be getting to you. You have to work to overcome it. Well, let's get going.

Greg followed Ben back to Art, who was standing by the equipment. Art said and thought nothing to either of them, but he did not hide an expression of abhorrence. Greg felt a momentary pang of guilt at this look, then he remembered why he had decided to come this far and quickly shrugged off the guilty feeling. He had a stunnor in his suit and had no plans to use the nullor except as a last, desperate measure. They had done no damage by using the nullors, so why should Art care?

Equipment okay? Ben asked.

Yes, replied Art's thought.

Okay, let's get started before we run out of time on the monitor, Ben continued. *Art, you take the relay unit. Greg and I will take the rest of the equipment. We'll stay on foot in order to conserve power and to gain some protection from the channel. Rich, for your benefit, we'll stop about midway where the channel starts to wind enough to block communications. We'll set up the relay unit near the top of the wall to cover us the rest of the way. If we have to, we'll use reflectors or ourselves to finish the job of relaying messages back here and scanner support to us.*

As expected, there was no acknowledgment from the concealed ship.

The three men picked up their equipment and carefully covered traces of their presence. Then they left the clearing for the narrower channel.

Almost as soon as he entered the channel, Greg felt confined. The ash-laden mist swirled above the tops of the ominously dark walls, almost cutting them off at the top, leaving the walls and weird pumiceous floor of the channel to complete their prison.

They walked in silence. Ben was in the lead, Art was in the middle and Greg followed in the end position. Greg wondered if Ben had again maneuvered the two of them so that Art, whom he obviously no longer trusted, was hemmed in. Greg dismissed his thought. He was not certain what he would do if Art did try to disrupt their trek.

Despite the omnidirectional data provided by his suit sensors, Greg found himself "looking" often at the tops of the walls. He regretted that Sedmak had been unable to provide them with concealing screens. He felt vulnerable against an attack from above. He had grown complacent about the walls and floor because he could perceive no danger coming from material that was impervious to a nullor.

Like Art, Greg was puzzled about the walls. They showed no internal structure, as if they had been forged from a uniform lump of molten material.

Ben stopped about midway through the channel. With the exception of their starting point, the spot he now chose was considerably wider than the rest of the channel, and the walls were higher here. Ahead Greg "saw" that the passageway quickly narrowed and became twisted.

This looks like the best place to leave the relay unit, Ben flashed. *Art, do you think you can conceal the unit near the top of the wall so it can cover us?*

Yes, came the reply.

Greg noted that Art had a look on his face as dark as the walls. He wondered why Ben was trusting him, but he realized that there was nothing Art could do to interfere with the relay unit. Besides, as a skilled planetologist, Art was the likely choice to hide the unit.

You'll have to use your pellor, Ben said mentally. *And you'll have to move the rocks by hand. Be careful.*

Ben and Greg moved back as Art turned on his pellor and slowly rose up in the air.

It's running full power and I'm barely moving, Art thought over the link.

The ground must be taking up most of your power, Ben thought in return. *Watch your supply. If anything looks amiss, get down quickly.*

Ben sent another thought message to Art on the link: *When you get to the top, try to anchor yourself physically to save power.*

Greg watched as Art slowly reached the top of the wall, over thirty meters above him. Art quickly scrambled among some rocks and began setting up the relay unit. Greg saw Art moving rocks around to shield the relay unit. Periodically, Art took sightings to make certain the unit could still transmit to the ship and to the spaceborne monitor while covering them for the rest of their journey. He reactivated the link with the monitor.

Art started to come back over the side.

Got it? Ben asked mentally, seeking formal confirmation.

Yes.

Art activated his pellor again and stepped off the top of the wall. Suddenly, his suit flickered and he fell. He quickly reached for the sheer wall beside him. The suit came on again. *Losing power,* he flashed through the link.

Take the other belt to him, Ben commanded Greg. *I'll put my suit tractor beam on him and try to bring him down. Art, be ready to anchor yourself to the wall because I don't know how good my tractor beam will be with the power drain on my suit.*

Greg turned on his pellor and started the same maddeningly slow ascent that Art had made. He managed to increase his rate of ascent slightly by using the extra belt, even though the channel floor seemed to be sucking the life out of the two pellor rays almost as fast as it had out of one. He kept his eyes fixed upward on the figure enclosed in the flickering shield. Through his suit sensors, he was aware that Ben now held Art in a tractor beam. Greg was also aware that at his present rate of ascent, he did not have the necessary power to use either of his tractor beams effectively.

As suddenly as it had happened before, Greg "saw" Art's suit flicker off—*only this time it stayed off!* Greg watched in helpless frustration as his crewmate frantically and uselessly grabbed for the wall. Then Art fell to the life-consuming black ground below.

9

FAUNA

Prepare thyself to die; for I swear by my infernal den, that thou shalt go no farther: here will I spill thy soul.
—John Bunyan, *The Pilgrim's Progress*

*I*t was lying dormant in the dust of a small, concealed basin when the first signals reached *it*. Alert now, *it* savored each delicious sensation as the signals played over the hollow. But *it* did not move. As much as the excitement welled up within *it*, *it* did not allow the smallest hair to flicker.

Absolute stillness. *It* continued to recycle its gases internally through its respiratory tubules. There must be no external motion. Even its environment must behave as if *it* were not hiding here.

It had never known anything like this since the Creators left. *It* knew that this signal was important because it came from above, through the dense atmosphere. Something was coming from out there. Something was coming with those signals which brought such exquisite pleasure.

Like the rocks and ground about *it*, *it* soaked up the signals, relishing them, and *it* felt the juices starting to flow within *it*. Now that *it* was fully conscious, *it* was hungry. But *it* must be patient.

The signals were weak, and at times they almost faded away. But still *it* did not move. *It* knew that *it* could do nothing to bring the signals closer, nothing except remain the seemingly dormant creature *it* had been.

The signals weakened and then rapidly got stronger. The intensity was increasing at such a fast rate that its hungry body almost shook from the effects of receiving so much power.

Suddenly, the source was overhead. *It* was vibrantly alive inside with furious activity. *It* was almost overcome by the sudden direct influx of energy. Never had *it* experienced a source of prey like this. Energy emanated from the source, which seemed like pure energy. *It* would feed long on this source. Closer, come closer, *it* thought eagerly.

But the source passed by. The source emanations got a little weaker and then suddenly ceased.

It knew that the source had to be on the ground! The rocks and undulating ground cover must have swallowed the energy. The emanations had not weakened perceptibly when they ceased, so the source had to be nearby.

It continued to wait. *It* could not afford to move out too quickly. *It* would frighten the source. *It* wanted the source to feel that everything was normal. There was plenty of time to feed.

It was relieved that the source had passed over so quickly and had then vanished. Now *it* would not have to contend with the others, as they would be less able than *it* to trace the source to its destination.

Then *it* decided to act.

It opened its eight cognizers, the only parts of its body exposed above the dust, then *it* actively surveyed its surroundings. It was no longer necessary to rely solely upon the hazy sensory data received through the hard outer shell of its body. With its cognizers *it* could "see" through the mist and sense the same spectrum as that of the enemies of the Creators. Without moving, *it* could look down, ahead and up. Its body provided sensory coverage in all directions.

Slowly, *it* unfurled its four pairs of walking legs from beneath the front part of its body. *It* stretched them out, flexing each of the seven segments on each leg. *It* paid particular attention to the clawlike appendages joined to the seventh segment of each leg. These claws were useful in moving over the rough ground and in holding its prey.

It felt a tingle as the hairs and serrated bristles unfolded through the hard covering on its legs. *It* felt additional sensory data coming in through these hairs and bristles. The bristles also served as accessory claws.

It felt the power in its massive legs as *it* slowly raised its large, dimerous body off the ground. As *it* rose from the ground, *it* left a small nodule buried in the ash, which *it* had learned to do during the Creation. Later, if the feeding went well, *it* would retrieve the nodule. *It* stood there for a moment surveying its environs from within the protective barrier of the sclerous materials that covered its body and legs. Its body fluids were in movement everywhere: in both parts of its body, in the narrow pedicellar stem separating them, and in its appendages. *It* felt good to be active once more.

It opened its trachea to the respiratory devices located in the second, or posterior, part of its body. These devices brought in the rich, ash-filled misty air about *it* and allowed *it* to cleanse its respiratory system by purging the gases *it* had used while lying dormant. *It* felt renewed by the fresh, warm mist of dust coursing through its body again.

It paused momentarily for one final examination of its surroundings. *It* felt no signals and sensed no activity within its range of perception. *It* felt secure in moving.

It moved its saltigrade legs slowly at first, being very alert to possible detection. *It* must not be discovered until *it* had the source in its power. *It* would try to mentally control any organic material the source contained.

It was fully aware of each movement of its legs. *It* had the flexibility to move easily over the jagged landscape, and *it* could balance its entire body on any leg.

Its initial motion produced no detectable response from anything beyond the hollow, where *it* lay well concealed. Slowly, stealthily, *it* began to crawl out. Its body moved just barely above the ground, and its segmented legs curved in support of its motion.

The ground around the hollow was particularly rough, contributing to the concealment of the ground source *it* had sought earlier. *It* moved effortlessly in the direction of the airborne source, alert to anything that might interfere with its goal.

It knew no fear because *it* had never known fear. *It* knew how to conceal itself when necessary. *It* had a scleritic covering which had easily protected *it* from the enemies of the Creators, and *it* had no natural enemies. Its fangs and jaws had readily penetrated the few sources *it* discovered after the Creators had left. *It* had minimal synaptic delays and could respond instantaneously to any stimuli. If need be, *it* could activate repellant devices that gave *it* the advantage.

In short, *it* ruled supreme.

Instantly, *it* froze. Its cognizers automatically shut, and its body covered the exposed parts. *It* sensed a small source ahead. *It* must not move.

Again, *it* waited patiently. This was not the enormously powerful source that had come through the air, but the source had enough power to greatly stimulate its senses. *It* felt hunger well up within *it*. *It* wanted this small source, *it* wanted this rejuvenating flux of energy to course through its body and bring nourishment to *it*. Perhaps this small source would come to *it*.

It sensed that the source varied in strength and was therefore moving among the rocks. But the average source strength did not grow stronger or weaker, so *it* concluded that the small source was not moving toward *it* or away from *it*.

Then the source suddenly ceased. But *it* did not move immediately toward the position the source had occupied. *It* knew that *it* would soon close in on its quarry, so there was no need to alarm the prey by making a sudden move. *It* continued to wait.

To Greg, the whole scene was like a slow-motion nightmare: Art appeared to fall in a lazy somersault to the ground below. One part of Greg's mind seemed aloof, as if he were a dispassionate observer. Another part of his mind was filled with concern and a will to action. As soon as he saw Art start to fall, and when he knew Art's suit could not save him, Greg reversed the pellor and began to descend. He was tempted to cut the pellor so that he could simply fall to the channel floor, thereby getting to Art sooner, but he decided not to trust his suit to protect him beyond minimal limits on this unnatural planet. He silently cursed himself for not starting his ascent closer to Art's position. If he had, he thought he might have been able to maneuver into position to catch Art. However, the dispassionate part of his mind told him to forget his anger, since only marginal power was available for such activity. He had channeled so much power into gaining altitude that he did not have enough to operate his suit tractor beam or the beam on the spare belt. He felt totally frustrated. With two belts, he was able only to leisurely levitate while isolating himself from his treacherous surroundings.

He saw Art hit the ground limply, his legs striking the ground first. Some of the mysterious dust moved about, but the main motion Greg observed below was Ben leaping on his own pellor ray across the channel to where Art lay motionless.

There was no further sign of the small source. *It* opened its all-sensing cognizers and studied the milieu carefully. In an instant, *it* was running rapidly toward a small cleft in the twisted landscape. Once in the cleft, *it* concealed itself, leaving only the disguised pedipalpi, which projected from the front of its body, to rest above the cleft for sensory purposes. *It* had no concern about its pedipalpi getting trapped because the pedipalpi, like its other appendages, could be autotomized and still not hinder its overall functioning or movement. *It* was worried that the source might be suspicious; *it* did not want the source to return and investigate because *it* had barely had time to conceal itself when *it* first sensed the small source.

In this cleft *it* was closer to where the small source had been, so *it* was content to wait a little longer.

It considered what *it* knew about sources. *It* had learned that sources tended to come in groups: where *it* found one, *it* usually found others. *It* supposed that this source had companions. *It* even considered the possibility that the small, mobile source was somehow related to the large, airborne source. *It* was not given to deep reasoning, but *it* reacted to the obvious: a great deal of time had passed since *it* last saw a source and then suddenly a massive source arrived through the atmosphere, followed soon after by a small, ground-based source. The two events must be related; *it* was capable of some simple reasoning, and *it* suspected that the small, mobile source could lead *it* to the larger, airborne source. *It* had to be careful not to act too quickly, otherwise *it* would lose the larger prey.

Except in the final days of the Creation, when sources were less plentiful, they had not fought against *it* or its kind. *It* was vaguely aware that near the end some sources offered resistance by unknown means which caused pain. Generally, however, its experience taught *it* that sources were defenseless repositories of energy more prone to running (if they were mobile) than staying and facing *it* or its kind. Because of this fact and the nature of the surface of its world, there was no need for special weapons. Its strength was sufficient.

It also knew that there was an element of danger in its present pursuit. The large, airborne source was different and could conceivably counterattack. But *it* was not overly concerned. Was *it* not invincible? Had not the Creators made this world for *it* and the others? *It* ruled supreme here.

Soon, very soon, *it* would continue to stalk its prey by approaching slowly, ever so slowly, with its sensory system alert to everything around it. Then at the right moment, *it* would extend its front legs, make a sudden jump and devour its prey.

Ben was crouched, leaning over the prone figure of Art Cooke. Greg was aware that Ben was ministering to Art with special renascent methods derived from the medicator in his suit belt. He was also aware of a periodic flickering of Art's suit.

Ben glanced up at him. *Bring me the spare belt quickly!*

Greg decided to forget his caution. He quickly cut the pellor beam and fell to the dusty floor below him. He braced himself for the impact just in case the shield did not provide full protection, and he positioned himself for a safe distribution of the landing stresses. He hit the dust harder than he should have with the shield, rolled once and bounced quickly to his feet.

He felt a fleeting pain, but the suit was taking care of him now. He knew his abrupt contact with the ground had put a temporary strain on the shield suit but not enough to deprive him of total protection.

Ben was kneeling beside Art, and Greg ran quickly to them. At a nod from Ben, Greg knelt beside Art and made the necessary arrangements for getting the spare belt around his crewmate.

How is he? Greg asked on the link.

Still too early to tell. I've applied the medicator. Let's see how he responds with the new suit. I think the old belt can mend itself now that it is relieved of full operation. Ben moved away slightly. *Take over for me while I give Rich a quick report.* Greg nodded his assent as Ben stood up.

Ben's mental communication flowed through the link, a stream of thought-words and thought-images. *Rich, I assume you've monitored this whole episode. As you know, Art got the relay unit into place. It seems to be working because we can still 'see' what is going on.*

Somehow his suit was drained of some power, possibly from the combination of trying to stay shielded in this damned air and running a pellor beam. I don't know for sure. You can check it out by replaying the data. I tried to stop him with my tractor beam but when he touched the wall, everything shorted out. My belt couldn't support the shield and the tractor beam under those conditions. The whole place is draining us. Everything has to be done slowly and carefully, one sequence at a time.

We've got Art under full treatment now. There's nothing more we can do at this time. I think his suit may have momentarily come on just before he hit because outwardly he doesn't look too bad. He's taken in some of the atmosphere, though, and because of this he may have latent internal injuries. No sign of shock. Life support is improving.

We'll remain until he regains consciousness and then decide whether to proceed. I don't see any problem in staying right here.

Nothing! *It* sensed nothing. Its pedipalpi strained for a sign that the source was still near. But *it* sensed nothing. *It* speculated that the jumbled landscape which shielded *it* might also be shielding the source. But *it* did not worry. *It* had been over this ground many times in search of an elusive ground source and *it* knew that there was no escape. There were no tunnels near the place where the small source had been. Ahead lay a large rift that ended in a large cavern. The source must have gone into the rift, *it* reasoned. If so, the source was helpless because *it* would command the ground above the rift. If everything went right, this source would lead *it* to other sources.

It pulsed internally in anticipation of the forthcoming feast. Its legs were poised and ready for the resumption of its trek across the rough ground between *it* and the rift. Its claws extended, ready to snatch its prey.

Art stirred slightly and sighed as he consciously took control of his breathing. He opened his eyes and "looked" at Greg and then at Ben. His color looked good to Greg.

"How do you feel?" Greg asked. Ben quickly knelt beside Art.

"Okay. What happened?"

"Your suit apparently failed," Greg answered. "Ben thinks it couldn't take the strain of supporting both the pellor and the shield. He tried to stop your fall with his own tractor beam but that shorted to the channel wall when you touched it."

How are the life-support readings? Ben mentally asked.

"Everything is normal," Greg answered orally. Turning to Art, he added, "You should feel as good as new."

"Except for a little mental disorientation, I feel all right," Art said. "Thanks for not using the link to communicate. I need a moment to get my thoughts in order." He smiled wryly. "After all, it's not every day one gets a second chance at life."

Greg stood up and stretched. He stepped back a few paces to "look" back along the channel in the direction of the *Odyssey. Looks good, Rich,* he thought quickly.

Art propped himself up on his elbows and "looked" around. His gaze came to rest on his belt.

"I thought my suit failed," Art said quietly as he shifted his eyes to Ben.

"It did," Ben answered warily.

"Then what is *this?*" Art asked in a surprised tone, pointing to the jeweled belt encircling his waist.

"The spare," Ben replied simply.

"Oh, hell!" Art grimaced. "You've given me that damned nullor!"

Time was running out. Soon *it* would have to return to the basin and reclaim the concealed nodule.

It decided to act. *It* moved quickly up and out of the small cleft. Its eight legs pumped up and down, forward and backward in rapid sequence. The landscape skimmed by without drawing its attention. *It* stayed low to the ground for maximum concealment, blending naturally and skillfully into its environment.

It climbed easily up ridges and leaped across fissures. The chaotic debris and undulating ground were of no concern to *it. It* moved effortlessly over and around the battered rocks. Only one thought concerned *it* now: ahead in the rift was a source—*food!*

"Damnit, Art, that's all we had," Greg said in an exasperated tone. "Ben couldn't have held you in his suit. Be reasonable—it was either *that* suit or death."

Art glared at Greg but said nothing.

Ben glanced from Greg to Art and then with an uncharacteristic placating tone said, "If you feel strongly about it, Art, we'll return to the ship now and get a belt that doesn't have a nullor. Or we can wait awhile until your old belt repairs itself."

Greg took a deep breath and rocked slightly on his feet in an effort to control himself. He could not believe his ears. Art owed his life to that suit and now he rejected it. Greg looked away from the two men, blotting them out of his mind. He felt as if he was in some sort of abode for the insane. Nothing seemed to make sense. All the rules of logic he had tried to live by were being torn asunder by every action they took on this planet. He wondered how much he could take before becoming as insane as the planet.

A scanner image tore into his brain. He froze, his eyes unconsciously fixed on the wall above him. Some huge, dark shape had just moved into place there! *It had moved into place!* Without the suit's physiological controls, he felt an icy sweat break out over his body. Whatever it was, he knew it was big. He guessed its height at four meters and its length even longer.

Ben! Art! Don't make any sudden moves. There's something above us on top of the wall!

Instinctively, their eyes darted to the top of the wall, even though the scanners had already provided mental images of the shape. No one moved.

Suddenly, like some monstrous Demogorgon, the black shape scurried over the edge and raced vertically down the wall toward them. Before they could move, the awful creature leaped upon them with flaying legs and tearing claws!

10

UNDERGROUND

Even in the first long days of our beginnings we held in our hand
the weapon, an instrument somewhat older than ourselves.
                                  —Robert Ardrey, *African Genesis*

Greg instinctively ducked the vicious grasping claws and tried to move out
of the way of the trampling legs. Burning pain ripped through him as he
darted around one moving serrated leg and hit another. The impact sent him
rolling helplessly through the hot dust across the channel floor. He reeled from
the jolt and the intense pain. His suit filled his mind with warnings of all types.
One warning stood out like a scream: *Penetration! Penetration!*

He winced as he hit the base of a large, pockmarked boulder. His rolling
stopped. A dull ache now added itself to the pain racing through his body. His
suit was badly weakened and provided only a partial barrier. He coughed up a
mixture of foaming blood, phlegm and, to his dread, the deadly black dust. He
felt the icy sweat forming again. Frantically, he wondered whether the dust
would suck the energy from his body before his suit could expel it.

Shouts and screams filled his mind and ears, as visual images from the scanners were lost in the dust stirred up by the battle. He tried to get up, only to
collapse back into the dust. His body ached from the searing torment.
Anxiously, he realized that the suit was not helping. Somehow the creature had
temporarily or perhaps permanently disrupted some of the functions of the
jeweled belt. Since he had been operating without the emotional controls of
the suit, he knew, depending on what had been done to him and despite his
mental conditioning, that he could go into a state of shock.

With an agonizing physical effort, he rolled over just as the scanners penetrated the dust, showing the hideous thing advancing toward Ben's now prone body. The remaining clouds of dust concealed the space behind and beneath the creature, so Greg could not see Art. Even Greg's scanner and sensor data became intermittently fuzzy. The burning pain caused by his impact with the creature's leg grew so intense that he no longer felt the bruises caused by his collision with the boulder.

The only thought in his fevered mind was to gain altitude. He cut his remaining suit functions to a bare minimum and channeled all available power to his pellor. He had to get above this monster to be safe, and he had to do it quickly or the monster would remember where he was.

He needed to reclaim his will to action. He mentally screamed at his suit to move. For the first time in his existence, he felt that his life was in danger. He now knew fear, a chilling fear which catalyzed a deep hatred. He hated that creature! He wanted to destroy it. *He* wanted to be the one to live.

The pellor ray slowly lifted him above the channel floor. His scanner and sensor input diminished rapidly. He twisted around to help his mind overcome its lethargy so it could focus the remaining input on what was happening to his crewmates. The scene he beheld only added to his fear—the creature held a writhing Art to the dusty ground with one leg and had picked Ben up from the dust with its two front appendages. Ben's suit flickered—it was losing power! The creature quickly drew Ben toward what Greg presumed was its jaws.

His hatred and fear reached a blinding emotional peak, coalescing into a sunburst of fury. Instinctively, as if reaching for some Chellean handaxe, Greg fired the nullor. He held the disintegrating ray on the creature as he mentally told the suit to funnel all unneeded power, even from the pellor, into the destructive force he was applying to the demon below him. He knew only one thought: *Die! Die!* His mind seemed to channel this hate-filled death wish into the nullor beam which in turn delivered it to the horrible beast below.

The creature screamed in Greg's mind and dropped the limp form of Ben Wilson. The agony and hate entwined in that scream almost sent Greg's mind recoiling in terror. He could not accept the thought that the creature still lived! It charged toward him, knocking Art out of the way. Greg regretted his choice of taking power away from the pellor ray. He quickly changed the distribution of power to enable him to move upward again. With startling speed, the creature stood upright on its rear two legs and reached out to grab him with its front legs and appendages. The claws tore savagely at him, but he managed to elude them by less than a meter. Like an avenging spider supported by an invisible web of force lines, Greg continued to float above the monster while holding it in his searing nullor beam.

It screamed its terrible fury at him again and then leaped up to catch him. Greg desperately maintained his assault with the nullor beam.

Suddenly, in midair, the creature went limp and collapsed onto the dusty floor below. Greg kept the nullor on the creature as it began to shrivel and the legs began to collapse and coil about the body. Again and again Greg wished death for the creature. He ignored the power drain on his suit. He ignored everything except the urge to kill this thing which had dared to take his life.

Stop it, Greg! Stop it! Art's message became part of the "noise" in his mind.

The creature's body collapsed upon itself at such a speed that it appeared to implode. The final debris of death looked like the environment which had nurtured the original body.

Greg shut off the nullor and allowed the pellor to take him down to the channel floor. He was physically and emotionally exhausted. As he hit the dust below, a wave of nausea and disgust overwhelmed him. He was shaking slightly, and he leaned against a small ashen boulder for support. He felt sick and depressed. His body seemed to have no energy left, not even enough to worry about the intense pain he felt, nor about the possibility that he might still be in danger.

Greg, are you all right?

Greg nodded dumbly to Art's question. He could barely marshal his thoughts to respond. Dimly, he sensed messages being sent back to the *Odyssey* that the danger was over.

He stood there, limply supported by the boulder, for what seemed an indefinite length of time. He was not conscious of anything until his suit told him that it was being given additional power from the outside. A feeling of wellbeing quickly spread through his body.

Greg looked up to see Art and Ben ministering to him by channeling the power from the three remaining suit belts to his belt. Greg saw pain in Ben's face and suspected that Ben had halted his own healing in order to help him.

Feel better? Ben asked.

Yes. Don't worry about me—help yourself.

Ben did not respond. At a nod, he and Art carefully pulled Greg away from the boulder in order to minimize the power drain.

Can you walk? Ben asked.

I think so.

Okay, we're going back to the ship. Pick up everything we brought.

The trip back was an ordeal of stumbling over rocky debris and picking up equipment which his suit could not hold. Greg felt as if it took a lifetime to reach the *Odyssey,* an eternity of slow motion down a never-ending channel of rock shrouded in an ashen gray mist. He was conscious of standing beneath the *Odyssey*, then he was beamed inside.

He awoke in his recliner in the control room. His first sensation was one of vitality and an absence of any pain. His attention was quickly drawn outside of himself by the sound of angry voices.

"That was a stupid thing to do!" It was Art.

"Damnit, we're alive, aren't we?" That was Ben.

Greg opened his eyes. Richard was leaning over him, adjusting the medical controls on his recliner. "Okay?" Richard asked quietly.

Greg nodded. He became aware of the mending operation on his right side. "What are the damages?"

Ben and Art had stopped arguing and were watching him.

"Well, for a starter, you had your side torn open by that friendly native," Richard answered with obvious sarcasm. "You took in quite a bit of poison, which kept your suit working overtime to keep you alive. Also numerous bruises and cuts. But it's all taken care of now."

Greg smiled thinly at Ben and Art. "You two seem to be okay."

Neither one acknowledged his remark. Ben looked at Richard and asked, "How about the other problem?"

"Everything checks out normally. Too early to tell for certain."

Greg looked at Richard. "What other problem?" Greg asked.

Art moved quickly to Greg's recliner. "I'll tell you what other problem," he replied angrily with a finger pointing accusingly at Greg. "Despite my pleas, you broke one of the most sacred rules of the Federation—*you killed another living being!*"

Art's words were like a trigger which released the same nauseous, depressing feeling Greg had experienced outside. He was only peripherally aware of Richard springing to his feet and confronting Art.

"Shut up, damnit!" Richard shouted. "He's got enough problems without your mouth."

Greg could not concentrate on the ensuing argument. Now he understood fully what he had been too numb to know before: *he had killed!* He, Gregory Sheldon, the man who prided himself on his mental control and his belief in the sanctity of life, had deliberately taken the life of another creature. He felt an awful guilt creep into his mind.

He had killed an inhabitant of another planet. He had performed this terrible act despite years of conditioning that life forms should be left alone. He had not stopped to use his stunnor—no! he had chosen to kill. He had, by a conscious effort, overcome all the barriers to such action. *He had killed another being!*

Greg felt the sickness worsen. One part of his mind told him that he had no right to live, that he must be punished. Another part fought back—he wanted to live. This mental battleground soon became littered with learned morality and tangled rationalizations of his actions. He held on to life and forced himself into believing that he was right in killing the creature. Whereas before he sent his hatred into the nullor beam, now, he sent out bolts of thought proclaiming his desire to live. He filled his mind with life-sustaining thoughts, which blotted out depression and guilt. As Coni had done before him, he won his fight to live.

He was aware of a hand on his shoulder. He looked up and saw Ben kneeling beside him. "Got it under control?"

Greg nodded.

"I have a pretty good idea what you're going through," Ben said. "Just remember: it's been programmed into you to feel this way. If you can keep positive thoughts fixed in your mind, it will help you overcome the bad feelings. There's nothing wrong with your mind. What you did out there was right"

Art muttered an obscenity and hurriedly left the control room. Ben glanced after him. "Rich, keep the ship on full alert. I'm going to talk to Art." Ben looked back at Greg. "I want you to rest so your mind and body can continue to heal. We all need some time to think out this situation. We have to make sure there are no more problems." Ben mentally activated a part of the medicator on Greg's recliner and got up to follow Art.

Greg watched him leave. His mind was still troubled and Ben's words had not completely soothed him, nor was he entirely successful in overcoming his Fleet conditioning. He knew that his depression and guilt had deeper roots than what he had been taught to feel, and he suspected that the violence those feelings aroused were learned responses. Out there on the alien dusty floor of that mysterious channel he had known fear and hatred. These forces, which he and his civilization thought were controlled, had broken loose within him, and he was afraid of the awesome torrent of emotional energy. He began to understand the wisdom of Coni's remark on the union of mind and body. He dreaded the realization that his revered intellect could be so easily overwhelmed by intrinsic forces more basic, more primitive and more powerful than he had ever imagined. He was no longer certain that in the final throes of his battle with the creature he was any more advanced or moral than his brutish adversary. This thought was profoundly unsettling, and it was not readily amenable to intellectual rationalization.

He took a deep breath and concentrated on relaxing his body. He knew that Ben had done something to his medicator in order to make him rest. He also sensed the salutronic fields of the medicator continuing to work on his body. He turned his head to look at Richard. His friend was back at work in the link.

Richard smiled at him and signaled with his hand that everything was okay. With that, tension finally left Greg, and he felt more relaxed than he had in a long time. He drifted quickly into a sleep as dark as the landscape outside.

He had one brief dream about Coni. He saw her smiling face surrounded by her long, blonde hair, and he felt himself engulfed by her shining green eyes. It will be good to get home, he thought and was amused by the realization that home was now Earth, where Coni was.

When he regained consciousness, he felt good. His body and mind were alive and refreshed. The recliner was taking care of all his needs.

He saw that Richard was still at his station and that Ben was now also on duty. He glanced over his shoulder but could not see Art. "Anyone care to tell me what has been happening?"

Ben rotated his recliner and faced Greg. "You look and sound like you'll live," Ben said with a smile.

"I hope so." Greg smiled in return. "The question is, do I still have my original mind?"

Ben laughed. "Yes. All we did was fix up your body and let you rest. You took care of the mental part and admirably, I might add. Not too many people could withstand Fleet conditioning as well as you did." He smiled teasingly. "I suppose if I were a dedicated Fleet officer, I'd note your ability to overcome your conditioning and mark you down as a problem." He laughed again. Greg had never seen his ship commander in such a good mood. Ben appeared to be enjoying the trials they had been through.

Richard looked over and smiled.

Ben continued talking in a friendly but serious tone. "You killed that creature, and it was fortunate for Art and me that you did. The creature managed to penetrate my suit and was well on his way to making me an *hors d'oeuvre* when you took care of him. I don't know how you did it. When I last saw you, you were laid open on one side and rolling across the channel floor."

"You and Art must have been hurt."

"Art suffered some deep gashes on his stomach and chest. His suit was only momentarily penetrated because the creature was more interested in you. And I took a few cuts also. But we were able to use what was left of Art's original suit to get our suits back into operation.

"That was quite a feat you performed. You even cut off your medicator to channel power into the nullor. It took a real effort to overcome the built-in interlocks and override the basic functions like medical aid."

"I'm not sure I knew what I was doing out there," Greg said. "And I still don't feel right about it. I should have tried the stunnor first. If that had worked, we, the creature and us, might all be alive now."

"Stop worrying about it," Ben said in a consoling tone. "You didn't have time to try all the options. Don't you remember how long it took to kill that thing? If it took that long with a nullor, think how long a stunnor would take just to knock it out; that is, if a stunnor could have worked on it at all. As it was, that thing almost got you." Ben smiled warmly. "Look at the bright side of it—that leap may have saved all our lives. My guess is the creature had the capability to channel the energy of a nullor or any destructive beam into the planet, much like a giant electrical grounding strap." A monstrous Antaeus, Greg thought to himself. Ben reached out and put his hand on Greg's arm. "So stop worrying, okay?" His smiled broadened. "Under similar circumstances, someone once told me that it took one hell of a lot of guts to do what you did. I'm sure that if he were here, he'd say that to you."

"Sedmak?"

Ben nodded.

Art entered the control room. "Everything is all set for departure. I've got that rock sample well shielded."

Ben looked at Art and said, "We're not leaving."

Art stopped himself from sitting in his recliner. "What do you mean? I thought we were finished here. We've got our sample."

"But we didn't find what we came for," Ben replied in a quiet, determined voice.

"The *Leos*?" Art asked in amazement. "It doesn't exist. The signal? It's some natural phenomenon."

"There is a very real reason why we should leave—we have killed an indigenous life form. We have no idea what that means to the local life cycle, but it is certainly against Federation principles. We have a duty to return to the Federation and accept the punishment due us."

Ben snorted. "Will you stop that crap? What was done out there was necessary for our survival. You wouldn't be here now if Greg had not acted."

Art laughed caustically. "We wouldn't be here now if Sedmak hadn't decided to ignore Council. One illegal act led to another until we finally committed the ultimate sacrilege."

"Which is no more sacrilegious than taking control of another's mind," Ben said in a quiet, tight voice.

Anger flushed Art's face. "What has been done in the name of Syncretism has been done for the good of all humanity. What you have done here is destroy life and interfere with the affairs of another planet."

Ben smiled mirthlessly. "You'll be an ideologue to the end. I don't see how you can call it interfering when this planet has already been violated. Furthermore, that thing you call life was about as natural as this planet. If it lived in the normal sense, why didn't any of us—including Rich, who had the best sensors in the Federation—detect it? How does it live?"

"I'm sorry, Art, but I'm not willing to write this planet off because it doesn't agree with my views. I intend to finish what I started. You can either help me or finish the mission stunned. Now which is it?"

Greg sensed the icy derision and commanding presence in Ben's voice. He saw Art glare at Ben with hatred, but Art said nothing.

Ben looked at Richard. "Anything?"

"Negative."

Ben glanced at the three of them in turn. "I've been deliberately waiting to see what would come of our first trip outside. So far nothing has happened. I'm convinced that that creature, whatever it was, acted alone. I want to finish exploring the channel and then we'll leave. We can do it if we're careful, alert. Greg picked up an image of the creature before it struck—this time we'll all be more receptive. Any questions?"

Art asked, "What's my duty station?"

"I want you to accompany Greg and me as before," Ben replied. "We'll need all the help we can get if another one of those things shows up. I intend to take spare belts for everyone. I'd appreciate it, Art, if you used a nullor belt."

Art shook his head.

"Do as you please," Ben said dryly. Greg sensed from Ben's look that he would have to be especially diligent in watching Art once they left the ship in view of Art's reluctance to use a nullor.

Art cast an accusing glance at Greg. "I have a request to make." He pointed at Greg. "If he's to accompany us, I want him to use the full mental and physical controls in the belt."

"What are you getting at?" Ben asked.

"You know as well as I do that he was operating without those controls when he killed the creature," Art angrily retorted. "I don't want to compound our crime by allowing him to crack up again and kill the next living thing we see. I don't have any faith in his conditioning."

Greg felt rage build within him. He quickly cut it off. He started to reply when Ben interjected. "He'll use the controls." Greg wanted to protest. He had an aversion to anything which could affect his mind. But how could he argue? His own mind contained demonic forces which even he could not control. He said nothing and merely nodded his agreement.

Art looked at Ben and laughed coldly. "Considering you're a treasonous criminal and anything I do, even betraying your trust, would be justified by Council, you certainly have a lot of faith in me. What is to stop me from sabotaging the rest of this mission?"

"Your desire to see us and a lot of others punished when we get back," Ben replied in a voice as cold as the other's laugh. With narrowed eyes, he added, "Perhaps you should ask yourself why I have not sabotaged *you.*"

"You need me," Art answered. "You need me more than I need you. But you won't be able to use me as you think."

"Maybe, maybe not," Ben said matter-of-factly. "If you keep an open mind, you might be of tremendous use to yourself and to a lot of other people."

Art snorted his contempt.

Ben briefly rubbed his forehead and eyes with his left hand, as if tired of the whole conversation. He glanced at Richard which acted as a signal to Greg that Ben was through with the fruitless arguing and was now ready to resume the mission. When he looked back at the others, Greg had the feeling that Ben was somehow looking at each of them simultaneously, holding them to him through the power of his dominating brown eyes.

"Let's take a few minutes to review what we plan to do and what we've learned about this place," Ben said. "We have accomplished just about everything we possibly could, except discovering the source of the mysterious signal. That may be our only hope to learn what happened here and to the *Leos.* Everything else has defied analysis or explanation.

"Our only choice is to go back through the channel and resume our search from the narrow far end, where we suspect the signal source is located."

With the aid of the link, Ben reviewed for them all of the available information on the planet. Concurrently, the computer restudied this information, then developed probabilistic models and again estimated the likelihood of both the various causes of these events and the possible scenarios of the immediate future. If the crew had inquired, the computer could have selected, from its knowledge of their individual value profiles and their willingness to take risks, the best decision path to follow to reach any preselected outcome. Or the computer could have calculated each person's optimal strategy. But the crew had no need of this assistance, for their minds could perform equally well such analytical decision-making.

The computer warned them that there was a high probability that the creature, coupled as it was with the planet, had sufficient field-penetrating capability to puncture the shield of a starship. (There were audible murmurings of surprise and disbelief when this information entered their minds.) Following up on the warning, the computer gave them the details of several credible models of the creature but noted that none of them satisfactorily fit into any biologically balanced system.

Most chilling to Greg was the computer's assessment that there were probably more creatures waiting out there. Moreover, the computer did not dismiss the possibility that the Fleet Alert signals might actually be a lure set by other hungry demons. The computer could not reasonably explain the planet, the signals and the creature; rather, it projected that the explanation involved some form of alien intelligence very likely associated with the monster and its cohabitants.

Since the creature appeared to seek out sources of energy, the computer recommended the obvious: using the debris of the planet as a screen against detection. For the crew, the visual band of the scanner-enhanced sensory spectrum offered the best means of detecting the creatures. Their single encounter argued that all other means of detection offered almost no chance of success.

Art grimaced as the computer noted that nullors were the preferred, and very likely the only, method of repulsing an attack by another monster.

To further complicate any defense against an attack from additional creatures was the computer's assessment that the first creature had operated by instantaneous neural signals.

The computer confirmed that the mentally received death screams of the creature indicated its telepathic capability, which in all likelihood had been used to slow down or thwart the defensive measures used by Ben, Art, and Greg during the initial assault.

No immediate defense against such strong telepathic attacks was suggested, although the crew received some consolation in learning that the first attack had, except for the memories, left their minds unaffected. (While the uninvited telepathic penetration of the shield suits raised the probability that the crew were victims of an enormous illusion, the computer still came to the cross-checked conclusion that their environment was real.)

Ben laid out his plans for a second search and concluded, "The rules are the same as last time, only now we will move faster and be alert for anything." He looked hard at Richard. "No change in orders—leave us if we get trapped. Someone has to get the word back." He paused briefly. "While it may seem superfluous in view of what has happened, I still want to maintain comm silence from the *Odyssey*." He looked at Art. "Get the equipment ready to beam off. As soon as Rich gives us the final clearance, we'll leave." As Art stood up, Ben turned to Greg. "Make one last systems check for Rich and then we'll join Art."

Greg nodded in agreement. He was glad to be active again. He felt in wonderful shape and even desired a little excitement. He quickly went through the full-alert systems checkout of the *Odyssey.* He felt elated that his mind was fully operative again.

When he finished, Greg got up and exchanged a look of assurance with Richard. He turned and started for the door. He heard Ben get up and say, "Good luck, Rich. Remember what I said."

"I will," Richard replied. "Good luck and good hunting to both of you."

Ben caught up with Greg in the corridor outside the control room. The door to the control room had already closed behind Ben.

"Wait a minute," Ben said. "I'd like to say a few words before we join Art."

Greg turned to face his commanding officer. Ben looked at him closely and said, "I want you to know that I appreciate what you did in the channel." Greg sensed sincerity and warmth in Ben's voice and eyes. This surprised him because when he had first met Ben at Carson's reception, he had felt that Ben was incapable of expressing warmth. "You've done a damned good job on this flight," Ben continued. "I'll admit that until you took on that creature, I had my doubts about your abilities, but now I consider you one of the best officers in the Fleet.

"You know you could refuse to join us because of your injuries?"

"I feel fine," Greg responded, knowing that Ben was graciously offering him a way out even though he was completely healed.

Ben said, "I realize that you haven't always agreed with me or my reasoning, but I appreciate your willingness to get the job done. I don't think I've compromised you, Greg. What we're doing *is* very important to our civilization. I hope you realize that."

"My judgment awaits the final results," Greg replied. With a smile, he added, "Anyway, I'm curious to see this through to the end."

"It may not be pleasant," Ben said. "I've got an awful theory about what may be waiting for us at the end of the channel." He shook his head slightly. "I don't want to talk about that now. Just be prepared for anything. I'm counting on you to help pull us through. Art is still an unknown quantity to me. But we need him, so don't let anything happen to him. I'm expendable. Do you understand me?"

Greg nodded. He heard the words but was not certain he had the blind obedience to accept that decision. He was not prepared to make the choice Ben had just commanded him to make. He had no intention of surrendering any lives.

"Now, if we run into trouble," Ben continued, "and you believe it is necessary, I want you to cut off your emotional controls. I want everyone to function at his best."

Greg nodded again. It helped to know that Ben supported his action against the creature and believed in him. He knew since Art first insisted that he use the emotional controls that he would, in an emergency, break loose from them. He had never liked mental controls or manipulations no matter what their purpose. Still he was aware that without some controls he must face an inner furnace of raw energy which, under threatening conditions, could again sweep up to engulf him. Despite his life in a civilization which had never experienced war or disaster, he now knew in a very personal, believable way that he carried within him the same genetic drive as his drought-stricken, starving prehistoric ancestors—if his life was threatened, he would kill to live.

Ben reached out and grasped Greg's hand. He had a firm handshake. Ben smiled warmly and said in a voice verging on a strong whisper, "Good luck." Ben quickly turned and started walking to the teleporter room.

Greg stared after Ben for a few moments and then followed him. He was a little bewildered at the change which seemed to be occurring in Ben. Up until their brief conversation, he had felt that Ben needed only Ben to complete the mission. He had assumed that Ben believed his crew were more like hindrances than helpers.

Once outside the ship, the three men checked their weapons. Ben gave a mental status report to Richard, then all three jogged warily into the channel.

Greg moved to the right and scanned the walls above him. He "saw" Art doing the same on his left. Their motion was slowed down by the rocks and boulders. Back in the ship, Greg felt that Ben's idea of a rapid trip to the other end of the channel made sense: they would explore quickly and then leave before being discovered again. Greg also considered that they could move too fast and fall into another trap. Then Greg remembered Ben's reference to his "awful theory" and decided that perhaps Ben had a very good reason for making haste.

Greg darted from rock to an occasional scallop or overhang in the wall and then back to rock. He tried to keep something solid near him for a shield. At any moment, he expected to "see" that ominous black shape move out of the swirling atmosphere above him.

There was little communication between the three of them. Greg made sure that he knew where Ben and Art were at all times. He wondered as he "watched" Ben move down the more open center of the channel floor whether he was acting as a decoy.

Reaching the scene of the battle, Ben ordered them to survey everything. Greg could still "see" signs of the battle: some dust disturbed here and there, but there was nothing left of the creature. Greg grimaced as he thought about the soil sucking up and boiling the blood which they had spilled from their penetrated suits.

Anything? Ben asked on the link.

Negative, Art answered.

Greg gave the same answer.

The relay unit still checks out, Ben thought. *From here on, we're in new territory and the channel gets smaller. Let's go.*

Ben started ahead, moving as fast as he could. Art fell into step behind him on his left.

Greg followed on the right. He grew more and more apprehensive as the floor narrowed, making the walls appear to increase in height. He felt imprisoned again and at the same time more vulnerable than he had felt in the clearing. He ceased his mental ramblings and concentrated every thought and sense on the channel.

The dark, foreboding walls grew closer together as they moved along the rocky, dust-covered floor. At several places Ben left reflectors so they could be reached by the relay unit in case they lost the required line-of-sight contact. Even though the channel was winding more now, the combination of wall height and twists did not interfere with the relay unit or the reflectors. Greg was thankful that Art had done such a good job. If they lost contact with the relay unit, they would lose the data from the special scanners in the *Odyssey* and would also be thrust into total darkness. They would be without direct support from, or link to, the *Odyssey.*

The three men were forced to walk in single file, moving with more difficulty, like shimmering sperms swimming against the dark current in a narrow, writhing oviduct of rock. Ben took the lead and Art took the center position. Greg deliberately brought up the rear. He wanted to "watch" Art.

What a funny life, Greg thought ironically to himself. Art and I meet because of a beautiful woman and a wonderful party only to end up tramping through this near lifeless planet in mutual distrust.

The channel narrowed until it was barely wide enough for a man to pass.

Ben thought, *According to our original scanner survey, the channel should end around the next bend. Be careful. I'll leave a reflector here in case we get cut off. So far everything is okay, Rich, but from here on be ready for anything.*

Greg "watched" Ben set up another reflector and then "glanced" up at the tops of the uniformly dark walls, despite the presence in his mind of the all-encompassing visual data the scanners fed him. He turned to follow the walls all the way back as far as he could "see." Nothing.

I'll go first, Ben thought. *Art, you stay at the bend where you can cover both Greg and me. Greg, you stay back behind those rocks and cover Art and the way back.*

Greg moved back and crouched behind the indicated pile of rocks allowing Art to "see" only a small part of him, just enough for direct communication. Art stood near the bend, monitoring both Greg and the channel ahead.

Ben stepped around the bend and was lost from sight.

Greg received Ben's thoughts and other suit transmissions, so he knew Ben was all right. After a few minutes, Ben signaled for Art and Greg to follow him. Greg was still getting up from the rocks when Art stepped out of his view. Even though he could still receive Art's communications, Greg silently cursed Art for moving out of direct sight.

Greg ran quickly to the bend. He did not want to leave the others uncovered at the end of the channel. He dashed around the bend.

What the hell! His muscles ceased to function. He could not walk. His arms and legs refused to obey him. But he *was* moving!

Ahead he "saw" the motionless figures of Ben and Art being drawn down the narrow channel toward the large ovarian cortex of a rock at the far end. In his mind he sensed their thought messages describing the channel as if nothing had happened. Then he received his own thoughts from outside himself! Even these were routine messages of exploration, giving no hint of his predicament. The three suits were transmitting false data. Greg wanted to scream about what was really happening but could only "watch" and receive the deceitful signals. He could not activate his belt functions. He was reduced to a passive observer. He was like some soon-to-die insect trapped in an invisible spider web.

As Ben drew closer to the large boulder, it suddenly rolled aside, exposing a gaping black hole in the wall at the end of the channel. The hole was larger than a man's body but considerably smaller than a starship. Ben was pulled into it and vanished.

Greg struggled furiously now, but his body would not respond. Helplessly, he "watched" Art vanish into the hole. Only his suit's emotional controls, which still functioned, kept him from experiencing real fear. He silently cursed those controls—he would not be permitted to even die with feelings.

The hole loomed larger, and suddenly Greg was engulfed in Rhadamanthine darkness.

11

DESTRUCTION

And the fourth angel poured out his vial upon the sun; and power was given unto him to scorch men with fire.

—Revelation, 16:8

The darkness was total. Greg could not detect anything. He prepared himself to die in the jaws of some demon.

And the silence was total. Greg was mentally aware that his belt was performing only basic functions. He was no longer aware of the three telepathic mimics. He assumed that the boulder had been rolled back into place, sealing the three of them from communication with the outside world.

Richard would be totally deceived. Perhaps, Greg thought with angry frustration, Richard was being stalked at that moment, unaware that the others were in danger. Greg wondered whether Richard would leave them here, as he had been ordered. With a sardonic mental laugh he realized that the whole question was academic—in a few moments he and his two crewmates would be dead.

Greg could no longer tell whether he was moving. His only sense of motion outside this tunnel had come from his visual impressions. He assumed that he had been hit by some kind of a stunnor and was being maneuvered by a tractor beam. He could be going in several directions, including down, and teleportation was not out of the question.

He had a brief, horrible thought that he might be in a feeding nest. And Ben and Art might be being eaten right next to him and he would not know it. Maybe the mental and physical controls will serve some purpose, he concluded.

When nothing happened to him, Greg relaxed a little and began to review his problem. Whatever had been done to him had not affected his mind. He analyzed everything he could think of that related to his predicament, but he could not find any answers. He tried again to move his arms and legs. Nothing. He focused his mind on moving just one muscle. Nothing. After repeated attempts, he turned to his belt. He could not control it. He felt like a disembodied brain.

A *light!*

His mind was alert. Yes, he had seen a light. It was dim but was getting stronger. Was he approaching it, or was it approaching him?

He could not judge the magnitude or the size of the light, nor could he determine if it was of a constant strength, but he sensed, more intuitively than analytically, that he was closing in on the light at a rapid rate. He was encouraged by one fact: he could see the light and from this he guessed that he had been freed of the energy absorbing material on the surface.

As the light grew brighter, covering more area, he was able to make out his two crewmates. He was relieved that they were all right. He would not have to face the immediate future alone.

The light increased in size and strength until Greg was able to make out its origin. They were being drawn into a large cavern filled with advanced scientific equipment. There was some hope now. Surely, he reasoned, this could not be the home of any eight-legged monster.

As suddenly as he had been drawn into the darkness, he came into the light-filled cavern. To his amazement, he found that he could move his head, but he could not use the communications functions in his suit. He immediately took advantage of this by signaling to Ben and Art that he was all right. He saw that they were all right, too. Then he looked around the cavern while receiving the sensory data from the scanner in his suit.

The center of the cavern was dominated by a large, black, oblong device mounted on a pedestal. The walls of the cavern were filled with scientific apparatus, and the equipment seemed to be operating. Greg was startled to note the similarity of the designs to equipment he knew and understood. He quickly catalogued everything: scanners; specialized sensors, some different from those he knew; exploratory probes; communications equipment; elaborate mensatronic units; consoles for the control of stunnors; nullors (he noted this with some concern); tractor beams; and life-support equipment. He knew that this was not a den for simple, brutish carnivores. All the necessities for life and its defense under hostile conditions were here.

He observed that the walls had not been formed out of the mysterious surface material, which explained why his suit scanner operated without support from the special scanners on board the *Odyssey*. Somehow, as he had suspected earlier, the three of them had penetrated the layer of energy absorbing material. This fact was worth noting. At least the whole planet had not been cremated, most likely just its surface.

Greg also noted that several tunnels entered the cavern. He suspected that nullors had been used to make these tunnels and the cavern. The walls showed evidence of having been formed in this manner.

Suddenly, he felt something in his mind. It was a presence, a sensation of another being. It was a passive presence, but it was there nevertheless. To one steeped in the sanctity of the mind, this was the ultimate transgression. He fought back but to no avail—the presence remained, quiet, waiting, aware.

He looked at Ben and Art. He could tell from their puzzled and alarmed expressions that they, too, were aware of the same sensation.

Something beckoned him to look at the black hexahedron. He turned, lifted his head and faced the large, black object. From the corner of his eye and from his suit scanner he noticed that Ben and Art were also staring at the oblong device.

Instantly, the blackness vanished from the hexahedron, revealing a towering, green-skinned biped staring down at them with a single, large Cyclopean eye.

Greg's training prevented him from consciously feeling revulsion at the ugly giant reptilelike creature. His trained mind quickly assimilated and catalogued the anatomical details of the creature: it had two legs and two arms, was capable of standing upright, was covered by reptilian scales and its hands and presumably its feet were slightly webbed. He estimated that the creature was about three meters tall. The dull greenish color of the naked creature stood out in sharp contrast to the muted tones of the cavern. But that eye! Never on the hundreds of Federation-explored planets had such a creature been sighted. The eye (if that was what it was; it was like no eye he had ever seen) filled most of the creature's face, dwarfing the line of a mouth. It seemed to stare unblinkingly into his mind with a white chitinous sheen.

Then Greg observed that the creature had not moved from its original position. He wondered whether he was looking at a tridem or quad-dem image rather than at a real being. Then a coherent message came to him, slowly, carefully, in a pacific manner:

Good thoughts be with you, sons of Earth. Do not be alarmed. No harm is meant. Be patient and everything will be explained.

Greg looked at Ben and Art and he could tell that they were receiving the same message. Greg was puzzled: the creature had not moved. He concluded that they had in some way become attuned to a mental link, but he did not see evidence of it. The message continued:

I was called Rana Klagor in your language. I was the last of the Lacerti which lived on this once wondrous planet we called Nelumbo and which the men from your worlds called Neriton.

You have been brought here to hear our story and then you shall be permitted to leave. The methods of your conveyance run counter to the desires of the Lacerti, but I fear it is necessary to operate in this manner in order that you may learn what we have prepared for you. It was not our desire that you should act impulsively before you had a chance to see and know us. It is also for this reason that our communications devices are even now deceiving your companion in your ship.

At this very moment all of you are in terrible danger. Your presence here was not desired under these circumstances, but it was prepared for. Those who preceded you had hoped that you might respond differently. The actions which you have taken here will soon initiate a chain of events that may cause not only your own deaths but also that of your Federation. For this reason, too, I must continue to hold you immobilized so that I may quickly and efficiently tell our story. Then you will know what to do.

Despite his grave concern, Greg felt at ease. Someone or something was spreading a sensation of relaxation throughout him. His suit's emotional controls were turned off. All distracting thoughts fled his mind, as if he was being prepared to concentrate totally on something new. Soon he felt like a being deprived of all thought and feeling. It was at this moment that the images and thought-words came, slowly at first and then rapidly until he was filled with them.

Tall trees, supported by massive dark-brown trunks and bulbous roots, rose up out of the black-water swamp in front of him. They were capped in limp, green covers. Small, tufted mosslike lichens grew in abundance around the bases of the trees, and large, leafy ferns and grasses carpeted the open spaces with soft-green fronds and spear-shaped blades. The farther Greg looked into the distance, the more the trees and foliage appeared to merge into a vast greenish haze, modulated only by occasional multicolored flowering plants and steaming, white mists arising from murky warm water. He was surrounded by verdurous trees, vines, ferns and dense foliage that gave forth odors of wet mud and growing and decaying vegetation. At his feet, he saw soft grasses and sedges nurtured by moist soil. Overhead, weird, shadowy reptilian and insectile shapes glided or flew through the white, misty sky veiled by large, green leaves. He heard the occasional hissing and buzzing of animal life, punctuated with an infrequent slap of water. This was a world of even, quiet sounds.

He felt sticky from the heat and humidity. He looked up again through the green growths and palmlike trees to see a hot, whitish-yellow main sequence star lighting the albescent mist-shrouded sky.

Sangraal! A thought-word implanted itself next to that of Sangraal: *Omphalos,* which in his own language was the name given to Sangraal by the Lacerti. He knew that star well now. But where was he? This was not a planet in the Sangraal system.

He moved like a spirit over the ground, passing through the dense foliage as if it—or he!—did not exist.

Water was in evidence everywhere. This place was a hot, moist swamp. The soil was muddy. He saw animal-like creatures slither through the grasses and into the dark water. They were as green as the plant life around them, and they looked reptilian.

Even the rocks were green with growths! And amidst the verdure, he saw abundant animal and insect life. The green growths were interspersed with large, placid bodies of dark water. Here, too, life flourished.

The moist, misty atmosphere, which only occasionally hinted at blue through its normally white haze, and the ever-present greenness worked to alter his sense of spatial and temporal relationships. Time and place seemed different somehow. The life process on this planet operated as he knew it, but the pace seemed less determined, less driven. Here was a world at peace with itself. Somewhere on the fringe of his mind which he still controlled, he recalled some long-forgotten lines about a people which "trust to providence, and neither plant nor plow, but everything grows without sowing or plowing; wheat and barley and vines, which bear grapes in huge bunches, and the rain from heaven makes them grow of themselves." A place where they "have no parliament for debates and no laws…" Surely those lines described this idyllic place. It was a uniform and stable world, perhaps a few hundred million years older than Earth.

Now he moved back into the dense, green growth. He knew that something was waiting for him. He peered between the vines and leaves of the tree in front of him and saw one of the Lacerti!

Closer examination showed that the arboreal creature was not quite like the creature which occupied the large hexahedral container in the cavern. This creature was smaller and less developed. In particular, Greg noted that the eye was much less pronounced.

Then, in a flash of revelation, Greg knew that he was part of some Archean journey and was witnessing the rise of the Lacerti. But this was no reconstruction of the past as his own kind was capable of through the recallers. This was a reconstruction based on the intact racial memory of a species older than humanity!

Greg felt himself drawn to the eye of the creature's face. Just as he seemed to merge with the eye, his mind took on a new awareness of his environment. He sensed the life about him in a vibrant fashion which made him feel happy at being alive. He was aware of everything happening about him even though his vision was shielded by the leaves and foliage. He felt the primitive emotions of the life around him. Greg realized that these impressions and images were remarkably similar to those he sensed with a scanner. But how? Where was the power?

Through the creature he sensed the presence of another one like it. These sensations were almost primordial. There was no thought and no order. The sensations offered a silent means of communication with their kind. Greg reasoned that this eye was more than just a scanner, it was also a rudimentary telepathic link. A thought-word appeared in his mind: *perceptor.*

Even as he, in the far uncontrolled regions of his mind, puzzled over such an organ, he realized the advantages of the perceptor. Sangraal II, which he now thought of as Neriton, had been a tropical planet. Life had developed in the primeval, nutrient seas, and by some whim of mutation, one creature was given the first vestiges of a perceptor. These early creatures sensed their environment more completely than their fellows; they could see, smell and hear more fully than the others. And they could *feel* what was happening around them. At first, their sense of awareness was dim, but gradually over the thousands of millennia, their awareness grew to that displayed by the creature Greg had seen in the tree.

Greg moved forward in time. He saw the arboreal creatures collect into happy, peaceful communities, where they lived on the nutritive fruits and plants. These gave them the energy to support their evolving perceptors. The changeless nature of Neriton offered no incentive for advancement as humanity had known it, yet the perceptor continued to develop. By human standards, it was a maddeningly slow development. Transitory emotions became partial thoughts. These merged into organized thinking shared by all of the community. As each advancement was perceived as good by the community, it fueled further advancement. Greg had difficulty discerning the dividing line between natural and induced development.

Yet, there was no need for such development, Greg thought. Neriton was peaceful. The Lacerti had few natural enemies and these it learned to control mentally. By nature the Lacerti were herbivorous and passive. Greg suspected that their development began accidentally and was nurtured, particularly in its later stages, as a kind of intellectual exercise.

Greg found it uncanny to be around these early Lacertian communities. Whenever one of the Lacerti experienced something, his comrades were immediately aware of it. This fostered a communal life and permitted the early development of a complete racial history.

As time passed, Greg observed the differences between the rise of humanity and the rise of the Lacerti. He knew that humanity was pushed by its environment, while the Lacerti enjoyed the serenity of a blissful, unchanging world. The Lacertian telepathic powers led them to a wholly different approach to life and civilization. Because they were fully aware of the other life around them, they were not cruel or aggressive. Because they thought as one, they lacked the need to develop sophisticated mathematical and scientific methods, as humanity had. The elaborate Lacertian thought processes, when suitably coupled, could function like a computer and describe and transmit the whole system. Such a method of thinking favored the social sciences. The Lacerti did not make the distinction imbedded in Tellurian language between what a thing *is* and what it *does*. The Lacerti saw the total relationship.

The Lacerti eventually built beautiful cities in total harmony with their jungle environment. Greg marveled at their mastery of environmental architecture. Their cities merged and blended with the foliage and were designed to enhance the natural lighting received from Omphalos/Sangraal.

The only word Greg could find to describe the social and political structure of the Lacerti was anarchistic, yet somehow this word did not quite fit. Anarchy connoted lawlessness, which did not describe the Lacerti. The Lacerti lived in a controlled state of anarchy. They had no laws and no government, yet they knew how to work and live together.

As a scientist, Greg could not pass judgment on these creatures. Their society existed and they were successful. He admired their ability to live in consonance with their world, but on a personal level he was repelled by their total lack of privacy. Greg knew he could never sacrifice the sanctuary of his mind on the altar of this peaceful, ordered society.

He appreciated their tranquil, harmonious existence, with its concern for the immediate and what was within them. But he was the product of a race which had long been concerned with the world beyond it and with the future. He applauded their cerebral pursuits, but their nirvana was not for him, not yet, anyway.

Greg's trip through time slowed. With a hint of trepidation, he knew he was nearing the present and that he was going to have the chance to see the recent past in full detail.

He observed that little technical advancement had occurred in the last few centuries. And he puzzled over the presence of the lush, green jungle and swamps. When had this beautiful world ended? he wondered. What had happened?

As if to answer or acknowledge Greg's question, he was transported to the largest of the Lacertian cities. All around him the Lacerti contentedly pursued their daily tasks and pleasures with their controlled disorder. Nothing was amiss here, but Greg sensed a dreadful anticipation building within his guide, Rana Klagor.

A pulsating saucer of energy suddenly burst through the mist above the city. In unison the Lacerti "looked" up at this anomaly in their sky. Greg mentally started: *It was a starship!* And it was different from any he knew. *This ship had not come from the Federation.*

The telepathic message came swiftly from the ship:

People of Nelumbo, we have come from beyond your mists to bring to you the rewards of a new Creation, a new life free from the banality you follow. We have wandered the pathways among the stars searching for those like yourselves capable of appreciating our elevating gifts. We wish to demonstrate our intentions by establishing an experimental station near this city at a place we shall mark. We ask that you grant us permission to land and operate freely. We shall return after ten dawnings for your answer.

A blinding flash of energy leaped from the ship to the ground. The Lacerti recoiled in agony, their perceptors injured. The flash was gone as quickly as it had come. Swiftly and silently, the saucer of pulsing illumination climbed into the mist and vanished from view.

The Lacerti responded in unison. They sought out their injured and healed them with telepathic techniques.

The Lacerti were aware of the threat to them, yet they still moved in a casual manner. Greg wanted to scream at them to defend themselves. He wanted to shake them out of their lethargic lifestyle. Could they not see that they faced the most dangerous menace in the Universe: an intelligent race armed with the penultimate weapon of destruction?

The starship returned, and the Lacerti signaled their welcome to the glowing craft. The ship landed in the center of the circular region of death and was silent for two dawnings. The Lacerti knew that it was exploring and taking samples. Only when an invited delegation of three Lacerti disappeared into the craft did they show real concern.

The ship asked for another visitation. Collectively, passively, the Lacerti resisted, requesting first some knowledge about those who had entered the ship. They were told that these first entrants were members of a new and marvelous race and would soon be rejoining those outside. Still, the Lacerti maintained passive resistance. They knew that the web of life which connected them to their three companions had been severed.

The star creatures, tiring of this resistance, reached out with tractor beams and collected ten more Lacerti.

The Lacerti mourned again. But this time their mourning catalyzed a thought—they had reached into their long history for the techniques they had so successfully used to survive. One giant thought formed from millions of shining parts, and they reached out to control the occupants of the starship.

They mentally beat at the shields of the ship, using all the cerebral tactics they had learned from millennia of need. They provoked the ship to issue a warning. They ignored it. Like some mental battering ram, they pummeled the shields in frustration. Greg doubted that the aliens were disturbed by the Lacertians's puny mental assault. In contrast to the protective power of the alien shield, this mental assault amounted to very little.

Without warning, the ship lifted off the ground and rapidly climbed into the misty sky, where it hovered long enough to unleash another lethiferous flash.

Greg screamed in agony. He cried and pleaded for release from his pain. His mind teetered on the edge of destruction. *He had felt the death of the city!* Only Klagor's rapid ministrations saved his sanity, but he was left weeping like some traveler on Cocytos looking at the smoldering emptiness which had once been the largest city on Neriton.

He again felt the sensation of relaxation spread through his mind and body. He was thankful for release from his sorrow.

Neriton was at peace once more as the Lacerti adjusted their thoughts to accommodate the horror they had experienced.

Then the *Leos* arrived.

After making the initial contacts, all according to Fleet procedures, and being welcomed, the Federation starship arrived at the chosen landing site. It came through the mists like some ghostly bowl of light, leaving Greg with the impression that the starship was more at home in the vaporous Neriton skies than were the Lacerti.

The human explorers soon learned that they were not the first visitors on Neriton. The humans were disturbed about the earlier visitors and their use of a nullor-type weapon. Such an alien visitation from another star system had never occurred in the history of the human race. Humanity had grown slightly complacent because of the knowledge that they alone in the known Galaxy possessed the means of star travel and the weapons of total annihilation.

The crew debated the available options. Richard's father passionately argued that the crew had two major responsibilities. First, they must tell the Fleet what had happened, and they must do so in the most careful way possible because signals could be monitored by the other visitors if they were still present or if they had left hidden sensors. Their second responsibility was to the Lacerti, who assumed that the aliens from the stars would return; therefore, it was essential that they find some way within the laws of the Federation to prepare the Lacerti for a third alien visit. Surely, he argued with those who wanted to leave Neriton immediately and let Council make the decisions, there was room for compassion between the inhabitants of the handful of living worlds. He observed that if humanity remained neutral about the Lacertian predicament, it was doing so to soothe the culturally induced human conscience. The decision to leave the Lacerti alone was just as damning as unleashing the weapons of death.

Greg was caught up in this man's singular commitment to life. With little effort, he traced the same vital spark from father to son. And he understood more and more the sadness of his friend at losing such a father and experiencing such pain on the first ill-fated mission he and Richard had made in the *Guardian* beyond the Perimeter.

Gradually, Richard's father persuaded his crew to accept his views. He quickly assigned a team to devise some means of covertly signaling the Federation. Then he ordered a study of what could be done to aid the Lacerti without violating Federation restrictions on intercourse between culturally and technologically different civilizations. Finally, in obvious sadness, he ordered an increased alert status and assigned part of his crew to prepare defenses for the *Leos*. Greg shared his sadness, and he relived his own personal guilt because he understood what Richard's father meant to do. *With the vast equipment and knowledge on board the* Leos, *the crew was going to attempt to build a nullor weapon.*

This plan was accepted with great reluctance mostly because the laws were not as strict in the days before the establishment of the Perimeter. Greg knew that the crew would need a nullor weapon in case the aliens returned, but he wondered if their stay would be long enough or their resources and knowledge sufficient enough to warrant such a decision. Influenced by a wave of guilt over his recent action, Greg sadly concluded that despite the many handicaps, the crew possessed the capabilities to develop the weapon, a capability the human race always had.

With the introduction of humanity's technology, Greg saw that a culture had changed. The Lacerti now had the rudiments of a simple planetary defense system, one that was nonlethal in keeping with the precepts of the Lacertian philosophy. He could imagine Coni's sorrow at learning of this technological change in a culture, but he felt that she, too, would understand the need for the change. He recalled her plea for cultural diversity, and he now knew the wisdom of having that diversity. Here on Neriton, the perceptor had worked against diversity, and now humanity must provide what nature had not. He only hoped that humanity was right. Then he remembered the present form of

Neriton and dreaded what Klagor was about to show him. He was helpless to warn the *Leos.*

Their work done, the humans prepared to depart when the fateful signal came from their ship:

Ten alien starships exited just beyond Sangraal system. On fast approach to Neriton.

Unable to escape, those crewmembers still onboard the *Leos* used the nullor to burrow deep beneath the surface of Neriton. A large number of nearby Lacerti, including Rana Klagor, were invited to join them on the voyage underground. Here, they hid undetected inside a cocoon of screens.

The aliens maneuvered their craft into position about Neriton and announced their presence. There were no discussions of a new order for the Lacerti. The aliens were blunt. They announced that they were taking control of the planet and that any resistance would be dealt with harshly. Greg felt ice flowing in the veins of his hands, neck and back as he received their next announcement.

We are aware that you have been visited by others from the stars. We know these others are still with you and that they have added to your technology. We wish no harm to our fellow travelers from space. We wish to meet with them and exchange information with them. We ask that they remain neutral in the affair between our civilization and that of the Lacerti. The Lacerti attacked a peaceful, unarmed exploration ship from our world, and we seek retribution for this immoral act. Please acknowledge receipt of this communication. We assume you are capable of deciphering Lacertian thought messages.

There was no acknowledgment from anyone on Neriton.

The aliens repeated their second announcement in different forms of communication. After considerable waiting, they continued, using many forms at once.

Please do not be alarmed by our presence. Like yourselves, we are a race of explorers. We came to this planet bringing the gifts of our civilization, gifts which would have given new life to the Lacerti even as your gifts have changed them. We offered them a new civilization and a chance to join us. Instead, they resisted and attacked our exploration ship. We seek only to settle our differences with them. We ask that you join us as fellow explorers. There is much to benefit both our races.

The aliens elaborated upon this theme. They described the benefits they planned to give the Lacerti. They sent out images of a vast, new Lacertian culture replete with technological riches. Against this image of positivism, they showed how the treacherous Lacerti had tried to destroy their first ship.

Greg admired Klagor's candor in showing these scenes but caution warned him that he was still being guided by another and the candor could be a cover for devious activities.

The images of the aliens' creation faded as the communication concluded with a final plea: *We desire to be your friends. Please join us. We know that you are here. Our probes sensed your arrival. We must apologize for inconveniencing your activities, but we were forced by the Lacerti to seal off this planet. We regret that this prevented your communications from being received by your home world and that your home world cannot detect us. If you will lift off, we will conduct you beyond the seal so you can contact your own people.*

To show our good faith we will land one of our craft near the largest Lacertian city and await your coming.

The urgency of the communication was almost irresistible. The aliens had mastered the same psychological techniques that the Fleet used in some of its alien communication equipment.

Greg felt like a one-person audience in a gigantic theater. Through the power of the perceptor, he could simultaneously be with the *Leos* and anywhere on the planet. He watched the Lacerti as their scanners showed one of the alien starships break out of its pattern of deployment and descend to the surface of Neriton. The remaining nine ships moved to cover the space it had left.

The crew of the *Leos* was aware that the aliens were now actively and vigorously probing the planet. So far their disguise was holding. Greg sensed a slight loss of hope aboard the *Leos*. The crew's predicament was obvious: they could not leave while the aliens were there, and they had no hope of signaling the Fleet—they were alone and had been alone since their arrival. Very likely, the Federation thought they were dead, and Neriton was now a marked planet.

Despite Klagor's access to many minds, the next few moments were confusing to Greg. The alien craft signaled its intent to land and that it planned to clear a space for the landing. For the first time, the Lacerti replied, insisting that such an act was unnecessary and unwarranted. The aliens responded (more to the unknown *Leos* than to the Lacerti, it seemed to Greg) that a clearing was necessary to avoid any traps. Appealing to the unknown *Leos* for support or neutrality, the aliens unleashed a vivid burst of rending energy upon a spot near the remaining largest Lacertian city. At that moment, a series of large stunnors beamed their paralyzing rays at the alien starship in concert with tractor beams of voraciously ripping forces. The suddenness of the Lacertian response, coupled with the concentration of stunnor and tractor beam energy, seemed to have a momentary effect on the alien ship. The craft wobbled briefly then instantly darted above the misty clouds, followed by a convergence of stunnor rays and tractor beams.

The alien response was as swift and terrible as it had been the first time. Devastating beams flashed from several alien ships to impinge upon this Lacertian city and every other place on Neriton where the Lacerti had assembled enough stunnor and tractor devices to pose a threat to the alien space-craft. Blinding light, a crack of explosive fury and the dying thoughts of millions of Lacerti flew through Greg's mind, as if all Lacertian defense centers were one in their moment of destruction. This time Klagor was mentally there to act as a buffer. Too much was happening too fast for Greg's guide to permit him to be engulfed in the terror of the moment.

The alien craft rejoined its nine companions in patrol above Neriton. For almost a standard hour there was no communication between the two sides, then the aliens announced:

We consider the recent act of hostilities to be a declaration of war by the Lacerti. While we know that the means for this act were provided by others not of this world, we shall overlook it if the others will desist and lift off so that we may settle our affair with the Lacerti. We have no quarrel with our fellow star travelers. We have not tried to conceal ourselves, although we could have done so easily. We have remained openly in view, vulnerable to your weapons. Can this be an act of war on our part? Can you not see that the Lacerti have attacked us again? Do not be deceived by them.

We know what has happened on Nelumbo and we know where you are. Our landing craft captured one of the Lacertian enemy in its teleporter, and we have learned of your shielded tunnels and weapons. We beg you to leave now before we retaliate against the Lacerti. You are one of us and must not be caught in this Lacertian web of deceit. Please acknowledge our communication.

As if to show the veracity of their statements, the aliens concluded this transmission with a series of images of humans and Lacerti working together on the tunnels. Greg observed with the same sigh of relief as the crew of the *Leos* that no images gave away the location of the *Leos*—the Lacertians had been able to keep part of their promise of mentally blocking such images. Greg imagined the mind-wrenching torture which the captive Lacertian must have experienced before giving away what little information he had provided the aliens. Greg was certain that the captive Lacertian must have died before revealing more, perhaps by a built-in suicide technique that kept the aliens from trying the same scheme on other Lacertians.

Realizing that their location was at best temporarily unknown to the aliens and that the *Leos* could not remain hidden from detailed inspection, Richard Highstreet, Sr., ordered the crew to gradually extend the disguising fields so that the *Leos* could bore deeper, eventually reaching the discontinuity between crust and mantle, where he hoped to establish a better network of concealing screens.

Shortly after the *Leos* began to move deeper, the aliens announced that they would give the Lacerti and their visitors one day in which to surrender and permit the alien craft to land or travel at will without resistance. The communication ended with an ominous warning of disastrous consequences if the Lacerti did not acquiesce.

Upon receiving this ultimatum, the crew of the *Leos* offered to do whatever the Lacerti desired, short of giving away the location of the Federation. Their Lacertian passengers, who in a passive, concealed fashion were part of the great Lacertian mental link, refused to accept further participation by the Federation crew. They realized the crew had done its best to help them, and they made it clear that the problem was one between the aliens and the Lacerti. They agreed to accept whatever help the crew could provide but firmly stated their consensus: the *Leos* must now save itself and forget Nelumbo. The Lacerti concluded by stating that their decision was final since it was based upon the collective consideration of all the Lacerti.

Greg's earlier premonitions flashed before him again. The pattern was established, and he knew the result. The Lacerti realized from the behavior of the first alien starship that they had no future in surrendering. Sadly, Greg observed to himself that they had no future in resisting either. To Greg, the Lacerti were like a herd of cattle trapped between a sweeping fire and a cliff. They were not conditioned for such dilemmas, and almost by instinct they seemed to be gathering the momentum to charge something. On a coldly intellectual level, he agreed with their decision to resist, since it offered an infinitesimal chance of success. The aliens meant to enslave, if not destroy, the Lacerti. Such creatures only understood the use of power and so if it were used against them, they might cease their warlike actions. Greg doubted that the aliens would really notice the resistance, but it offered some hope. Emotionally, he was not sure that under similar circumstances he could have made such a quick decision. It was not clear whether the cattle were stampeding toward the cliff or the fire, or if it made any difference. With a tremendous effort of will, Greg turned his concern to the crew of the *Leos*. The Lacerti had made their choice. Now the harsh reality of galactic power politics dictated the escape or total destruction of the *Leos*.

During the period of grace given by the aliens, the *Leos* had moved into position beneath the crust of Neriton and cleverly disguised itself within the inner planetary morphology. Now the crew and their Lacertian passengers waited anxiously in the tense, passive silence of the ship.

On the next day, the aliens repeated their demand for surrender. The Lacerti refused. And Greg learned why the aliens had returned with so many ships when only one would have sufficed to conquer.

Five of the larger alien craft, every other one in the orbital flight pattern, began to teleport unshielded Lacerti and other living creatures aboard. In fear and desperation, the Lacerti flocked to the surviving cities, where they hoped to escape this fate by remaining inside the protective shields.

Several days passed. Most of the Lacerti gathered in the cities. Then the aliens returned their captives to the surface of the planet.

The shock of their return aroused despair in Greg. He saw grotesque shapes writhing in terrible, unending pain. He saw organs and limbs interchanged, producing a kaleidoscope of biological horror. How they continued to live was beyond his comprehension. The aliens had understood the Lacertian philosophy of life and beauty and had exacted their insane, unjustified punishment in a manner designed to cause psychological as well as physical pain.

Greg had no energy left to feel rage. Seeing such twisted, pained creatures liquefied him with frustration, like an aimless current in Acheron. He could not imagine a mind that could develop a starship also creating (if that word could be so defiled) such pain and ugliness. There was no logical pattern to what was happening. Perhaps triggered by these thoughts, he remembered another place populated by similar monstrosities, a planet called Ahriman, where beauty and life no longer reigned. A planet where the woman he loved had almost died, her body violated by satanic tortures. A planet which had fueled the idea of demonic forces presently at work in the Galaxy.

So this is the new creation, he thought bitterly. Some of Greg's sickening deadness yielded to anger and fear. If what he had been told by Tom Lippert and Coni was true, if what he was seeing now was true, then humanity had at last met the abominable Apollyoni!

Upon reflection, he remembered that what he was witnessing on Neriton antedated the Federation mission to Ahriman. Greg thought that if the *Odyssey* returned, he and the others could make a drastic change in Coni's view of human history. The Sanderson party would not go down as the first recorded contact between humans and the work of the Apollyoni. The crew of the *Leos,* wherever they were, could claim that.

The Lacerti and the human crew were pulled out of their state of horror and revulsion by the actions of three of the five alien ships. Each beamed down a series of shielded containers next to the remaining major Lacertian cities. The Lacerti unsuccessfully probed them and futilely tried to penetrate them with stunnors and tractor beams. As soon as the matter transmission ceased, the shielded containers opened to reveal...

The giant eight-legged demons!

These ugly, tenebrific creatures raced out of their containers in unison toward the shielded cities like ferromagnetic particles attracted to a magnet. With their poisons and claws, the multilegged beasts ripped apart these beautiful cities and killed the Lacerti on contact. Greg watched in helpless horror as a crewmember was trapped by one of these creatures of destruction. The man activated the pellor ray on his shield suit but did not move fast enough—the creature leaped and easily caught him with its claws. The crewmember fired his stunnor at full strength, but the creature's sclerotized plates protected it. The jaws easily penetrated the shield suit and sucked up its energy, causing the field to collapse. The crewman was the first to be exposed to Neriton's environment. His thoughts were open to all of the Lacerti and to Greg. The creature punctured the body of the screaming crewman and injected it with its poisonous digestive fluid.

The crewman burned with pain and nausea; his organs became rigid obstructions to life. His suit and life-support system were nonexistent now, and no medical assistance could aid him. The crewman went into convulsions and died, whereupon the creature mashed his body into a reddish-pink pulp and regurgitated digestive fluid over it. The creature quickly completed its meal and went after other prey. There seemed to be no satisfaction for these creatures except more feeding. Their appetites were insatiable, as if each intake of energy charged them up to a point where they desired more.

Greg no longer felt any guilt about his actions in the channel. He felt vindicated. These creatures were the artificial constructs of the aliens—the Apollyoni. They were lifeless ghouls sent to terrorize a planet. Remembering the awful destruction of this fellow human, Greg was glad he had used his nullor. When he subdued his emotional response to the crewmember's death, Greg reflected that the man may have been lucky—he could have suffered a more terrible fate if he had been beamed aboard the alien craft. In the process, unless he committed suicide, he would have betrayed the *Leos*. In a sense, the implication of the killing of the crewman was more terrifying to Greg than the actual deed itself. Greg concluded that the aliens, who had shown by their images that they knew what the humans looked like, were either so confident of their success that they did not have to make concessions to the *Leos* by sparing any humans (was this part of some larger plan, or had the aliens concluded that the humans would kill themselves rather than submit to interrogation?) or else they were so uncaring that they unleashed their Demogorgons with no further control.

The Lacerti quickly organized a defense against these demons by using several high-power stunnors in concert against a single target. Given enough time, this procedure proved an effective means of stopping the creatures, since they had no way of channeling the extra stunnor energy to any absorbent material.

The Lacertian counterattack was short-lived. Every time a creature was paralyzed, the alien craft would destroy the stunnors which had incapacitated the creature. It was a losing battle. Greg almost wept in frustration; he wanted to use *his* nullors on these monsters. The aliens were slowly torturing the planet to death.

The terrible nightmare on Neriton lasted for nearly a standard week before showing signs of abating. When it seemed to Greg that the dismemberment of the Lacertian culture was almost complete, the aliens once again signaled the planet. They repeated their plea for the *Leos* to lift off. They stated that they knew the ship was still there, hidden beneath the surface, and they warned that the ship might be damaged when they destroyed the Lacertian tunnels. They apologized for any human lives that may have been lost. They pointed out that they had not intentionally fought the humans. They again urged the *Leos* to lift off while it was still possible.

The crew of the *Leos* did not even consider the aliens' suggestion that they leave the planet. They knew that a race which could so wantonly kill a civilization could and would easily destroy them. This latest alien ultimatum did surface a debate which had been tearing at the crew since the alien attack began. Influenced by the horror of what they had seen through their instruments and the minds of their Lacertian passengers, many of the crew argued that the *Leos*, with its nullor weapon, must go to the aid of the Lacerti. Others in the crew argued that the time for emotional commitment was past. Looking at their situation in practical terms, these crewmembers reminded their comrades of the ten-to-one odds against them. If the *Leos* started to leave its position, it would be detected and annihilated before they could aid the Lacerti. Under the most optimistic circumstances, they could envision the *Leos*, with its crude nullor, destroying only one of the better-equipped alien craft before the *Leos* was destroyed or captured. These crewmembers argued that their only hope lay in hiding. They would try to contact the Federation, otherwise it would be left dangerously ignorant of the alien terror. The Lacertian passengers had also considered the human dilemma through their organic mental link and agreed that the humans should remain hidden.

The *Leos* remained as it was.

After repeated pleading with the hidden *Leos*, the final two alien craft began destroying the Lacertian tunnels and the few remaining cities. The sum of the mental agony and horror which Greg had known until that moment was only a fraction of what he was to experience. The earlier attacks were a mere preparatory ritual to the hideous final act.

In systematic fashion, the two spacecraft played thermolytic beams across Neriton. The remaining cities and their surroundings flashed into flames of fierce intensity. It was a strange fire, more befitting a sun than a planet. Its light overwhelmed Sangraal, bleaching the landscape of Neriton to a deathlike white. Greg mentally started as he realized that the aliens meant to slowly ignite and burn off the beautiful surface of Neriton. The final torture was under way.

Loud detonations assaulted Greg's ears with such rapidity that he could not distinguish the individual contributors. A solid wall of flame marched slowly across Neriton, preceded by a rushing cloud of glowing, superheated gases and incandescent particles. Whatever this cloud touched also caught fire. The gases were so hot they easily melted through rocks. Frothy, liquid remnants of the planet were ejected thousands of meters into the atmosphere along trails of fire. Fierce winds blew with terrible force, and the ground trembled in its death agony. Overhead, the misty sky grew dark until Omphalos/Sangraal could no longer be seen. Black clouds laced with vast, raging lightning storms rose up for many kilometers and spread out like deadly canopies to reflect back the fires below.

Ahead of the fire, the trembling ground became a series of severe, large-scale quakes which tore open fissures and lifted mountains. The quakes penetrated deeply into the planet. Everywhere basins and fracture lines formed. Gas-filled lava flowed from the fissures, accompanied by explosions which threw out incandescent ash and clots of frothy lava. Steam jets issued from other fissures and torrents of rain mixed with ash followed these emissions until a monstrous, fluidic mass of boiling mud engulfed the area about the fissures.

Intense electrical storms flowered all over the planet, and lightning signed its deadly signature to the black clouds. The living were surrounded by fiery aureoles, and their bodies emanated sparks until they looked like the spirits they were destined to become. These electrical discharges and the advancing fire were all the light that was left for those terrified few who struggled through the acrid, poisonous gases and the crashes of thunder. Ash and pain were all they felt and tasted.

One by one the remaining Lacertian communities and underground shelters vanished in the holocaust. The shields failed to function. The sight was ugly. Death came before the fire. Death came from the blast of the superheated cloud and from the scorching and asphyxiation caused by the hot, poisonous gases in the cloud. There was little or no free oxygen left, leaving many substances carbonized ahead of the oncoming wall of stellular flame. Those bodies which had not yet carbonized were discolored and inflated. The ones who survived the scorching were left in writhing pain until suffocation ended their misery.

Blinding acids formed from the rains and vapors. Winged reptiles and insects fell dead from the skies, and the water creatures died where they swam.

The seas explosively boiled like some hideous brown brew. The violent forces lifted waves of steam into the atmosphere, where they merged with the exploding black clouds of ash.

The fiery hurricane continued to march across the face of Neriton like some terrible wind from Pyriphlegethon. Behind the flame swept furious winds, sucking up everything into an immense updraft.

The crew of the *Leos* were rapidly losing contacts with the surface. As each enclave of Lacerti was destroyed, another mental link was broken. The crew were in no immediate danger, since the flame seemed confined to the upper part of the crust, and the shields offered adequate protection against the planetological forces at work around them. The passive sensors detected nothing in the places where the fires had been.

With this energy-sealing trap tightening around them, the crew immediately realized the need for a secure escape route. They activated the nullor under the cover of the flames overhead, boring a passageway to the surface. The crust vanished without warning along a carefully designed pathway, yielding a fused tunnel, twisted and contoured into a weird protective labyrinth. At a selected point just ahead of the flame wall, the nullor burst through the surface and protected the opening as the fierce Abaddonese flames passed by. The flames had no purpose other than mindless destruction, and so they easily accommodated the destructive anti-force which purposefully guarded the tunnel. The nullor held undetected against the torrential forces around it, and the crew sat back in their recliners with relief. They had a pathway to the surface if anyone wanted to return there.

Their relief was short-lived. The sensors told them that the passageway was open, but it was too small at the end for the *Leos.* They might walk as individuals on the wasteland above, but they could never leave it, nor could they risk contacting their home worlds. And the Federation could learn nothing from its sensors of what had happened to a planet known only to it as Sangraal II.

For the crew of the *Leos* and their Lacertian passengers, there came a period of enervating despondency. They performed their tasks more like automatons than intelligent beings.

Overhead, the aliens finished their gruesome task and froze the surface into the twisted, blackened mass that Greg knew as Sangraal II. He could no longer bring himself to apply such names as Nelumbo or Neriton to the dead world above. Like the crew of the *Leos,* he puzzled over the weapon which the aliens had used. The weapon had carefully controlled the extent of energy release, thereby preserving the inner planetary features during its passage across the planet. The surface was quickly cooled afterward to a temperature high enough to keep all water off the surface. But most puzzling of all to the crew was the type and extent of the trap they were in. The crust and the ash-laden atmosphere were energy sinks. Only gravity penetrated this barrier, as if the aliens desired to leave the blackened planetary hulk intact; however, the crust filtered the gravitational field, rendering it useless for communicative purposes. No longer did the magnetic forces act to restrain the deadly space radiation, while the surface remained sufficiently hot to prevent the accumulation of water. These environmental changes worked to ensure that Sangraal II would stay dead.

The crew of the *Leos* had no more success than the crew of the *Odyssey* in probing the energy sink. They did not know if the energy sink was a natural aftermath of the thermolytic weapon, or whether the aliens had cleverly laced the surface and the atmosphere with shields and other artificial barriers before cooling it. The latter theory, if true, would explain the use of all the energy soaked up by the surface. Their single consolation was the knowledge that the energy sink was so complete that even its builders could not penetrate it.

Here and there in the days following the final destruction of the surface, the crew of the *Leos* made contact with other Lacertian survivors who had managed to tunnel deep enough to escape the doom of Hephaestus. In the ensuing weeks, some of these survivors found passageways to the surface, and plans were made for a gathering of all who were left. But even here the aliens had anticipated such a possibility, and before they departed, they left the surface populated with their multilegged companions who sought out the passageways and destroyed the survivors.

The crew of the *Leos* acted quickly to cover their tunnel with the energy-absorbing debris of the surface so that the demons could not find them. Subsequently they built an elaborate entrance system and guarded it with the nullor, designing it to fire automatically at any Apollyoni spacecraft which got too close to the entrance. They planned no aggressive actions against the eight-legged creatures with their weapon for they had learned from the creatures' earlier attacks on the cities and from the recent attacks on other survivors in the tunnels that the immobilization or destruction of one of these brutes brought an immediate, deadly response from the aliens. Even in their absence the aliens had devised some manner of permanently monitoring their beasts. Greg felt the ice in his body again. Now he knew why Klagor had said they were in terrible danger. Even now, an alien craft might be speeding toward Sangraal II.

But Klagor did not release his passengers on this journey through time. Greg "watched" as the Federation crew expanded their hiding place so they and the Lacerti could live outside the ship. They used the materials of the planet and their converters to set up additional screens and warning devices. They built an elaborately concealed transmitter to send a coded warning once the alien screens were down: the *Leos* would not be a lure for others. Greg observed that the humans no longer hid their technology from the Lacerti—the two races were partners in their prison and both races shared in the work and the planning.

The years passed slowly for the human crew. They continued to try to reach the surface, only to be frustrated at every turn. It was on one of the larger expeditions that the final act was played out. An improperly built tunnel collapsed during a sudden, unforeseen quake induced by the stresses built up in the planet during the final alien attack. The human crew and most of the Lacerti perished in their alien prison, crushed in a rubble of energy-absorbing debris from the surface. The remaining Lacerti could not beam them out. Greg now felt the pain of loss which must have been Richard's so many years ago.

Rana Klagor and the few remaining Lacertian survivors continued to perform the functions they had been taught by the humans. Realizing that their civilization was dead and that the human devices could perform without them, they seemed to lose all purpose in living. Quietly, they died.

Klagor was the last. Greg was not sure whether this was by accident or by the will of the others. Klagor had turned on the transmitters to send out coded messages at random intervals. He used powerful bursts to penetrate the ashen energy barrier in the atmosphere. To Klagor, it was of no concern whether the aliens were still screening off the planet. Sooner or later, the Federation crew had told him, the aliens would tire of their vigil and let the screens down, perhaps as the final bait.

Then Klagor died, the last of his race, alone among equipment he had not understood a few years earlier.

Klagor's thoughts continued in Greg's mind: *I was the last. What you see now are my remains, preserved inside this tank for your direct view and examination. The equipment about you, including my thought messages, is automatically operated. My thoughts have been collated by a computer which now thinks for me. No one lives on Nelumbo except you.*

I have taken you on a journey that lasted millions of your years. You have seen in minutes of your real time the rise and fall of our civilization. You have seen the beauty and life which was ours. And you have seen the pain and death which came to us. You can believe what you will but take these mental images back to your Federation.

I will now release you from my control to do as you please.

The effects of the stunnor quickly left Greg, and he reached out to some consoles to support himself. He was completely exhausted. His emotions had run through their full range, and his mind was filled with the history of another race, a history he knew better than that of his own. Every nerve in his mind and body screamed for relief.

The cavern was now fully in view again. He saw Ben and Art showing similar signs of exhaustion. Had they been on the same journey? Greg had not been aware of them. His suit chronometer mentally told him that Klagor was correct in his time—the whole mental journey had taken only a few minutes.

He looked up at the giant reptilelike shape towering over him in the hexahedral container. "I'm sorry," he whispered. His eyes were moist. He looked down and saw his hands and feet through the faint shimmering field of his shield suit. Everything seemed the same, but he felt different. He had different thoughts. He did not attribute these thoughts to Klagor; rather, he saw pieces of his life coalescing and taking form like the birth of a star. He saw Ziol and Ra. Earth and Sol. Frey and Jotunnheim. Coni in all her beauty, with her sad, shining viridescent eyes, so reminiscent of the plants of Frey and Nelumbo. Ahriman. The *Odyssey*. The battle in the channel. The death of Neriton. The events of his life spun through his mind like a cerebral Omphalean wheel leading into a swirling catharsis. What is it all about? he asked himself. Why has all this happened?

Through his suit, he felt a hand on his shoulder. He looked up. Ben was smiling at him with a lined face, tired and aged like the men of ancient times, and Art was staring at the creature that had been Rana Klagor.

Ben walked around the cavern, examining equipment with his suit probes. "It looks genuine," he said after he completed his circuit. "And it looks like standard Fleet gear, a little dated in places. Some modifications here and there. The crew or the Lacerti probably altered the basic Fleet design."

Greg finally amassed enough words to ask, "Did you both experience the death of this planet? Were you there for all that destruction?"

Ben nodded. Art simply shifted his uncanny stare from Klagor to Greg.

"Klagor used some kind of mental link and gave us the full tour," Ben said. "I imagine this whole process has been in readiness for years, just for us." Ben turned to the body of Klagor. *I want you to give us the flight recorder of the* Leos. *And I want you to return us to our ship.*

A receptacle opened in the pedestal and the flight recorder materialized. Ben picked it up, examined it with his suit probes and then stored it in the field of his suit.

Klagor's thoughts came to them again. *You have the flight recorder. If you have any questions, I will answer them. But your time is short. Use it wisely.*

Did you take us all on the same trip? Greg asked.

Yes. It was our hope that when you returned you would let your mental links extract our story for the benefit of your people.

Greg asked, *But is it real? Did it happen?*

The proof is in your minds and on the surface.

Can you show us where the crew of the Leos *are buried?* Art asked, his features coldly molded.

One of the tunnels lit up by unseen illuminators.

Down that tunnel almost around Nelumbo. I can take you there but your time is short. There is nothing to see. The tunnel is sealed. I can also take you to the Leos *if you wish.*

"I think we had better return," Ben replied firmly, his words intended more for the living than the dead. He looked at Art and then at Klagor. *May we come back later?*

It may already be too late. Even now your friend is trying to contact you, and my imitators will not deceive him. I will relay his signal to you.

Greg looked hard at Ben and Art. Richard was sworn to maintain communications silence. If he was trying to contact them, then something must be drastically amiss outside.

Richard's thought message poured into their tired minds. *Ben! Greg! Art! Do you receive me? I'm picking up a new transmission from near the channel. It's coming through the relay unit, and it's unlike any signal we've received on this planet!*

12

BATTLE

Hell is empty,
And all the devils are here.

—William Shakespeare, *The Tempest*

Ben frantically looked at the lifeless yet undying Klagor. *We must communicate with him now.*

The means are there, Klagor answered. *Use your links.*

Rich, we've found what we came for, Ben thought. *We're returning immediately. We suspect the signal is related to the creature Greg killed, so stay on full alert and be prepared for more of those monsters or even alien starships. If anything goes wrong, lift off immediately. Acknowledge.*

Acknowledge, came the reply. *What's happening?*

We'll explain later. We're on our way back now. Ben turned his attention back to Klagor. *Return us to the surface. We'll take our knowledge home with us. If you are right, we thank you for what you have done. Our worlds may live because of you. And we will remember Neriton. And avenge your civilization.*

You know what must be done, Klagor replied. *This place is of no more use to you. I will immobilize you again in order to transmit you quickly to the surface. Go with good thoughts.*

The silent stunnor took effect again with nerve-blinding speed. Then the tractor beam whisked them from the cavern, leaving it bereft of life, and plunged them into the Stygian black tunnel. Their return seemed faster to Greg, perhaps because he had been through the tunnel once and knew what to expect.

Ahead of them, the large guardian boulder rolled to one side, exposing the artificial light produced from the enhancing scanners aboard the *Odyssey.* They emerged into the blackened channel like renascent zygotes to find everything just as they left it. The stunnor and tractor beams ceased to enfold them, and their scanners showed the boulder rolling smoothly and silently into place. Nowhere could they "see" the concealed antenna.

Already, Greg was having trouble deciding whether what he had been through was real. The images persisted, and his trained mind told him that it was real. What it could not tell him was whether the events were all true.

Ben's thoughts on the telepathic link interrupted Greg's mental examination of his experience in the tunnel. *Rich! Give me a report on the signals!*

Richard's reply came back immediately in Greg's mind. *It was a single pulse, much like the signals we've been chasing, but the pattern was totally different. Here is a sample.* A burst of static entered Greg's mind. *It's definitely not a natural signal. But I can't decode it and like the other signals, it has no identifiable receiver.*

Can you locate the source? Ben asked.

Not from where the Odyssey *is. The relay unit also picked it up so it must be on the ground above the channel and judging from the strength, it must be fairly close to us.*

Ben continued, *Rich, from what we've learned in the last few minutes, that signal may be a call for more of those creatures, or it may even be a call for alien spacecraft. We're picking up our gear and will be with you as soon as we can. Be alert and ready to lift off without us if necessary.*

Ben…what did you find? Richard asked. *Anything on the* Leos?

Ben "looked" at Art and Greg with cold, dark eyes that seemed to suck up light just like the ground around them. *From what we've learned…the entire crew was destroyed. I'm sorry, Rich. I'll explain when we get back. I'd like to set up a data link, but we've got to devote our thoughts to getting out of here.*

Systematically, they retrieved all their equipment then made their way through the twisted scar on the face of Sangraal II. Only the hidden relay unit was left because too much time would be involved in getting it back, and without the scanners on board the *Odyssey,* the relay unit was useless. By design, the relay unit would not provide any clues to the unit's origins. Moreover, as the power of the relay unit was sucked up by the planet, its shield would eventually collapse and destroy the unit.

The dust-filled channel with its sheer black walls assumed new meaning for Greg. After seeing Nelumbo/Neriton, he felt the death of this planet even more personally than before. He was repulsed by the thought that the dust he walked on was once living plants and animals. How total the destruction had been that one could no longer differentiate the forms of the living! And the murky, ash-filled atmosphere seemed to mock Neriton's once beautiful misty skies.

Without further incidents, the three men returned to the *Odyssey,* their suits containing all the equipment (except the relay unit) they had taken with them.

"Greg, why don't you hook up a link with Rich and transmit Klagor's story," Ben suggested once they were back in the control room. "He's as involved as the rest of us and might as well know the story now. His link filters should protect him from any mental controls that may have been subconsciously implanted in us by Klagor." Turning to Art, Ben said, "Take the flight recorder from the *Leos,* run a quick examination on it—I couldn't find anything wrong with it—and beam its contents to the monitor along with your evaluation of its condition. Also send Klagor's story. I'll get the ship ready to leave and review what has been learned about the new signal. I'll need your help, Art, in concealing the fact that we were here." Art silently took the proffered flight recorder and stared intently at it for a few moments before doing as Ben requested.

Greg set up a mental data transmission link with Richard, and they both settled in their recliners. Greg turned to Richard. "It's not pretty, and we don't know how much is true, so keep your filters active." Richard nodded, and the link transmission began. Greg watched pain and suffering write their ugly lines across Richard's handsome face. Greg did his best to ease the flow rate of information so that his friend and fellow crewman suffered as little as possible.

When Greg's difficult task was done, Richard withdrew from the link. He put his hands to his eyes and slowly shook his head. "I don't believe it!" he repeated to himself softly along with almost silent cursing.

Greg went to his side and placed a firm hand on his arm. "We don't know how much is true. I'm sorry."

Richard looked at him. "What an awful way to go. A whole planet destroyed. Why? For what reason? So much life, so much good, all gone!"

Greg could not find the words to ease Richard's burden. Greg felt closer to him now that he also knew his father. "Sometimes life makes no sense," Greg said, then looked away from Richard. "I got to know him, too. He was a good man, and it was a good crew. At least now we know what happened."

"I keep wondering if my brother was right," Richard said almost absently. "So much sorrow has accompanied our flight to the stars—my dad's death and the problem we had on the Perimeter."

Greg tried to soothe him. "If Klagor is right, had we not made this flight we could have been tied up by the Perimeter waiting helplessly for these…Apollyoni."

Art laughed derisively. Greg and Richard turned to see him watching them. Art said, "I wondered how long it would take for you to make a connection between what Klagor told us and what Coni told you."

Greg stood up, defiance rising within him. "Whether the terror Coni faced is related to what happened here makes no difference. Her father's theory fits Klagor's story and the name suits. This world was utterly destroyed."

"But by whom?" Art asked in a penetrating tone. "And why? We have only one version and possibly a rigged version at that. Who knows what mental traps may have been buried in our link with Klagor."

"You seem to have resisted any traps," Greg replied with barely concealed sarcasm.

"Perhaps I fought better than you or Ben. You already half-believed the Apollyoni theory. And Ben wanted to believe in some anti-Federation conspiracy."

"What about the flight recorder?" Greg asked in a cutting tone. "Ben said it was okay."

"So it seems. But even that could be a cover."

"Does it verify Klagor's story?" Greg asked angrily.

Art shrugged. "There's a relationship. But the recorder could have been tampered with."

"Oh, shit!" Greg turned away and walked to his couch.

"Damnit! Listen to me!" Art yelled. "What do we really know about Klagor's story. *Nothing!* Not one damned thing, except for this flight recorder."

"And one burned-out planet," Richard added coldly. "Explain that, Art."

"Maybe there *was* a war," Art replied. "But it doesn't concern us. It was a private matter between two alien civilizations. The Lacerti may have been as guilty as Greg's Apollyoni."

Richard gave a short, mirthless laugh of rebuttal. "Does the *Leos* concern us?"

"The *Leos* may have been trapped in someone else's war or tricked into participating," Art replied. "For all we know, the Lacerti may have been the villains Greg talks about. Maybe someone finally got their just revenge. In fact, our presence here may lead these aliens to believe that we sided with their enemies."

Ben turned around in his recliner. "There's only one flaw in your theory, Art. We know from our sensors that there were no Sangraal-based starships operating around this system before the *Leos* arrived, and everything was screened off. Even if they could have concealed such ships, which doesn't make sense, they couldn't have known we spent years passively monitoring the system. There was no evidence that the life forms *on* the planet had the necessary space technology. We found no evidence anywhere in the Sangraal system to show that the inhabitants of this planet ever left it. They didn't even have a space defense system. As far as I'm concerned, every fact points to the conclusion that the Lacerti were as they portrayed themselves—innocent, planet-bound victims of some terror, call it the Apollyoni or whatever, from space."

"What you are saying doesn't make sense," Art said. "I can't visualize a race which has advanced to the point of star flight traveling about the Galaxy destroying life. There's no reason for it."

"That same thought has puzzled me, too," Greg said quietly. "But I've done a lot of thinking about it since I killed that creature in the channel. I've got a few ideas, but I'm not sure they all fit together.

"If we assume such a race as the Apollyoni does exist, their actions may not—in fact, they don't have to—make any sense to us. But who knows what sense it makes to them? Our own history is replete with societies that seemed to revel in dealing out death and destruction. Maybe the dominant social pattern of their period of spaceflight was devoted to spreading the kind of hell we have seen here.

"Who knows how it is justified? Maybe they believe they are purifying the Galaxy by cauterizing undesirable races. It may even be some kind of religious fanaticism. Maybe their biological makeup is such that killing gives them a thrill. I could list a dozen other reasons for their actions."

"The discussion is academic," Ben said. "Our job is to return to the Federation and let the probes settle the question. If Klagor is correct, we will have to act quickly to prepare the Federation."

Art glared at Ben, his blue eyes afire. "That's all you can think about. Prepare for war. Killing. I think this whole mission was contrived to provoke some sort of incident and undo the peace humanity has achieved. You're no better than the Apollyoni."

"Ease off, Art!" Richard heatedly interjected. "Ben said nothing about going to war. He said that we must alert the Federation. When contact comes, I'm sure Council will encourage communication between our two races so that we can understand them. But we must be prepared to ward off what happened here."

"We don't know what happened here!" Art retorted angrily. "We only know the story of a dead lizard. And you're letting sentiment enter the picture."

Greg was furious now and swore loudly. "We know a planet has died! Damnit, there's no sentiment in that fact! You speak of emotional biases—does that include xenophobia? 'Dead lizard'—shit! Did nothing in that tunnel mean anything to you?" He turned away in disgust.

Ben focused his eyes on Greg. "Take it easy," Ben said in his quiet commanding voice, then he looked at Art. "Greg is saying what has disturbed me. We have a dead planet which defies natural explanation. Our Federation sensors would have noted any natural event which caused this planet to die. We know Rich's father came here and from all the evidence we have, he and his crew died here."

"We don't know that for sure," Art said. "We never got to explore that tunnel, and the flight recorder could have been altered."

"Rich received a signal which cut short our exploration, or have you forgotten?" Ben retorted, his features grimly etched with emotional acid.

"Another trick of Klagor's to keep us from exploring the tunnels," Art said coldly. "The *Leos* and its crew may still be there, prisoners of the Lacerti."

"Do you want to go back and look?" Ben asked incredulously. "You know the risk."

Art shook his head.

"The *Leos* is not the first ship to vanish mysteriously," Ben continued. "You know Coni Sanderson. Do you believe her?"

"I'm not going to be led down that path again. We've argued these points before. The seeds of doubt and destruction have been planted in our minds."

"I don't believe that you truly think Council would be so naive as to turn a first contact into a war," Ben responded. "We'll be a lot more alert, that's all."

"No, it goes beyond that," Art said. "When this story gets out, people will clamor to arm the Fleet with nullors. We'll be on war footing again. Humanity will be violent again. Everything Syncretism has worked for..."

"Is that all you care about?" Richard asked in disbelief. "Are you telling us we should withhold our story because it doesn't fit some preconceived political or philosophical theory?"

"He wants a Procrustean fit," Greg murmured cynically.

"What kind of a scientist are you?" Richard asked.

"One who believes in peace," Art replied with the assurance of one steeped in *novus ordo seclorum*.

"The only peace we seem to have is here," Richard said with a wave of his hand, encompassing the planet outside. "If the aliens consider us enemies for opposing such terror and destruction, then so be it."

"I think we've argued this point enough," Ben said. "I've examined the signals and can make nothing of them. But then if they are a warning, they do not have to make sense. The *Odyssey* is ready for liftoff. Art, did you complete the transmission of the data on the flight recorder?"

"Yes," Art replied, his tone subdued. "The monitor has it all now."

"Okay, you and I are going to see what can be done to conceal our presence here. Maybe high-power, short-duration bursts of the tractor beam will do it. Rich, let's get airborne over the channel. Greg, check out all systems and back Rich up. I want you both to pick several jump points in case we need them." It was quietly understood by all that these jump points could not reveal the location of the Federation. As Richard began the final operation, the crew silently reactivated their suits, protectors of life in this deadly, insentient world.

On the stillness of its pellor rays, the *Odyssey* moved over the concealing rocks and out of the black cavern and climbed above the debris-laden gash of a channel. From its ghostly position in the swirling clouds of ash and vapor, the ship sent bursts of its tractor beam to the blackened surface.

"Nothing!" Ben muttered in disgust. "We'll have to leave it as it is. Let's get out of here."

As the *Odyssey* began to climb rapidly into the atmosphere, Greg exclaimed, "Ben! I ran a final closure check on the scanners and sensors. *The whole Sangraal system has just been screened off!*"

"What about the monitor?" Ben asked harshly.

"It's inside the screen," Greg said. "With us." Even to himself his words sounded hollow in the quiet control room.

"I think the trap is being sprung," Ben said grimly. "Full speed to the nearest jump point. Kick on the impellor."

Richard mentally established the necessary confining and stabilizing fields, then he activated the engine injector. Phase mixing and stability were quickly achieved. The fields focused the energy flux and ejected the awesome energy into the black void of Sangraal II. The *Odyssey* soared out of the atmosphere on a trail of galactic fire.

Ben was on the link. *We stay on full link hookup. No voice. Monitor the scanners for any disguised spaceships entering the system. Full alert!*

The *Odyssey* streaked away from Sangraal II and "above" the plane of the Sangraal system toward the nearest gate to metaspace.

A familiar, ominous shape burst into Greg's mind like a glowing meteor. It was a fleeting image that darted through his mind like some Protean wisp. He attempted to hold on to it. *Ben! An alien exited ahead. It matches Klagor's description . It's coming on fast! The damned thing is slipping all over the spectrum, but the scanner has it.*

Richard quickly fed Ben the alternate gate locations. Ben turned the *Odyssey* away from the closing alien spacecraft.

Another glowing shape flamed into being in Greg's mind. *There's a second! They're trying to take us!*

Ben turned the *Odyssey* again. They were nearing luxon speed and had not yet escaped from the inner region of the Sangraal system. Suddenly, the *Odyssey* slowed its pace. Its shields flickered.

Greg: *Some kind of tractor beam! Very powerful. Fortunately, it was just a burst.*

Richard: *What have they got? They almost penetrated! If they get our range or slow us down enough to use an area-wide beam, we're finished!*

Ben: *They're trying to stop us. Also trying to test our shields. Can't make meta-space now, and we're cut off from Neriton. They'll destroy or capture us if we run for it.* Ben turned the *Odyssey* a third time and started a series of rapid evasive maneuvers. *Got to get rid of them. Our only hope is that they want to capture us alive. We responded to the bait. They may never get this chance again.*

The *Odyssey* darted effortlessly through space along the only path open to it: Sangraal.

Art: *This is insane. They only want to capture us. Let's not start a war!*

Ben: *Shut up! We can't take chances. If they mean us no harm, they'll leave us alone. We can't afford to be captured, and now that the monitor is also sealed off, we can't let them destroy us. We've got to get our message back some way.*

Art: *From the middle of a sun?*

Ignoring Art, Ben thought, *Rich! All surplus power to the shields. We're going into Sangraal. They won't try to capture us there. Hold the engine under control so we don't blow the star.*

The *Odyssey* sliced through the vacuum of space like a glowing fish surrounded by invisible feelers. It sped along a randomly twisted path, darting quickly around the oncoming flashes of tractor beam energy sent to ensnare it.

In unison, the two alien craft swung around to cover any possible path of retreat. Like deadly eels, these ships sent out pulsed tractor beams, guiding the *Odyssey* and forcing it to reduce speed.

Greg felt his insides go cold. He locked his emotions into the control he had learned from the Fleet. Events were happening too fast for thought or emotion. This action was for real, and the stakes were their lives. He responded as one with his crewmates and his ship.

Sangraal loomed ahead, its incandescent, raging surface threatening them with flaming dissolution in a huge, seething cauldron of blazing gas. But Greg worried more about their ability to control the whirling maelstrom inside the *Odyssey*. If they were not careful, they could cause a nova with their engine, adding the destruction of a solar system to their list of crimes. Briefly, he remembered the image of cattle trapped between a cliff and a fire. Where were the cattle headed now?

The *Odyssey* easily penetrated the albescent, glowing gases of the corona, as if they were an ephemeral substance, a mere ionized wisp of pearly light. The ship slipped quietly among the vast pink prominences which hung like evanescent curtains above the pale, salmon-colored chromosphere of Sangraal. As seen in profile by the scanners, these curtains became like reddish sheets of flame that played in glimmering patterns, twisting and writhing into the graceful arches and curves of a mythical Gheberan dwelling. Some coalesced in the corona, only to fall back along the field lines of Sangraal like long twisted ribbons of incandescent gas. Others surged upward with geyserlike ferocity, reaching hundreds of thousands of kilometers into space to make seething loops of reddish nuclear flame.

Viewed from the outside through the scanners, Greg saw the *Odyssey* as an insignificant glowing ellipsoid of stability lost among the interlacing networks of turbulent gases. Intense radiant pressure and gases, which were heated into incandescence, assaulted the *Odyssey's* shields in unison with charged particles riding on powerful fields. Inside, he and the others worked feverishly at staying alive. No one had any concern about the dangers raging in the huge nuclear furnace outside their tiny ship because the potent shields easily overwhelmed the vast fury of Sangraal. Greg sensed the same nervous concern in all of them, for in the bowels of their small shelter of life they held the power to destroy this tumultuous inferno with its clouds of luminous nuclear smoke, and they fought mightily to keep that power under control.

With gradually decreasing velocity, the *Odyssey* plunged deeper into the turbulent atmosphere of Sangraal. Hot gases and charged particles continued to race out of the cataclysmic chaos to beat at the *Odyssey's* shields. Eruptions of stellar energy burst around the ship as it glided over the "surface", falling deeper into the red-hued chromosphere, battered by intense shock waves, where bladelike jets of gases squirted up several thousand kilometers. Absorbent temperatures continued to increase outside the ship. Everywhere, brilliant, hot gases swirled and danced in tremendous turmoil amid ghostly wisps of radiant energy.

Near the lower level of the chromosphere, Richard sent, *We can't go much deeper without diverting energy from the shields to the engine fields. I can sense an effect already on the gases below us.*

We'll stop and wait, Ben replied. *This stratum may be the best place.* He put the ergon impeller on standby, using the pellor rays to control the motion of the ship.

The *Odyssey* leveled off above the tenuous yellow-white photosphere where profuse, seething geysers of hot gases rose from the visibly opaque lower levels. Hydrogen ions streamed out of the opacity through the flimsy cloak of gases, ramming futilely against the shields. Greg felt the whirling interchange of particles trapped between the forces of flaming heat within Sangraal and the gravitational attraction without. Swirling eddies formed within the gases, their amorphous masses becoming twisted by the incandescent turbulence. Flaming white-hot gases spun into violent whirlpools, forming vast magnetic hurricanes to spin out their fury across the "surface" of Sangraal. Throughout most of the total sensory spectrum, Greg experienced a volatile entity engulfed in tremendous turmoil, a thing alive with brilliant change and crackling noise. And he remembered the death of Sangraal's second planet.

Almost automatically, for they all knew the answer, Ben asked, *Where are the aliens?*

Greg responded, *They're still with us but staying beyond the corona. They're monitoring our every move.*

We wait, Ben thought. With thought-words and images, he quickly explained, *If they are the Apollyoni, they'll try to capture us so they can find the Federation and destroy it. If we've made some kind of colossal mistake and they mean us no harm—we have not harmed them—they'll realize we want to be left alone and leave. I'm gambling that if they do want to capture us, they'll want to badly enough to avoid killing us. And if they use their tractor beam again, they'll destroy us and their chance to find our home base. This is our only way of proving we have a self-destruct capability that will automatically function if put to the test.*

No one replied. Each man continued with his assigned job. Greg shifted his body in his recliner, oblivious to the many bodily functions it performed for him. His attention was focused inward, to the flaming ball within his mind. With the aid of the scanners, he saw every prominence, every sunspot, every flare, and he could plunge into the multimillion-degree heat of Sangraal's center. Physically, he had never been this close to a star. Most ships lacked the extra margin of safety to risk coming this close without damaging the star. Even though he knew that he controlled more energy than had ever been associated with Sangraal, he still felt in awe of this mighty sphere of glowing, swirling gas. He remembered Ra. And Sol. Here was the origin of life. A baptism by fire in the most literal sense. Now the question he pondered was whether their final rites would also be by fire.

His mind simultaneously focused on the two alien spacecraft. Despite their constant attempts at concealment, their images were also implanted in his mind by the scanners. For several minutes the two ships hovered just beyond the delicate streamers of the corona, then they separated. One moved farther away from Sangraal until it was visually shielded by Sangraal's disk. It was still "visible" in their minds. No one moved inside the *Odyssey,* as each man concentrated on the multifaceted third eye within him.

The remaining ship moved.

Ben! Greg flashed.

I 'see' it! Ben replied. *Stand by for trouble. I think they've decided to take us. They're gambling that we lack the ability to harm them and that our desire to live is so great that we don't really want to destroy ourselves. Rich, I'm taking control of the impeller and the tractor beam. Hold the* Odyssey *steady with the pellor ray and watch that other craft. When I signal, take the* Odyssey *back to Neriton—as fast as possible!*

Richard acknowledged his orders. Greg saw that his friend was as puzzled as he. Self-consciously, Greg glanced back at Art. Art ignored his glance, his vaporous eyes fixed on the back of Ben's recliner like some damaged but still operative scanner.

Greg, what can you tell me about that ship's shields? Ben asked.

My data show they have about the same strength as ours, Greg replied.

The alien craft sped through the luminous atmosphere of Sangraal straight toward the *Odyssey* on a path that kept it clear of the sensed direction of the ergon impeller. Through the link, Greg felt its sensory equipment probing the *Odyssey* for any sign of weakness.

Richard: *Between the engine, Sangraal and those probes, the shields are working overtime.*

Ben: *Just keep that path to Neriton open. And keep us away from that second ship.*

The first alien ship was in the chromosphere now, and it was slowing down rapidly, as if preparing for a rendezvous.

Art spoke slowly, his voice filled with quiet pleading, "Ben, don't do this. If they're friendly…"

I said no voice, Ben replied. *We stay on the link until this is done. The only friendly visitors to Sangraal were the crew of the* Leos *and they're dead.* Almost as an afterthought, he added the damning thought, *Do you want to be relieved?*

No!

Ben: *Greg, you back up Art. Rich, are you ready?*

Yes.

The alien craft closed slowly on the *Odyssey.* It was very close.

Art: *There's been no attempt at communication.*

Ben: *Why should they? They know that we know about them. For what other reason have they come visiting with concealing screens and tractor beams that can tear a shield apart? And I have no interest in talking to anyone like that, except to tell them to get the hell out of here.*

The *Odyssey's* shields gave a little, then quickly readjusted.

Greg: *They're probing. They're going to try to coax us out by weakening our shields.*

Richard: *I see now why they took the chance of coming in here with us. Clever bastards! At this range, they can tamper with our shields as slowly and carefully as they want, using their tractor beam to manipulate us out of here.*

Ben did nothing. He continued to hold the ship firmly under his mental control.

The alien craft probed again and again with its powerful tractor beam, now feeling with the delicate touch of a masseuse for some soft spot, now thrusting with the skill of a swordsman. The shields were rapidly shifting to cope with each new onslaught in this intense fencing of energy. *And they were moving slowly away from Sangraal!*

Simultaneously, Ben fired the ergon impeller at the luminous photosphere, and focused the *Odyssey's* powerful tractor beam on a single spot in the alien shields. Richard struggled with the pellor ray as the hellish torrent of energy released from the confining fields of the engine tore through the photosphere and lower levels of Sangraal, releasing a seething ocean of hot gases and radiant energy. Driven by the intense radiant pressures below, a massive surging prominence rose up like some colossal fiery amoeba from beneath the photosphere, accompanied by blasting radiation, bursts of energy and high-speed charged particles. The two starships were enveloped by this tremendous scorching tumescence.

The alien shields weakened under the sudden focused attack of the *Odyssey's* tractor beam. The power drain forced the alien tractor beam to withdraw and its engine to power down. Instantly, Ben maneuvered the *Odyssey's* field structure to focus both the tractor beam and the engine flux on the alien ship. With savage abruptness, he fired both systems. The alien shields fought to stabilize against the *Odyssey's* dual swords of battle and the erupting stellar energy surging about them. The alien ship wavered…it flickered…

The craft vanished in a flare of radiant energy.

Ben's mind screamed: *Get us out of here!*

Richard instantly took control of the *Odyssey,* sending it bursting away from Sangraal like a lost soul scurrying across Al Sirat, leaving the stellar surface to boil in uncontrolled violence. Greg breathed a little easier because the alien engine had evidently collapsed upon itself, leaving Sangraal and the *Odyssey* safe. The *Odyssey* arced away from the second ship on an evasive path to Neriton.

Greg worked frantically to keep up with the demands placed on him. He checked their course. He monitored all the systems. And he monitored Art's activities. So far, the other was cooperating. But Greg knew that Ben had wanted him to do more than just back up Art.

We have only one chance left now, Ben thought. *On Neriton, amid the channels and rocks, we may be equals. With Klagor's nullor we may be more than equal. Out here, they know what we can do and more importantly, what we can't do. That second ship could hold us on Sangraal until it got help, if it hasn't already used its pseudo-concealed position to send out a disguised signal. In any case, we'll just have to hope that these two were advance scouts who just happened to be close by and that the main fleet is some time away.*

The erupting disk of Sangraal etched itself in Greg's mind like a burning circle from hell. What they were dreading was now happening: over the flaming disk flashed the second ship with a velocity greater than that of the *Odyssey.*

Ben: *That crazy bastard will blow the system yet! Keep hard at the evasive maneuvers!*

Like some dazed insect flying away from the light, the *Odyssey* flew along its insanely erratic path toward Neriton.

A blast of energy tore through the nearby space, quickly followed by another.

Greg: *They've got the tractor beam going again. Damn! That beam is powerful!*

Again and again the *Odyssey* jerked away from the intended targets of the lancing beam, while ahead loomed the clutching Mephistophelean hole of Neriton. Behind streaked a glowing saucer that hurled short, lethal bolts of stabbing energy as it tried to capture the *Odyssey* or penetrate its shields.

Silence dominated the link except for the mechanical communications between crew and ship so necessary for their flight. Attention focused on two objects: Neriton and the alien tractor beam. Repeatedly, they dodged around the beam, unaware of these maneuvers inside their secure inertial system.

Time froze for an instant as the *Odyssey* shuddered in its rush for safety.

We've been hit! Richard flashed on the link. *The shields are damaged! We can't make it!*

13

RETURN TO NERITON

No poet but is twisted by my hands, twirlers of light,
From countless colored strands that merge at last in white.
— Robert Graves, *Watch the Northwind Rise*

To hell with the shields! *Keep the ship moving!* Ben's thought commands pierced Greg's mind with the rending thrust of an alien tractor beam.

Ben and Richard forced the *Odyssey* onward. Lines of strain and concentration grew like gnarled roots across their faces, seeking some source of sustenance. The *Odyssey* twisted around pulse after pulse of energy, its scanners providing advance warning and its computer providing the necessary randomness of movement.

Ben: *I'm placing all unneeded power on the shields. Power down the inertial system and payload area to minimum levels. Better hope our suits can take it.*

Greg double-checked his suit and redistributed the power by shifting it as Ben had ordered. Operating under reduced power, the inertial system readily transmitted a greatly attenuated version of the ship's motion to the control room. Greg felt the random wobbles, turns and twists, as if he were dancing in swirls on a whirling, vibrating, Corybantic carousel. It was little comfort to know that he felt only a fraction of the total motion or that his recliner and suit absorbed most of what got through to the control room. Greg forced all his thoughts to the flight.

The alien ship pumped out repeated bursts of its tractor beam like blood spurting from a severed artery. Only this blood could rip a shield apart and freeze a ship in midflight.

Neriton was closer. Seconds of flight remained. Art preceded the *Odyssey* on the scanner, pointing the way to Klagor's tunnel. The alien ship rushed after them with no sign of decreasing speed.

Art: *Ben! This speed! The engine! We'll tear up the planet!*

Ben: *It could suck us dry and never know we were here. Greg, are we clear for making the channel?*

Greg: *Yes.* He knew now why Ben had asked him to back up Art. By implication, Art had just been relieved. Ben had ceased to argue.

The *Odyssey* streaked into the enigmatic darkness of Neriton's noxious and corrosive atmosphere like a whizzing torch of hyperluminous energy, its engines trailing a torrent of controlled devastation. The energy-starved ash of Neriton's atmosphere clawed at the shields for relief from this hurtling bolt of power. The potent scanners battered through the vast, unbroken blackness, revealing the bleak landscape below. Nightmarish images of the wild, tortured face of Neriton rushed through Greg's mind: scenes of blasted rock, scorched basins, contorted ridges and winding channels, dominated by hulking heights, the protuberant scars of the original shattering blast of death. A carpet of dust and ejecta mantled the alien wasteland like the terminal ashes of some tortured phoenix. Superimposed on these accelerating views was a single, rushing saucer of penetrating light: the alien ship was still with them!

Greg: *Ben! Rich! The alien is in with us. Seems to be having no trouble following us.*

Ben: *We 'see' him.*

Richard: *That's no surprise—we left a trail as big as Sangraal! The bastards made this place, they should know their way around it!*

Swiftly, the *Odyssey* moved around Neriton while its altitude dropped until it barely skimmed the distorted, hummocky surface.

Richard: *The shields are taking a helluva beating. They could collapse!*

Ben: *Hold them, damnit!*

Several times the alien ship tried to force the *Odyssey* from its path, but Ben stubbornly held to his course. The alien tractor beam continued to thrust out at the *Odyssey,* only to be thwarted now by the parrying effects of the ash-filled atmosphere.

Ben laughed aloud, the coldness of his tone echoing eerily throughout the otherwise tomblike control room. *The rotten bastards have undone their own weapon.* Then he added, *We're going in before they get nasty.*

The *Odyssey* swooped down from its flaming path and dashed toward the rocky incision they knew so well.

Ben: *Power up the inertial system!*

With the inertial system on full strength, Greg felt at ease again, as if comfortably seated at home witnessing the sequence through some link-fed adventure tale.

Ben forced the *Odyssey* out of its twisted path long enough for it to race the length of the winding channel in less than a second. The *Odyssey* instantly dropped into the clearing, as if sucked into this mephitic black hole. Now level with the floor in the clearing, it shot into the huge, screening cavern.

The alien craft flashed after the *Odyssey,* its engine blazing. It hurtled across the channel after its prey...

A flare of energy pierced the ashen sky, its tight beam tearing through the alien ship. A brilliant flash of light ripped from this meeting of force and anti-force, and the alien ship froze in flight, then reeled slowly away from the channel in a blazing torrent of dissolution.

Greg: *Klagor got the son-of-a-bitch!*

Ben: *Don't bet on it. Cut in the relay unit. Let's see what we get.*

Immediately, the scanners were alive with views of the alien craft. Grumes of luminous energy broke away from the rapidly descending alien craft, and these were quickly swallowed by the hungry planet. The craft wobbled erratically, a dream shape moving though a highly viscous fluid, then it suddenly fell from view behind the ever-concealing milieu of Neriton.

Ben swore angrily as he broke voice silence. "The main part of the ship was still intact when it vanished behind that rise. The nullor must not have been properly calibrated for this damned atmosphere or for a craft moving like that. Now we don't know if that bastard is sitting out there waiting for us or whether he's finished." Ben turned his recliner around to face the rest of the crew. Greg could see that the tense look on Ben's face was giving way to an expression of concern and a hint of fatigue. "We can't leave until we know if the alien ship is destroyed," Ben said. "Judging from its flight path, it must have landed close-by, probably just over that rise. If it is mostly intact or even partially disabled, it could finish us if we tried to lift off. I'm sure they've decided to quit playing games with us. Since they can't capture us, they've got to eliminate us so that the human race doesn't do something about them. We know they have nullor-type weapons on their ships. I just hope like hell they haven't signaled for help." Ben stood up erectly and with an aura of power which made him seem taller than he actually was. "Rich, I want you and Art to repair the ship as best you can so we can jump. Can you do it?"

Richard nodded, his face grave. "We can rig up something that'll hold for a while. We may have to scuttle a few systems for power and parts, but the computer will fix it." Richard checked the computer's diagnostic feedback. "We'll need about five hours to do it, though."

Ben looked at Greg and with entreating eyes said, "Greg, I'd like you to join me on a scouting trip to see how the alien fared. Okay?"

Greg nodded, somewhat surprised at the ease with which he acquiesced to Ben's request. They all knew the choices and the slim odds for success given to them by the computer. "Okay," Greg said simply.

Ben turned to Richard. "The ground rules are still the same. If we get in trouble or don't call or don't come back within five hours, get out of here. Five hours should give us plenty of time to get to that rise, look around and come back. You had all better hope that they're too damaged to get a signal through this atmosphere because five hours is a damned long time to be stuck here in our present condition. If you have to leave, Rich, don't look for us or try to contact us. Your best bet is to move out low and hope they can't get you. And keep watching for those damned creatures and alien ships. Understood?"

"Yes," Richard replied in an automatic tone. With more feeling, he continued, "I think you're taking too much of a risk. We could all stay here, fix the ship and get out."

"Too much is riding on this mission now," Ben said. "The whole Sangraal system is screened off, including the monitor. It's anybody's guess what the Fleet is sensing about all of this. These aliens are clever, so everything here probably looks normal back home. But just one mistake on our part, or if that ship is still in a position to get us, particularly with a nullor, then we've lost the only chance the Federation has. The next planet to look like this could be Armstrong or Ziol or Earth." Ben looked around at each of the crew. "Any questions?" No one spoke. "Let's get going." He started out of the control room toward the teleporter room. Art stood up as Ben passed his recliner.

"Ben, I want to go with you," Art said quietly.

Ben stopped and looked hard at Art. "Why?" Ben asked without emotion.

"I've got my reasons. You don't need two of us in the ship. Rich can handle the repair work and fly out of here if he has to." Art's voice took on a tone of urgency. "Let me come with you. Three of us stand a better chance than two."

Ben turned his body so that it faced Art. Ben's brown eyes penetrated Art's like two nullors. "Why do you want to come?" Ben asked. His voice was demanding.

Art's hands and arms moved as if framing each word, "Ben, we may have made a serious mistake today. Suppose that despite all that has happened these aliens are innocent. I want to make sure we do the right thing out there. The contact must be correct. Maybe we can help them. Maybe we can undo this damage."

Ben turned away from Art. "I'm not arguing with you anymore, Art. You don't make sense. If you won't accept the facts, then go back to your damned dream world." Ben started to walk away, then apparently changing his mind, he paused and swiftly whirled around to face Art again, his eyes flashing anger. "Reality is out there!" he said with a wave of his hand. "You deny that at your peril. We have to live with *that*, not with what is in our minds. How can anyone undo that?" Ben started to turn away again. "You're too much of a risk out there."

Art moved quickly to block Ben's path, his voice reflecting Ben's anger. "You said you wanted me to return with the whole story. You need me because of what I represent. No one will believe that the rest of you weren't link-fed a bunch of lies. My people will accept my version. But if you keep me here at this crucial moment, you lose the whole mission. Think it over, Ben. Do you want to go back without what you really came for?"

Ben paused, his mouth tight, his eyes ablaze with black fury. "All right, you sonofabitch," he said finally. "You can come. But one wrong move out there or one argument and by my Fleet oath, I'll kill you. Just remember: I need someone, anyone, to get back with a message more than I need to indulge your idiosyncrasies. Is that understood?"

Art nodded, his face twisted with anger and hate. Greg personally felt every aspect of the conversation, in particular Ben's unprofessional and unethical resort to cursing a crewmate. At that moment, Greg realized the source of power Ben held over the others: it derived not from his official position but from within him, for he conveyed very clearly his message of making his own way in the Universe regardless of the social and legal customs of his society. His dominating and threatening independence, particularly noticeable when his will was challenged, constituted his ultimate power over people. Greg understood fully both the true strength *and* the danger of his ship commander. Ben was above their prosaic checks and balances; he had not idly threatened Art's life. *Ben seriously meant to kill Art if Art got in his way!*

Ben turned to Richard. "Can you manage by yourself? I can leave Greg."

Richard glanced at Greg, seeking an answer, but Greg signaled with his eyes that he wanted to go. Looking back at Ben, Richard said, "I'll manage."

Ben gave the briefest of nods and quietly left the control room. Art glared momentarily at Richard and Greg, then he turned and quickly left.

Greg expelled a breath of air and shook his head. "Ben should have stunned him."

"You've probably cut your chances of success by a factor of ten," Richard said quietly. "I don't envy you your trip. We could switch places or I could use you here. I'm serious."

Greg shook his head. "No, I'm going. I think Ben needs me on this trip."

Without mentioning Art by name, Richard said, "Frankly, I'm glad *he's* with you. I wasn't sure how I was going to handle him here. The mood he's in, he's liable to try to fly over and say hello to the aliens."

Greg started to leave. "I'd better get going." Then he paused. "Rich, this sounds stupid, and I'm not much on emotion, but if you get back without me, find Coni…and tell her what happened…no Fleet bullshit…and tell her that I loved her. Maybe you and Jan could…"

A brief flicker of pain crossed Richard's face. "We'll take care of her. But you're coming back." He grasped Greg firmly by the hand. "If it gets tough, I'm coming out after you."

"No, Rich," Greg replied firmly. "Ben is right. Get out of here. Hell has claimed enough souls here."

"Good luck," Richard said simply.

Greg smiled dryly and walked rapidly to the teleporter room, where Ben and Art had assembled the necessary communications equipment, scanner enhancers and link reflectors. He saw that Art was wearing one of the special belts with the nullor. From Art's face, Greg imagined the argument which must have led to Art's wearing the belt.

Ben looked at each of them with his fierce stare and hardened face. He spoke slowly, his tone sending forth icy winds, "The aliens have the advantage on us out there. Based on Klagor's story, they must know what we look like. That gives them several advantages. They know what to look for and how to kill us. We have no such knowledge. We're relying on the shipboard scanners and one relay unit, and we better assume they know we're operating our scanners. Just be alert to any scanning on their part. Remember: they could be anything, and they probably know how to operate in concealment here." He paused briefly, then continued, "Just plan to use your nullors on the first shot."

"They'll know we're coming before we get close," Art interjected. "The scanners will give us away."

"They know we're near anyway," Ben replied "They saw us land, and they probably suspect we'll attempt to search them out. Our scanner enhancement of the landscape will only confirm their suspicions. What they don't know is whether we are conducting an investigation by remote control or whether we're actually going out there.

"One additional problem: there is a remote chance that they may have learned from their early studies of Neriton how to decipher our communications. We'll use directed line-of-sight mental communication as much as possible in order to take advantage of the natural shielding against interception. Also—and Rich, I want you to do likewise—turn on the standard scrambler code. It won't help much if they pick up our signals, because then they'll know we're outside. But it will give us some time before they actually figure out our message content."

Each man activated his scrambler circuit and tested it. Ben went on: "We each wear a spare belt. And set them both for nullor self-destruction in five hours. Mark D minus five hours. If anyone tries to tamper with them or us, it'll blow. I know this is new and goes beyond the usual annihilator scheme, but we've got the nullor capability and a clear, identifiable threat. I think we should be prepared to go for complete destruction of ourselves and everything around us rather than be captured. Nothing about the Federation must be learned from us. We either get back or we're finished. One way or the other."

Art and Greg did as Ben instructed, setting a special bypass on the nullor belts which would provide a well-controlled annihilation of its wearer. Only by returning to the *Odyssey* could the wearer stop this time bomb. After inspecting everything, Ben spoke again: "I'll go first. Then Art. Then you, Greg." Ben stepped into the teleporter unit and vanished. Ben did a quick reconnaissance outside the ship then signaled for Art and Greg to follow.

Within minutes, the three of them, encased in their ghostly sheaths, were running across the clearing toward the shortest part of the channel wall, where Ben had them check their weapons.

We go up here, Ben signaled after selecting the spot. *Once over the top, no communications except line-of-sight when we're shielded by the rocks. Stay under cover as much as possible. Only one man moves out at a time. We'll spread out a little but always stay in sight of each other. Okay, let's go!*

D minus 270 minutes came the eidolonic mental voice of the nullor chronometer.

Using the pellor rays of both belts, they each started the slow rise up the sheer face of the channel wall. Ben reached the top first and jumped quickly behind the scattered remains of some large, broken rocks. As Greg and Art joined him, Ben mentally said, *We'll set out the enhancers and reflectors where we start to lose the boost from the relay unit.* Then he scurried around the barren rocks and ran quickly across a slag-ridden open space and dropped from view into a small, black depression.

Greg and Art "watched" carefully for any alien response. When nothing happened after a few minutes, Art rapidly followed Ben. Greg watched Art slide into the depression and suddenly felt the awesome loneliness of Neriton. It was his turn now. The vast, enervating stillness of his grim world swirled up like clouds to engulf him. He "peered" into the murky atmosphere, which suffused everything in a grayish-black gloom. His distant surroundings were a blur. He could imagine alien shapes moving just beyond his range of scanner vision, shapes as monstrous and amorphous as the ashen clouds. He could feel their nullors burning through him, flashing him into vaporous luminescence.

Greg got up quickly and ran swiftly to the depression. His mind was frozen now, locked into the rigid Fleet discipline he had learned so well. He was not using the automatic mental and emotional controls of his belts. Art had not brought up the subject, and Greg had no intention of obliging him if he had done so. He focused his powers on getting the job done and on surviving.

Ben said nothing when he arrived. Instead, he stood up and dashed over the rise in the depression and ran to the next energy-absorbing obstruction. Art and Greg followed in turn. The circuitous trip continued, first one man then the other and the other running from chunks of rocky froth to ash-filled hollows to ropy sinews of fused blackness. Up and down and sideways. Look and run. Look and crawl. Look and jump. Look and hide. Their only direction was based on the last scanner impression of the falling alien craft, now lost from view in a landscape perpetually immersed in a blackish gloom.

D minus 210 minutes.

Greg leaped into a jagged, dusty crevice, where Ben and Art were already hiding. The barren walls, which rose slightly more than two meters above him, were like the shriveled hide of a dead animal. Greg saw instantly that this was not a typical gouged depression or battered hollow since the walls ran parallel as far as he could "see" in one direction. In the opposite direction gaped a fractured hole, a sardonically contoured mouth of stone enveloped in blackness.

Looking at Greg from his kneeling position, Art observed, *Collapsed lava tunnel.*

How about the remainder of the tunnel? Ben asked.

It could run all the way back to the channel, Art replied. *Or it could end near here. We didn't record any breaks like this when we were in the* Odyssey, *so it's safe to assume the tunnel has no major openings to the surface.*

Ben looked carefully at the shrouded tunnel. *If this runs straight back to the channel, it would be a safe, fast way to return to the* Odyssey. He turned to Greg. *Care to turn on your random number generator to see who goes in? I think we've got barely enough time to check it out.*

Greg collected his scanner enhancing equipment and stood up. *I'll go.* He knew that Ben wanted him to go—Ben had more important matters to tend to, the aliens and Art.

Ben: *Make it fast, we're running out of time on our belts. If it gets too difficult, just return. If the tunnel is passable, be sure to leave enough concealed equipment on your return so we can 'see' our way through the tunnel in case we need to use it.*

Greg nodded and cautiously entered the dark, dismal hole, his body precariously protected from the energy vampires by his talismanic shield unit. He moved carefully over the dusty, rocky debris of the tunnel floor. He "peered" closely at the ropy walls and ceiling, a giant worm tunnel devoid of color and frozen forever from the hellfires which had made it. He was concerned about the possibility of the tunnel collapsing around him. Visions of entrapment swiftly darted through his mind—he saw himself suffocating like the crew of the *Leos* under a massive pile of rocks with each rock attached to him like some devilish lamprey sucking his life fluids from him, while all the while the belt timer moved on its silent, inexorable path to end in a brilliant flash of energy/anti-energy, instantaneous incandescence, the vaporization of Greg's being, his essence, and then the snuffing out of the flash by this enfolding, engulfing, encompassing world. He mentally shook his head, forcing out these thoughts. If they did not contribute to solutions to events, then he had no use for them. Quietly, in the recesses of his mind, he admitted that the vision had helped in one sense. He had donned two belts and activated specially built self-destructive devices on each belt. He had not thought much about this operation at the time, there had been too much to worry about—beaming off the *Odyssey*, finding a way to the top of the channel, finding the aliens. But now seemingly shielded, albeit temporarily, by the tunnel from these concerns, he realized the double death he wore. His race was not with the aliens or with the repair of the *Odyssey*. His proper concern was the latent, nova-rivaling destroyers encased about his waist which would envelop him instantaneously within *D minus 200 minutes!* His trained eyes "saw" that the blackened tunnel walls and ceiling were in no danger of collapsing.

Greg had no trouble moving rapidly through the tunnel because its course broadly meandered and was not intricately designed as he had at first feared. The tunnel ended in a collection of jagged, black blocks and talus, the cracked remains of some demonic operation on the other mouth of the tunnel. *No wonder we couldn't see this tunnel from above.* He discovered that he could climb over the colorless debris, and he soon was crouching again on the surface of Neriton. A few hundred meters ahead lay the savage fracture where the *Odyssey* was concealed.

Greg swiftly climbed back into the tunnel. He felt uncomfortable being so exposed near the edge of the channel. *Mission accomplished.* He also sent an image of the second opening as he walked rapidly back through the tunnel.

Ben smiled his thanks as Greg emerged from the tunnel. *I've followed the collapsed part a little way ahead. I think we can get fairly close to our destination by following what's left of this tunnel.*

Greg nodded in agreement, and the three of them continued their journey. The stillness and swirling gloom seemed less ominous now that they were shielded from the imagined or real terrors of the surface.

D minus 145 minutes.

The collapsed part of the lava tunnel ended in a shallow pile of rocks. Without waiting, Ben climbed to the top of the wall, "peered" around and then signaled for Greg and Art to follow. When Greg reached the top of the wall, he "saw" Ben and Art crouched behind some congealed boulders. Beyond these monuments to Siva, the ground rose gradually to a broad black hump of a hill topped with a jumble of rocks.

Bent low, Greg ran to join his two companions.

Ben briefly transmitted a mental image of the map made by the *Odyssey.* Superimposed on the map was the trace of the alien ship. *It ends just over this hill, which is evidently the ridge of a large basin or hollow. From here we spread out, but stay in sight of one another. We'll crawl to the top of the hill. If it isn't here, we'll regroup and keep moving until about D minus 60 minutes. That's a damned tight schedule.*

Carefully, the three men crept up the hill, leaving behind them three trails resembling inverted molehills that meandered back to the sheltering boulders like some trimurtian path radiating from the Divine Ground.

Greg disliked having the energy-sucking dust so close to so much of his body. His shield suit worked strenuously to overcome the leeches seeking to penetrate his body. Feelings of the gritty surface were transmitted to his mind. He wanted to shut off these feelings but resisted the temptation. His survival depended on every part of his being sensing his harsh, deadly environment.

D minus 130 minutes.

Greg reached the top of the hill which served to ridge a broad, deep, hollow depression, with the raised circular rim rising over two hundred meters above its rounded bottom to reach a diameter of about one thousand meters. His senses were only peripherally aware of this dust-filled panorama of gently sloping, craterlike walls, which held the sporadically placed boulders like a catch basin for the clotted black raindrops of Armageddon. As he lay among the rocky ruins, his senses magnetically locked onto a glowing saucer of light at the bottom of the depression.

The alien spaceship!

It rested in the dusty basin like a large, menacing unicellular eye blinking against the stinging air. There was no sign of life outside the ship and no evidence of other scanners.

Ben signaled with his hands that Greg and Art should climb back down from their places on the ridge and join him a few meters below the rocky crest.

Shielded by the hill and surrounded by swirling clouds of dust, the three men conversed in thought-words and images.

Ben: *We're in luck! The alien ship is badly damaged. It's resting in the dust, not above it, and it's flashing like crazy. I don't think it will last long. Shields must be almost gone.*

Greg: *You realize we're sitting next to a potential nova?*

Ben: *On any planet but this one I'd agree with you. Our job is to get rid of that thing so we can lift off before it brings more ships on us. If we spread out along the rim and set up a constant triangular crossfire, we may catch the shields on a down cycle and get through.*

Greg: *This could be a trap.*

Ben: *That's why I want us separated. Less risk of all of us getting it at once. Rich knows what is happening. If it's a trap, he can still get out while we fight here. If the ship blows, taking us with it, then he's got a clear shot home. And if we survive, we all have the clear shot.*

Ben looked from Greg to Art. *Any questions? Okay, we'll split up. Greg, you stay on the rim here. Art, you swing around to the left about 120 degrees and I'll do the same to the right. Leave reflectors so we can communicate around the rim, not across it. That way they can't monitor our communications. I'll start firing when we're all safely in place.*

Each man scrambled along the dusty hillside to establish Ben's trigonal figure of death. Greg, with only a few meters to crawl, settled promptly amidst the broken rocks sprinkled along the rim. He squirmed around to achieve maximum concealment from all sides, having considered the possibility that the aliens may have already set up some weapon to catch him. He scanned the rocky rim and the walls below. Nothing. No movement. His scanner-received images showed only an empty basin except for the blinking thanatopic jewel below.

Like a phantom wind, the stillness came again. The stillness and the desolation. Greg felt like the only man alive in the Universe. Alone and threatened. Even if Sangraal II had not been physically dangerous, its depressive gloom made it psychologically dangerous. Depressive—yes, that's the word, he thought to himself. Depressive and desolate.

Ready? Ben's query brought Greg's attention to their real problem. The thought-message came like a welcomed beverage in this desert of silence.

Ready, Greg answered. His whole being tensed in anticipation, his concentration focused intently on the flickering craft below.

Art?

Hold it, Ben. Something is happening on this side.

Pause. Greg strained to "see" what Art was "watching". He was vaguely aware of Ben's probing through the link.

Ben, the ship is opening some kind of port in its screen. There's a tractor beam ramp.

Greg could "see" the port now without any assistance from Art. What the hell is going on? he thought to himself.

Forget it, Ben commanded. *On my signal, start firing.*

Ben! Stop! The words tore through Greg's mind like a piercing scream. *Someone is coming out of the port. It must be some kind of emergency exit. Their teleporter must be damaged.*

Ben: *I said forget it.*

Greg: *They've got scanners operating!* He felt them probing everywhere.

Ben! The frantic cry again.

Pause. A gust from the silent, phantom wind.

It's human!

The words seared into Greg's cortex, penetrating the core of his mind. Never in a thousand worlds…He could now "see" the shape emerge from the portal. It walked erect on two legs. Like him, it was sheathed in a diaphanous cloak of protective energy. Greg examined the creature closely. *It looks just like a human!* The features, the body—everything fit. The alien's shield suit flickered momentarily. The creature stumbled.

Art: *He's injured. Ben, he's one with* us. *You were wrong, damn you, wrong! I'm going to help him.*

Art! Stay where you are! Ben's mind screamed its fury like a lightning bolt aimed at Art.

A flurry of dust appeared at Greg's left. Then Art emerged from a cluster of rocks and openly showed himself to the alien below. Immediately, Greg received Art's standard recon signal calling out to the alien in peace and friendship.

Art! Get down! Ben's thoughts merged with Greg's in a pleading command. Only the emotion was lost in the filtered link. Greg wanted to stun his crewmate and force him back into hiding, but Ben cautioned against this, *It'll give us all away.*

Art disregarded them. He had the alien's attention. Slowly, Art started down the dusty wall while continuing to send his message of peace.

The alien stood motionless near the bottom of his ethereal ramp. His eyes followed Art's every move. Greg, who had the only direct view from the rim, was keyed to fire his nullors at the slightest provocation.

Midway down the craterlike wall, Art vanished from Greg's direct view behind a group of broken boulders. Greg focused part of his attention on Art, waiting for him to emerge into the open again.

A sudden flash of light streaked from the alien, and it vanished into the rocks. Art screamed in agony. Greg futilely fired his nullors at the alien. The creature had vanished from the ramp and the portal was closing. Greg wanted to blast into the portal, but he checked himself. Art was still out there. If he succeeded in penetrating the alien ship even from his awkward angle, everything could be destroyed. He dismissed the possibility that killing the alien might be sufficient to destroy the ship.

Art screamed again and again. His thought-messages were filled with scorching phlogosis. His pleas for an end to his pain came as one bathing in Phlegethon. Greg was momentarily stunned by Art's agony, and he pleaded, *Ben, we've got to do something!*

Stay put, Ben commanded. *They know where you are. I'm coming around. Can you see Art or the alien?*

Negative. My life-support readings on Art are very confused: his suit must be damaged or…

Greg remained motionless, his mind drinking every image poured into him. He fought to silence the angry frustration nurtured by Art's screaming cries for help.

Ben was just below and behind him. *I'm going part of the way around from up here, and then I'm going down into those rocks.*

Ben, you can't.

Just as Art was hit and despite some portable alien concealing screen, I received a fleeting image from him of the alien leaping off the ramp. He's got to be outside, hidden by the ship. Evidently, their ship is too damaged to use its nullor so they're resorting to suit nullors. If I approach the rocks from this side, he won't be able to 'see' me directly. You cover me. But stay out of sight—your firing has given away your position.

Can't we try some remote medical link-up? Greg asked. *It's suicide to go down there.* Ben did not answer. Greg knew that Art was probably too shielded from them for anything but direct medical help. Greg's frustration mounted. The screaming continued. Agony. Pain. These feelings were written in flaming paints upon his mind.

Cover me, Ben repeated. *If anything happens to me, try to blast the ship. I hope Rich is ready to lift off. The Federation takes precedence now.*

Through the scanner hookup, Greg watched Ben crawl along the rim. *Good luck,* Greg called after him. Ben clambered among the energy-absorbing rocks on the rim and vanished, reappearing as a crouched apelike being stealthily moving from boulder to boulder on a diagonal path around the wall toward the screening rocks enveloping Art.

Greg's mind received a flicker of motion at the right-hand edge of the alien ship. Concealing screen! he thought. Can't make it out! *Ben! Get under cover!* Something was coming around the far side of the ship, trying to line up with Ben.

Greg fired at the same time as the alien, being careful not to hit the alien ship. Greg perceived two blinding flashes of released energy—one engulfed the alien, the other came from his left and below. His life-support system told him that Ben had ceased to exist.

A third evanescent burst of light swallowed him, dancing in sparkling and crackling fury about his shield. He was thrust backward and tumbled disjointedly down the hillside inside the dying pulses of his main shield suit.

Half-running and half-tumbling, he slid behind the rocks where only a short while ago his two companions had joined him for the final assault. Stung by his stupidity at exposing himself when firing, he cursed as he fully activated his second belt, leaving his dying first belt buried in the concealing soil as a trap. Fortunately, the rocks had shielded him, leaving his suit to take only a drastically reduced, indirect blast from the alien nullor weapon.

There was at least one more alien out there somewhere. He was certain he had killed the alien who had fired at Art and Ben. But now he was vulnerable behind this array of rocks, precariously placed between the craterlike rim and the collapsed tunnel. He could not go back up to the rim now. *They* were waiting for him up there.

The screaming had ceased. Was Art dead, or had it all been a trap baited with a screaming simulacrum?

Greg swiftly scouted his surroundings for any signs of trouble, then he ran hurriedly toward the open remnant of the tunnel.

Scanner image: *motion above and behind him on the rocks.* He automatically fired the nullor, its beam spurting out from the back of his shield suit, instantaneously ending at the source of the motion. With a pellor assist, Greg dived headlong into the tunnel just as an intense blaze of rending energy tore over him.

He landed in a clump, his flight dignified somewhat by his suit and the last minute reverse activation of his pellor beam. He scurried among some rocks, frantically "watching" the tunnel wall above him. Can't stay here, he thought. They can probably find a way to get me from the rim. He looked down the shielding tunnel. *Rich, get out of here. I'm coming back down the tunnel and will try for Klagor's cave. Ben and Art appear to be extinguished.*

Knowing there could be no acknowledgment, he crouched and trotted down the tunnel, keeping as much detritus as possible between himself and the rim. The alien or aliens had him now. They must know about the channel where the *Odyssey* was hidden. His job was to lead them to the other end of the channel. Some remote part of his mind found it weird that he had so simply and with full knowledge selected his own death, as if wondering whether his mind was filled with nepenthe.

Behind him the collapsed tunnel glowed with the fires of destruction. They're trying to kill anything left alive back there, he thought. He ran faster. Speed was important now. Satisfied that they had nothing to fear at the end of the collapsed portion of the tunnel, the aliens could now simply walk along the tunnel wall, bathing the debris below in the disrupting flare of their nullor-type weapons.

Run!

The schismatic walls converged ahead on a void-filled rent. Greg leaped into the opening of the tunnel remnants, relieved at having additional protection about him.

D minus forty minutes.

Richard sat in his recliner, his face lined with tense muscles that channeled beads of sweat down it. He had worked feverishly to repair the *Odyssey,* spurred on by the events occurring above the channel. Exerting his Fleet training, he separated the schizophrenic images pounding in his mind. He was coursing through the life stream of the ship on a phagocytic mission to repair its damages while his attention focused on the activities of his three crewmates outside.

He felt the agonizing loss of Ben and Art. Life was too precious to be wasted. *So much has been wasted here!* He followed Greg's frantic rush to divert the aliens, and Ben's final orders floated into his conscious thoughts: *"If we get in trouble, get out of here." Get out of here. Get out of here.* The words echoed in his mind. *Shut up!* Richard screamed in defiance. His mind was calm now, functioning with amazing rapidity, compressing everything into seconds, sifting, evaluating, deciding. The *Odyssey* was essentially repaired. Greg was in trouble. Richard could not beam him back through such grasping debris. Ben had said to leave.

A new scene welled up which unraveled in maddeningly slow fashion. A scene from his and Greg's intentionally forgotten first trip beyond the Perimeter.

A Fleet spaceship floating silently…the *Guardian*! Nearby, another ship, this one obviously a trade ship. Inside stood two Fleet officers looking at the remains of four people who had dared to defy the Federation. One officer kneels in sorrow beside one of the dead men.

A flight recorder unwinding its threaded tale…a message from the dead to the living. Certain sentences are forever engraved in his conscious mind—the jointly prepared plea from four lifeless individuals.

"We have lived for years in a civilization bounded by the lack of imagination of its members. We have seen humanity's dreams die, withering in the sterile soil of stagnation. The agony of this death has been slow in coming.

Many do not recognize it, even though it relentlessly chisels its gruesome mask upon the face of humanity…

"What have you left for us to live for? What aspirations may we have? What dreams may we dream? What goals may we strive to achieve? Today you have erected the Perimeter in defiance of all that is known about humanity's wanderlust and its accompanying renascent powers. Tomorrow you will undoubtedly turn within, seeking to find something that can only be illuminated against many different backgrounds. But once the slow rollback has begun, there will be no stopping, for nature will not aid those who quit.

"Is life worth living at this price? Some will argue that life is worthwhile regardless of the terms. We think not. We cannot condone a life with no hope, a life mocked by those who secretly prefer the security and tranquility of the dead. To be full, to be realizable, a life must be free to seek expression…

"Like seeds we have gone beyond the Perimeter seeking escape from the barren soil that humanity has become, seeking to grow again under a new sun: Ormazd, the creator and guardian. Here we have met the very poison we sought to escape in the form of a Fleet ship sent to capture us. We have made our choice to be free of the shackles fastened about us by a society determined to control everything. Will you make the same choice for freedom?"

Superimposed upon this view of the flight recorder floated the image of Jerry Whittaker, Mary's brother and Richard's best friend at the Academy, his face vacant in the final view of death.

Richard had made his choice then in that far-distant Fleet ship and gradually learned to live out that choice in a new understanding of his life with Jan. He affirmed that choice now.

D minus thirty minutes.

Greg stumbled through the tunnel, clawing with hands and pellor ray to keep his footing. The deadly glow suffused through the rear of the tunnel, cutting off his aft scanner connections. Only the meandering course of the tunnel saved him from dissolution. The glow acted like an emotional pulse, pressing him faster through the tunnel.

D minus twenty minutes.

Greg crawled among the rocky remnants of the tunnel at its second mouth. He could "see" no sign of pursuit. He dared not hesitate. He sprinted up from the rubble toward the yawning black channel. He darted between several cauterized boulders standing near the edge, turned on his pellor ray and leaped into the abyss.

His shield again crackled with angry fire. He spun aimlessly in the ashen clouds, falling toward the channel floor.

It was a second grazing hit! *That son-of-a-bitch!* The rocks, and perhaps the cloud thickness, protected him. But now he had only one shield belt, and it was dying on him. He nursed it, screaming in mental agony for enough power to break his fall.

The pellor beam flickered on several times, buffeting him in his plunge.

Greg hit the floor in a cloud of dust. Instantly, he was rolling, crawling, running for shelter. His body ached. His suit was almost finished. The blackness was rushing in toward him. Was this caused by the failure of his suit, or had the *Odyssey* left? He would never make it to Klagor. He would never make it anywhere. An inner desire to live just a little longer drove him to shelter behind several angular boulders at the foot of the opposite wall.

D minus fifteen minutes.

He laughed mirthlessly to himself. The belt was quitting for lack of power, yet it still had enough power locked separately inside to annihilate him. The insanity of his predicament was too much for rational thought. Where was that power now that he really needed it? *We're always preparing for death, never for life,* he thought bitterly. He laughed silently again, seeking relief through emotion.

A movement to his right in the direction of Klagor's tunnel and along the wall he had just left caused him to focus his limited scanner powers toward it. *What the hell was that?* Had he really seen something, or was the enveloping blackness playing tricks on his weakened scanner capabilities? *No! There it is again!*

His emotional dike fell before the onrushing waves of fear. He had suffered through the battle in the basin only to be trapped by alien beings in this geologic gash while his suit was preparing to destroy him. But now, crawling stealthily down the far wall came another of the Argus-eyed demons.

Had the aliens summoned it? No matter. He had to find a better hiding place. *Relax. Think.* He looked about. To his left, in the direction of the cavern where they had hidden the *Odyssey,* he saw a crack in the wall on his side of the channel. It looked big enough to hold him. Would it be narrow enough to keep out the monster? What about the aliens? The futility of his situation was obvious. But if he had to die, it would be by his own hand, not by the jaws of that huge, eight-legged demon and not by an alien nullor.

Cautiously, Greg started to creep toward the crack.

Blinding torrents of energy seared a barrier in front of him.

He leaped back, shaken by his short venture.

Utter hopelessness washed over him. He fought it, subduing the emotional currents. He had learned something. *Need confirmation.* He crawled in the opposite direction, toward the demon. Again a flash. Greg laughed again. *Same point of origin! You bastard! You dirty, stinking, lousy bastard! There's only one of you. Do you hear that, Rich? There's only one left. If you're still here, get out while he's 'watching' me.* Greg realized that Richard could have left while he was incommunicado in the tunnel. That might partially explain his declining scanner capabilities.

The monster was on the channel floor now, prancing hypnotically toward him on eight gigantic legs. He felt curiously entranced by the approaching eight-legged vision of death. Was it really so bad to die this way? Was it really death to merge one's energy, one's essence, with another? Painless oblivion. Peace. *Fight it! Got to fight it! The thing is trying to take over my mind. Get out, damn you! Get out!* He built mental barriers. He filled his mind with images of Coni: an exquisite amulet with stellar yellow hair and verdurous eyes warded off the idea of death. He channeled his cerebral stream toward one goal: staying alive as long as possible.

Greg thought fleetingly about rolling a stone toward the crack. Then he could move beside the stone and be sheltered. He dismissed the idea as too risky and too late—the monster would surely catch him even if he could stay hidden from the alien's nullor. Frantically, he clawed into the dust and pulled rocks in around him. Maybe if he completely concealed himself, he would be safe.

Greg! Above you!

Startled, Greg "looked" up at the wall above him. A belt floated down through the mist. *It's Rich!* A nullor beam lashed out from the opposite wall seeking something above him.

Greg grabbed the belt as it hit the dusty floor. With instantaneous reflexive movements, he encircled his waist with the new nullor belt. This must be Rich's spare, he thought to himself. All the others are dead or dying. The ministrations of his new belt immediately eased his pain.

Nullor beams crisscrossed above him with dazzling brilliance, creating a network of filamentary death. The ashen air was alive with lancing lights. Richard fired several diversionary blasts at the oncoming destroyer. Demogorgon paused, apparently puzzled by the intense play of energy overhead.

Get back to the ship while I hold them both off, Richard commanded.

No chance! The beast would get me before I moved ten meters. I'll head for that crack in the wall and see if I can climb up to you. Keep that alien down!

I'm trying! Get going!

Greg dashed from his cover, feeling like a man shrouded in a black thundercloud within which vast bolts of eye-stinging lightning played in some macabre dance. He was gambling that the alien had no automatic traps set for him.

The beast decided—it wanted him. It was almost flying over the ground on its eight pounding legs of fury.

Greg reached the crack first. He could not fit in. Frenziedly "looking" up, he "saw" a wider spot less than a meter above him. Boosted with his new pellor ray, he climbed and clawed his way into it. With obvious relief, he moved back into the crack as the beast desperately tried to catch him. The demon tore mightily at the crack, trying with all its furious strength to widen it. Outside, the duel of nullor beams continued, casting frightening shadows across the channel of the dead.

Greg "looked" up into the crack. Bitterly, he observed that the crack did not run all the way to the top of the wall. He was still trapped. If the alien shifted position, he could "burn" Greg where he stood.

D minus five minutes.

The belt! The fukken belt! Got to get rid of it! In his panic to put on the new belt, he had forgotten to remove the old one. The belt, in order to fulfill its mission without alerting enemies, was not designed to give any special warning as the deadly countdown proceeded. Greg was momentarily relieved that his new belt was not set for self-destruction, even though he knew that he could not stop the timer on his old belt without returning to the *Odyssey*. He ripped off the old belt, held it over his head to toss it outside the crack. Then he stopped, sparked by an idea so simple that he almost laughed at his stupidity in not seeing it earlier. He reminded himself that the idea was also deadly.

He waited for the timer to run its course.

D minus two minutes…

D minus one minute…

Seconds now. He tensed and then hurled the belt to one side through the crack high into the swirling clouds. *Now hide!*

A brilliant flash. A controlled, miniature nova. The confined energy/anti-energy danced across the grounded monster, cajoling, pleading, drawing the creature's attention to the various energy beams above it.

The beast paused and then instinctively leaped for the new and more powerful source of energy hovering above it. As its feet cleared the ground, Greg fired. He had no more remorse about using his nullor. He knew about Klagor and Neriton. He had "seen" the end of the *Leos* and knew firsthand the loss of his two crewmates. Along with the full searing disruptive power of his nullor, he sent a controlled but raging torrent of his hatred, depositing it in this creature as he had in its kin.

The beast screamed in his mind as its kin had done before it. It screamed and it died, a shriveling black hulk upon the graveyard of its victims.

Greg moved to the crack opening. No conditioned sickness plagued him this time. He was his own master. He was in control of his fate.

Outside, the nullor beams continued to flash at each other. With calculation, Greg climbed out of the crack and ran to the protection of the opposite wall, where the alien would not be able to "see" him directly. Silently, he rose on his pellor beam toward the remaining source of his problems.

He ignored the crackling beams of destruction that silhouetted this infernal world. He knew Richard understood what he was going to do.

He reached the top of the wall and scrambled between the rocks. Coldly, methodically, he sought out his enemy. It did not take him long to find the focal point of the alien lances.

From behind several closely spaced rocks, he "watched" the alien fire at Richard. Up. Fire. Down. Sideways. Fire. Back. Greg waited calmly for what he knew must come. He was not concerned with his weak rationalization that this was the surest way to end their nightmare. He no longer cared that he was looking at a duplicate of his own kind. The demon below could not have inspired more loathing.

The final act was beginning.

The alien sent a terrific barrage of rending energy/anti-energy across the channel toward Richard. Then, still concealed in the aftereffects of this barrage, he leaped toward another boulder to resume the attack from a different vantage point.

Greg caught him in midair with his portable tractor beam. The alien tumbled unprotected into the space between the channel walls.

He's all yours, Rich!

A pause. Greg suddenly realized that Richard might still be suffering from the same conditioning he had undergone. The alien was trying to control his motion with a pellor beam while playing his nullor around the channel. Instinctively, Greg fired at the bipedal being dangling from its invisible vine. Simultaneously, a second beam laced out from the opposite wall, the two beams hungrily seeking the evil morsel floating above the channel floor. The beams fused with blinding fury then ceased.

Silence. Only the energy-starved clouds swung through the void where the alien had been.

Carefully, Greg scanned his surroundings for other adversaries, then he walked to the edge of the channel. *Let's go home.*

A sudden explosion lifted him off the ground and sent him tumbling down the side of the channel, his mind engulfed in the darkest Yuga of all.

Feeling. Motion. Fluids in motion. Sensation. Nerves functioning. *Where am I?* Check the system to see if it is functioning. *What happened?* Light, filtered but nevertheless light. Sounds. Open eyes. Tall man bending over him. Smiling. Face capped with black hair. Friendly, dark eyes.

Greg smiled weakly up at Richard, who said, "Welcome back to the living." Richard stood up. "To save you asking any trite questions, you're dead. At least you were and would still be if the old master here hadn't come through in time with his medicator. You're as fortunate as the fabled Tellurian cat.

"Also, in case you're interested in how you died, just on the outside chance you show signs of learning from your experience, you managed to be standing up when the alien ship blew. I'd say you've just about used up all the protection one person can ask of the planet. Not to mention three belts—and one of them my spare!"

Greg tried unsuccessfully to sit up.

"Take it easy. Even the many fabled Tellurian vegetation gods purportedly took a few days to rise again."

"Ben? Art?"

Richard's face clouded. "I flew over the basin. Nothing left. No chance for renascent techniques. Nothing to work on. Everything not of the planet was disintegrated and sucked up. The monsters were crawling all over everything, the basin *and* the channel when I left."

"I take it we're off-planet?" Greg asked weakly. Richard nodded. Greg closed his eyes briefly. Visions of the desolate basin, populated by those infernally demonic Gogmagogs, swirled up with frightening intensity. He opened his eyes again, seeing Richard in a teary crystal halo of multicolored refracted light.

"We're in metaspace. There was no trouble leaving. I've covered our trail well, including the monitor." Richard cleared his throat. "Now comes the truly rough part of our trip, convincing the Federation that it's in extreme danger. And we may have run out of time to prepare for an attack. We'll have to be the best proselytizers in ages to turn around over a century of Syncretistic ideology. Depending on your point of view, you and I are either the most important or the most dangerous humans alive."

Greg nodded in agreement. He was beginning to appreciate their difficult task. Despite all their evidence, they would still be subjected to the most intensive and extensive mental examination in history. Not a shred of either of their minds would be left unprobed. He knew he should be considering the future that was blasting toward him like a shockwave front, but he could not keep his thoughts from that deadly basin.

"I feel so damned rotten about it all. If only we'd kept Art here. If I'd fired sooner, Ben might be alive."

Richard knelt beside him and put a hand on his shoulder. "The decisions were made, the world lines established. Art felt he had to be there. Maybe, in a way, he did have to be there. No one could have saved Ben without possibly taking the alien ship and himself, too. That would have also killed Ben. There were just too many unknowns then."

Greg relaxed a little, letting his eyes close again. He felt his strength returning faster now. "So unreal," he murmured. "Even now, it all seems like a dream. We finally meet hominoids, and we find ourselves at war with them." He shook his head in disbelief, a cynical smile creeping across his youthful face. He saw the personification of what countless thinkers had tried to tell humanity. "Our own worst enemies…Art couldn't see it…Ben may have…I almost didn't. Why did Ben do it, Rich? He must have known it was a trap."

Richard looked away from Greg, his eyes focused on the rear of the control room. He shook his head slightly. "I don't know. Ben had a job to do, I guess. I could never get close to him, but I'd follow him back here again if necessary." Richard shrugged. "Even Art was needed: he kept us objective. And now I suppose he's achieved the only true merger possible for humanity."

Greg relented a little, feeling that he was probing too deeply too fast. "You certainly weren't good at following Ben's orders," Greg responded, his voice chiding good-naturedly. "He told you on several occasions to get off this planet if anything went wrong. 'The Federation takes precedence'—remember?"

"Screw the Federation!" Richard replied coldly. He walked over to his recliner and sat down. He quietly stared for several minutes at Ben's empty recliner. Greg looked away, regretting his callousness. He was alive. What more could he ask?

Richard spoke finally. His words came slowly, quietly. "I made my decision at Ormazd…for Jan…for you here. Dad said life at all costs. But that doesn't always hold true. I couldn't leave you. The price was too high."

Greg's throat was tight. "Considering the Federation?"

"Considering the Federation. Loyalty and duty are easy in our business. Friendship is hard. I never told you before, but you got me through that Perimeter assignment."

Greg shook his head. "You got yourself through that assignment." He smiled gently at Richard. "You were the wisest of all of us. It took me to the bitter end to begin to understand what you—and maybe Ben, though I doubt it—knew all the time." His eyes focused amicably on Richard's, and he quietly added, "Thanks."

Richard returned his smile. "You summed it up back there in the channel," he said, his voice evincing feeling, an inner calm: *"Let's go home."*

"In one sense, I think that was home," Greg said sadly, "and having recognized it as such, maybe we've finally earned the right to leave it."

ABOUT THE AUTHOR

Gary L. Bennett has worked on advanced space power systems and advanced space propulsion systems in support of the nation's space program. Specific missions he has supported include Voyager, Galileo, Ulysses and Cassini. He is currently involved in NASA studies to send humans back to the Moon and to Mars. He has received numerous awards from NASA and from national organizations. He is a Fellow of the American Institute of Aeronautics and Astronautics, a Fellow of The American Physical Society, and a Fellow of The British Interplanetary Society. He has a PhD in physics.

978-0-595-35540-2
0-595-35540-4

Printed in the United States
33795LVS00005B/127-174

9 780595 355402